She was . . . *beautiful.* Which made it all the worse, somehow.

"Shawn?"

He jolted in his own skin as those eyes turned back to him, luminously bright.

This car was too small. Too cramped. The air between them turned warmer, and as he took a deep breath through his nose, it occurred to him that she smelled like something fresh and clean. Rain without the acid tinge; a storm without the filthy undercurrent of refuse and mold.

Very carefully, Shawn peeled his fingers from around the steering wheel. *Do not touch.*

"We should—"

"Wait." She shifted in her seat, facing him, arms folded over her midsection. It bunched her yellow silk blouse against her body. Was it soft? It'd have to be. As soft as the skin beneath.

He watched, transfixed, as Kayleigh's tongue slid over her lips. A groan knotted in his chest; he forced it down. Swallowed it back.

She raised a hand to pull tendrils from her face, absentmindedly self-conscious. "I don't know you at all. But I'd really . . . I mean, I'm wondering. Will you . . . Can I test something on you?"

He managed a hoarse note of inquiry.

"Will you kiss me?"

By Karina Cooper

The Dark Mission Series

ONE FOR THE WICKED
SACRIFICE THE WICKED
ALL THINGS WICKED
NO REST FOR THE WITCHES
LURE OF THE WICKED
BLOOD OF THE WICKED
BEFORE THE WITCHES

The St. Croix Chronicles

GILDED
TARNISHED

KARINA COOPER

ONE
FOR THE
WICKED

A DARK MISSION NOVEL

AVON

An Imprint of HarperCollinsPublishers

This is a work of fiction. Names, characters, places, and incidents are products of the author's imagination or are used fictitiously and are not to be construed as real. Any resemblance to actual events, locales, organizations, or persons, living or dead, is entirely coincidental.

AVON BOOKS
An Imprint of HarperCollins*Publishers*
10 East 53rd Street
New York, New York 10022-5299

First Avon Books mass market printing: May 2013

Avon Trademark Reg. U.S. Pat. Off. and in Other Countries, Marca Registrada, Hecho en U.S.A.
HarperCollins® is a registered trademark of HarperCollins Publishers.

Printed in the U.S.A.

10 9 8 7 6 5 4 3 2 1

ONE
FOR THE
WICKED

CHAPTER ONE

Footsteps crunched on the gravel behind him, counter to the streaming patter of rain slapping the rooftop lot. Four stories below, the pitted and broken strip that was all that remained of a leveled tenement glistened beneath a corona of neon fluorescence. Red pooled like blood into the cracks, purple flashed and sparked off the occasional skeletal finger of metal rebar and twisted hunk of cement.

Shawn Lowe didn't turn around. Only one person knew where to find him on this day.

"What?"

His greeting, cursory as hell, spiked hard. His dark brown hair dripped into his eyes, too long these days but Shawn hadn't bothered to hack it off. Maybe he'd grow it out. Maybe he'd take a pair of scissors to it later.

Maybe he'd be dead before it mattered.

The odds were about even any which way.

"Your comm is off." The gravelly reprimand behind him didn't need to fight for dominance over the rain and permanent hum of New Seattle's electrical grid. She had a voice like sandpaper and a way with orders that put him in mind of an old dog long past the point of common courtesy. Raspy enough to stand out, it cut through the white noise like steel wool.

Shawn's shoulders moved. Apathy.

The footsteps shifted, easing to his right, and the woman who was all the family Shawn had left stepped into view.

May's profile was nothing particularly flashy or awe-inspiring. A woman of sixty, maybe more or less, with iron gray hair kept buzz-short, and features lined with age and experience that bit deep. With her ten-pack-a-day voice and runner's physique, she was tough as old nails and twice as sharp. Nobody could ever accuse the woman of being soft.

Shawn had learned a long time ago not to try.

Her eyes, a brown almost as dark as Shawn's, had perfected the art of steel implacability long before he'd ever met her, and she used it to damned good effect.

Years ago, she'd once told him that he reminded her of herself. He looked enough like her grandson to warrant the distinction.

Similarities between the two men ended there.

"I assume you're here for a good reason?" His voice, deeper than hers, clashed with the faintest echo of thunder. This far down into the depths of the city, the sun never reached and the rain didn't fall so much as leak off the higher tiers. The fact that he could detect the rolling boom told him there was one hell of a storm raging overhead.

Fitting. It matched his mood.

May mirrored his pose, toes inches from the edge of the roof, hands jammed into her coat pockets. She wore synth-leather, like him, though hers was more protective than street-style. Most denizens of the lower streets wore it, if they could afford it.

"Been here long?" she asked.

"Long enough." Forever, even. Seemed like no matter how many years went by, Shawn still found himself here. Overlooking the cratered patch of land that was all that remained of his parents' place after the fire.

"Find anything?" She asked it every year.

Every year, the answer was the same.

No funeral. No bodies. Just a handful of ash and a vendetta.

His jaw tightened. "What do you want, May?"

She shifted, turning her back to the lot. Rain slicked down her short hair, painted her weathered face in reflected flashes of neon. "Your team lead's been trying to contact you."

Shit. Of course today. Wrenching his gaze from the pitted scar, Shawn looked up. The lights and signs and irregular bursts of color would forever be the closest thing they'd ever see of stars down here. "If she wants more drills, tell her to go fuc—"

Her hand flashed, a pale blur trailing water, and Shawn winced as it skimmed the back of his wet head. "Watch your mouth."

He had about six inches on her, but the woman had reach. Ducking, he rubbed his skull with a callused hand, slanting her a wry, wary grimace. "Where do you think I learned it?"

"I'm sure I don't know." A bald-faced lie if he'd ever heard one. The resistance leader had a mouth on her that rivaled most anyone else he knew.

How she'd ended up with such a polite grandson in Danny Granger still posed one of life's greatest mysteries.

Shawn swore enough for the both of them, but not around May. Usually. Today was a sensitive day. "She can still take a flying leap."

"Usually, I'd agree."

He heard the word she didn't say, so filled it in for her. "But?"

"But I know you'll want in on this, and I need your talents."

Shawn's gaze slid away from the woman's unreadable profile, vaguely aware that somehow, his face had settled into the same lines. May wasn't his grandmother, not by any stretch of blood or marriage, but she'd practically raised him like one. He owed her his life—owed her a lot more than that, given the direction he'd been headed when she rescued him from the Mission orphanages.

Sixteen years in the resistance had taught him a thing or two about debts.

"Fine." A reluctant concession. "Tell her—"

May's profile turned, and Shawn spun as another set of footsteps crunched on the gravel behind them. His fists clenched at his sides, a rapid pounding settling in his head as two more people crossed what had been his rooftop vigil.

And his own private hell.

Shawn's jaw clenched so tight, even he didn't know how the words made it out from between his teeth. "What the fuck are they doing here?"

Sizzling pops of green and orange neon picked out Jennifer Davis and Kevin Horner, two of his assigned team. Jennifer led them, though he didn't care one way or another who got called what. She raised a hand, slick with rain, and rotated a comm in silent greeting. The screen glowed blue, signaling its connection to someone on the other end.

Wiry fingers circled his forearm, bit into the muscles he'd clenched in preparation for . . .

For a fight. A brawl. Something.

This was *his* turf. His hell. Nobody else got to look at it.

Not like he did.

"Time's short and we didn't have the luxury of playing tag," May said tightly, her voice a graveled order buried in steel. "They're catching you up and then you're leaving."

"Five minutes," he growled, his gaze pinned on the intruders but his voice lowered for her. "You couldn't give me five goddamned minutes to meet them on the street."

Jennifer hesitated, her own eyes flicking between them both before she murmured something to Horner.

They both stopped. Waited.

"No." And that was the end of May's sympathy.

Shit. Of all the days to hijack, whatever this was had to pick now. Turning his back on the crater long since broken and covered with debris, Shawn forced his attention away from the graveyard with no markers.

Out of the past.

He strode toward Jennifer, ignored the way she backed up a step, and nodded curtly. "Make this fucking fast."

"Hi to you, too, sunshine." The crystal-clear voice from the comm earned Jennifer a withering stare, but she raised her chin, eyes narrowed, and held it up as if Shawn had trouble hearing it.

"Didn't know you'd made it to the inner circle already," was Shawn's greeting. Not much of one. Even Horner winced at the implication.

The voice hesitated.

"I know this is a bad day," May said as she dragged a wet, gnarled hand over her short hair, "but that was your freebie, kiddo."

Shawn's fists jammed into his jacket pockets. "What's this about, Stone?"

Jonas Stone had been part of the resistance for only three weeks. Word on the street was that he'd been rescued from the Holy Order he used to work for. In exchange, he'd rescued Danny from his old employers.

Rescued, patched up, and then some.

Shawn didn't buy it. The Holy Order of St. Dominic wasn't anything so innocuous as an *employer*. Once they got their hooks in a man, they owned him. Body and soul.

His father had learned that the hard way.

May didn't share his reservation.

Or his hatred.

"We've got an in." Jennifer's voice was softer, more feminine than May's. She was shorter than May, with a heart-shaped face and ruthlessly scraped back, frizzy blond hair. Nice enough girl; didn't have the chops to stand up in a room full of dominant personalities.

Still, she organized the same way he breathed: without effort.

She'd do. Long enough to get what he wanted.

This team had been on standby for months. Only one thing—one person—could pull them into active duty.

Lauderdale.

A predatory smile pulled at his mouth. He forced it

back, intensely aware of May's acute study. "What are we looking at?"

The comm crackled as Stone cleared his throat. "In exactly thirty-seven minutes, I'm going to get one shot at the quadplex security."

Horner, a tall man with a barrel chest and balding brown hair, folded his arms across his belly. He looked at May, mouth beneath his handlebar mustache pulled into a frown. "I thought we had no way of getting in there."

A man of few words; Shawn had no problems with him, as long as he stayed out of the way.

May's eyes gleamed in the neon-infested shadows, sparked purple and green. "Jonas?"

Shawn scowled at her; she returned his annoyance with relentless expectation. He'd never heard her pass technical details to another person. Ever. She'd been Shawn's go-to for as long as he could remember.

How had Jonas taken on that role? When?

Maybe sleeping with the woman's grandson earned a man more points than Shawn thought.

"Been chatting with Parker and we found a loophole," Jonas said, effortlessly translating to English without being prompted. Shawn met Jennifer's gaze, shrugged when she raised her eyebrows. "Some of the backup systems she had installed to keep herself organized do a routine check every— Yeah, you don't care. Listen, we get one shot at getting someone inside, and that's the point."

"Wait." Shawn's gaze pinned May. "Inside?"

"Where you're going to track down Kayleigh Lauderdale and bring her here," May finished.

"*Kayleigh* Lauderdale?"

"Yeah," Stone answered, nearly drowned out by a

sudden and freakishly loud clap of thunder. Everyone looked up in surprise, except Shawn.

He snatched the comm from Jennifer's flagging hand.

"Hey!"

He ignored her. "What do you mean 'yeah'? Why the fuck are we kidnapping the daughter?"

There was a moment of silence, a patter of offbeat clicks he recognized as strokes on a keyboard.

May watched him silently. Unblinking despite the rain.

"Your mission," Stone replied slowly, his easy voice cautious, "is to extract her. We wouldn't do it if it weren't important."

We. And that was the problem, wasn't it? Somehow, this Church dog had become a *we*.

"Shit."

Kayleigh Lauderdale. Shawn raked his wet hair back with one impatient hand.

He didn't want a shot at the daughter.

Jennifer's hand darted out, plucked the comm from his grip before Shawn's fingers could lock around it. The look she shot him simmered, but her voice pitched to carry over the splatter of the pouring rain. "What does the rest of the data coming out look like, Jonas?"

"Lots of chatter," he replied without missing a beat. "And I mean, like, ice cream social, somebody nobody likes just won an award kind of chatter."

"What are they saying?" Shawn demanded.

"Sorry, it's encrypted tight enough to take me a week to crack."

All three pairs of eyes turned to May. Her smile flickered, a fast curve quickly gone. "Minimum of five days." She was better at it, but if she meant it, not by more than a hair.

"They've changed every encryption," Stone explained. "We've lost every last plant up there and we've got no interior access to their closed system. All we have is mid-low sources and they're drying up fast after Danny's jailbreak. What I can tell you is that something big is going down. Not now, but soon."

Shawn's lip curled into a snarl. "Why aren't we taking the opportunity to plant something in their systems?"

"May?"

The woman shrugged. "We won't have the opportunity to smuggle in you and a tech to do the planting. It's a plant or the objective. Once you're up there, it's closed comms 'til you're out."

And they thought Kayleigh Lauderdale was worth more than a jack into Church systems?

Shit. He had nothing to argue with.

"What do we have on the daughter?" Jennifer asked.

"Not much," Jonas replied. "All I've got is what you already know. She's Lauderdale's daughter and the newest scientist in charge of the Salem Project."

The witch factory. A place where Laurence Lauderdale bred witches for his own use.

One of the most closely guarded secrets of the century. At least until a few months back, when a Mission operation had gone sideways and details started leaking into May's hands.

Nasty business. Made all the nastier when Shawn started putting pieces together himself. The lab, the timing.

Lauderdale's presence at his parents' house sixteen years ago.

Shawn had learned long ago how much the Holy Order of St. Dominic pissed on things like morality and ethics. And *truth*.

Good to know the daughter didn't stray far from her daddy's crooked path.

Even better to know he had an opportunity to dish out his own brand of payback to the man who had forever scarred Shawn's world.

"All right," Jennifer said, squaring her shoulders, "we're a go. Kevin, pick up Jim and Donald. We're going to have to set up camp near enough that we can provide support."

"On it." The man shook himself, splattering raindrops in a wide arc, and turned. He loped to the edge, where a ladder bolted to the far wall creaked beneath his weight.

Shawn turned to May. "Why her?" He didn't mean Jennifer, and May knew it.

"She's the only option we have."

"For what?" he demanded, ignoring the team lead as she raised the comm to her ear and spoke into it. Procedural crap, probably. She was good at that stuff.

"She's Laurence Lauderdale's daughter," May said, steel once more buried in her voice. Her stare. If she was at all put off by the rain, by Shawn's looming challenge, she didn't bend even a little to show it.

Sixteen years earned her a lot of leeway.

It didn't earn him quite as much. Not as much as he needed.

And what he needed was Kayleigh's father. He wanted to get his hands around the man's throat so badly, he could taste the raw edges of a violence he'd kept simmering, festering, for over a decade.

He could make do with *her*, if he had to. *Lever-*

age. He lowered his head against the fat drops sliding out of the neon sky. "Have you heard from Amanda?" The abrupt change of subject didn't faze her.

He didn't realize he was holding his breath until sympathy colored her frown. "You asked me that yesterday."

"I'll ask until the answer I want to hear comes in," he said, but roughly. Anger filled his chest where pain had settled only an hour ago. "Have you seen anything about Amanda and her team?"

She blew out a hard breath. "No."

"Damn it, May!"

Thirty-seven days imprisoned up in the Mission cells. The resistance—even May, with all her technological savvy—had no eyes on the group that had been ferreted out and arrested by missionaries. No ears in the topside Church quad. Nothing.

If anyone was still alive, would they be worth saving?

Yes. Hell, yes.

"We have one goal, here," she said, a lashed reminder. An order. "One. Concentrate on that. Let me worry about Amanda and the others."

"Are you still trying?" he demanded, staring down at her. Willing her to crack, just a little. Let him see what filled her head, her heart.

Show him that she cared as much as he did.

"Yes," she said, so matter-of-fact that he wanted to snarl. To shout. To swear.

But that was May. Iron-willed and steady.

She cared. He knew she did. But in the scheme of things, half a dozen resistance fighters were expendable if it meant saving more.

That's why they operated they way they did. Only a

handful of cells knew of May's existence. Fewer knew her name.

No one, not even her grandson, knew where she lived, or how many cells she operated. The less a member knew, the less he could spill his guts at the hands of the Mission interrogators.

The Church was always on the lookout for insurgents. Rebels. Heretics, they called anyone they dragged in for questioning. Witches or witch sympathizers.

Heretics, his ass. Maybe a quarter of the resistance claimed any sort of magical hijinks. The Mission just slapped that name on anyone they wanted.

Amanda Green was at least a witch of some skill, but her team were all like Shawn. Normal.

Resistance members. Protestors.

He'd known her for years. Partied with her, fought by her side. He owed her more than just a *try*.

Fine. He couldn't get his hands on Laurence Lauderdale for a crime sixteen years old, but he sure as shit could get his daughter.

She'd be worth more than a few resistance fighters. She'd be worth the whole damned lot.

"Jonas says the system swap is going to happen soon," Jennifer called. "We need to go."

His guts rolled. Fury. And fear.

Would May understand?

Shawn swallowed it down. Frowned as he asked, "How long do I have up there?"

Eyes glinting, May turned back to the scarred lot at the foot of the tenement. Her mouth, a thin line, settled into a grim slash. "A few hours, maybe. You're lacking real credentials, so you'll have to move fast. We've prepared what little we know for you, including the location of her personal lab and what Parker remembers of the quad layout." A beat, a ghost of a smile. "That girl remembers everything. Any questions?"

Lots. Too many, and none of them with easy answers.

Shawn didn't turn; couldn't bring himself to face out over that lot again and see what it used to be. The rooftop garden before the city had gotten too damned tall to let the sun through. The paint splashed on walls to hide the wear.

His mother's smile, when she was wrist-deep in washing.

Fuck. His heart squeezed hard.

"Go get her, Shawn," May said quietly, turning up the collar on her coat. It hid half her profile, muffled her voice. "Bring her back. It's imperative we get her intel."

"What intel?"

"She's the daughter of a Church director," May said, no answer at all. "She'll have intel."

"Intel that Mission director couldn't give you?"

"Ex-director," May corrected, not for the first time. "And yes. Exactly that."

He narrowed his eyes, but she didn't look at him.

Grunting wordless annoyance, he spun, strode across the lot, and didn't care that he kicked up gravel and sodden dirt in his wake.

Jennifer frowned into the patchwork neon sky at whatever Stone said in her ear. As Shawn grabbed the ladder, turning to step down, he watched the woman approach May, touch her arm.

May bent to listen.

Her face a pale blur, the team lead gestured as she shaped words he couldn't hear. When her eyebrows knitted, Shawn recognized the signs.

May had just won a debate. Probably with her usual end-of-discussion say-so.

With a glance toward him, Jennifer threw up her hands and stalked to the ladder.

He didn't bother to wait.

This was where things had to change. For Amanda and her team; for him, and all his nebulous plans.

For everyone.

He had to put on his good little sheep face.

CHAPTER TWO

"**A**re you sure you're feeling all right?"

Dr. Kayleigh Lauderdale unfolded the lab coat laid out with the rest of her belongings, smoothing out the wrinkles seventy-two hours had creased into the starched fabric. It was easier to concentrate on that little detail than the embarrassment, the irritation, the harmless question caused.

No. No, she wasn't feeling all right. She hadn't felt *all right* in days. Months, maybe.

"I'm fine," she said, not for the first, second, even third time. "Really, Dad, I feel much better."

Yet, like the first, second, and third time she'd said it, Laurence Lauderdale looked less than convinced. Worry lines bit deeply into his wizened features, his pale blue-gray eyes intent as he studied her from the hospital suite door.

He didn't help her pack what few things she'd

needed for her too-long stay in the observation suite. She didn't ask him to help.

Her father had never been young, not in her memory. Always distinguished, even in her childhood, now he hovered on the brink of ancient. Deep trenches scored a face more often set to stern than gentle, carved brackets around a mouth whose lips had vanished over the years. His hair, once the same honey-toned blond as hers, had faded to pure white, thinned until the age spots mottling his pink scalp nearly overwhelmed what hair was left.

He was eighty-three to her thirty, but the generational gap had never bothered her so much as when he watched her with concern, with care. As now.

He looked so frail. So much more brittle with every passing year. He needed less stress, not more. He needed her to do her part.

She sighed, pausing with a comfortably worn sweater in one hand and her digital reader in the other. "I'm sorry for worrying you, Dad. The doctors assure me it was only a migraine." A bad one, sure, and not the first of its kind. The first was enough to cause her to faint in her own lab.

Subsequent episodes proved too intense to safely ignore.

But two days of sedation and two more of observation, while mind-bogglingly dull, hadn't offered any more insight than what Kayleigh already knew.

She was exhausted, worn out by an ongoing bout of insomnia and an ulcer slowly eating through the lining of her stomach. When she closed her eyes, her mind repainted graphic images across the backs of her eyelids: a tiny, stifling room, screams reverberating in tandem with the crackle of an intercom.

It had been only three weeks since the Holy Order agents had interrogated Parker Adams in her own Mission cells.

More days than Kayleigh liked of her hospital stay were spent staring at the white ceiling, replaying the events of the Mission director's betrayal over and over in her head.

Parker, cold as ice in every previous meeting Kayleigh had ever had with her, lived up to the challenge. She'd screamed—God, she'd screamed—but Kayleigh remembered her accusations more.

Your father is butchering people.

Wild claims, anger and hatred and envy, for all Kayleigh knew. But they stuck. They echoed.

On bad nights, she found herself back in that room, staring down the barrel of Simon Wells's gun.

Suffer the consequences with the rest of them.

Simon was one of her Salem subjects. A man bred from witch and missionary DNA. He'd always been a wild card; an agent who skirted every rule she'd ever laid out.

Her half brother, Parker had claimed. The first of her dead mother's secrets.

Exhaustion. Sure. It was as good a word as any.

She hadn't mentioned any of it to the doctors of the Magdalene Asylum. When it came to her health, she'd learned long ago that they reported to her father, and he had enough to worry about. Especially now, with the Mission in disarray and the Church demanding solutions.

When Laurence smiled, he revealed teeth that had long since been replaced by dentures, but his eyes crinkled. "If you're sure, I should go handle this press release." And just like that, it was back to work.

She winced. She'd been a late-in-life baby, but Kayleigh had never really felt unloved.

Just . . . sometimes a little invisible. When she wasn't being smothered.

"Kayleigh?"

Her stomach cramped. "Yes, absolutely." She zipped the small overnight bag closed, adjusted her hair with a quick hand through it. She ran a critical eye over her small suite. Rumpled bed, machines no longer beeping at her with every heartbeat, a vase of expensive flowers her father had sent a day ago.

That was it. A brief stay, inconclusive tests, and a bunch of hothouse blooms. Talk about wasted time.

"I have a field trip, anyway," she added briskly.

"Oh?"

She turned her back on the room. "I want to go down to the GeneCorp facility, see if there's any—"

His face clouded. "No."

Kayleigh frowned back at him. "Why not?"

"That place is dangerous and near to collapsing." He shook a gnarled finger at her, emphasizing his point. "You should have access to all the data the techs were able to pull. You don't need to go yourself."

Except she did. Because techs knew only one language, and it wasn't hers. They'd never know what they'd be looking at. Kayleigh would.

"But I can—"

"The answer is no, Kayleigh. Get it out of your mind."

Frustration gnawed at her.

His worn, arthritic fingers curved over her shoulder. "You should go home, get some rest. You've earned it, sweetheart."

If only. "I can't." Especially not now that he'd taken away her one shot at a lead.

He frowned at her, thick, wiry eyebrows knitting. "I haven't looked over your charts yet. What did the doctors say?"

For the first time in what seemed like an eternity, a smile worked its way to her lips. She touched his hand gently. "Same thing the doctors always tell you, Dad. Rest more, work less, eat better."

He snorted. "Smart mouth. Like your mother."

Twenty-two years of coming to terms with Matilda Lauderdale's death meant she no longer flinched at the reminder of her mother. Her rueful humor eased into something quietly sad, instead.

Something slightly bitter.

Her mother. Half the reason Kayleigh was even in this predicament. "Speaking of," she said, frowning over her father's stooped figure. The clock on the wall told her it was only just after one. Her techs would be leaving, an hour before the next shift change, but there was plenty of time to get some work done. "If I can't go down to the old lab, I need to go to mine. The Eve sequence won't patch itself."

"Are you sure you don't want to take the day off?"

"To do what with?" she asked wryly. "You know I'd only work from home."

"I know." His smile went crooked. "That's my girl." Laurence shifted, elbowing the door wider and gesturing a faintly trembling hand to the hall beyond. It was quiet in the recuperation floors, empty of personnel. "I knew you'd pull through."

She usually did. Anything else would only disappoint everyone counting on her. Kayleigh slung the bag over her shoulder as she matched her father's halting steps down the pristine white hall. "Will the press conference be complicated?" she asked, looking down at his mottled head.

Once upon a time, he'd stood taller than her. She couldn't remember exactly when that had changed.

If he felt his years, he didn't show it. Dedication; that was the Lauderdale way. "Bishop Applegate and I are working out the details," he replied. "That Adams woman left the Mission a mess. We've had to plug the holes with our own."

Our own. Once, the witch-hunting arm of the Holy Order of St. Dominic had been completely separate from Sector Three, the research and development division. The Mission had housed their headquarters in the Holy Order's central quadplex, across from her father's Sector Three and flanked by the Holy Cathedral and the New Seattle civics center on either end. At the peak of the metropolis, these four structures comprised the seat of power in the city.

A seat Parker Adams had tipped over.

With so many missionaries gone traitor or killed in the ensuing fighting, Kayleigh wasn't surprised to learn her dad had filled in the missing agents with subjects from Sector Three's ongoing Salem Project.

Regardless of everything else, there was always the threat of witchcraft in New Seattle's streets. The Coven of the Unbinding might have been dismantled, but that didn't stop so-called resistances from causing trouble in the rest of the city. A full missionary force needed to be ready at all times.

Still, it seemed wrong to her. The Salem witches weren't a long-term solution, not as long as they kept breaking down. Dying.

But that was *her* responsibility.

Kayleigh nodded, but slowly. As her dad stabbed the elevator button, she stared sightlessly at the silver door and wondered how many of their "own" would make it through the transition phase.

The project combined the best of witch DNA with the hardiest of missionary samples. The whole process had been started by Laurence and Matilda Lauderdale before the quakes that had crumbled the old city of Seattle five decades ago, continued through the rebuilding, through Matilda's death, even through Kayleigh's meteoric rise through the classified ranks of the research and development sector.

They hadn't made new subjects in twenty-five years, but time was ticking. The subjects were dying. Science demanded progress.

Her father needed her to come through.

"I need to meet with the planning committee before the conference," her father said as the doors slid open on a faint hiss of compressed air. "You'll be all right?"

"I'll be fine," she promised, summoning as reassuring a smile as she could. She resisted the urge to rub her stomach. It wouldn't help. "Will you be home for dinner?"

His face clouded. "Not tonight, sweetheart."

He didn't offer an excuse. She didn't ask. The excuses all started to sound the same, anyway; work, work, and more work. She did it, too. "Okay. I'll just have something delivered."

"Don't work too hard." He patted her hand, dry skin of his palms rasping against hers. "Oh, before I forget. I've arranged for someone to keep you company—"

That got her attention. "What? Dad, no."

"Don't argue with me," he said over her. Old he might be, stooped and gnarled, but when he spoke like that, his faded eyes sharp as glass, even Kayleigh recognized a lost cause. "You work longer hours than your techs and I don't want you alone until these migraines go away. The material you're working on is too sensitive to risk another lapse, am I clear?"

She gritted her teeth, forced herself to keep from flinching. "Yes, sir," she said, because he wasn't speaking to her as her father now. He spoke as Sector Three's director, her superior in every way.

"Security will meet you at your lab. I've pulled from Bishop Applegate's complement, so don't give them any lip." Gesturing her inside the smooth, reflective elevator, he added, "Keep me apprised of the project."

"I will."

"And, Kayleigh?" He thrust a hand against the panel edge, glowering at her from beneath his protruding eyebrows. "Take care of yourself, sweetheart. I worry about you."

Her mouth drifted up in one corner. "I will," she repeated. The doors slid shut on his nod, and Kayleigh allowed herself the luxury of leaning back against the paneled wall.

The reflection staring back at her looked tired. Even taking the time she'd had—showering away four days of immobility, fixing her hair into loose waves, putting on a bit of makeup to offset the shadows under her eyes—didn't wholly help. Her navy blazer, yellow sleeveless blouse, and khaki slacks looked both sunshiny and professional; her bright red flat shoes provided a flash of contrast that she'd hoped would cheer her up.

It didn't work. Her father's concern, his obsession with his work, her own workaholic tendencies were catching up.

As soon as she completed this project, she was going to take a vacation. A long, do-nothing vacation where she holed up in her suite, never got out of her pajamas, and slept for as long as she wanted.

There were days when her job sucked.

She'd followed in her parents' footsteps, was good at it. She loved the challenge of mapping the witch-craft allele in human DNA, loved the puzzle of fitting the pieces together. But then, along came one she couldn't solve.

The Eve sequence.

The one thing that could stop the catastrophic breakdown of the Salem subjects, the thing her mother had died before she could finish, became Kayleigh's responsibility.

Working on it made her feel closer to her mother. Talking about it made her feel closer to her dad, whose eyes would light with the challenge. Just as hers had, once.

It seemed a lifetime ago.

She'd started banging her head against the problem only a few months ago, when her predecessor had un-expectedly died. Nadia Parrish had been one of her father's contemporaries, but she was no Matilda Lau-derdale in capability.

Neither, for that matter, was Kayleigh.

To have her father—to have the director of Sector Three trust Kayleigh with such a monumentally im-portant task, to be thought of as not just an adequate replacement but even on equal terms with her mother before her . . .

Kayleigh scrubbed her face with one hand.

So much pressure.

At least her vision was clear today, no low-key corona hanging over the lights or flickering wildly. Going back to work might just be enough to trigger another migraine, but at least she'd have a babysitter to catch her this time.

Going home didn't really appeal. She hadn't slept much in months, anyway, and she'd long since learned there were no answers written on her bedroom ceiling.

The elevator doors slid open. She strode into the hall that was like every other corridor in the Magdalene Asylum, faceless and marked only by indecipherable numbers. Though New Seattle's premier hospital took up the first dozen or so floors, Sector Three claimed the rest. Labs filled the building, large to small, from the theoretical to the experimental.

Lab Seventeen—her lab, specializing in whatever genetic projects she fancied—occupied a good portion of this hall, though she didn't need that much space. Most of the time, the equipment remained dark and under protective wraps. Since being handed the Salem Project responsibilities, she hadn't had any opportunity to play with her own endeavors.

If all went well, if she could crack the anomaly cutting the lifespan of Salem subjects tragically short, she'd have more data for her own use. If she could get inside the single, tiny allele responsible for the abilities the rest of the world called witchcraft, she could have the foundation for the greatest scientific breakthrough in decades.

If. Big if.

So far, she was coming up empty with a whole lot of

degenerated subjects fed to the incinerators. Just like Mrs. Parrish's attempts before her. Her own father's before that.

So many failed.

Her footsteps slowed as she rounded the final corner. Maybe she should have stopped for coffee. And lunch, for that matter. Hospital food, premier or not, left a lot to be desired.

Before she could decide one way or another, motion drew her attention to a figure standing just outside Lab Seventeen's secure door. The fluorescent lights, unkind even without the hovering threat of visual impairment, painted the man's back in matte black; a broad, large frame.

She frowned. Her very own security agent, huh?

At this distance, she picked out athletic shoulders. Thick arms encased in a black synth-leather jacket, which surprised her. His denim, worn in the seat—and stretched comfortably enough across a backside as strongly defined as the rest of him—seemed wildly out of place up here in business-dress civilization.

His hair seemed black in the same light, but as he turned, glints of rich, dark auburn flickered through the strands. She blinked as she realized the open jacket did nothing to conceal a muscular chest that tapered down to lean hips, clad in a plain dark blue shirt that also surprised her. She'd expected something in black, to suit the whole dangerous-missionary vibe he had going on.

Her gaze trailed over him, narrowing. His jaw was not only chiseled in every way she'd ever thought of the word, but darkened by a five o'clock shadow she found wholly unnecessary at one in the afternoon.

His hair—longer than she expected from any kind of security force—curled faintly at the ends, which brushed his collar and fell across his forehead.

It looked soft.

She didn't need to be thinking about how soft it looked, either.

And when his eyes, the same dark shade as his hair, met hers across the hall, she couldn't help but think that he knew what she'd *been* thinking.

A surge of annoyance, as unwelcome as the sudden jolt of awareness, flickered through her.

This man didn't exactly scream *danger*, no more so than any other athletic man in street-ready clothing, but something about the way he looked at her took the fine hair on the back of her neck and raised it on end.

This was a man she'd think twice before tangling with. In any way except one.

Kayleigh liked men she shouldn't like. Enjoyed looking at the agents whose paths she sometimes crossed. Liked, specifically, the rough-and-ready ones, the men who looked as if they could get into a back-alley fight with a posse of angry witches and come out on top.

Like this one.

It was one of the many reasons she didn't date. Her father had long since made his requirements as to her social life clear.

No scandal. No one who couldn't live up to dinnertime conversation.

No nonscientists, really.

This man was not a scientist. If she started talking DNA sequencing and genetic therapy, his eyes would probably glaze.

She could think of a half dozen more interesting ways to make his eyes glaze.

Damn it, Kayleigh.

Mouth tightening, she fished her comm out of her bag, snapped it open, and stabbed her father's code. Laurence answered quickly. "What is it?"

"Are you sure I need a keeper?" she asked, her eyes pinned on the man's own. His expression revealed nothing. Not even an eyebrow rose at her obvious rudeness.

"Yes," came her father's sigh, crackling faintly on the line. "A security detail is necessary. As are any of the other personnel I send to you."

"What if I need to do classified work?" Specifically, on the Salem Project, which still hadn't hit mainstream channels. Yet.

"You're a smart girl, Kayleigh," came her father's firm response. "You'll figure it out."

Her nose wrinkled. "I can't talk you out of it?"

There. A flicker of something at the corner of the man's mouth—she might have called his lips feminine on anyone else, but surrounded by all that raw masculinity, she didn't dare. His hands slid into the front pockets of his jeans, thumbs out, as if he could wait all day long.

"No," Laurence told her. "And that's the last time I'll say it. Be courteous when the agent arrives."

Augh. She wanted to stamp her foot. "Fine," she replied, barely managing not to snap. "Good luck with the conference." She clicked the comm closed, ending the connection.

Tucking the device back into her bag gave her the opportunity to run her options through her head.

Easy. Leave, or get to work.

She was a fully capable adult. Whatever signals her body sent her, she was the one in control.

Besides, she was already here. If she turned around

and left now, he'd know he discomfited her. Add that to another restless night and she'd kick herself in the morning.

She raised her head as she approached the door. And its guard. "So you must be my babysitter," she said dryly, as if he hadn't just witnessed that entire exchange. At least her part of it.

"Guilty as charged." His voice, not completely lacking in humor, was slow and deep. Cool, but at least he didn't try to pull the usual overly charming tactics Kayleigh had gotten used to from men like him.

The color of her hair had nothing to do with her level of social acuity.

He stepped aside as she approached, his arms folded over his chest. "I take it you aren't happy with this." It wasn't a question.

She pressed a finger to the security lock. "What's your name?"

"Lowe, ma'am. Shawn Lowe."

"I'm Dr. Kayleigh Lauderdale." The computer ticked softly. "What are the odds, Shawn Lowe, that you'll be one of those babysitters that finds a corner and occupies yourself while the geneticist does her job?" She didn't look at him, bending to fit her eye to the small retinal scanner just over the thumb lock.

If he smiled, if he frowned, she had no idea. All he said was, "Good odds."

"Great." The door hissed open, revealing a swath of protective plastic.

This time, when she straightened and glanced at him, a faint haze of light clung to his skin. His hair. Turned his swarthy skin to something sheened with gold.

She scowled, digging a thumb into one eye. She'd

only just gotten out of the freaking hospital; could her body give her one day without complications? Just one.

He didn't notice, studying the open door. "Do I need to wear anything in particular?"

Less might be nice.

She cleared her throat. "No. Just don't touch anything, and try not to distract anyone."

When his mouth slanted upward, she repressed a hissed breath. She did *not* just call him distracting. "Okay. How many?"

"What?"

He raised a strong-looking hand, idly scratched the side of his whiskered jaw. "You said 'distract anyone.' How many people am I dealing with?"

No one, if she had her way. She wanted him in a corner, away from everything inside. Away from her. Instead, she shrugged. "Two techs at any given time, at least until ten o'clock."

"Closing time?"

Not for her. "Something like that." She pushed in ahead of him, one hand curling into a fist against her stomach. It sizzled.

Maybe skipping lunch was a good idea after all.

•

CHAPTER THREE

Too easy. That worried him like hell.

Shawn followed Dr. Lauderdale into the laboratory, ducking beneath a folded flap of plastic that only just grazed the top of her blond head. She didn't give it any notice, which told him that she was used to the lab and its security measures.

He wasn't. He'd have to pay close attention before he gave anyone the impression that he didn't belong here.

"Dr. Lauderdale!"

He hung back as a portly man with a black goatee approached, brown eyes bright.

The doctor smiled, but from Shawn's diagonal vantage point, it seemed strained. "I'm fine, Gerry, before you ask."

"You sure? Can I get you anything?"

"No—" She shook her head briefly, cutting herself off. "Yes, you can start with anything important I need to know. Have the results from the latest projections been calculated?"

"Calculated and run through the system," he replied immediately. "No immediate improvement. Two out of seven projections suffer catastrophic breakdown before fifteen."

A muscle jumped in her left temple, so subtle Shawn wondered if he'd imagined it.

The man slanted Shawn a suspicious, skeptical glare.

"Ignore him," she said, distracted more than rude. He bit back a grin. "He'll find space in a corner somewhere."

Only until he coaxed her out of this thinly concealed prison.

"Sure," Gerry said, not as convinced as she seemed to be.

"Welcome back, Doctor!"

He watched as Dr. Lauderdale greeted another lab-coated professional. Petite, silver-haired, with glasses perched on the end of her nose and a beaded chain affixing them to her white lapel.

The lab was big, spacious enough to accommodate more than three people, but most of the equipment was shrouded beneath protective plastic and white cloth. A few machines hummed, as alien as anything Shawn had ever seen, and a handful of monitors gave evidence to the work going on in the lab.

He'd need a translator to know what that was. Something genetic, no doubt. Maybe even something to do with the witch factory.

It didn't matter. That wasn't his focus here.

"Doctor?"

Shawn transferred his study to the older woman,

then flicked it to Dr. Lauderdale. She hadn't moved, studying the lab with something he couldn't read shaping her expression. Uncertainty? Pensiveness, definitely.

He cleared his throat.

She blinked, turned a questioning, distant glance past him. "Mm?"

"Rachel and I organized your last three projects. The data is on your computer and copies are on your desk. It includes your next seven projections," she added.

Gerry nodded emphatically, chin wobbling.

"Thank you, Paula." So polite, Shawn thought. Weirdly so. "This is Shawn Lowe, he's going to be our guest for—" Her gaze flicked to him briefly. "Hopefully not for that long. He's only partially briefed, so keep classified material secure."

Paula flashed him a smile, brackets appearing around her pink-painted mouth. "Nice to meet you. Do you want us to wait for a while before we leave, Doctor?"

"No," Kayleigh said, shaking her head. "Go on, the others will be in soon. I'll get to work on the backlog."

Aware he hadn't made it far out of the foyer, Shawn stepped aside, clearing room for them to pass.

Gerry hesitated. "Before I forget, the last analysis you sent out on the contents of that syringe came back."

The doctor's shoulders tensed. Imperceptible, save that Shawn stood right behind her.

"It's with the rest of the project material," Gerry continued, speaking as if it wasn't strange at all to find random syringes around.

"Results?"

He shrugged. "Junk, junk, and more junk."

A syringe full of junk? What did that mean?

"Did the analysis fail?" she asked.

"Not that I can tell. We thought about running more tests on it here, but with no instructions on it and no labels . . ." A note of censure colored the man's trailed-off explanation.

She didn't seem to notice. "No, that's great," she murmured. "Thanks, Gerry."

But then, it was a lab. Maybe syringes weren't all that uncommon. God only knew what they got up to in here.

Shawn wasn't going to find out. He needed to pack up the doctor and get her out immediately.

Before the real security detail came calling.

Paula shrugged out of her white protective coat, folding it over one arm. "Do you need anything before we go?" When the doctor didn't automatically respond, Paula cast Shawn an exasperated look he took to mean she was often like this. He shrugged.

"Dr. Lauderdale?" Paula pressed. "Coffee? Food?"

"Oh." The doctor's hand slipped between the flaps of her lab coat, pressed against her stomach. "No, thank you. See you tomorrow."

When the other woman's gaze turned to him, penciled-in eyebrows rising, Shawn shook his head silently.

With a shrug and a last suspicious stare, Gerry and Paula stepped out of the lab, through the plastic siding.

The door hissed closed behind them, mechanical tumblers snicking quietly into place.

For a long moment, Shawn watched the tense line of her shoulders. Was he expected to go in ahead of her or wait?

What was she thinking?

Shawn didn't know. He didn't care, really, except that it provided him with ample opportunity to study her. Watch her.

Laurence Lauderdale's daughter didn't surprise him in any way. Her wealth of tousled blond hair, her professionally cool demeanor, even the designer brands she wore—all of it was everything he expected from a rich man's kid. The top of her head only just reached his chin, which placed her at about five-foot-seven. Her eyebrows were fine, a few shades darker than her hair.

She was pretty, in a polished sort of way. Only a blind man could miss it. Had he been some random guy—or Gerry the portly scientist—Shawn could have taken the time to appreciate the slender body beneath her shapeless lab coat. He might have taken some time to watch her mouth as it moved, soft lines and full upper lip.

But she was Kayleigh Lauderdale. No matter how innocent she *looked*, she wasn't. End of story.

So he looked away from the profile of her high cheekbones and her downturned mouth.

If she seemed a little forlorn standing alone in the now-empty lab, that wasn't Shawn's problem.

"I'll just—" His voice fractured the heavy silence. She jumped, startled, and sidestepped into him, hard enough to rattle the air in his lungs.

"Oomph!" Her body rebounded against his, a distinct impression of feminine warmth slammed into kinetic reverse. One of his hands curled around the back of her neck by habit. Her elbow jammed into his side as he snaked his other arm around her waist, steadied her on her feet.

She sucked in a breath.

Every nerve in his fingertips lit. Warmth, subtle heat from her nape, slid into his skin, trailed into tingling awareness at the pads of his fingertips. Shimmered up his fingers, into his palm.

He was seized with a sudden, aggravatingly sharp urge to tighten his grip. To press his palm flat at her nape, feel the delicate hairs there tickle his sensitized skin, smooth as silk.

To hold her still while he—

Let her go.

He did. Fast.

Shit. There would be no handling of Kayleigh fucking Lauderdale. Not unless it involved her neck in a completely different kind of grip.

Color filled her cheeks as she backed away. "I'm so sorry. Are you all right?" Polite. Carefully conscientious. "I'm not used to having someone so . . ." She gestured vaguely. "Close."

Tense as hell, he noted, eyes on the fist at her side.

That made two of them.

He forced his expression into even, unreadable lines. Resisted the urge to run his still-humming hand through his hair to wipe the feel of her skin from it.

It would take more than a mild collision to put him down. "Tell me where to sit and I'll get out of your way," he said, throwing courtesy to the wind. If it came out hard, she'd deal with it.

She blew out a quiet, steady breath, gaze flicking to the lab again. "There." She pointed.

He almost laughed, except he didn't find anything funny about Dr. Kayleigh Lauderdale. "An examination chair."

The color at her cheeks heightened. "Sorry. We

don't have anywhere else comfortable for long periods of sitting." When he said nothing, she added, "It's never been used. I don't know why we have it, really, except one never knows."

Never knows when a cadre of butchers would need a living specimen? Sure. He'd buy that.

"I'll try the stool," he told her, ignoring the sudden, diamond glint in her eye. The way her mouth flattened.

"Suit yourself." She shook off whatever lethargy had grabbed her and strode around a covered batch of strange devices.

Just like that, he was on his own.

That worked for him.

Shawn took a seat at one of the tech chairs, settling into the round, padded seat with a grimace.

How the hell would he get her out of this place?

The team had known going in what kind of chances they faced pulling this off. Shawn had gotten lucky enough to be in the right place at the right time, which was a hell of a lot better than trying to break into the vaultlike security of her lab.

"Computer," she said, and his eyebrows rose. "Print out latest analysis of unknown viscous contents." Blue-gray eyes flicked to him. "Print out reports of generational degeneration from current projects as of two weeks ago."

Interesting.

"Powering up," said a pleasant automated voice from somewhere near her. A bank of monitors beside her flickered on. "Printing."

Well, hell. He knew at least one computer geek who'd sell her right kidney for this setup. He'd have to send word to May about this. Eventually.

If she ever forgave him.

Kayleigh Lauderdale bent over the table, using a finger to scroll through the data on the monitor. Within less than thirty seconds, her posture shifted. She gathered her hair into a loose tail, wrapped an elastic band around it.

The end result left her looking like somebody's fresh-faced kid sister, all blond tendrils and bright eyes and playing at scientist.

Except the Holy Order didn't play.

Her shoulders tensed as she pored over the data.

Shawn got the impression he'd been forgotten.

Workaholics. They were all the same.

This one breathed a whispered, "Damn it."

"Problem?"

She straightened, shooting him a look over her shoulder he couldn't decide was frustration at him or whatever irked her. "You wouldn't know."

Ouch. "Try me," he coaxed, deliberately affable. Just a buddy eager to lend an ear.

Except her gaze snapped to his, clashed. Whatever she'd heard in his words, it crackled between them, an electric intensity that sucker-punched him in the gut.

Before he could react—decide how—she looked away.

One hand flourished at him, a dismissive wave as she reached across her worktable and retrieved a stack of paper. She pulled the first few off the pile, skimmed through them quickly. "Damn it," she said again, sharper.

He stood. "Doctor?"

"It's just junk." Almost a snarl.

She was cute when she puffed up. Like a kitten.

Wait a damned minute. Cute? The hell she was.

Focus. "So you don't know what it is?"

"I know what half of it is," she said absently, glaring down at the paper. Shawn circled the table, leaned a hip against the edge.

She didn't seem to notice, chin lowered, brow furrowed.

"Maybe you ought to get out of the lab," he offered dryly.

"I just came back from out."

The preoccupied way she dismissed the idea almost made him smile. That same tone came from May all the time.

He didn't have the luxury to appreciate the similarities. He needed her out. "I mean," he clarified, "of the whole quad. When was the last time you had a change of scenery? A cup of coffee that didn't come from a vending machine?"

Now her gaze came up, eerily fog-touched. He expected her to have brown eyes, or maybe dark green. The shade of blue cut by gray seemed too direct; a frisson of surprise—of a strange sort of interest—skimmed through his system. "Mr. Lowe, are you asking me out to coffee?"

If she were any other woman, it wouldn't be coffee on his mind. The fact that it *wasn't* coffee on his mind was something he deliberately ignored. He did not need to be considering her that way. At all. She was a tool. A means to an end.

He forced himself to sound relaxed. Even friendly. "Coffee, sure. 'Out' is the relevant point. A walk around less"—what the hell would he call this?—"sterile environments might jog something loose for you."

She stared at him.

When the silence stretched to uncomfortable levels, when he found himself studying the curve of her top lip and the way her heartbeat pulsed at the side of her slender throat, she dropped the papers onto the desk. "You're a genius," she said, spinning as she shrugged out of her lab coat. "Let's go."

Getting out of the quad had been easy. Her silent bodyguard had followed her down the elevator, to the parking garage where her champagne-colored sports car waited in its designated slot.

He'd whistled at it as she popped the locks, then looked stunned when she'd handed him the keys. He didn't even ask why.

Men and cars.

Twenty minutes later, easing away from the sec-line checkpoint Kayleigh's identification allowed them to sail through, she decided that there was only one problem with being trapped in a car with a man whose worn jeans inspired all the wrong thoughts.

Notably, all the wrong thoughts now filling her head.

Kayleigh allowed the silence to grow, her gaze on the city passing her window. The heaters hummed softly, filling the car with warmth to combat New Seattle's autumn chill, and rain pattered against the windshield. As they moved deeper and deeper down the byway, the daylight took on a strange, counterfeit quality that—to her surprise—didn't seem to trigger her ocular issues.

Since that hallway moment shortly after her medical discharge, it'd been smooth sailing.

Instead, as true sunlight faded away, the streetlights glanced through the car windows, slid over the interior and lit up parts of her ruggedly handsome security agent. A flash of his fingers, one wide shoulder clad in matte black, his face, the grim edge to his mouth.

Shawn handled her car smoothly, large hands curving over the steering wheel like he held something precious. Aside from a brief moment when he'd folded into the seat and fumbled for the height adjustment, he drove her car like he owned it.

Like he had a right to it.

He still didn't ask why he drove. She didn't volunteer the details.

"Are you thinking about your work again?"

His dark voice filled the interior, smooth and dangerous. She shivered, suddenly aware that she wasn't looking outside anymore.

He'd caught her staring. Devouring, she admitted silently, and dropped her gaze to her hands, fisted around the straps of her purse.

"Not . . ." Her throat dried. "Not exactly."

Her insides churned, a sudden ache low in her belly unfurling, heating.

Bad move. Very bad.

She knew the drill. Close quarters created a false sense of intimacy. Include the stress from her work, the additional pressure of doing something she'd already been forbidden to do, and she was a basket case of raw nerves.

Kayleigh didn't date. She didn't sleep with many men because most of them were colleagues. Nice men, or at least brainy men who were great on the lab floor and about as exciting as hothouse tomato juice anywhere else.

To say nothing of her job getting in the way.

Headlights cut through the windshield, pooled into the car. One hand left the steering wheel. Touched her arm.

It was gentle, and under the navy blazer she wore, it wasn't as if she'd felt his skin, but her blood didn't care. It surged through her body, circled around that small touch, and brought heat to her cheeks.

"Are you all right, Dr. Lauderdale?"

No. At the moment, she felt like the slumming child she'd once been accused of being.

Because all she wanted to do was jump his body like a raw piece of meat.

Her father would be horrified.

"We should be arriving soon," she blurted, a desperate attempt to focus.

"Arriving where? I'll have to get directions if I need to get off the byway."

"Oh." Hadn't she said? Kayleigh winced. Way to come across like a complete fool. "We're going down to the industrial sector. There's a place there, the old GeneCorp facility?"

His eyebrows winged upward. "I know of it."

That didn't surprise her. Everyone in the Mission probably knew of it, by now. "We're headed there for some data."

"You think it'll have the answer to your whatever it is?" As she watched, he reached to his hip, picked up his comm, and scanned it quickly. Checking in with his people?

Probably. He was, after all, responsible for her safety. She tucked tendrils of her hair back behind her ear, gaze drifting again to the window. On the farthest lane, nothing but a guardrail and a sheer drop off the edge of the city met her gaze. The massive wall protecting the city from the ravaged world beyond it blocked everything else.

"I hope so," she murmured. Because if not, she was out of ideas.

She didn't want to think about work right now. Despite the distraction it posed from her entirely too attractive companion, it would only make her stomach hurt. Again. Still.

"So," she offered, drawing it out. The comm vanished into his pocket as he glanced at her. "Where are you from, Shawn?"

It was another full minute before he answered, eyes back on the road. "Down here."

No details came, and it took her another moment before she slapped her forehead with one hand. "I'm so sorry. Orphanage, right? Missionaries all come from there."

His gaze flicked to her again, a glint of obsidian until another streetlamp set his brown irises with gold. "Something like that."

"And so I did it again." Kayleigh's hand lowered to cover her mouth. "I'm sorry, I don't mean to bring up bad memories. Or anything."

His mouth quirked. "Anyone ever tell you that you need to relax?"

"Once," she answered without thinking. "Right before he stuck his tongue in my mouth." Not that she'd been complaining, at the time.

"That great, huh?"

Her brain caught up with what she must sound like to him, a total stranger babysitting the director's daughter. She cringed. "You don't want to know."

"Try me," he said, repeating his earlier offer and evoking all the same physical responses.

She'd like to.

Kayleigh looked away. "It's . . . not important."

"Let me guess," he said as he navigated across two lanes of thinning traffic. "Your boyfriend."

There was a word for it. The sound she made, torn between embarrassment and unstoppable humor, snorted. "He wasn't exactly that."

"Lover?"

"Once," she confirmed again, squirming in her luxury seat. It was all she'd been allowed before getting caught.

The disappointment in her father's eyes, the anger and sorrow, had been enough for a lifetime. She'd focused on school after that, on her studies, her grades. Later, her work, and the occasional seemingly nice man whose eyes didn't glaze over when she started talking about it.

"Sounds like he wasn't all that successful."

His voice curled into her skin, dug in nails that made her shiver.

She gripped her purse tighter. "It was a long time ago," she said, lifting her chin. "He got the job done."

For an eternal moment, silence reigned. Then, all at once, his laughter filled the car. Found all the secret places she very specifically hadn't been thinking about and stripped her defenses away.

She lusted after men who could laugh like this. Deep and solid, unabashed humor.

Even if he laughed at her.

"Why am I telling you this?" she groaned, looking away. "This is none of your business."

Except she knew why.

Laughter muted to rich, deep-chested chuckles, Shawn didn't reply.

Her heart slammed against her chest as Kayleigh stared fixedly out the windshield.

CHAPTER FOUR

He hadn't expected to laugh.

Hadn't expected the buttoned-up Dr. Lauderdale to actually confess to a virtual stranger to having a man who'd, Jesus, *gotten the job done.* He sure as hell hadn't expected the sudden, aching knot formed under his solar plexus at the mental image of his oblivious captive letting a man past her professional armor. Into that lab coat she'd worn so easily topside.

His humor drained away, leaving something else in its wake.

What would she be like, stripped of her expensive designer clothes, her shell torn away by the hard hands of a man who wouldn't be intimidated by the diamond-sharp intelligence in her fog blue eyes?

His guts clenched. A fiery kernel of something harsh and hungry slid tendrils of heat through his chest. Under his skin.

Would she moan his name? Or was she, as he suspected, a quieter lover? A woman who shuddered silently, sweat on her skin and her muscles clenched tight around—

God damn it. He reined in the visuals so hard, his hands cramped around the steering wheel.

It didn't matter. In less time than it'd take to inject her with the syringe in his jacket pocket, she'd be his prisoner. Not his fantasy.

Sure as hell not his lover.

The comm in his pocket thrummed silently. Without taking his eyes off the road, he reached down, grabbed the device, and raised it to eye level. Jennifer's directions glowed.

Let her look for her data. We can use it. It'll give us time to reconvene at the rendezvous point.

Use it? A bunch of decades-old information?

If he weren't already betraying May, he might have ignored the opportunity. Shot her full of the sedative, hauled her off to let his team sweat the sudden and unannounced change in plans.

Except the thought of his plan—a plan that didn't involve laughing with Dr. Kayleigh Lauderdale, teasing her—still made cold sweat break out on his shoulders.

Maybe if she found something, he'd hand it over to the woman he owed his life to. Maybe it'd soften the blow.

"Turn here." Her husky voice rubbed over his skin like something slick and expensive.

He set his jaw. "I know where it is," he assured her as he cut across the byway. Down this far, and he was practically home. Very little traffic made it down here by midday. Most would come later, when night fell and the clubs picked up the beat. Slummers from the mid-lows to the topside reaches. Drugs, drink, music, skin.

A lot of skin.

Did she dance?

She smiled, a crooked thing that didn't read as amusement so much as wryness. "I guess you did your homework."

Just enough to know the general details. Shawn navigated the sleek car through the dark streets, aware of how out of place the flashes of gold-shaded paint would be to anyone searching for an easy mark. The lights in the old industrial sector weren't as regular as the better-maintained levels above the mid-lows, but there were enough to make him hyperaware of the siren song of topside money.

At best, there'd be squatters in the district. At worst, any of the usual prowlers who called themselves a gang.

The gun holstered under his jacket would only be useful if he saw them coming.

"What's the plan?" he asked as the closely nestled warehouses abruptly widened into a series of gritty, broken asphalt and abandoned gravel lots. Structures hunkered at the farthest edges, many framed by rusted fences or the remnants of cement walls.

This district hadn't seen use for at least twenty years. Maybe more. Hard to tell when the neglect set in.

"Here," she said suddenly, her pale hand flashing in the ambient light filtering from the city rising high above them.

He followed her gesture, guided the car into one of the broken lots. The engine shut off. "Plan, Doctor?"

he coaxed. "Or will we kick down the door, guns blazing?"

Her surprising snort of amusement turned into throaty apology as she admitted, "I hadn't considered that. Do you . . ." Her head turned, gaze aimed at the abandoned complex at the far end of the lot. "Do you think there are people inside?"

The light loved Kayleigh Lauderdale. He couldn't help the thought. It touched her profile, skimmed silver-blue across her skin, made paler by the ambient luminescence dusting the sector around them.

The shape of her mouth, already full at her top lip and made all the more lush by the shadows in the car, pulled slightly to the side.

Shawn got the impression that she was always thinking.

Did she ever stop?

He got the job done.

He could do more than finish a job.

Already half aware of her every breath, his dick stirred—something between anger and panic clutched his chest.

She wasn't a woman. She wasn't a *person*. She was Kayleigh fucking Lauderdale, daughter of the man who'd murdered Shawn's parents. Related to one of the most secret and atrocious crimes against humanity since the witch fires fifty years ago.

She was . . . *beautiful.* Which made it all the worse, somehow.

"Shawn?"

His name on her lips sent another shaft of heat to his dick. Another fist around already too-sensitized flesh. He jolted in his own skin as those eyes turned back to him, luminously bright.

This car was too small. Too cramped. The air between them turned warmer, and as he took a deep breath through his nose, it occurred to him that she smelled like something fresh and clean. Rain without the acid tinge; a storm without the filthy undercurrent of refuse and mold.

Very carefully, Shawn peeled his fingers from around the steering wheel. *Do not touch.*

"We should—"

"Wait." She shifted in her seat, facing him, arms folded over her midsection. It bunched her yellow silk blouse against her body. Was it soft? It'd have to be. As soft as the skin beneath.

He watched, transfixed, as Kayleigh's tongue slid over her lips. A groan knotted in his chest; he forced it down. Swallowed it back.

"That boyfriend? The one that . . ."

He couldn't help himself. "That got the job done?"

Color slid into her cheeks. Shawn's hands curled into fists, tension locking them by his thighs before he did something stupid. Something purely driven by the hormones he hadn't expected to have to put a lock on.

"His name was Mark," she whispered, lashes lowering. Concealing the fiercely sharp glint in her eyes. "I was nineteen."

Why? Why did this matter? "Doctor—"

"Not that it's been that long since," she added hastily, looking down at her knees. "It's just that the men I date aren't usually so . . . They don't—"

Oh, Jesus. Shawn stared at her as her mouth worked around the words he was suddenly desperately afraid of hearing.

"This is not—" he began, and broke off when her

face came up, her eyes bright in cheeks so red, they were nearly purple in the blue-tinged light.

She raised a hand to pull tendrils from her face, absentmindedly self-conscious. "I don't know you at all. But I'd really . . . I mean, I'm wondering. Will you . . . Can I test something on you?" He managed a hoarse note of inquiry. "Will you kiss me?"

Kiss her. In this car. Her, a Lauderdale.

He wanted to.

"Fuck," he breathed.

She cringed, hands rising to cover her face. Embarrassment obvious, she blurted, "No, you're right, it's stupid, I don't know what—"

"Oh, no, you don't." Shawn didn't even really give himself the order. He caught her wrists, pulled her hands from her face, jerked her half out of her seat. As her surprised sound filled the cramped interior of her car, he slid one hand around her nape, trapped her half sprawled between the two seats. Her hand braced on his thigh, so close to his suddenly aching dick, he could barely concentrate.

Her eyes filled his vision. Bottomless, beautiful. So close, he could trace each individual lash framing her too-wide stare.

Anticipation filled him. Why not? A taste of her. Just one. He deserved it. And it'd make his revenge all the sweeter.

"You play chancy games with strange men, Dr. Lauderdale." His lips skimmed hers as he spoke, his threat flaring her eyes even wider. "You don't know anything about me."

"I know," she whispered. The fingers at his thigh tensed as he skimmed his own across her cheek. His thumb lingered at the corner of her mouth, so close to his. Her breath shuddered, peppering his skin with damp heat.

His cock hardened to near-pain. Even before he'd kissed her.

"I could be dangerous," he warned her softly.

Her nostrils flared as she inhaled. "I know."

Annoyance bit hard; infected the heat of his arousal with something fierce. Aggressive.

His fingers tightened on her nape.

"For a woman whose boyfriends don't satisfy her," he growled, "you claim to know a lot."

Kayleigh flinched, but he didn't give her the chance to back out now. She wanted a case study? He'd give her one.

He was the most dangerous thing she'd ever meet.

A sharp tug, and his mouth seized hers in a kiss that he didn't bother to start gentle. The instant her mouth touched his own, warm and soft, that spark of aggression intensified. Burned a path from lips to chest to dick, curled claws into his brain and ripped out everything that wasn't about her mouth, her skin under his fingers.

Her hand beside his crotch.

She gasped into his mouth as he tilted her head forcefully, swept his tongue between her parted lips to taste her. To coax her tongue against his, slide flesh to flesh and hear her muffled whimper as he drew back.

Pride flicked through him.

Her mouth, parted and damp from his kiss, gleamed as she stared in hazy bemusement. One of her hands braced against the dashboard, white-knuckled with effort, while the other still propped half her weight against his thigh. If she was uncomfortable in her half-sprawled position between the seats, he didn't see it.

All he saw was her flushed face, heard her panting breath as she struggled to slow it.

The pulse beneath his thumb hammered rapidly. Telling detail.

She swallowed hard, throat moving with the effort. "That . . . I, um . . ."

A smile tugged at his mouth. Predatory as hell. "Need more study, Doctor?"

She blinked. "No. No, I think I'm . . . good."

"Get what you need?"

He read the answer, watched the lie fill her features moments before she took a sharp breath and said quickly, "Yes, everything. Thank you."

His smile deepened. "Liar."

"I am n— Oh!"

Quicker than she could react, Shawn slid his hands under her arms, fingers spanning the delicate cage of her ribs, and hauled her across the rest of the gap.

This was not happening. This was completely not happening. Kayleigh froze as her knees came down on either side of Shawn's hips, as the steering wheel gouged into her back and forced her pelvis against his.

Long fingers spanned her waist under her jacket, burned through the silk of her blouse like it wasn't there.

Her lips tingled with the memory of the kiss that had already rocked her down to her obviously deranged soul. She couldn't take any more. Not without breaking every pact with herself she'd made over the years.

She flattened both hands against his chest—tried not to thrill as the contours of well-defined muscles flexed beneath her palms. "I'm good," she said, somehow managing stern. "Scientific inquiry well and truly settled." Her face burned with embarrassment.

And not just embarrassment.

"Is it?" His hands left her waist. A small relief torn away as they skimmed up her arms, over the sides of her neck, to ease into the loose knot of her hair. He tugged gently.

She resisted. "Shawn, this isn't—"

His eyes sparked, a strange mix of humor and implacable resolve. "Relax," he murmured.

Oh, God. The word melted like chocolate in her belly, intent pooling between her legs. The same legs cradling his hips.

The ridge of his erection, hard proof of his own reaction to her, only weakened her resolve further.

He wanted her. He couldn't hide it.

Kayleigh loved being wanted.

The fingers in her hair pulled harder. Her spine bent. His eyes filled her vision, nearly black in the dim light, until her lips brushed against his. Hesitated.

Shawn didn't wait.

She groaned as he pulled her face to his, as his lips nudged hers open for another deep, openmouthed kiss. Lips, tongue; he employed everything he had, turned Kayleigh's mind into a melted pool of immoral need, desperate craving. His whiskers, too rough to ever belong to any of those nice men, rasped against her sensitive skin, sending jolting little bolts of pleasure through her body.

He held her head like she was the most precious thing in the world, but he pulled her tight to his body as if she were nothing more than a nameless woman on the prowl. Hungry, wanting.

She wanted.

She shouldn't, but as he feasted at her lips, as his teeth nipped at her top lip and sent sparks through her vision, her mind, she groaned her surrender and tunneled her fingers into his hair. The ends tickled her skin, long enough to grasp, to hold him still as she tilted her head just so and deepened the kiss to something vulgar, something unrestrained and demanding.

She didn't know. Didn't care about anything except that he made a rough sound in his chest, let go of her head to grab her hips and pull her tight against his erection, nestled so squarely against the hot place between her legs.

More sparks. More need.

Rough and dangerous and more than illicit.

"Oh, my God," she whispered against his lips.

"Keep begging for help," he replied hoarsely, his voice as sensual as a rough hand between her legs.

Nice boys didn't do that. The nice men she'd sworn to date, the men she'd chosen to please her father, didn't pull her shirt from her waistband in a car parked in an abandoned lot. They didn't splay a callused hand across her ribs, hot and hard, or lift it to palm her breast, squeeze her sensitized, aching flesh over the beige lace of her bra.

Her head fell back as raw sensation swept under her skin. Sweat bloomed beneath her jacket, sent conflicting shocks of hot and cold in a trail of gooseflesh.

His hand left her breast, two fingers easing into her waistband. "I want to see you come."

Her eyes flew open. "What? No!"

"Let me get the job done." Shawn's expression,

ruthless in the dark, didn't soften. Didn't alter from the merciless intent of his fingers as they unsnapped her slacks. The zipper, delicate as it was, all but unzipped itself as the fabric pulled.

One hand fisted in the back of her jacket, pulled her shirt tight to her chest. Held her still. His hand slid between her splayed legs. One finger drew a thick line down the center of her matching lace panties, and her muscles clenched.

Her back hit the steering wheel. The dashboard shuddered. "Shawn, please."

"Jesus, you're already wet." The mutter wrapped around every nerve center in her brain and squeezed. Mortification warred with fierce pleasure; she arched back against the wheel as he traced her flesh, as his fingertips skated over damp fabric and sent shock waves through her.

She was shameless. And she was so damned close already.

As his palm covered her, as he held her still against the wheel and ignored her short, sharp, panting gasps for mercy, Kayleigh's body tightened. Writhed.

Fingers tight against her lace-covered flesh, his palm pressed up, ground against the aching bead of her clit.

She cried out as her orgasm swamped her, as the tension in her body uncoiled on a rush of wild sensation; wicked gratification shot into the stratosphere as her elbow hit the steering wheel.

The short, sharp burst of the car horn echoed across the empty lot.

Shawn's sudden gust of laughter was all she heard as he freed his hand from her slacks, caught her arm, and removed it from the steering wheel.

Shaking, gasping for breath, she didn't struggle as he pulled her away from the wheel. Tucked her against his chest, one hand flat on her back, the other smoothing her hair.

Reality curled in around the sound of his heartbeat.

Oh, my God.

It was true. All it took was a hard-eyed man and a dark corner to get her begging for it.

Her father had never said it, never even hinted, but he must have thought it. His disappointment, his watchfulness had all been to save her from this. Hadn't she promised herself?

Obviously, Kayleigh didn't know how to be the woman she wanted to be.

Never again.

All right. That was the dumbest thing Shawn could have done.

The doctor pushed away from him, color hectic in her cheeks as she scrambled off his lap and into the passenger seat. The air was thick with the smell of her, musky with arousal, and it was taking everything he had not to finish what she'd—what *he* had started.

His balls ached with the need to take her, to bury himself in all that wet heat he knew he'd find between her legs. She was damned sweet. Eager for it.

And embarrassed as hell.

She didn't know the half of it.

"One job done," he made himself say, breaking the silence with forced levity.

Her laugh was strained. "Thanks." As if the single

word could make it any less awkward. "Um." Her hand stilled at the door latch. "Shawn, if you could avoid telling anyone . . . ?"

No threat of that one. He nodded. "Okay."

Relief filled her still-pink features. Her eyes, cleared of the fog of arousal, darted to the window. "Listen, if you want to stay out here—"

"You're not going in alone," he cut in, and pushed open the driver's side door. Unfolding his body from the car hurt like a son of a bitch, his aching cock demanding retribution for the hell he was putting himself through, but the slap of early autumn cold helped.

She stepped out of the car, adjusted her clothing with abashed care.

Idiot. Out of the hundreds of scenarios he'd ever played in his head, seducing Laurence Lauderdale's daughter had never once crossed his mind.

He was supposed to hate her. Hate her whole family.

He wasn't supposed to fuck them. Or think about fucking them, at least not in any literal way. So what did he do first chance he got?

Forget that she's the enemy.

He raked a hand through his hair as she turned to the building. "I guess, after you," she said.

Maybe if he was lucky, damned lucky, the place would be filled with angry squatters looking for a fight.

He needed to lose some steam.

CHAPTER FIVE

The place was empty. Not only of people, but of anything Kayleigh had hoped to find.

Ten minutes on the remains of a computer in the main lab told her everything she needed to know. It wasn't here.

She stared at the bank of monitors painting the interior of the abandoned facility with an eerie, sickly blue. Four of the six computer screens had long since blown out, and the neat hole in the frame of one—exactly the size of a bullet—gave evidence to at least one reason why. Shawn had pointed out the signs of a fight.

Fortunately, the power source and at least some of the drives remained intact.

Not that it helped.

It wasn't here. The answer she looked for—the solution she *desperately* needed—wasn't in the system.

Common sense suggested that she'd prepared for this possibility.

Her stomach burned, splashing acid up into the back of her throat as her eyes skated over the corrupted batch of characters scrolling across one of the three remaining screens. Her fingers bit into the desk, sending spasms of pain up her hands that barely registered.

~~She didn't know how to prepare for despair.~~

Somewhere beyond the reach of the flashlight she'd brought with her—the sturdy base standing up on its end at her elbow and pointed at the ceiling—something clanged dimly. The old GeneCorp facility had been making noises since they'd stepped inside, strange clangs and clinks and the occasional metal groan. After the first few turned out to be nothing, Kayleigh had stopped paying attention. She'd barely noticed when Shawn had made his excuses to look around.

Everything she was, every sense she possessed, had been pinned on this. This one chance. Her final effort.

A failure.

"Lauderdales don't fail," she muttered. The ulcer in her stomach echoed the sentiment, sizzling in mingled reprimand and dismay. One hand fisted against it as she straightened from the table, but it didn't help.

Stress was doing its level best to eat a hole through her stomach lining while she gallivanted around, flailing in the dark.

Assaulting strange men in her own car.

She bit back a groan, covering her face with both hands.

Kayleigh worked hard. She worked *very* hard. Nobody could ever say that Director Laurence Lauderdale's daughter didn't put in her hours. Being placed in charge of her father's Salem Project had ensured she'd never do anything but work again. Was it any surprise she was losing her mind?

Her eyes closed in exhausted disappointment. She was running out of time. Out of energy.

Her father's lab rested on her shoulders.

Her lab, really.

She'd had high hopes for the project. High hopes for her mother's legacy.

But the body count . . . the *stress*. It was eating at her. Breaking her down in a way she found laughably similar to the physical degeneration affecting the Salem subjects.

The cosmic imperative had a sense of humor.

She needed a break. She'd been so desperate, hoped so badly to find it—the sequence itself, even a *clue* about it—that she'd disobeyed her father.

Why had she thought that information about Parker's syringe could be found here?

Turned out her dad was right. "Next trick?" she murmured, her voice echoing eerily in the dark.

She was out of ideas. Done. Months of banging her head against the riddle of the broken DNA sequence had taken its toll. She had nothing left.

Laurence Lauderdale's daughter was a big, fat disappointment. The end of his life's work . . . of her late mother's entire world.

A slummer with more success in the bedroom—*a car*, she corrected herself, bitter—than with saving lives.

Tears burned through her too-dry eyes, a crust earned from staring too long at incandescent screens. As another faint groan echoed from the settling interior, she forced her fingers to unclench, reached for the switch that would power down the computers and once more leave the facility in abandoned shadow.

The echoes didn't fade.

Her fingers stilled. She tilted her head, a slow frown pulling at her brow, her mouth, as her vision began to shudder. Another sign of ocular deterioration?

"Shawn?" The flashlight next to her purse jiggled, causing the shadows and reflections to dip and sway.

A deafening clap of thunder tore through the dark. The monitors shattered one by one.

Kayleigh jerked away from the bank of old computers, tripping over her own feet as her knees wobbled out from underneath her. Her heart launched into her throat; glass sprayed in an arc, and she threw up her arms over her face as shrapnel glittered wildly. The sound of it tinkling to the old facility floor drowned beneath an ominous, howling rumble.

The world shifted.

Her body folded. Partly the fault of the floor as it rippled underneath her like something alive, and partly raw, stark terror. Kayleigh wrapped her arms over her exposed head. Every cell in her body gave over to a nightmarish blend of memory, of experience too recent to have to suffer again so soon.

Fire. Screaming.

Walls shaking.

Not again.

Her teeth gritted so hard, both joints in her jaw cracked, but she couldn't stop. Couldn't do anything but hold her breath and wait for the ground to stop rocking, the walls to stop groaning.

The ceiling to come down.

Just as in the Mission quad only three short weeks ago. Chaos, all over again.

A sob tore from her throat.

"Get up!" Shawn's gritty order caught on a grunt as something crashed to the floor beside her. Tinny echoes ricocheted in her ears, over her exposed nerves. Hard, desperate fingers curled around her forearm and yanked her to her feet. "Fucking *move!*"

The flashlight hit the floor and cracked. Overhead, the wiring detonated in an explosion of sparks. Bulbs burst from the power surge she could all but feel as the charge ripped through GeneCorp's remains. In a half second of pure terror, she glimpsed the glint of brown eyes, a flash of dusky skin, and bared, gritted teeth before everything went dark around her.

This time, it wasn't her own body throwing her senses into disarray. It wasn't stress or fear or insomnia-induced. The world was literally falling apart around her.

The fingers biting into her arm dragged her in an unknown direction, though God only knew how Shawn could navigate as the shriek of metal on metal ripped through the lab. "What's happening?" she screamed, unable to keep a pleading note from infecting her frightened demand.

The world juddered; one flat shoe snagged on something metal and sharp. Something gave—her skin or the snag—pain lanced through her leg and she cried out, only to inhale sharply, choking, as the hand at her arm flattened over her chest. His body shifted, another arm curved around her waist.

"Hold on!"

She didn't get to ask to what. Didn't have to guess. His arm tightened, and all of a sudden, her feet left the floor, her weight suspended in the grip of a man who had come from nowhere. She had no choice but to trust him to navigate them both through hell.

Another shudder jarred the walls in ways solid metal walls should never have moved. The whole facility rang like a gong, as if a giant hammer slammed against the outside. Dust billowed, turning nominally difficult vision to near impossibility. Her nose rebelled, eyes watering, but she clung to Shawn's broad shoulders, fingers hooked in his shirt, and struggled not to scream as something cracked, groaning, and collapsed nearby.

The rumble stopped.

Just as quickly, so did he.

For a long moment, only the staggered echo of settling debris filled the tomblike silence.

Shaking, trying hard not to let the sound of her own terror fill the gap, Kayleigh buried her face against his shoulder.

Would the fire come now?

Would the screams?

Weak. She could do better than this.

She was a Lauderdale. Eve sequence aside, impossible odds was what they *did*.

"Put me down." The order that came out of her mouth wasn't as strong as she would have liked, but given the circumstances, she'd settle for shaken over struck dumb with terror.

In the near-perfect darkness, she couldn't see his face.

Instead of answering, instead of even acknowledging her demand, he shifted her weight until an arm banded at her lower back, another trapped her legs at the knee. She flinched as pain pulsed through her left leg. "Ouch!"

"Are you hurt?"

Did he care? The flat way he asked it jerked her chin up, forced her to stiffen against his binding grip.

That he had suddenly become a line of warm, male muscle from knee to breast was something she didn't want to explore too deeply while the dust settled around them. While her heart settled.

He rescued her. That earned him some leeway. *Some.*

"You're hurting me," she pointed out, just as evenly. "And I think I cut my leg."

"Fuck." His arms flexed underneath her, and the hand splayed over her ribs tightened. "Keep still, I'm going to get us out of here."

Kayleigh had no choice but to hang on to his solid shoulders for the ride. "Let me go," she pressed. "I can walk."

"No."

Her mouth dropped open. "What?"

"No."

Not even an excuse, no apology. Just . . . *no.* In a taut, firm voice that held no tolerance for argument. *No.* And that was that. "Are you serious? Shawn!"

"Stop struggling, Doctor."

Heart in her throat, she twisted; the corded steel at her ribs tightened, making it abundantly clear exactly who had the upper hand in this silent debate. She hissed. "In case you missed it, whatever exploded out there rocked this place down to the foundation. You need to let me go!"

"These things aren't related," came his terse rejoinder. "Hold still."

Kayleigh shuddered, closing her eyes as something large and heavy clattered to the ground behind them. One of the conduits decorating the ceiling, maybe. Or the frame for the monitors she'd been studying before everything had gone topsy-turvy.

The dust billowed like a gritty wave and she felt smeared with it, coated by sweat and the cloud of decades of abandonment. As Shawn made his way through the old GeneCorp building, obeying some inner map she couldn't imagine, Kayleigh tried hard not to let herself panic any more than she already had.

She was alive. He was alive. More or less unhurt. Things could have been so much worse.

Still, she wanted to stamp her foot. Aside from the fact that he wouldn't put her down, she knew the action would net her the same thing it always had when she was younger: nothing. Not even disapproval.

She'd learned long ago not to bother.

Instead, she concentrated on breathing. Forced in air, filled her lungs, let it out again. Adrenaline, trapped in her skin with nowhere to go, burned a hole through her stomach.

Where was he taking her?

They'd started in the largest part of the facility, where the only working mainframe had somehow withstood the dual tests of violence and time. Damn it, she couldn't even remember which way they'd come *in*. Where were they now?

"Shawn, are you hurt?" He ignored the question, and she glared at the faint outline of what she thought was his jaw. The angle was right. "That better be a no."

There, a tilt of his head as he stepped carefully over something she couldn't see. "I'm fine," he said.

The relief filling her only compounded the surge of wayward adrenaline. Burying her face against his shoulder, she murmured, "I'm glad."

A curse hissed over her head.

Trusting in her rescuer seemed easier than it should have been.

Being carried, drained to the point of exhaustion by the adrenaline now leaving her feeling battered and empty, proved even more an obstacle to good judgment than nervous anticipation. The intense heat of the man who carried her, his body warmth cutting through her clothes to combat the chill of shock, stole the rest of whatever protest she might have had left.

She was tired. Suddenly so very tired. And his arms were strong, his chest firm.

To her consternation, her lashes lowered, eyelids suddenly heavy. Impossibly heavy. As her cheek nestled against his shoulder, as her brain struggled to comprehend the shock turning her limbs to lead, she could have sworn that he murmured something else over her head. Something much gentler.

Her heart throbbed in her ears as pain lanced a fiery hole through her stomach lining.

When the first whisper of what passed for fresh air in New Seattle's lower industrial district wafted across her face, she sucked it in gratefully.

An exit. Thank God.

She didn't expect to be carried across the border into hell. A vicious haze wrapped around her head as her vision blurred; that corona that always signaled the beginning of one of her stress episodes.

She closed her eyes.

The destruction of the old witch factory wasn't part of the plan.

Shawn stepped out of the encompassing dark, grateful to see the incandescent glow of lights overhead as he broke cover from the teetering building. New Seattle soared high above, just as it always did, with its sky full of neon lights and humming electrical grid. The layers of each subsequent tier hadn't toppled from the tremors. Hell, he couldn't even tell if they'd noticed.

He couldn't say the same for the old industrial center.

The mysterious rumbling had torn apart already cracking pavement, crumbled the warehouse directly across the lot into a skeletal foundation. Dust billowed from the lot; the air smelled of damp rot disturbed and the constant acrid note associated with New Seattle's acid rain.

He turned, Kayleigh's light weight shifting in his arms as he studied the mutilated façade of the abandoned building. It listed dangerously, fractured down the middle.

What the hell had caused it?

One moment, he'd been poking around in the back rooms off the main lab he'd left her in, the next, the whole place tried to come down around them. His chin dropped, brow furrowing tightly as he studied her pale, strained features.

Whatever she'd been looking for in this place, he doubted *this* was it.

She opened her eyes. The color still surprised him: a blue edging more to cloudy sky than true blue. It took her a moment, but when her gaze focused on their surroundings, her gasp echoed his silent, grim dismay. "Oh, my God." The same thing she'd uttered in the car. Softly feminine in a way he intrinsically recognized, hot-blooded male to female.

His chest kicked hard. "We are damned lucky to be alive," was all he managed. "I take it you didn't find your information?

The dismay in the blue-gray eyes meeting his told him everything he needed to know, but his jaw tightened when her lower lip quivered, then firmed deliberately. "Put me down, please."

If he needed a sign from beyond, this had to be it. No data, no luck for either of them. Or for May.

This was it. Now or never.

The hard slash of his mouth curved up. It wasn't a nice smile, and he didn't soften it as he dropped her legs, keeping one arm tight around her back. She slid against his chest until she found her balance. Hectic color appeared high on her cheeks, combating the sickly pallor painting the rest of her.

The drag of her against him, the feel of her hands on his shoulders, almost made him reconsider.

He'd already watched her come apart once. It had to be enough. She'd never forgive him after this.

Not that he demanded forgiveness from a Lauderdale.

Reaching into his jacket pocket, he located the tube he'd placed inside, relieved to find it hadn't cracked. He didn't strictly need it, but beating Kayleigh Lauderdale to within an inch of consciousness factored right up there with fingering her to an orgasm. He'd managed one, despite himself; he wasn't the kind of man who could justify the other.

This is where he proved how badly he wanted the end goal.

"*Was* that an earthquake?" she asked breathlessly. Her hands, braced against his chest, shook. "Or did something blow up down here?" When he said nothing, her eyes darkened. Her hands went taut against his chest. "Shawn?"

With his thumb, he flicked the cap off the needle.

It hit the gravel lot, a faint click she picked out from the ambient noise—the sirens in the distance, the constant thrum of millions of volts of electricity crackling through the metropolis. Her own rapid heartbeat, obvious at the pulse hammering in the base of her throat. Her gaze flicked to the discarded blue plastic.

Sharp ears. Good sense of awareness.

Too late.

She stiffened. "You— Shawn, what are you doing?" Her fingers dug into his chest. Curled, then slammed into his sternum. "Let me go!" He grunted, twisting her arm to force her into an awkward arch. To pin her in place. Her feet scrabbled in the gravel lot, whimper cracking as she wrenched at his grip.

Lauderdale should have invested in a few self-defense courses for his daughter. Not that it would have helped much in the long run—maybe her pride.

Shawn reversed the syringe in his palm and slid the needle through her lightweight blazer, into the fleshy part of her upper arm. She cried out, fear and shock twisting her features. Betrayal.

Just the first of many.

His teeth ground. "Good night, Dr. Lauderdale."

Another fisted wallop knotted his right pectoral. He blew out a wincing breath, dragged her tighter against him as he depressed the plunger the rest of the way. Her hips turned into his, gouged into the soft flesh between his legs, and he hissed a curse, wrenching the needle out of her arm before she managed any other accidental feats of useless bravado.

The sedative wouldn't take long. Already, he could see the wild light in her eyes begin to dim. Her lips peeled back, bared her teeth as her nails dug into his upper arm, but he'd worn synth-leather on purpose.

Aside from New Seattle Riot Force flak jackets, nothing beat synth-leather for casual personal protection on the streets.

He'd learned that lesson the hard way. All because of her family.

Women like Kayleigh Lauderdale didn't belong down here with the scrappers. Pampered, spoiled by topside living, she would have made easy pickings for anyone else. He couldn't imagine what she would have done if he hadn't been there to escort her down here.

Lucky for her, the resistance got her first.

Now he'd take her even from them.

The tension in her legs, heels dug in to the gritty lot, abruptly eased. Instead of falling back against his arm, she swayed forward, head lolling. She collided with his chest, hands sliding between the flaps of his jacket, tangling in his shirt and pulling the worn fabric uncomfortably tight across his back. "Why," she whispered thickly. Her mouth tightened, curved down as she struggled to fight, to stay awake. "Why . . . Shawn?"

He dropped the syringe and said nothing.

Her lashes fluttered closed, and with a soft exhale, her hands loosened. Her cheek fell against his chest. Just over the too-calm beat of his heart.

Shawn held her in silence.

In the chilled autumn damp, she was something warm and alive in his arms. He already knew how she'd respond to him—how she would have, before all this.

Her breath saturated his shirt, sank into his skin.

His scowl tightened. Sympathy pangs had no place here.

Breathing was fine. She needed that. Two fingers

notched against her throat, but no satisfaction filled him at the knock of her pulse, steady and slower with sleep.

She looked innocent in sleep. Artlessly sweet, like a child. Hers was not a face used to the strain of survival. And why would it be?

Even smeared liberally with dust and grime, her soft, pink lips slack, Shawn couldn't deny her physical appeal.

He smoothed back her hair from her face with a rough hand, peeled open one eyelid to find her pupils wide in a thin band of misty blue, her breathing steady.

Her skin burned into the nerves at the ends of his fingers.

"Stop it," he muttered between clenched teeth, curling them into a fist. That was over. All over.

He'd done what he needed to do to ensure her trust. That's it.

That's all he could tell himself.

Turning roughly, he pulled her over his shoulder with less grace than he could have and no more than she deserved.

Kayleigh Lauderdale was the enemy. It didn't matter how soft her skin was, or how prettily she came under his touch. Any touch. She was a monster, descended from monsters.

Soon, she'd be the ticket to freedom for people a thousand times better than her.

And his ticket to revenge.

As if on cue, the comm in his inner pocket thrummed. Shawn cursed under his breath. It took a moment, but he managed to fish out the unit with one hand to scan the frequency number.

Jennifer. Checking on the status of the operation, no doubt.

His smile thin, Shawn banded an arm across Kayleigh's ass, securing her over his shoulder. He took his time turning the unit on. "Yup."

"What the hell was that?"

"Near as I can tell," he replied, "an earthquake."

"One that only hit a single district? Impossible."

"Either that," he replied, shifting his grip on the doctor, "or something exploded. I'm busy, what do you want?"

She cleared his throat, the sound uneven on the comm. "Did this mess up the plan?"

Not even in the slightest. "I found her. She's sleeping like a baby." Balancing the doctor's dead weight, he strode for the car still in the lot.

"Great." The relief in her voice was palpable. "Jim and Donald are already out to the rendezvous point. Did she find anything?"

"No, place is clean."

"All right. Hopefully she'll have some info for us at the base."

"Mm-hm." It wasn't a confirmation. But he wasn't any less of a dick for it, so he added, "Should see you in fifteen."

Her sleek car huddled under a broken security light. Dust and debris scattered across the glossy paint, but it didn't look like the shakedown had affected much else.

"Great," Jennifer said, relief again displaying more of her softer side than she should. Shawn shook his head. "Drive safe."

"Yup," was all he bothered to say, and closed the comm unit with a sharp click. He'd have forty-five minutes before they assumed the worst. If he was lucky, he'd have even longer to make a clean getaway.

Whatever it was that rocked the lower streets of New Seattle, it hadn't hit a district wildly populated with people. Squatters would get up and move. Abandoned, unused factories and warehouses would crumble.

New Seattle had moved on a long time ago.

It was time he did the same. Before the rest of the resistance came looking.

CHAPTER SIX

Something had crawled into her mouth and died. There could be no other excuse for a taste this bad, her throat dry as sandpaper.

When her eyes fluttered open, two flickering lamps glared down at her in twin warning. Kayleigh groaned, squinting beneath the double-halo surrounding each one, and raised a hand to rub at her gritty sockets.

Her shoulder popped, but her hand didn't move.

She tried again, willed her muscles to clench, her tendons to leverage her arm up to her own face.

She couldn't move.

Her spine snapped straight. All thoughts of sleep—of lethargy, and what felt suspiciously like a hangover—fled. The two lamps to her left jerked, then merged into a single burning corona, forcing another groan from her chest as she realized two things simultaneously.

Her leg throbbed in time with the pressure building in her head and stomach, a long line of pain, and she was tied down.

Tied. Down.

Fear dried what little saliva had pooled in her mouth.

"Oh, God," she rasped, staring at the restraints. Her forearms fastened to the stiff arms of a chair, her ankles to the legs. The unforgiving light, a lantern of some kind powered by batteries, picked out other details to add to her waking nightmare—the metal floor coated with grime, the bare walls surrounding her, and overhead?

Sweat bloomed on her skin, a shuddering sweep of ice and fear.

Nothing but black. No roof of any kind that she could see. A tall room? Vaulted ceiling?

The light didn't reach that far, and as her heart pounded, as she twisted and pulled her immobilized limbs in every way she could, Kayleigh couldn't keep a sound of raw dismay locked behind her teeth.

"Don't bother. You'll break before it does." The masculine voice pierced the gap behind her, a void in her spatial awareness she desperately needed to fill. She tried to turn but only succeeded in cracking the fine bones of her neck. Her wince fractured on a gasp of echoed pain from nape to tailbone. "Warned you," he added.

Only shadows filled her peripheral sight, but she remembered that voice. "Shawn! What's going on?" she demanded, her throat closing around the words.

Alone. In a dark place. With a man who was, in the end, just a stranger. A stranger who she'd . . . that she'd . . .

Oh, God. She was tied down. *Helpless.*

Her fingers curled into fists, nails tight against her palm and knuckles bruising against the metal. "If that's even your name," she added, snarling her hurt.

"My name *is* Shawn Lowe, but I don't expect you to know or care why it matters." His voice, richly hued with all the deep resonance of masculinity, managed a level of even chill that sent gooseflesh rippling down her arms. "Despite appearances, you aren't exactly the one I want, Dr. Lauderdale."

Every fine hair on her nape rose. The way he said her surname, with a cold menace only thinly leashed, slammed her heart into overdrive.

Bad. This was so bad.

She tried to lick her cracked lips. Fear coated her tongue, drenched her skin in icy sweat. "Why am I here?"

Footsteps on the metal flooring echoed eerily through the dark. A figure entered her peripheral vision, skirted across the circle of light, and she sucked in her breath as all broad six feet and four towering inches stepped into view.

Her stomach pitched, and when that wasn't enough to convey the depths of her stark terror, sizzled. Agony locked her teeth together until her eyes watered.

His dark eyebrows rose, powerfully shaped arms folding over his chest. The fabric of his dark blue, long-sleeved shirt went taut across muscles she didn't need to see flex to know how strong he was. "Tears already, Doctor?" His mouth quirked. Victory.

That *ass.*

"Screw you," she managed. "I get migraines and I've got a freaking ulcer."

Whatever ghost of a smile existed hardened. "You want a medal?"

"I want an answer. What do *you* want, Shawn?"

"What anybody wants. Life, liberty, and the pursuit of happiness."

The old words surprised her.

When his lips curved higher, a smile with a sardonic, angry edge, she realized she'd let it show. "Yeah, there are people living in the low streets who know history. Try not to die of shock."

She winced guiltily. "I didn't—"

"Yeah, you did." He didn't move, didn't so much as lean toward her, but no amount of distance soothed the painful gurgling in her belly. The corona hazing the light had faded, thank God—she wasn't in any position to lose ground to another migraine—but the harsh light did nothing to make him seem less . . . *present.*

Wherever they were, their voices echoed hollowly in chilled silence, she didn't hear the everyday sound of the city around them. They were alone.

"I'm sorry for the perceived offense," she managed, at least a facsimile of calm. "I don't mean to imply anything. I just want to know why I'm here. And where is here?"

The scornful hike to his mouth twitched. "You're here because your father has something I want."

She blinked. "Something you want?"

"Oh, yeah."

For a long moment, she could only stare at his face, into his eyes.

Was he serious?

He was.

A roar began in her ears. Her vision tunneled; not the migraine-induced pressure she remembered, but something darker. Furious. "My . . . father?" The words barely made it past her lips, tight with strain. "You kidnapped me . . . You did all those things . . . because . . ." Because of *money*? Because of some kind of . . . "Are you *kidding me* right now?"

This time, he leaned forward, his arms unfolding, hands settling at his knees as if she were a child to be talked down to. "Your father is going to give me what I want, and in exchange, you go free. Unharmed."

Oh, she knew how to pick them, didn't she?

Anger swamped self-preservation. The restraints rattled as she thrust her face out to meet his, fury to his obstinate calm. "I trusted you!"

"Says the spoiled little girl tied to a chair." He straightened, glancing overhead for a moment. When his gaze returned to her, there was nothing kind, nothing remotely compassionate in it. Nothing even close to the raw, expressive way he'd watched her as he touched her. As she came from his fingers.

She'd been so *stupid*.

"He has two days to respond to the demand. After that, we'll revisit the 'unharmed' topic and add 'mostly.'" He straightened. "After three? I start sending fingers. Am I clear?"

Fear filled her spine. Her thoughts. With the shadows encroaching on him, saturating his eyes to black pools of malice, she believed every word. He'd hurt her. And for what? Money? She bit back a crack of laughter, certain it'd feel and sound more like a sob, and firmed her jaw. "You're crazy. My father will rescue me. He has agents at his disposal you've never even dreamed existed."

His eyes crinkled, but the venom in them did more to terrify her than anything he'd said to date. "Oh, I don't know." He didn't come close to her, didn't try to crowd her. He hadn't even touched her since carrying her out of the shaking building. He didn't have to.

Kayleigh had a good idea what he could do—what he would have no problems doing—just from the rigid tension in his body. The way he planted his feet. The line of his hard mouth, and his callused hands.

And to think, she'd all but thrown herself at him. Such a fool.

She looked away. Then thought better of it and met his eyes direct. "You're just a bully." An eyebrow twitched. "I deal with your kind every day. You don't scare me."

"Is that a challenge?" He didn't move, didn't raise his voice, but Kayleigh wasn't as stupid as she felt. She said nothing, simply matching his stare with the same steely glare she'd used on every Holy Order official who'd ever thought he had something on her. Bulk, brains, social authority.

Except this man had something most of them didn't.

The upper freaking hand.

She looked away, after all.

"Good girl," he said softly.

Fierce heat flooded her cheeks. It almost matched the intensity of the ulcer in her stomach.

"While I've got you at my mercy—"

She inhaled sharply, winced when the echoes of the strangled sound she made darted into the dark.

His chuckle grated. "Relax, Doctor. I'm not interested."

Liar, she thought in mute rebellion, her lips tightening. She remembered vividly the feel of his hardness under her lap, remembered how he'd kissed her.

Was all that a lie, too? Was she just an easy lay?

She didn't want him touching her. Not ever again.

"Why don't *you* tell me about these agents dear old Dad has?"

She bit her tongue, said nothing, and stared at a dark spot of grime away from his looming silhouette. Her limbs trembled, her body and mind very much aware that she couldn't move even if she wanted to; it was taking everything she had not to flex against the restraints, scream until her oxygen-starved brain went black on her.

She couldn't, *wouldn't* give him the satisfaction.

"No?" This time, when he closed the distance, her heart stuttered. A hand reached across her thousand-yard-stare, caught her chin, and forced her head to turn. She struggled; it didn't matter. Her gaze collided with his. "Are you sure you don't want to talk to me? I'm the nice one, Dr. Lauderdale. I think I've proven how *nice* I am."

Fear, shame, swelled in her throat. She fought the sensation of choking, swallowed hard as it threatened to overwhelm her. "Let go of me," she spat, wrenching at his grip. "I've got nothing to tell you."

His fingers bit into her cheeks. "I don't think so. Like you, I'm well aware of what your precious father is capable of." His voice, softer, scored as painfully as his grip. "Like him, I also know the value of my collateral."

She scoffed.

Then choked on it as the rough pad of his thumb scraped across her lower lip. Her eyes widened. "You really are pretty," he murmured, his gaze pinned on her mouth. "It's a shame."

The threat inherent in his observation, in the leashed aggression in his grip, spiked raw and ragged into her chest. Her lips firmed under his heavy thumb, knuckles popping audibly as her fists tightened. "I wouldn't expect anything else from the likes of you."

A muscle leaped in his cheek. "The likes of me?" he repeated, but she ignored the quiet warning. Fought through the visual vapor that seemed to settle over his skin like a soft nimbus.

Scared, sure. Alone, fine. But now she added anger, brutal anger, to the list, and she didn't have it in her to play the frightened little damsel as it coursed through her veins.

The feel of his fingers at her jaw, the looming threat of his silhouette blocking the light, none of it could stop her. Scorn, bitter and venomous, welled up. Flooded out of her.

"Obviously, you're a product of your miserable life," she found herself saying. "What happened, Shawn Lowe? Were you poor? Did your parents kick you into the streets?" The cruel words fell from her lips, each one a poisonous dart. She couldn't stop, even as his eyes darkened. As the hard planes of his face tightened until he could have been carved from granite. "My dad loves me. Don't blame me if your mother never— Oh!"

Too late, she realized her error. The fingers at her cheek bit cruelly, each one a sharp point of pain.

She stared up at her captor, every ounce of furious courage draining out from the tingling soles of her feet as she stared into the face of raw hatred given form. His eyes glittered, dangerous shards of ice and obsidian. His mouth, generally softer than she'd have expected on any man, thinned to almost nothing.

The corona hovering strangely over his skin faded.

"Don't." The word was a violent warning, punctuated by terrible pressure at her chin. "Don't *ever* talk about my parents. You of all people never get that right."

Her mouth dried with raw terror. The restraints rattled, even as she struggled to keep it from showing, keep her body from shaking with it.

Her of all people?

He let her face go, but she didn't count it as a victory. The memory of it throbbed painfully. He backed up, every step thudding in defiance of the brutal control shaping his rigid shoulders, ripped the lantern from its hook, and strode away.

For a long moment, she held her breath. Watched him until he turned a corner. Until she was sure he wasn't coming back.

Her exhale shook violently.

What was wrong with her? How close to "mostly unharmed" was she willing to get?

The darkness filled in the deafening silence behind him.

Her heartbeat scudded into overdrive as she stared into a yawning void and heard no signs of life. No cars. No snap of electrical power.

Alone.

He'd left her in the dark, tied down and unable to defend herself. Unable to run.

She closed her eyes, but it wasn't any better. Then again, she thought with a bitter crack of muffled laughter, she figured it really couldn't get any *worse*.

Her nails bit into her palms. She sucked in a breath through her nose, let it out hard through her mouth.

As her brain spiraled into a sea of tangled sensory memory, she told herself that the air didn't reek of smoke. There was no fire or bullets or screaming. She wasn't ignorant. She knew post-trauma when she saw it, even if what she saw it in was her own eyes. Her own reflection.

This is where the screaming starts, whispered the terrified voice that had taken up residence in the back of her head. *Just answer their questions.* ·

Her ulcer burned.

"Think," she whispered, jaw aching with the effort it took not to scream. *Just think for two seconds. . .*

There was opportunity here. There always was.

Shawn stalked away from the fragile target she'd made of herself, fist clenched so tight around the lantern handle that a joint snapped against his palm.

Fuck. Just . . . *fuck*.

Shawn had never in his life come that close to hitting a woman. It tangled with everything, with the lust still simmering in the base of his skull, the memory of her body arching into his.

The fear he'd felt when the building threatened to collapse on her.

Undone by the raw, brutal rage riding him now, he struggled to find his mental equilibrium. Maybe it said something that he'd have put his fist to her face if she'd been a man. Something ugly.

Almost everyone who knew him knew better than to talk about his parents. His past.

She taunted him. Stuck her sharp-nailed fingers into the wound, provoked him into behaving like a thug; an animal.

He hated the Lauderdale name, but he was better than that.

He ducked out of the two-room structure, every

step away from the temptation of her feeling like a rubber band snapping taut behind him. Stretching, tightening.

Doing its level best to yank him back into that room, snarling his rage, his accusations, into her wide, haunted eyes.

Temptation. What a perfect word for the devil's own daughter.

It didn't start out that way. It wasn't temptation that rode him as he'd planned this. It wasn't temptation that he saw when he watched Laurence Lauderdale's precious daughter fight her restraints, no matter how soft her hair looked, or how wide those eyes were as they met his stare with flat challenge that did nothing to hide her fear.

Fear. That was the word. That was better than anything else.

It would keep her alive. Keep him focused.

Her sainted father knew a thing or two about fear.

Shawn stepped over the broken rubble of what had once been a porch stoop. The icy chill settled into the very heart of Old Seattle rose up like a fist, wrapped around his chest as he took a deep, cleansing breath of musty air and forgotten spaces. Damp and cold and idle, even delicate rot.

The light in his hand bounced off jagged angles and broken corners, remnants of what had once been a bustling district filled with people. Fifty-some-odd years wasn't a long time. Not in the scheme of things. Shawn was born thirty-three of those years ago, more than half the time since the cataclysmic events that shaped the city.

This city. Old Seattle.

Named because the rest of the world moved on,

rebuilt, locked the ruins of the destruction beneath a couple thousand square miles of concrete and supports and built New Seattle right on top. Bigger, better, higher than the clouds.

Like that always ended well.

The insistent cold plucked at his skin, tunneled beneath his long-sleeved shirt as if the fabric didn't exist. He looked up at the darkness enfolding the small bubble of light that was all the lantern could manage, considered going back to retrieve his jacket.

She'd be there. Watching him. Judging.

Talking, because he didn't think she'd shut the hell up long enough to let him get in and get out without graphically considering letting loose his temper.

Or giving in to the demon riding his back and kissing her into silence.

He grunted as he eased his weight down to a ruined half of broken step. The cement held, crumbling bits of the edges clattering to the ground. When he was sure the stair wouldn't dump him on his ass, he allowed his shoulders to slump; his forearms draped over his upraised knees as he stared blankly into the black.

Old Seattle. A death trap on a good day, and today wasn't a good day.

Farther out, toward the final edges of the new city border, he knew cracks had developed in the paved tomb. He'd seen the rays of daylight, feeble and determined, poking through. He'd been to the edge of the Old Sea-Trench, heard its rushing current, and had no trouble imagining the wholesale destruction the fault line could cause if it chose.

He hadn't expected to feel it up in New Seattle's lower industrial district.

He sure as hell hadn't expected to dodge falling

debris and rescue the girl he'd managed to steal out from under the nose of his own allies.

His first impression stood: he wasn't surprised by her at all. Not *her*. Exactly.

What surprised him was the fact that his body seemed drawn to hers. That even after he'd touched her, sampled her, she'd felt warm and right in his arms, the way a woman *should* feel when a man touched her.

That even though she looked at him with fear and fury, the light burning behind her blue-gray eyes only made him want to challenge her, tease her until it shifted to something else. Something human.

He knew what it looked like when she laughed. Everything about her softened; her face, her voice. Her eyes sparkled when she smiled. Did she know that?

Why did he?

He liked women. He liked women fine, but maybe he ought to have spent more time liking them and less time shelving them with the other distractions he'd told himself he didn't need.

When Lauderdale's perfect daughter started to look like easy pickings, he knew there was a problem.

Shawn's muffled snort of laughter, edged with self-deprecation, gave way to a whisper of sound; a hum thrummed against his hip.

That was one of the reasons he'd chosen this abandoned whatever-it-was. Just close enough to a comm buoy overhead to get reception. His smile tightened as he plucked the comm unit from his hip and cracked it open. He didn't bother to check the number. It'd only lie.

He didn't get the first word. "What the hell are you doing?" came a demand both raspy and edged.

"May."

"Don't 'May' me," she snapped, anger infiltrating every sharp word.

He eased back against one elbow, grit grinding against the dirty stoop. Closing his eyes, he said nothing.

She wasn't the type to let silence stand. Not for something like this. "Why aren't you at the rendezvous point, Shawn?"

"Change of plans."

"Don't get cute," she said tightly. "What scheme have you concocted now?"

"Heh." She knew him well enough. After sixteen years, she of all people knew what it was that drove him. Every minute of every day. "I know you're tracking this frequency," he said instead. "So you have thirty more seconds."

"Shawn." May's voice didn't soften. But it didn't harden, either, and he recognized that for what it was. Years or not, she *knew* him. Like no one else. "Whatever you've got planned, you need to bring Kayleigh Lauderdale to the rendezvous. This is too important to let go to waste."

His grip tightened on the comm frame. "If I do that," he said, so quietly that even he couldn't hear the venom in his own voice, "it *will* go to waste."

She blew out a breath on a word that didn't make it through the static, but he didn't need to hear it to know he frustrated her. He always had. "She's not responsible for—"

The frame cracked. "Don't."

"Shawn!"

As fury welled in his throat, filled his chest with ashes, he swallowed hard. Forced his voice to icy calm. "The Mission has held on to our people for thirty-seven days. Thirty fucking seven. In three hours, May, it'll be thirty-eight. What do you suppose they're going through? How many do you think are still alive? Three? Five? Who cracked first? Amanda? Digs?"

Silence thrummed on the line, sizzling with tension.

He didn't let it hold for long. She knew him better than he knew her, but he knew enough. "Don't try and find me, May. If you do, I'll kill her."

"If you kill her," May threw back, "we lose our shot at a cure."

"For what?"

"For people who are dying, Shawn."

It took him a moment. When the thought calcified, bypassed shock and disbelief, laughter cracked from his throat.

A cure for a dying killer.

He covered his eyes with one hand, blocking out the shadows pressing down from every direction. "For the missionary. Are you kidding me? That's what all this is about? Some genetic witchy bullshit?" He shook his head sharply. "*Fuck* him. He can die with all the rest of the Church puppets."

"For God's sake, listen to yourself. Neither Simon nor that girl are responsible for your parents' death!"

"Murder." His throat closed around the word. Squeezed until red climbed in around his vision and he realized he'd stood, feet crunching on grit and debris. "It was *murder*, May, and the hell she isn't."

"She was just a child! So were you."

He was seventeen, and more than old enough to have done something. Anything.

He didn't then. He could, now. "She's in charge of that fucking lab, what do you think she's responsible for now?"

"Shawn—"

"She will return to her precious father when he returns our people." And gave himself up, but Shawn didn't say that aloud.

It surprised him, still, how hard it was to give voice to premeditated murder.

"Damn it, Shawn—"

"Sorry." And he was. Not enough to forgo the plan that would end in the return of a half-dozen resistance fighters, not enough to give in to the woman who'd saved him from a fate like them—a fate like his parents—but enough to give her that much. "One goddamned missionary isn't worth them. He isn't even worth *one* of them."

"That's not how this operation—"

He snapped the lid closed, severing the connection. For a long moment, only his breathing—fast, tight, a thin veneer of calm—filled the silence.

Two days. Laurence Lauderdale got two days. Jenkins, Amanda, Collers, Digs, and the others he didn't know personally would be home, safe and surrounded by people he knew they'd need to patch them back together. He'd face the music then.

If Lauderdale played hard to get?

Shawn's fingers crushed the comm to the point of pain.

He'd start sending reminders of the stakes.

Kayleigh Lauderdale.

Maybe the woman knew what her father had done. Maybe she didn't then, but she sure as shit had to now.

It didn't matter. She was the enemy. He had to remember that. Let the Church-born witches implode. His people, his friends, mattered more than a bunch of indoctrinated slaves.

Obviously, you're a product of your miserable life.

His feet moved before his brain gave the command; he stepped over broken steps and the shattered remains of wood long since rotted beneath the ever-present damp. Mud and moldering residue squelched beneath his boots. It didn't pay to wonder too closely what a man strode through down here. Enough people died in the quakes that ripped up the fault lines that he could be walking through a whole slurry of flesh fertilization and never know it.

Since they worked for the Church, he was positive that the Lauderdale family knew a thing or two about disposing of the dead.

He uncurled his fingers from the lantern haft, impassively dropped the piece he'd broken off. It clinked behind him, the tinny echoes swallowed up by the eternal night. Unlike the lower streets of New Seattle, no light filtered here that wasn't brought.

He'd walked out with the only source of it.

Was she afraid of the dark?

A flicker of unease, something that felt suspiciously like sympathy, corded along neural pathways he'd thought himself long since done with.

It shouldn't matter. It *didn't* matter.

But he'd better go check on her. Just in case.

CHAPTER SEVEN

She wasn't going to sit here like some kind of ritual sacrifice. If *he* wanted her to be good little bait for her father's money, he had another think coming.

But what were her options?

The dark closed in around Kayleigh, a muffling fist squeezing her ribs until even breathing sounded overly loud. Her eyes strained, wide enough to hurt as her brain desperately sought something, anything in the dark. The restraints at her ankles and wrists refused to budge.

"Okay," she muttered, the sound of her own voice the only comfort she could find in the pervasive black. She felt it watching her, staring at her.

She wasn't going to come up lacking.

The dark wouldn't bite. Nor was it doing anything at all but sitting there, filling up the space. She could breathe. Kayleigh forced herself to take a deep breath, just to prove it. See? In and out. Just like normal.

That left her with only one major problem to solve. How to get out?

She was a smart woman. All she had to do was put all that brainpower to use.

She turned her head in either direction. Her neck, stiff and sore, complained, her hair drifting over her cheeks, but she saw nothing but the ongoing void around her. She twisted her hand gingerly. The unforgiving strap ground against the fine bones of her wrist; she flinched as one hit a nerve and zinged all the way up her arm.

It hurt. It hurt bad enough to bring tears to her eyes, but the alternative was worse.

Adrenaline spiked through her veins, jostled her heart into a frantic beat. Setting her jaw, Kayleigh tested the other wrist, turned it faintly in either direction.

Was it just her imagination or did the strap give some?

Another turn, another zinger slammed up her arm, but there it was. The faintest tug, a slide of her skin beneath the fastener. She bared her teeth fiercely in the dark.

Before she could talk herself out of it, her smile became a clamp of teeth on her lip, a deterrent against any sound she might make as she wrenched her arm toward her body. Pain immediately jangled through her wrist; she clenched her fist, realized the added bulk to her stiffened wrist wouldn't work, and forced her hand to relax.

She knew how this worked. There'd be pain, more

of it, but her dad hadn't raised her to quit. Giving in now seemed somehow worse.

Her jaw ached, chest tightening with a groan she struggled to stifle, but it was nothing compared to the raw agony surrounding her wrist. The skin pulled, tighter and tighter, until it was so taut she imagined it stretched like paper across her bones. The restraint rattled, stuck hard.

Her fingers pulsed, tight with pressure.

"Come on," she hissed between her teeth, and with a muffled cry, she jerked her arm, slammed it again and again through the restraint until something gave, torn or lubricated by sweat or blood.

Her hand slid out from the restraint, sending tingling pins and needles all the way up to her elbow. It throbbed from wrist to fingertip, and she was positive she'd taken off a few extra layers of skin, but she'd done it. Maybe her duplicitous, son of a bitch captor was trying to be kind; she doubted it. More like, Shawn Lowe didn't think she had the gumption to hurt herself to get out of the restraints. A little pain, and the rich blond cheerleader would give up. She'd given up her body easy enough.

Asshole. Showed what he knew.

Triumph dulled the bite, allowed her to reach for the latch on her other arm, fumble the buckles free. Positively barbaric, this chair.

Within moments, holding her breath as she stiffly worked the restraints at her ankles, she was free.

Her fingers skated across a bandage under the hem of her slacks. She stilled.

He'd wrapped up her leg. Why?

If it were her—not that she'd ever considered kidnapping a helpless woman and holding her for ransom—

she didn't see a point to wrapping up a minor injury.

Was it for her benefit?

Or his?

It didn't matter.

It wasn't her only injury of this escapade and she couldn't dwell on it now, bandaged or not. Her left hand thudded in time with her heartbeat. Until she got somewhere with light, she wouldn't know if she'd caused real damage or if her limb was just reacting to the temporary loss of blood flow to the region. She could move her fingers, though. A major enough win, given the stakes.

Now for the rest of her plan. Of which, she realized as she studied the darkness with grim desperation, she had none to speak of. *Escape* didn't cover much by way of details.

Her fingertips pulsed. Wincing, she glanced from side to side, screwed her mouth into a hard frown, and *willed* the shadows to lessen.

A warehouse, maybe? If it were insulated well enough, it could explain the cool temperature and musty air. Soundproofing would make the rest of the city fade away, just her and the insane man who'd kidnapped her.

Was her dad searching for her even now? Frantically mustering agents to locate her, gathering whatever money he could?

She had to get out. She had to make it home before he worried himself sick.

Before she disappointed him any more than she already had.

The first step she took wobbled. Clenching her fists sent shards of pain through her wrist, echoed by a dull ache in her shin, but she didn't fall. Didn't run into anything. She used the chair as guide, aware he'd left by striding immediately away from her. Yet he'd initially come at her from behind.

That meant, she thought very carefully, eyes painfully wide, that there was a second way out. Or maybe an avenue circling around. She couldn't be sure until she reached the far side.

Grimacing, she forced her hands out, concentrated on taking step after cautious step. Half expecting to stumble over crates or discarded boxes, she pressed on. The silence mocked her shuffling progress. Her senses, blind and deaf in the dark, screamed that she should stop, turn back, fall into a useless pile of quaking limbs, and wait for rescue.

No. Her dad would be looking for her. The least she could do was meet him halfway, skin intact.

She wasn't afraid of the dark; Kayleigh never had been. She'd spent enough time lying awake in the darkness, counting down the hours until she could justify getting up again. Working again.

But this? This wasn't just "dark." This was a living, breathing force, a smothering shroud sucking the air from her lungs, filling her nose with old, musty aromas that tickled her sinuses and stung her eyes. She smelled . . . things. Things she didn't recognize, things that put her in mind of old air, forgotten corridors. Like dust and mildew. Old wash left too long.

Wherever she was, however far from help she might be, she couldn't be that far from an exit.

She could do this. She'd done things with genetics everyone else had considered impossible. She'd seen miracles—*performed* miracles, watched her father build on the miracles her mother had begun. This? This was child's play.

All she had to do was walk into the dark.

Her fists jammed into her stomach as it twisted.

A muted clink behind her, tinny and hollow, made the decision easy. Light gathered, slowly lighting the pitch-black to something murky and thick. Throwing a wild glance over her shoulder, picking out nothing but more black just ahead, Kayleigh threw caution to the stale air and darted into the unknown.

She'd expected more than six feet before the floor gave way to nothing.

She didn't have time to cry out. Her tongue snagged between her teeth as gravity yanked her over the edge of the missing floor and into oblivion. For the longest second of her life, she hung in suspended animation; a thousand outcomes flashed through her mind, lightning calculations that ended in shattered bones, bloody abrasions, splattered brain matter.

"Oomph!" Each scenario ended abruptly when she hit the ground, knees folding, wrist twanging like a tightwire as she jutted out her arms to keep from planting face-first into the dirt.

Flailing for a handhold back up, she found it painfully, abruptly, when her knuckles scraped against cement.

The foundation of the floor jutted in a semicircle arc around her, ragged to the touch. Only four feet up.

Relief and adrenaline conspired to send her gasping for breath, giddy laughter rising to her throat. A tiny fall. Not even worth writing home about. Abrasions would heal, the shock would wear off in a matter of seconds, and she'd survived the first step. *Take that.*

Over the rim of the jutting floor, the light solidified into a blinding orb.

She swallowed hysteria down hard, blinking furiously as the light shredded what little night vision she'd succeeded in cultivating. Heart pounding against the bruised cage of her ribs, she half ducked, hunching in an awkward limping stride that took her away from that oncoming light and—she coasted on a surge of triumph—the dangerous man that held it. Breath held, Kayleigh sprinted into the gloom.

"**T**he hell?"

A shimmer of gold at the farthest edges of the light jerked his attention away from the empty chair. Shawn leaped into motion, sprinted after her as her shape vanished into the dark recesses of Old Seattle.

She was going to get herself killed.

And fuck all if he was going to let his collateral get away that easy.

The half room he'd stashed her in should have been enough. He'd found it years ago, staked it out this time as the perfect prison for his unwilling guest.

He hadn't expected her to magic herself out of the thing.

Shawn's feet hit the dirt, light swaying as he caught his balance on the edge of the fractured floor and pushed off after her. "Stop," he shouted. "Don't go any farther!"

Like he expected her to listen to him.

Son of a bitch, he should have seen this one coming.

She darted away at the very edges of the light, a willowy ghost playing dodge with the rubble dotting the landscape. The ruins were bad news on any day, but at her reckless pace, she could break a leg, fall headlong into a pit; hell, find the trench and tumble in. The place was a bona fide death trap, and the little fool sprinted through it without care.

If he were half the man he wanted to be, he'd let her kill herself and never let on. Force Laurence Lauderdale to relive every moment the way Shawn did. The way he always would.

If only.

To his disgust, he wasn't that man. Even now, with the odds stacked against her and the solution to his aggravation laid out right in front of him, Shawn firmed his grip on the lamp. He jumped over the stacked remains of fallen walls, his boots kicking up grit as he navigated the steep slant. Keeping one eye on her and one on his path was a bitch, but he had no choice.

He knew how easy it was to disappear here. To die here.

Bracing a shoulder against a broken cornerstone in a sharp slide let him rebound off it in a hard right angle, which allowed him to duck under a broken cornice and shave off a few feet between them. If he played his cards right, he'd intersect with her before she could do much damage to herself or—his shin bounced off a jutting metal tank; he cursed long and hard—to him.

She stumbled. His guts jerked hard in response as he heard her sheared-off cry.

Idiot. *Idiot* of a woman.

A haunted look over her shoulder showed him the faintest glimpse of her face, a pale oval with wide, hollow eyes. Her hair caught the light swinging in his hand, threw it back in that glinting web of gold, as bright as any flare he could have wished for.

The light still loved her. Still clung to her, a beacon in the dark.

He forced his legs to eat up more ground than ever safe in the ruins. Years of cautionary care, gone.

Slowly, the rest of her body came into focus. She was limping.

But damned if she was giving up.

Admiration fizzled beside stone cold fury.

Shawn cursed under his breath, sweat dampening his shoulders. A quick scan of the environment gave him nothing to work with—more rock, more fallen buildings, more skeletal foundations thrusting the remains of walls and rooms and barriers into the dark. She stumbled again.

He watched her pale hand catch the edge of half-tilted doorway. Her arm clipped the frame; she sucked in a ragged breath he heard even through the ear-rattling slam of his pulse as he picked up speed.

Close. *Closer.* The light painted the ground in front of her, now, providing her with as much opportunity as it did him.

Dirt smeared down the back of her blazer, a flash of a pale hand as she flung it behind her for balance provided him all the opportunity he needed.

With monumental effort, he crouched low, leaped over a pile of treacherous debris she tried to skirt, and snagged that hand. It jerked hard as he landed, twisted in his grasp as he flailed.

Her eyes flared, threw back the light like diamonds. "Let me go!"

"Stop— *Shit.*"

The scrap gave way beneath him. The light went flying, a flickering globe arcing into the shadows.

He lost his footing; she lost her balance. As he wrenched Kayleigh in a semicircle with him, it was all he could do to catch her waist in one arm, tuck her hard against his chest, and grit his teeth as every jagged edge, point, prong, and rivet slammed into his side, his back, his forearms wrapped around her back. Metal screamed against metal as his body weight jarred it loose; a line of fire carved itself into one arm.

To her credit, she didn't scream.

But as they came to a stop, debris clattering to stillness around him, Shawn found himself cradling her against his chest, staring up into nothing as he struggled to pull in air through his bruised and battered body.

The rasping, panting echo was hers.

Lights sparkled somewhere beyond the scope of his vision, pops and crackling feelers made of shock and pain as his nerves checked back in. Spine, limbs—*Christ*—fingers, skull . . . Intact.

Rocks jammed into his back. His tailbone ached like a motherfucker, one elbow throbbed in direct counter to everything else, and yet . . .

"Shawn!" Heat filled his hands. Pressed down on him. Heat and flesh and *her.* "Are you okay?"

Was that concern in her voice? Worry?

Impossible. He'd given himself a concussion. Obviously.

One of his hands, curved over her head to protect her skull, now tingled as he realized that her hair was every bit as soft as he'd remembered. Her scalp was warm, her body fit to his in all the ways he shouldn't have noticed.

But he did. As his muscles sent out prickling assurances of functionality, as adrenaline pooled and frothed and slammed through his veins, he *noticed.*

Shawn wasn't that man. The one that could take everything human about himself and compartmentalize it. He wanted to be, had spent too damned long telling himself he could be, but he lied. Right now, as he inhaled through his nose and found the air a strangely intoxicating blend of wet metal and woman, he couldn't find it in himself to hate. To forget.

She'd made him laugh. Caught him off guard. She'd made him run like hell, too.

Brave girl. Stupid, but brave.

~~Are you okay?~~

Why did it matter?

She shifted. Her hip dug into his thigh, too close to his dick, which had absolutely no sense of timing or taste as it stirred. Hungry, eager to remember the feel of her in his hands.

"Jesus," he muttered from underneath a wave of scented silk. She smelled like soap, clean and fresh. "Stop wriggling."

As if suddenly aware of her own precarious position, of the erection he couldn't hide pressing into her thigh, she stiffened. An elbow dug into his ribs.

"Don't you dare!" she hissed. Like a ruffled kitten.

His grip firmed. "You aren't going anywhere," he said tightly, banishing all thoughts of fragrance and femininity and *soft*. "What the hell were you thinking?"

A shudder rippled through her. "What the hell do *you* think?" she tossed back. "Run for help? Get away from you? Take your pick."

"In the ruins? You idiot."

The elbow at his side eased. A hand insinuated itself between his chest and hers. Though she pushed at him, he had nowhere to go between her weight and the ground, and he wasn't letting go of her head or the warmth at her lower back anytime soon. Not until she knew the score.

He would win. The end.

"Let go," she huffed.

He could. But he didn't. Instead, slipping his right hand from her hair to curl over her nape, he gave her just enough room to push her head up, glare into his face with a scowl so fierce, he almost laughed outright.

The light, hidden somewhere behind debris, painted her dimly in shades of blue and gray. Shaped her mouth in ways that drew his attention. Her eyes, paler in this light, turned to silk and shadow.

Shawn's urge to smile faded.

Hectic color stained her cheeks. Sweat plastered tendrils of her hair against her forehead, caught a strand against her mouth. He wanted to tuck a finger against the corner of her lips and stroke the glint of gold away.

And then he wanted to taste that bit of skin with his tongue. Follow the curve of her lower lip and find out if she was as indifferent to him as he should be to her.

He wasn't. Maybe that other guy would have been, but Shawn definitely wasn't. He'd proven that already.

Her shoulders tilted as she shoved at his chest. "I said—"

"I know what you said."

Those eyes flashed. "I'm warning you."

"I know you are."

Panic twisted her mouth, swam behind her eyes. Another shudder slammed through her. He felt it sweep through her body, felt the way her body shivered into his. "Shawn, don't . . ."

One knee slid between his legs, her thigh suddenly tucked even closer against his rapidly hardening erection, and he hissed in a breath.

She froze.

"Fact is," he managed somehow through the jolt of sudden, adrenaline-fueled lust spiking through his senses, "I didn't expect this. Any of . . ." His gaze skimmed to her mouth, to the gaping neck of her blouse. "*This*. Maybe I should have."

That color deepened in her cheeks. Swept across her forehead, her jaw. "You had your chance," she said, unsteady, trying so hard for angry.

He deserved angry. "I know. Believe me, Doctor, *this*"—because he had no other name for it—"isn't what I want."

"Then let me go."

"I can't."

"Well, you can't—" Her husky denial broke as his thumb dug into the soft skin just behind her ear. Her eyes flared. "You shouldn't . . ."

When she trailed to silence, wild gaze glittering as it shifted away from his, Shawn almost groaned outright.

This wasn't part of the plan. It had never been part of the plan, in any incarnation. He'd never imagined that his dick would find the concept of Kayleigh Lauderdale worth considering, much less thickening for.

Until she'd turned to him in her car. Until she'd kissed him. Now, as her weight shifted—as that leg pressed hard against him and she swallowed a wary, awkward sound—he wondered if her mouth would be cool and remote if he tried to kiss her again. If she'd respond the way she had in that car, a whole other lifetime ago.

Murderer, the vicious part of his brain whispered. She came from a line of them.

It didn't help. The blood leaching out of his brain

arrowed right for the greedy flesh between his legs, and he needed to reverse the flow. *Now.*

Only he didn't want to.

"Wait—" The hand at his chest stiffened.

Too late.

He hadn't even realized that his fingers curled into her hair. That he'd wrapped the tousled length of it around his fist. "Okay," he murmured.

Her lashes flared, delicate fans around the wild panic in her eyes. "Shawn, stop."

He wouldn't. Not until he absolved himself of this temptation, this ridiculous need to taste her again. Mark her, brand her with his kiss as if he could burn it out in one go, get it the hell out of his system and off his mind.

It wouldn't work. Shawn didn't care.

Adrenaline surged as he tugged her closer, inexorably closer, until the wide shape of her diamond pale eyes filled his vision and her breath puffed against his mouth in rapid, shallow alarm.

"Just one." A promise, a threat to his unruly body, each syllable ghosting over her lips as he framed the words. Her mouth parted on a gasp; she shuddered in his grip.

Just one fucking kiss.

Her leg jerked.

Pain lit up the inside of his skull like a blown fuse.

"Fuck!" A snarl, a wheeze, and then he couldn't hang on to her anymore, too busy balancing the dual need to vomit with bone-deep agony spiraling up from his brutalized testicles. She flung herself backward, wrenched out of his lax grip, and crab-walked so fast, grit skittered out from her flailing limbs.

"Never," she swore. A promise, an accusation. "Never again."

He didn't—couldn't—answer, every inch of his body fighting the urge to go fetal, wrap around the soft flesh she'd jammed her knee into. Fucking hell. It'd been a long time since he'd let himself get caught that badly by anyone, much less a woman.

Much less *this* woman.

Racked by Kayleigh Lauderdale. For *fuck's* sake.

CHAPTER EIGHT

"**Y**ou have forty-eight hours."

Director Laurence Lauderdale folded gnarled, shaking hands on top of his desk, stared blankly out the window as the recorded threat came to an end.

It wasn't the first threat he'd ever fielded. It wouldn't be the last, given his history. In his eighty-three years of life, in the years before the earthquake had destroyed everything he'd held dear, he'd handled death threats, litigation threats, even threats of prison time.

None of them came as close to his heart as this one.

His daughter. They had Kayleigh.

How?

Outside his window, some forty-odd stories above the ground, he had a clear view of the silent side of the Holy Order quadplex. Situated at the top of New Seattle, home to the Holy Cathedral, the civics side, the remains of the witch-hunting Mission, and his own

Sector Three research and development division, the area was the safest place in all of the metropolis.

He'd made sure of that. The last of the traitors were dead or would be soon. The Mission was filled with loyal agents of his Salem Project, run by him with oversight, for now, by the Bishop of the Holy Order of St. Dominic.

There was nobody on the roster he didn't personally approve. Nobody who could have kidnapped his daughter, and definitely nobody with the wherewithal to smuggle her out of the quad security without him knowing.

His hands shook, pain flaring in arthritic joints.

That left only one option. One way that Kayleigh could have escaped his cautious eye.

She must have left the premises. Ignored his orders and gone on her fool's errand.

Disappointment; sharp as a knife. With effort, he flattened his hands on the desk, pushed himself out of the chair that was supposed to—according to the doctors—provide him more back support and lessen daily stress on his spine. Kayleigh had insisted he use it. He'd obliged her, but he didn't care for all the modern luxuries and high-tech devices his daughter foisted on him.

It was a chair. It did its job. That was all he demanded of it—and everything else.

Make a better world. That had always been the plan.

He walked carefully to the window, reaching up to feel the chill surface of the glass against his fingers.

Kayleigh was out there. Somewhere. In the hands of a monster.

How much was he willing to sacrifice to see this through?

A perfunctory knock on the door preceded his assistant's respectful greeting. "Do you need something, sir?"

Patrick Ross was a good boy. Clever and efficient, though transparent in his bid for power in the kinds of office politics Laurence didn't much engage in.

Why bother when he was already at the top? Or close enough that it wouldn't matter soon.

"Yes." He beckoned the young man in, turning away from the window to hobble carefully back to this desk. "There's a small matter that needs to be handled with discretion."

"Of course, sir."

Lauderdale expected nothing less. No other answer would satisfy. "You heard the message." It wasn't a question. Patrick, lovely boy that he was, was one of the privileged few who had earned that right. That trust.

"Yes." The cover on Patrick's digital reader—similar to the type his daughter always carried—flipped open, and the young man tapped a few keys. The reflected light gleamed off his thick glasses. "I have the techs already attempting to run a trace. It's a short call, however, which tells me the kidnapper knows about signal tracking."

Smart boy. Eager to please. "Any luck?" he asked, easing his bony frame back down into his chair. With care, of course. Everything he did was with care, these days. His daughter often warned him about taking it.

Things were so much more fragile these days. Much different from when he was younger.

Everything was different then.

"Not yet," Patrick replied simply. No sympathy. He'd learned. Laurence didn't want sympathy; he wanted results. "I assume that answering his ransom is out of the question, sir?"

"Unequivocally." Half of the people the kidnapper demanded go free were already dead. Unfortunate, but not unexpected. Some people simply weren't suited to the demands the Holy Order placed on them.

And some were all too eager to live a little bit longer. "Organize a rescue team, Patrick." Lauderdale rubbed at his forehead, digging at the loose flesh there. His wedding band, long since dulled with age, was warm against his skin. "Put Amanda Green in it."

"What?"

He dropped his hand, frowning. "The team," he clarified slowly. "Put her in it."

"But . . ." Patrick cleared his throat, dark eyebrows knotted. "Sir, she's virtually untested."

"So, test her. I can't think of a better time, can you?"

His assistant hesitated. Then, shaking his head, he keyed in a few more commands to his reader and confirmed, "It'll be done. They'll be ready to go at a moment's notice."

"Give them two goals," he instructed quietly. "Bring my daughter back at all costs, and end this mongrel who put his hands on her." Rage. It'd been a long time since the flickering heat of it warmed the cold, empty hollow beneath his skin. He nursed it, fists tightening, knuckles popping. "I want every last shred of his existence burned out, am I clear?"

The younger man nodded slowly. "Yes, sir."

For a moment, neither moved. Lauderdale blew out a wavering breath, forced his brain to turn to less emotional tasks. Just as important.

He needed to shape the world his daughter was coming back to, didn't he?

He flattened both hands on the desk. "Speak to me of the Mission repairs."

"The damaged sectors need to be gutted entirely, but once everything is settled, round-the-clock work shifts will be ready to go. There's been no problem from the remainder of the original agents." If the boy had any problems keeping up, Lauderdale detected nothing.

Pleased, he folded his hands neatly—over the copy of the press release he had paused in approving—and gave Patrick his full attention.

"Right now, the Salem agents have stepped into the gap and there's been no trouble with integration." Now, he paused.

Lauderdale nodded. "Except when degeneration commences."

"Except that."

Another problem Kayleigh had caused. Or rather a problem she hadn't fixed. Yet. He needed her back for that reason, too. Not only because she was his daughter—the last of his flesh and blood, he thought with a pang in his old heart—but because she was the only key to a riddle his late wife had left him. Matilda was brilliant, there was never any doubt about that.

And wily. She'd always been three steps ahead of him.

He waited for anger; all he felt was a sadness so keen, it was as if razor blades bit into his chest. His head drooped, bloated knuckles whitening, cracking in protest.

His first daughter, missing after the earthquake. His second hadn't lived past twenty years of age. Kayleigh had been his own miracle, a gift from God. Yet, as if that weren't enough hell for one family, his wife had betrayed him, left him with a small child and a lab full of subjects he couldn't use.

All because he'd wanted to make a better world.

Kayleigh understood what Matilda hadn't. She recognized the potential where his wife had only seen madness.

Matilda was no longer a factor, but he wasn't a stupid man. He'd never been a stupid man. If he knew ~~Kayleigh's mother, she'd have left contingencies in~~ their ongoing game of chess. The queen had fallen, but a game could be won by pawns just as easily.

The solution was simple: clear the board. Knights, rooks.

Bishops.

And crown a new queen. "Patrick."

"Sir?"

"Do whatever you have to," Lauderdale said thickly. "Bring my daughter home."

"We will, Director."

He nodded, but when Patrick didn't immediately rise to leave, Lauderdale lifted his weary gaze. "What else?"

Patrick hesitated, as if searching for the right words. "Given the circumstances," he said slowly. "Do you want to hold off on—"

"No," Lauderdale interrupted, straightening his spine with effort. The chair underneath him conformed, supported the gesture. "We will proceed as planned. There is no room for delays in the schedule, Patrick."

"All right. Probably best," he added with a faint smile. "The lead specialist isn't, um, kind when he's interrupted."

The least of his problems. Lauderdale reached for the press release briskly. "You have your orders."

"Yes, sir." Finally, Patrick took his reader and left, the door shutting quietly behind him.

What would be, would be. The team would find Kayleigh, bring her safely home, end this annoyance of a threat, and the pieces would fill the chessboard like good little players.

At least until he found the right trigger to shake the board.

He was decades into patience. No reason to rush now.

CHAPTER NINE

What the hell had possessed him to kiss the devil's own daughter?

Shawn dragged his captive back to the dubious safety of the dark prison, ignoring her stiff gait and muttered, unintelligible complaints. His body hurt subtly enough to warn him that he'd really regret his life choices tomorrow, and his pride stung like a bitch.

Not that he didn't deserve it. It wasn't any worse than what he'd done to her.

"Do you *realize* we're in Old Seattle?"

Her shrill demand drilled a hole through his head, setting his teeth on edge. "That so."

"What kind of suicidal moron willingly travels through the ruins?"

"The kind with nothing to lose," he growled. He tucked his hands at her waist, ignored her sudden, shocked breath to boost her up over the ledge leading back inside. The light hooked around his wrist bobbed wildly. "Get up there."

Her options were obey or fall. To his relief, she made the smart one.

It took her a moment to find a grip, to edge a knee over the jagged rim. For every second the resistant doctor worked it out, his fingers transmitted exactly how soft her backside was beneath her dusty, grime-smeared slacks. How warm her body, how easy it'd be to span her waist with his hands and perch her on that damned ledge with her ass hanging over it and—

And what? Let her jam another lethal limb into his balls?

Hell, no. Lesson learned, thanks very much.

He'd gotten his one taste. Two, if he counted when she didn't consider him an asshole. He was done.

He shoved her over the ledge with a harder push than necessary, jaw locking as she bit back a startled gasp, something laced with what sounded suspiciously like pain.

She could join the club. The scratch on his arm burned. His body sang a note that would translate to sheer, balls-out aggression tomorrow. To say nothing of said abused balls.

No fucking sympathy.

Except that wasn't exactly true, either.

Catching the ledge in both hands, he leveraged himself over the rocky edge and caught her arm before she managed to do more than take two steadying steps.

It jerked in his grip. "I'm not an idiot."

He couldn't help himself. He snorted.

"I didn't know you'd taken me to Old Seattle," she shot back to his wordless scorn, the hollows of her face dark and eerie as she turned away from the light. "I've never been here in my life!"

"That's the point, Doctor."

Her mouth flattened. "It doesn't make it a smart move."

"Like kissing a stranger in a dark parking lot?" She said nothing to that, her jaw thrusting forward. Stubborn. He expected nothing less from a spoiled topsider. Especially her. "Let's go."

But when he marched her across the short distance, as the chair she'd escaped once already loomed large and imposing in the light, she balked. "No way."

"No choice."

Her sensible flats scraped across the floor. "I'm not going back in that chair."

The hell she wasn't. He tugged at her arm, forcing her feet to slide in the filth coating the floor.

She panicked.

"No!" Her elbow wrenched in his grip, forcing him to tighten his hold before she made another break for it. The cords in her slender throat stood out in sharp relief as she jerked her chin up, resistance thrumming through every tense line of her body.

She meant it. That much was clear. Her eyes skimmed the darkness, searching wildly for an escape or an excuse.

Rescue.

She wouldn't find it here. He couldn't afford it.

He shoved her forward, taking advantage of his greater strength to wrestle her bodily across the room. She fought like a feral cat, hissing and flailing as he dragged her around the chair.

"Sit," Shawn ordered. His fingers closed over her forearm as it swung at him.

Hers closed around his own, hard enough to leave white indents in his skin.

He glanced down. Frowned at the blotchy brown stain at her sleeve. "You're hurt."

"Screw you," she snarled.

Exasperation warred with a wildly inappropriate surge of humor. This was unbelievable. "Look." He tried for reasonable. "Get in the chair, and I'll look at your inju—"

"*No.*"

"This isn't negotiable, Doctor."

"I'm not negotiating," she panted, her voice thin. High. "I'm *telling* you. You'll have to sedate me if you want me back in that chair."

Shawn didn't have the patience for this shit. "Sorry, Your Highness, this isn't exactly a luxury topside resort. You intend to run. I can't let you. It's really that easy."

She opened her mouth. Closed it when he raised a challenging eyebrow at her.

"Get in the fucking chair."

Her face, already paled to near ghostly translucence by the lantern light, drained of color. "I'm sorry I kneed you in the testicles," she whispered. "Really." She shook her head. "But I'll do it again if you force me."

He gritted his teeth as the ends of her hair skimmed over the back of his hand.

So much for easy. He didn't have another damned needle.

He spun her in a hard semicircle, ignored her protest as he hauled her against his chest; backed her hard toward the chair.

She pushed against him, stepping into his space,

into *him*. As if she could push him back, use him as some kind of leverage or anchor.

It didn't have the effect she wanted. Instead, as his brain wised up, his body translated every detail of her small, tantalizing breasts pressed against his chest, of her hips against his. Her breath gusting out against the skin where his neck met his shoulder.

Damn it, he'd *known* better. Known that his body wasn't obeying his directives where she was concerned, that his imagination had already relieved her of that blazer and the flimsy silk shirt underneath. Painted her skin in shadow. His nerves crackled to life at the press of her body, teasingly close. Tauntingly forbidden.

His brain shorted.

That his dick, tragically abused as it was, took note of her—her warmth, her vitality—threw logic under the bus of rampant desire. Her fragrance, softer and more feminine than the dust and age and decay he'd grown accustomed to smelling, filled his nose. His senses.

Ah, what the hell? He'd try for three. That was a good, witchy number, wasn't it?

When the backs of her knees collided with the frame, her back stiffened. Her mouth opened again, eyes flashing pure fury. Dread. Warning so sharp, he wondered if he'd bleed by the end of it.

Maybe it'd be worth it.

Whatever she'd meant to say, whatever plea or threat or curse, died as his hand splayed across the back of her head and he slanted his mouth roughly against hers.

She froze.

Shawn didn't stop to consider niceties; he wouldn't

have listened to himself if he'd tried. Her lips weren't relaxed, he couldn't even say they were warm in the chilled Old Seattle air, but Jesus Christ, his body didn't care.

She tasted as good as she smelled. Sweeter than he remembered, after all.

Her shocked breath caught in her throat. Shawn's fingers slid from her hair, curved over her collarbone, thumb at the pulse hammering wildly in her neck as he slid his lips along hers. One of her hands found his side, curled into his shirt so tightly that he felt her nails score his flesh beneath, and it shot a bolt of pure pleasure to his hardening cock. Damage forgotten. Even forgiven.

One more kiss. Hadn't he promised himself that?

This was it.

And as his upper lip caught against her lower, as a low, strangled sound turned ragged in her throat, her mouth softened. Parted. Unmistakable invitation to his tongue; his accidental, unnecessary, unstoppable seduction.

The chair. This was about the chair.

Wasn't it?

The hell it was.

Shawn caught her tangled hair in one hand, wrapped it around his fist to hold her head still for a kiss that had nothing to do with names, with places, with *plans*. Abandoning finesse, he jerked her head back, bared her throat to him, and swore as wild color filled her cheeks. As her lashes shadowed them; her eyes closed, hid her thoughts.

He wanted to see her shock. Her arousal. Wanted it like he wanted to bend her over that chair and fill her body with his, feel her rise against him, her hips tilted, flesh slick with sweat. The memory of her wet flesh against his hand wasn't enough.

He'd never wanted anyone as badly as he wanted her.

And *she* was a Lauderdale.

Kayleigh shuddered. Her white teeth sank into her bottom lip, full and damp from his kiss, and it was enough.

Too much.

Groaning, Shawn bent his head to claim whatever hell he'd have to pay by sinning with the devil's own.

Her leg lifted around his thigh, curled. Like a moron, he didn't even consider how close to a second round of pain he'd gotten until it was too late, but she didn't follow through on the all too easy target.

Instead, one hand flattened against his thudding heartbeat as she pressed up, into his kiss. Into him. Her toes locked around the back of his knee.

Shawn stiffened.

Too late. She wrenched her face away, splayed both hands at his chest, and pushed him hard enough that he staggered. His knee locked into her leg, and he stumbled backward, swearing, flailing. The floor thudded as he landed ass-first.

"Stop *doing* that!" Her shout, muffled by the arm she dragged across her mouth, broke. Eyes blazing, feet planted, she glared down at Shawn, her body steel-straight and all but crackling with tension.

Distress. He read it easy in her stare, in the panicked speed of her breath. Distress, and confusion.

"You've made your point," she said again, quieter, but trembling. "Stop it, now. It's not funny."

Shawn stared, his mouth tingling, his brain trapped in a feedback loop of shock, lust, anger, amusement.

Guilt.

What the fuck was he doing? "I'm—"

The chair rattled behind her.

For a too-long moment, nothing made sense: the woman standing over him, fists tightly clenched, the slick ground under his palms and digging into his tailbone.

The rumble filling the silence.

Shawn bolted to his feet. Not fast enough.

The chair slid an inch to the left. Jerked back to the right. The rumble became a roar.

Not again.

"Shit!" The floor bucked beneath them. Balance destroyed, he yanked her away from the suddenly vibrating chair, tripped over her as she lurched into him.

Kayleigh flung both hands out for balance. Stone cracked as it jarred loose from rotted moorings, metal and brick and moldering remains rained down through the hole in the ceiling.

Dust exploded in a sudden cloud; dust and mold and fine particles of indefinable grit.

The remains of the structure listed violently. The chair spun, leaned on its axis, and toppled with a sharp crash. The foundation teetered.

"Get out," he roared, snagging her wrist as she flailed for balance.

Kayleigh cried out, pain and obvious terror overwhelmed by a substantial groan wrenching through the once-silent ruins. Brick peppered them, a stinging hail of shrapnel. She hunched, flailing for purchase with her slick-soled shoes, and with all his strength, he turned, fought the wild toss of gravity to shove her back the way they came.

She stumbled, toes catching against the floor, a pale blot in the dancing, juddering light.

He staggered, forced backward by the swaying floor. "Run!"

She tried.

Muscles bunching, he strained for purchase, desperately fighting the rolling surface.

She found the edge of the broken floor. Vanished over it, sinking into shadow.

With a powerful, desperate shriek of metal giving way, of foundation tearing free, the whole floor tilted violently upright. Shawn hit the grimy surface, twisted to his back just in time to ride the sudden slant down into the darkness.

Impact came almost immediately. He hit what he hoped was the ground, grunted as his ribs collided with something jagged and unyielding. White light detonated behind his eyelids, flashed red as pain lanced through his chest, his arms, down his spine.

When it all went black, Shawn didn't know if it'd stopped or if the fall knocked him out, but he'd take the breather.

At least until he inhaled a cloud of dust, choked on it, and found he couldn't take a deep enough breath to cough it out.

His eyes opened slowly. Light pooled somewhere beyond him, painting ripples through a dust cloud thick enough to eat.

Coughing, cursing, searing agony licked from ribs to shoulder.

His brain kicked back into gear only sluggishly. Jerking his hand up slammed his knuckles into a rough block of cement, and he swore some more. "Shit. *Shit!*" His exhale wheezed.

He was pinned. And he couldn't fucking breathe.

CHAPTER TEN

"Shawn!"

Kayleigh couldn't see much beyond the fine cloud of unsettled dust and grit, only the faint outline of his shoulder and chest silhouetted by the lantern light she could just make out behind him. A cloudy haze covered everything, coated him in a backlit nimbus, stung her eyes until they watered.

She half slid, half stumbled down the steep embankment that had, until moments ago, been a floor. She'd seen the floor, felt it underneath her feet. Flat. Sturdy.

Now it looked like nothing more than a steep incline lit by the abandoned lantern shining weakly from a pile of rubble.

All remnants of confused arousal, of panicked fury, had been brutalized into submission by the icy reality of terror.

The earth had, thank God, stopped shifting. That the

only sound now was the occasional echo of something snapping in the black, dropping to the ground, colliding with other ruins like it, didn't help her peace of mind.

An *earthquake*. Exactly like the one that had hit those lower streets. Was New Seattle in danger?

Why hadn't anybody considered that the quakes could come again?

Because the witches had caused the Armageddon. Wasn't that the truth?

The doctrine had always said one thing, but as Kayleigh scrambled down the newly formed gradient, she couldn't make it fit her reality. Earthquakes. Not just something that happened to strangers years ago, but to *her*? Now?

Rocks bounced and clattered beneath her feet, scraping along the steep slant as she clambered down to the base. The shadows filled the newly formed rubble with inky blots of nothing, secretive voids muffling the occasional shudder of rocky foundation or the rustle and snap of falling debris.

As she got closer, as the cloud of dust settled slowly, the corona clinging to Shawn didn't fade. It got worse, thicker, forcing her to squint, brace for the pain of a migraine she didn't have time for. Each step closer to him heightened the effect, solidified the nimbus until the shimmering cloud of lantern-lit gold colored the world. From within it, tense, raw pain tightened his features to the same harsh edges as the block of concrete trapping his shoulder to the fractured remains of a wall behind him.

She might be furious at him for his high-handed assumptions—for his betrayal—but he didn't deserve this. Nobody deserved this.

His shoulder twisted, streaks of white pressure

climbing up his skewed collar. "Shit," he growled, voice rasping.

"Stop struggling."

His gaze jerked to her. Narrowed before it turned again to the weight he fought to pull himself out from under. "I'm pinned." Taut. Strained, yet there was nothing in his voice, his expression to plead with her. Nothing that suggested anything but grim resignation.

She could run.

The knowledge filled the trembling silence. Caused the halo in her vision to dance and sway. She could run now, leave him to his fate.

Kayleigh hesitated.

Cataloging her own hurts took less than a second. Leg throbbing beneath its bandage, wrist stinging fiercely, even a dull ache through her abused muscles from the awkward run through the ruins. The rumble had scared her, his kiss had thrown her off balance, but she was hale and healthy.

Physically.

A muscle in her cheek twitched as she blinked at the glittering space between Shawn and the rock. Absently, she pressed two fingers to the twitching nerve.

Mentally, she had to be losing her mind. The evidence of her evaporating psychological acuity shimmered in front of her.

Shawn's dark eyes fixed on her, stared at her as if he expected her to turn her back. Judgment? Some. Acceptance, which surprised her.

He knew what he'd done to her. She had no doubts of that.

The world throbbed around her, a visual pulse assaulting her senses, but Kayleigh's head remained clear of associated pain.

Clear enough to recognize the opportunity. Run. Escape.

She took a step back.

Leave him to die.

Shawn's eyes glittered beneath the maddening nimbus of gold.

She'd never been in an earthquake before. Her father had. She knew the stories. Weren't the old ones caused by malicious witches?

She wasn't a witch. But . . . but was he? Was her captor a witch?

Could one man pull *this* off?

Why would he want to?

Another step back sent her vision dancing, sparklers of light flickering at the corners.

Framed by the halo she couldn't shake, his lashes lowered, jaw tensing as the muscles in his free arm bulged with effort to shift the concrete block. Blood slid in a thick line from a cut over his eyebrow, mingled with dirt and dust to turn black.

His vengeance could destroy her.

The certainty of it filled her thoughts.

Kayleigh turned, her heart hammering. One chance. This was it. She could run like hell. Common sense demanded that she leave him to his fate and . . .

And . . .

His growl caught on a sharp note. Rock and metal grated, fragments pattering like rain to the uneven ground.

She didn't know what made her stop. What made her pause long enough to look over her shoulder.

The air thickened with something indefinable. Turned heavier. Kayleigh's hand lifted to her head, smeared sweat into mud, but her vision didn't clear. The corona didn't fade. Blood and dirt coated Shawn's face, stained his shirt. His teeth, obscenely white against the grime, bared with effort as he strained. Muscles bulged in his arm, the skin at his eyelids tightened.

It was if she stared at two of him, superimposed. Similar, but different somehow.

His choices could right the past.

The thought—heavy with knowledge, serious—sounded like her own, but the words were alien. Confident.

How could she know with such conviction? Who was she to decide?

What was she thinking?

She couldn't leave him to die. Not like this, and not willingly.

Kayleigh's feet turned. Carried her over rubble, found purchase unerringly in the hazy light. His head jerked up in surprise. His eyes narrowed, breath coming in low, tight wheezes. "What are you doing?"

She didn't know. She had to be crazy.

As if she watched herself from far away, she crouched down, one hand curved over his shoulder. One pressed against the hunk of cement. Her fingers slid across his chest, eyes closing as she traced taut muscle and rumpled fabric. Found the seam where rock met flesh and felt for breaks. For trauma worse than bruising.

The latter would be unavoidable.

He stared at her.

"Is anything broken?"

"No." He paused, and she felt his chest bunch beneath her fingers. "No, I don't think so."

She took her own time, worked her fingers between the rough cement and him.

He stared at her, eyes narrowed. His lashes were coated with dust, glinting strangely in that nimbus she couldn't shake. "Why?"

She wasn't so far gone that she didn't know what he asked. It echoed the question she demanded of herself. Why was she helping him? Gaze focused on the dark seam where her hand vanished under the weight, she allowed seconds to pass while she considered it.

Why, indeed?

Because she'd never been a killer.

That's not true.

Her palms tingled, echo of the sweat already prickling across her shoulders. Slicking down her spine.

That was a warning she knew. She took a deep breath, fought the need to cough against the dust swirl, the pressure in the air. How would she explain?

When the words came, they surprised her. "Even if I leave you," she heard herself say with utter certainty, "you'll get out. You're smart. You'll find a way."

"Hunh." Not so much a word as a grunt.

"If I leave," she told him, frowning, "your hatred will be more than justified. So . . ." All at once, the weight vanished, sucked out of the air and leaving her grasping for her next words, fighting the urge to squirm under his gaze. "I don't hate you, Shawn. I'm furious, I'm betrayed, but I don't want to see you dead, hurt, or . . ." He flinched under her hand, a sudden tightening of muscle away from her probing fingers. His breath hissed out. "Sorry." She closed her eyes, the better to focus on the tender flesh beneath her fingertips. The ragged edge of his shirt rasped against them.

"Or what?"

"Does it hurt if I—"

He ignored her concern. "Dead, hurt, or *what?*"

What did she have to lose? "Humiliated," she whispered. "I'm not like that."

His chest stilled. Jerked as he sucked in a shallow breath. "Is that what you think? That *I'm* like that?"

He hadn't left her anything else to go on.

As if aware of it, he hissed, "Fuck."

Kayleigh's snort took in more dust than comfortable. It turned into a cough, and she opened her eyes, squinted when they stung. Swiping at one didn't help; the dirt encrusted on her skin only forced her to blink hard.

The dark was bad. The dust bit. But the freaking *glow* made her prefer dark and dust to the certainty of ocular deterioration.

Something shuddered in the distance, sending vibrations all along the slanted wreckage. Shawn's lips peeled back around his clenched teeth as the cement shifted.

Without thinking, she laid one hand over his forehead. The ends of his hair tickled her fingers, but his skin felt warm. Vividly so. "You aren't going into shock," she murmured. The doctor part of her brain, the one that remembered how to function, took over. "Good. Keep breathing, slow it down. We don't want you to hyperventilate."

He flinched as her thumb found the swelling at his eyebrow. "Listen to me. I didn't mean to humiliate you."

She froze.

He stared across the awkward circumference of his prison, gaze banked. Rigid with pain, but intensely direct and as even as his low, rich voice as he offered a quiet, "I'm sorry."

Sorry? That was almost worth another attempt at a

laugh. How could she possibly tell his truth from his lies?

Her mouth tightened. "I have no reason to believe you." She pulled her hand back, wiped her palm against her hip without consciously making the choice. It didn't help. Her palm radiated heat, fingers detailing every second laid against his skin.

He had the grace to wince. "I know. I blew that about five different ways."

At least he understood.

"This is how it's going to go, Shawn Lowe."

He waited in silence, broken only by labored breathing.

"No more kissing." She braced both hands against the rock. His gaze flicked to them, then back to her. Narrowed. "No unnecessary touching, no arguments punctuated with your oh-so-virile masculinity."

Humor sliced behind his eyes, and his lips hitched at one corner.

"That was sarcasm," she added flatly.

"Or what?"

The repetition of his earlier demand gave her pause, and Kayleigh frowned at him. "What?"

"No unnecessary touching, or what?" His shoulders shifted, knuckles white in the hand braced against the hunk of wall. "You don't want me dead, remember? Or hurt."

"No." That much was true. Kayleigh tipped her head back, gathering her tangled hair over her shoulder as she studied the vast emptiness overhead. "But I *can* sure make you as uncomfortable as possible for as long as I can. I can make your life a living hell while you keep me here, and if you kill me, well . . ." Her smile was wan. "I'd be beyond caring, wouldn't I?"

His eyebrows rose. "You drive a merciless bargain, Dr. Lauderdale."

"Take it or leave it."

He didn't disappoint. "You have a deal." The lines his almost-smile carved into the corners of his eyes softened his hard features. Made him look almost human.

Her stomach pitched.

She stood, blowing back dust in her wake. "And when you're out of here," she added, too loudly in the dank quiet, "you're going to let me go home."

He blew out a shallow breath that sounded suspiciously like a laugh. His head fell back, propped against the cracked wall behind him, and he closed his eyes. "No."

Just that one word, a single syllable. He was so *good* at it.

"What are your options?" she demanded.

"Make you watch me die," he returned evenly, as if it didn't matter one way or another, "slow and painful."

Augh. The urge to stamp her foot grew. Instead, pressing a fist to her forehead, one to her stomach, she considered her own alternatives.

There was no real choice here. As she studied the obstacle, forcing herself to focus—to ignore the racing palpitations of her heart and twisting burn in her guts—she told herself this was the only choice that mattered.

He'd lied to her, made her like him, laugh with him. She'd trusted him. Then he'd kidnapped her, imprisoned her. Sure, he'd apologized, but what good was an apology when he wasn't going to let her go?

Kayleigh didn't know.

He'd acquiesced to all her demands but one. Freedom. That should have been reason enough to leave him here, but could she?

He hadn't hurt her. He hadn't killed her. She was made of stronger stuff than that.

She took a deep breath. "Fine. You're a lucky man, Mr. Lowe."

His snort strained.

"This chunk of death got caught on that outcropping. If it hadn't snagged up there . . ."

"Paste, yeah, I get it." He threw back his head, staring hard into the shadows hanging over the wreckage. "And?"

"And," she repeated slowly, circling the block, "all I need is something for a lever and I see a way out." With this much scrap and debris around, finding the fulcrum for her makeshift lever was as easy as shoving at a hunk of metal and bonded cement until she'd wrestled it into place near the cement pin.

Shawn watched her silently, nostrils flaring with every shallow breath.

"Basic physics," she said, dusting her palms off against each other.

"Great." It was little more than a wheeze.

Kayleigh took her time searching through the nearby rubble and debris. She walked carefully, picked up various bits of metal, discarded them when they were too short, too flexible, not strong enough.

It took her five dedicated minutes to find what she needed: a perfect piece of rebar, twisted but solid. Smaller hafts of metal wrapped around it, and as she tucked it against the corner of a crumbling bit of rock and tested the durability, it didn't so much as flex a millimeter.

It'd have to do.

The rough metal scraped her palms as she lugged it back to Shawn's impromptu prison.

"Got it. This should—" She didn't realize he watched her until she looked up, her gaze clashing with the dark intensity of his own. Her voice halted mid-assurance. Her heart thudded, suddenly too loud in her ears.

The shape of his jaw, hard with the pain she knew he must be feeling, shifted. "Kayleigh."

It was the first time he'd used her name.

It shouldn't have mattered. Shouldn't have meant anything. But she flushed, looked away. At the long haft of twisted steel in her hands, the scrap hunk of metal she intended to use as the base for her impromptu lever. Anywhere but at him. "A-anyway," she continued, striving for brisk. "Don't move until there's enough space between you and the rock. I don't know if that anchor will hold, so be ready to move fast."

"Kayleigh, I meant it when—"

"No." She snapped it off, shook her head when his teeth came together, a muscle shifting in his jaw. "I don't need to go over it, okay? Just . . . don't move until I say so."

He closed his eyes. A bead of sweat trickled from his temple, barely even carving a line through the bloody stain across his cheek. "Got it," he managed.

He'd better. They'd only get one chance at this.

Kayleigh dragged the heavy rebar to her chosen brace, slid it over the peak and under the concrete weight. It rocked, enough that Shawn flinched, cursing tightly.

She halted, held her breath.

"Keep going," he ordered, voice tense. His eyes, stark and intense, met hers. Held. "You can do it."

He was reassuring her?

She wanted to laugh, but there was nothing funny about it. Because, as she braced her feet against the rock-strewn ground and prepared to shove all her weight against the bar, she realized she needed it.

His reassurance. His encouragement.

Any reassurance.

"Brace yourself," she murmured.

"Do it."

Kayleigh grasped the edge of the rebar in both hands. Tightened her grip until the metal bit, and pushed. Hard. Harder. When the opposite end of her lever ground against the concrete, she grunted with the impact. When it refused to budge further, she sucked in a breath, clenched her teeth, and threw her body weight onto the far end.

The concrete shifted.

Fragments peppered the ground, scattered from the building that braced it. The anchor that held it. She groaned with the effort, threw herself into it with everything she had. Her hands ached, nerves pinched until she felt the strain in her shoulders, her back, her legs. Her hair fell over her face as she bent nearly double, and somewhere beyond her shell of awareness—the effort and the raw grit—she heard him encouraging her. Goading her.

Praising her.

The block groaned. Concrete gave, just in time. With a screech of sliding metal against metal, the fulcrum collapsed.

Between one instant and the next—one wild heartbeat—the rebar slammed to the ground. Kayleigh toppled, fell on top of it, and barely registered the crack of one forearm against steel, gravel grating against her palms.

Dust billowed all over again, rocks bounced and shimmied. The light dimmed as she shoved her hair out of her face, squinted through the haze. Panic gripped her. "Shawn?"

Oh, God, had she killed him? She clambered to her feet, fist curled as sparklers of pain and shock licked through her forearm, and called louder, "Shawn!"

Please, please, please.

A cough tore through the ruins.

He loomed out of the billowing cloud, covered head to toe in gray and brown. One arm cradled the other, and he staggered, hacking out the choking particles.

Kayleigh couldn't help herself. Despite everything, despite the kidnapping and the fear and the pain, she darted into the miasma, flung herself at him so hard, he had no choice but to catch her with one arm.

Her cheek found his chest, his heartbeat loud and steady under her ear. "Thank God," she whispered. "I thought . . . I thought . . ."

It didn't matter what she thought. He was alive. Free.

She wasn't stranded in Old Seattle by herself.

A rough hand cupped the back of her head. Slid to her nape and tightened. "I'm fine," he rasped, his voice rough. Gritty. "Thanks to you."

At least he gave her that much.

She raised her head, frowned as she realized his face hovered only inches from hers. That she could rise on her tiptoes, close that distance, and—

And maybe she could avoid giving him mixed signals? *Fool.* "Sorry," she said quickly, easing away. The arm around her lower back tightened.

Cold metal banded her wrist, sent sparklers of pain up her arm as it dragged across the abrasions she hadn't had time to wrap. *Click.*

The tiny sound stole the rest of the question from her brain. Her eyes widened.

Features intent, unreadable beneath the layers of dirt and grime, Shawn held her gaze as he guided her hands together at his chest. As he locked the other metal cuff around her other wrist.

"But . . ." Her brain flailed. Why? All her vast intelligence, and the only thing Kayleigh could say was, "But I helped you."

His mouth hiked into a hard slant. Not really a smile. Wry, angry. "So you did," he said quietly, stroking a finger down her cheek. Tendrils of her hair slid free from the sweat trapping them in place, but it wasn't a tender gesture.

He wasn't capable, was he?

"You're unbelievable," she breathed, tears gathering through the irritated burn in her eyes. She blinked hard. "I can't believe I trusted you. Again!"

He spun her around, slid a hard hand around her upper arm. "You said no unnecessary touching." He pushed her. Gently, but impossible to resist. She didn't have it in her to try. "No kissing. Let's not make this more than it is, all right? You don't trust me—"

"With good reason!"

"And I don't trust you," he finished over her. "Now let's get somewhere more stable."

The dust swirled around them in eddies of gold and mud brown. As she stumbled up the steep incline, half supported by his unbreakable grip, Kayleigh called herself every version of stupid she could think of.

Whatever her idiotic hopes, Shawn Lowe was, after all, just an asshole.

CHAPTER ELEVEN

She managed to hold her silence for an eternal hour. Kayleigh's sense of time had always been good, honed by countless hours fighting to sleep and failing.

Down here, where no sun shone to note the passage of it and she had no access to her digital reader, marking the approximate length of every minute gave her something to focus on.

Something besides the angry ache at her leg and arm, or the uncomfortable position of the broken wall at her back. Or the gnawing hunger that had replaced the pain in her stomach.

She was starving.

Shawn hadn't done anything to break the silence, short of muttering a terse, "This is fine," once they'd found a fairly high vantage point near the utter ruins of his original hideout.

She was pretty sure he sulked like a champion.

She was *damned* sure she was tired of feeling like anything she said, anything she did, would earn his snarl. She'd saved his life, for God's sake!

At this rate, a kiss might just be preferable to this leashed aggression. At least his lust was honest.

She raised her cheek from her upraised knees, squinting automatically. When the light flickering up from the base of the hill didn't coalesce into any sort of haze, she breathed a sigh of relief.

Whatever was going on with her eyes, whatever ocular issues she needed to get diagnosed, she had a reprieve.

Then again, despite her location in the death trap of Old Seattle and her predicament as kidnap victim, she wasn't feeling all that stressed at the moment.

Even her stomach had settled.

She almost laughed at the incongruity of it—a forced holiday at the hands of a man who only wanted to trade her for ransom proved a viable vacation, after all.

But as her gaze settled on him, as it skated over the slanted breadth of his shoulders angled against a wide pillar and followed the taut line of his deceptively casual posture, the urge to laugh faded.

In its place, an ember flickered.

She had no right to be surprised, but she could go for angry.

She raised her cuffed hands, scraped back her hair from her face. "So." Kayleigh drew the word out until there was no doubt she demanded his attention. Old Seattle plucked the syllable from the air, tossed it around for a while before the shadows swallowed it.

His head tilted.

"I don't suppose you have some bandages?"

"I used all I had on your leg."

Of course he did. "Thanks for that, by the way." His wordless sound, almost a grunt, was so stupidly *male* in inflection that she sighed. "For the record, the leg was the earthquake's fault. If I die of some bacterial infection caused by your kidnapping," she pointed out matter-of-factly, "I'm going to haunt your every waking moment."

He didn't laugh. He only looked at her, scraping his hair back from his forehead. "How bad are you hurt?"

The visual reminder of his own scabbing injury above his eyebrow just made her wounds hurt more. He could have looked for himself, but she wasn't going to give him the satisfaction. "Never mind," she lied sullenly, looking away. "It's fine."

"Fine."

It wasn't fine. She was hurting and stupidly upset and the warm edge of her anger would last for only so long.

See if she ever saved his life again.

"What's your plan, then?" An innocent enough question. One she sharpened deliberately. "Wait around for a few days until my father drops off a few thousand dollars?"

The light wasn't ideal, but Kayleigh bit down on a surge of triumph as the silhouette of his jaw tightened. He didn't reply.

Fine. *Again.* "Is a few thousand dollars *enough*?" she persisted, deliberately leveling sheer scorn through her calculated needling. "I don't know how you people live under the sec-lines—" Her voice hitched as he pushed off the pillar, turned on her with a look of such animosity that her heart slammed into her throat. Beat wildly.

She swallowed it down. This one, she'd win.

"Topside, that's not that much money," she added casually, as if her guts weren't suddenly churning in a pit of their own acid. What was she *doing*?

Promoting communication.

Psychology at its finest. If he wouldn't respond to pleasantries, he'd damn well respond to provocation.

Kayleigh raised her chin. Met his eyes and didn't dare look away as he closed the distance between them. "How much are you asking for?"

For a long, tense moment, he stood over her, features shrouded in shadow. Unreadable but for the glint reflected in his eyes.

Kayleigh held her breath.

"It may surprise you," he finally replied, voice a dark rumble, "that I am not trading you for money."

It did. It must have showed, because his mouth twisted.

"You little snob." Annoyance, sharp and cutting. "You think I'd kidnap you, go to all this trouble, for *money?*"

"What am I supposed to think?" she shot back, stung despite herself. She'd started this. "You obviously don't want me for my looks."

His arms folded over his chest, which only made him look broader as he loomed over her. "Narrow-minded, too."

"I am *not*. The evidence speaks for itself!" She wanted to stand, but there was no room to maneuver. If she tried, she'd have to wiggle between him and the wall.

She considered that more than unnecessary.

He ignored her argument. "You can't be ignorant of your father's role in the Church."

That stopped her. Her mouth fell open. "What? His

role?" She scoffed. "Of course I know what he does. He's brilliant." Although how Shawn Lowe knew, she couldn't begin to guess.

If possible, his mouth got thinner. Harder. He didn't bend, didn't have to, but she suddenly felt as if he took up more space as he glared at her with such . . . such *hatred*. "He's a killer. A butcher."

The word slapped her in the face.

Your father is butchering people. . .

She lashed back. "He is *not*!" A weak counter, and she knew it. Damning caution, she pressed her shoulders back against the rough wall and struggled to stand.

To her surprise, to her consternation, he caught her elbow, lifted her with less effort than he should have, given his injuries.

It put her suddenly all too close.

As she found her feet, the oddly helpful gesture stealing some of her spark, he straightened. Folded his arms across his chest. "Your sainted father," he said quietly, "is holding on to friends of mine. Friends I want back."

"What friends?" she demanded.

He misunderstood. He must have, because as he quirked an eyebrow, he pointed out evenly, "Believe it or not, I do have them."

Kayleigh shrugged that away. "That's not what I meant. What does he possibly need with common street people?"

Both eyebrows winged upward this time.

In his silence, she replayed the tone, the words that had just come out of her mouth, and cringed. "I— That's not what I meant, either!"

"It's exactly what you meant." One hand palmed

the brick by her head as he leaned down. Just close enough that she couldn't escape his pinning stare. Nowhere to go. Nowhere to hide.

But he didn't touch her.

Her skin all but vibrated with anticipation.

"You're a spoiled little princess, Dr. Lauderdale." His scornful drawl scored where his earlier silence had only aggravated; heat suffused her cheeks. "For all your studies and university smarts, you're blind and ignorant, and you're happier that way, aren't you?"

"That's not true," she whispered. It couldn't be. Not knowing what she knew. "I just meant that my father has no need of outsiders."

His gaze slid to her mouth. Darkened, and lifted again to stare at her. Through her. "I know about the Salem Project."

Kayleigh opened her mouth. Caught herself.

He'd called her father a butcher. The same words Parker Adams had flung at her from her interrogation chair.

How did he know about the lab?

If he did, how could he possibly think his friends were involved?

Mouth drying, Kayleigh whispered weakly, "I don't know what you mean."

He raised one hand, but when she turned her face, wincing, she realized he only meant to wipe at his grimy cheek with the back of it. His gaze never left her face. "You're a terrible liar."

The chain between the handcuff bracelets rattled as she tucked her locked fingers against her stomach. "I . . . ." She blew out a shaking breath. "How do you know about it? Are you friends with Parker Adams?"

"No." His lips curved, hard and—her chin jerked up—pitying. "You really don't have a clue what you and your precious father are up against, do you?"

She glared.

"Tell me one thing," he growled. "Just one thing and I'll let it go." She doubted that, but he didn't give her time to say anything as he demanded, "Where does your outside DNA come from?"

"What are you—"

The hand by her head clenched into a fist. "Don't bother with the bullshit, Doctor. I *know*. I know about the witch factories and I know enough basic science to know you can't just combine the same crap from the same source and get a working model. *So where do you get it?*"

She stared into his face, her eyes wide and burning. Her cheeks felt clammy, but all she could say was, "Missionaries."

Not the answer he expected, obviously, as his features went harder than the stone that had pinned him; darkened with rage she saw reflected in the glittering depths of his near-black stare. "You're *lying*."

Kayleigh shot off the wall. "I am not— Oh!" His hand flattened against her chest, pushed her back against the surface, but a red haze licked at the corners of her vision. Her neck craned as she hissed, "I'm *not* lying to you."

"Wrong." He thrust his face close to hers, the hand by her head white-knuckled. "Your sainted father takes people off the street. He goes searching for his favorites, did you know that?"

Impossible. He didn't know what he was saying. She knew where the DNA samples came from; she headed the operation! She sucked in a breath to argue.

The hand between her breasts flattened hard, tightened against her body, locked her against the wall.

Her mind went blank. "I . . . You're wrong . . ."

"You, Dr. Lauderdale," he said evenly, anger a seething boil behind the taut lines of his face. So hard. Unforgiving. "*You* are wrong. You choke down whatever excuse Daddy gives you and I bet you never even question that bullshit the Church taught you to spew, do you?"

"No—" The cuffs clinked as she wrapped both hands around his wrist. "I mean, yes! Of course, I'm a scientist. I question everything!"

His eyes glittered, mere inches away. "I. Don't. Believe. You." Every word a terrible punctuation to the disgust she read in his stare. Heard in his voice.

Felt in her stomach, acid and fire.

Weak. She had to stop playing at weak!

Kayleigh's grip tightened against his wrist. Forcing her shoulders from the wall, a whip of grim triumph licked through her as surprise flickered under his so-superior scorn. As he took a step back at her shove. "You talk so big," she retorted. "But all you are is a kidnapper and a bully."

That surprise guttered to something Kayleigh swore looked like humor, then edged over to unreadable again. Just like that.

And just like that, he let her go. Jerked his wrist out of her hands and put space between them. "I'm saving lives, Dr. Lauderdale."

"Ha!" She didn't even bother looking for her equilibrium. Far as she could tell, she'd left it topside with the rest of her life. "Easy for you to say. All I can see is a grown man sulking because his life sucks."

Shawn stilled.

Never talk about my parents.

"Oh, I'm sorry," she sneered, "did I hit another nerve?" She took two steps from the wall, jerked her bound hands at him as if she could wave the truth into existence. Slap him with it. "You kidnapped *me*, Shawn. You felt me up in the front seat of my car knowing who I was, what you intended, and then you betrayed *me*." Another hard shove at his chest, but this time, he didn't budge an inch. "You're trading me for some criminal friends of yours who got caught—" Her harsh crack of sound wasn't a laugh. Somewhere in the back of her mind, she cringed at her own nastiness.

Why couldn't she stop?

Because he'd started it. Because he flung cruel daggers at her and her father, and he thought he was so perfect.

Shawn took a step closer.

She raised her face, met his eyes, and said flatly, "Whatever your friends did to get caught by the Mission isn't my or my father's fault. Pick better friends next time." The heat in his eyes congealed, froze to a solid bank of ice. His jaw set hard enough to cut glass, and had she cared, she would have stopped there.

She couldn't.

He'd called her father a butcher and she wasn't positive that he was wrong.

That she wasn't a butcher, too.

"Maybe," she said softly, all too aware of her perfect aim, "you should try friends who aren't criminals. Then the Mission wouldn't take them away from—"

He moved so fast, Kayleigh couldn't place more than a lunge, an *impression* of motion detailed by raw strength as a hand curled in her jacket collar. He lifted her off her feet like she weighed nothing, dragged her nose to nose with him so that she had no choice but to stare into his eyes.

If a gaze could cut, she'd be bleeding at his feet.

"Shut up," he growled, his breath hot against her cheek. "Shut up, or I swear to God, you'll go back to your father in pieces. Which is more than he ever gave *me*." She gasped for air, but he'd left her no room to breathe, one hand in her lapel and one tangled in her hair, forcing her head still. Every gasp thrust her chest against his, and her toes barely held her weight against his raw strength.

He held her effortlessly, gave her nothing to work with—no leverage, no momentum. Nothing but the rapid-fire beat of her heartbeat.

Her wide, straining eyes pinned on his face, taut and twisted. His teeth bared inches away, his eyes blazing.

Don't cry. She didn't dare give him the satisfaction.

She didn't get a say. A tear slipped over her lashes. Fear, anger, frustration.

His furious gaze fell to her cheek. Blanched.

Slowly, his soundless snarl eased, lips softening. The grip in her hair loosened, until the knotted waves slid over her shoulder and his thumb tracked a damp line down her cheek.

He hadn't hit her. Even after she'd been so cruel. She'd all but demanded he do it, knew she provoked him, but he hadn't done it.

The knowledge settled into her skin and simmered, a slow, uncurling certainty.

Shawn Lowe wasn't the stone-cold killer he made himself out to be.

He stared down at his fingers. Regret shaped his mouth, his features. The set of his shoulders. Something harsh and painful and so bleak, she shuddered. "Stop talking about it," he said raggedly. "I'm trying fucking hard, Kayleigh—I can't . . . Don't use it like a weapon."

Her breath shook as she took it in. "I'm not a butcher. I don't want to be." It came out on a rasped whisper, a tattered plea that she wasn't sure he'd heard. Or that she'd meant him to.

But his eyes lifted, bitter. Wary and veiled. "Sixteen years ago yesterday," he said quietly, barely more than a rumble of sound, "missionaries came for my father."

Another tear followed the first. Again, his thumb grazed her skin. Wiped it away.

"Laurence Lauderdale was with them. He—" His throat worked, golden skin tightening as he swallowed hard. "They spoke, my parents were gunned down."

She couldn't hear this. Wouldn't. Closing her eyes blocked out the sight of him, but did nothing to erase the bleak words from the air, from her mind.

"Your father was there. Kayleigh—"

Her sob fractured through her chest.

He let out a muttered curse, a hard sound that only made it all the worse as he rasped, "I'm sorry." Carefully, he let go of her jacket. Eased away until she found the ground with her own feet.

She didn't fall. Somehow, despite the queasy hollow scraping out her insides, through the dull ringing of doubt and dismay in her head, she didn't keel over on the spot.

"I didn't know," she whispered. She couldn't even be sure. Sixteen years ago? All she could think was that he'd been studying missionaries for the program, shadowing them to find the best of the new recruits. That her father had his reasons. He *always* had reasons. "Shawn, I-I'm sorry. I won't bring it up again." No matter how badly she wanted a response.

He turned away, once more cast into shadow. "Just for the record," he said over her, over whatever useless apology, vapid explanation she wanted to give, "I don't hate you, either."

People had killed his parents—*her father was there*, she repeated silently, dizzy—and he didn't hate her? Her laughter sounded sick. Wan. "Maybe you should."

"Maybe." His shoulders moved, a powerful slant that told her nothing. "Maybe it's not about you anymore."

Kayleigh stared as he strode from the pocket of light. His footsteps, marked by the crunch and clatter of rock and grit and debris, faded within moments.

Trembling, she allowed her knees to bend. Allowed her back to slide against the wall until her tailbone hit the ground.

Missionaries weren't supposed to kill civilians.

Then again, maybe they weren't civilians. Maybe Shawn knew less about his parents than he thought.

She buried her face in her upraised knees.

Maybe . . . maybe it was Kayleigh who didn't know as much as she thought she did.

CHAPTER TWELVE

What the hell was wrong with him?

Shawn glanced up as a droplet of icy water splattered against his scalp, frowned when more followed it. High overhead, where the paved ceiling covering Old Seattle gave way to New Seattle's foundation, a mass of twisted pipes drained collected water from the city base.

It was the only kind of rain the ruins ever saw, and the reason for all the rot infesting the moldering carcass.

That and neglect.

He stopped on the edge of the pool of light, fists clenching and unclenching at his sides. One throbbed, painful reminder of the real damage he could have caused his captive if he'd lost his temper completely. He'd almost slammed her against the wall behind her. Almost allowed his rage to overwhelm whatever decency he had left, a thin little thread.

That couldn't happen again. Ever.

So the question stood. What was wrong with him?

"I don't hate you?" he muttered, glaring up at the shrouded black ceiling again as another flurry of fake rain splattered to his shoulders. Of course he wanted to hate her!

Her father was responsible for the murder of his parents. He was *there*.

The man had watched it all. Instigated the damned order.

The chaos, the screaming as Shawn's mother fought off the men who'd come to take away her husband.

Shawn had killed a man that day. The first of a handful over the next years, but at seventeen, all Shawn remembered was fear and rage. So much rage.

His dad had been a union laborer, just home from a brief hospital stay after minor injury. His mom had been . . .

His heart twisted as it always did.

She was beautiful. Stubborn, loving, determined to make a good life for her family. Eager to have her boys to herself for a few days before both went back to work.

God, she'd been so pleased.

Then Lauderdale had come with his offer and . . .

He knuckled at his eyes.

May had rescued Shawn from the Church orphanage only days later.

Kayleigh's father was the reason for everything.

But God damn it, Shawn didn't want to hate her. He wanted to *like* her.

"Based on what?" he snarled, kicking aside a loose stone with savage frustration. It rebounded off a hunk of rusted metal, scored deep enough to light a spark in the darkness.

Because she was *pretty*? Because she gave up her body so easily to a few rough words growled in the dark?

No, that wasn't fair.

Because she had guts. Her bargaining chip, big enough to leave his shoulder aching where it had pinned him, proved she wasn't just some delicate little flower out for a good time. She was smart, resourceful. Intelligent.

It also proved she had enough presence of mind to lie to him, if she wanted to. And why wouldn't she want to?

He ran a hand through his hair, shoved it back from his face as the fake rain gathered momentum.

Another storm must have rolled in. Several hours ago, probably. It took time for the runoff to collect from the upper streets, pool to the lower, gather in the lowest pits, and seep through the twisted mass of haphazard aqueducts.

Now, it dripped to the abandoned city and saturated everything. Each plink as drops hit metal, each muted *thud*, grated.

He had a plan. A solid one. Although the coordinates he'd given Lauderdale now pointed to little more than rubble, Shawn had picked enough of a vantage point in the reshaped landscape to watch for the Church's agents.

Experimental ones, he'd bet. No simple missionaries to rescue Lauderdale's darling little girl.

Shawn wasn't without his own training—every one of May's soldiers learned how to fight. Some, like Stone, were shit on the street, but the things the tech could do with a keyboard stymied most.

Shawn knew the streets, the hard places in New Seattle. He knew the dives, the back-alley shortcuts, the unforgiving places where the wrong body wearing the right clothes was more likely to see a shiv than a friendly smile.

And he knew Old Seattle. Bits of it. Just enough to know how to get around.

None of old man Lauderdale's operatives could claim that.

Shawn crouched, flicking through a pile of stones in absentminded interest. He palmed two, but it wasn't the rough edges he saw, or the solid weight he felt.

Her eyes. He hadn't seen them under anything but fluorescence and battery-operated light, but he found himself wondering what they'd look like under the sun. Pale and cold like diamonds?

Cool and mysterious like fog?

Why did it matter? The obvious answer was that it didn't, but Shawn didn't usually make a habit of lying to himself. Not about women. He liked them or he didn't.

He liked this one. Maybe since the moment she'd made him laugh in that car.

How did this woman worm her way under his skin so fast?

Was that why her words hurt so damned much?

Up on that ledge, Kayleigh Lauderdale was filthy and covered in the same dirt that coated him, her nice topside clothes long since ruined. She hadn't complained of anything, not hunger or cold. She'd taken his jibes and dished out her own, held her ground even when he scared her.

And he knew he scared her. He'd gone out of his way. He'd scared himself, too, just now. The violence that had filled him, the burning need to lash out, to shut down her cruel barbs, to . . .

To not hear what she had to say.

He scraped both hands over his face, but it did nothing to wipe away the guilt. The only women he'd ever handled so roughly had been trying to kill him as part of thinly stretched Church doctrine.

Kayleigh Lauderdale came from that Church, but he'd stepped over the line this time. Fuck.

Still. She surprised him.

I don't hate you, Shawn.

Damn, he wished she would.

He rose, rotated one of the rocks in his grip, and drew back his arm.

A clatter somewhere in the dark held his throw.

Settling debris?

Every instinct denied it. Shawn crouched, eased back behind the teetering shield of half-crumbled walls and out of the light. Just in time. As the lantern flickered gently thirty feet away, motion drew his attention to the shadows just to his right.

He tensed, fingers tightening around the rocks.

Why didn't he have a weapon? Oh, right.

Because he'd left it in his goddamned jacket, which was buried somewhere at the bottom of a newly formed chasm.

Swearing silently, Shawn ducked his head, braced one hand against the damp earth as the rain picked up in earnest. Droplets bounced off the broken brick and bent steel, splattered across his shoulders.

A figure slipped just out of sight, a whisper of black on black.

Shawn eased around the corner, eyes straining. Part of him wanted to call out, demand confrontation, but he hadn't survived this long being the kind of idiot who relied on a fair fight.

Quickly, weight balanced on the balls of his feet, he moved through the shadows. Another pale flash on the other side of a broken wall gave him his target.

The rain, smelling earthy and coppery and acidic, dripped into his eyes. He blinked hard, jerked his dripping hair off his forehead.

Surprise was his weapon of choice.

He lobbed one of the rocks across the wall, heard it *thunk* in the shadows where the light couldn't reach.

The figure straightened, turned.

Shawn palmed the wall, leaped over it in a smooth motion that belied the exhausted, abused ache screaming from shoulder to hip, and landed beside a petite figure clad in black.

The operative turned.

Shawn's opportunity for surprise shifted into a strangled shout as the hooded woman—too trim to be anything else—ducked his grasp, sidestepped, and nailed a foot square into his back.

Shawn grunted as he planted face-first into the wall, pushed off it, and ducked, dropping to a crouch as a fist whipped through the air where his head had been.

The cowled figure looked down, tanned features twisted into a scowl, just as he looked up from his squat, leg muscles braced, ready to lunge.

Shadowed brown eyes widened. "Shawn?"

"Amanda!" He stood so fast, Amanda Green danced backward, her feet sliding in the rapidly thickening mud beneath them.

She found her footing with help from the broken remains of a chimney pipe, gloved fingers tight against the rusted metal.

He took a step, hesitated when she flung out a warning hand.

Amanda Green was a witch. The kind whose power had stopped bigger men than he in their tracks.

She was also supposed to be locked up topside.

"I thought you were dead!" The words tumbled out of him, surprise and confusion and—hell, elation. "Amanda, where are the others? Are you with them? Are they okay?"

Instead of answering, she stared at him, rainwater turning her naturally tanned skin to a golden shine. Beneath her hood, her sandy blond hair dripped across her forehead in neat spikes.

It was short. She'd always liked it short.

"Shit," she whispered. Her gaze flicked up, to the pipe rain as it sparkled and caught the light, then back to him. "They didn't say you were here."

"They?" He pulled one boot out of the mud, jumped the distance to rockier, less swampy ground. She watched him, mouth a white line beneath her hood. "Did May rescue you?"

"No." A faintest slash of a smile. "Not this time."

May had been instrumental in both of their histories. Shawn had been saved from the Mission orphanages, one of a small group of newly made "orphans" destined for the Holy Order's witch-hunting boot camp.

Amanda's family had kicked her out. Too kind to feed her to the witch fires, cruel enough to let her die on the streets.

May's people found her first.

As far as he'd known, she'd never looked back.

"Tell me you're all right," he said quietly, hands fisted at his sides. "And then tell me why you're here. How you found me."

She blew out a hard breath. When she looked down

at herself, he followed her gaze. Picked out the flak
jacket, the traces of body armor sewn into the unique
brand of uniform he'd only ever seen on one kind of
person.

Cold sweat replaced the acidic tang of rain. "Amanda."

"Thirty-eight days." Her eyes flicked to the side.
"You have no idea."

Oh, God. "They didn't," he said roughly, as if force
of will could undo what he desperately hoped wasn't
true. "Tell me they didn't turn you. Nothing could
turn you!" Shawn took a step forward; she raised one
hand. The sleek black weapon she held wasn't one of
the resistance's usual castoffs. This was menace given
metal form, a machine gun merged with a pistol.

"Stop," she warned. "They didn't brainwash me,
Shawn."

She didn't need a gun. He'd seen her strange witch
powers work with just a flick of her fingers. The fact
that she held a gun on him now was a riddle he didn't
know how to unravel.

Courtesy between fighters? Laughable. If it didn't
hurt too damned much.

"Come home with me, Amanda."

"Home?" The word was a sneer. "Which home?
The safe house over the First Avenue whorehouse or
the moldy, shit-stained studio outside the Second Cap-
itol ghetto?"

The force of her scorn, her hatred, fisted in his
chest. Sucker-punched him, until he couldn't breathe.
"How can you say that?"

"How can *you*?" Her eyes flashed, lighter than his
but angrier than he'd ever seen them. "We live at the
bottom of the pile, rolling in filth. Trying so hard to
fight the system because why?"

"You know why!"

"Because you think it'll make your parents less dead?" The words Amanda flung scored harsh furrows across his senses. Left him raw and bleeding. He flinched, teeth baring. "Look," she snapped, "I didn't want to come here, but it was either that or I join the rest in the fires."

He jerked, as if slapped. "The fires? Did they all—"

"That's enough." Her gun lifted, eyes flinty over the matte barrel. "I don't care about the resistance, Shawn. I never did."

Shit. *Shit.* The rain hammered, soaking him to the skin, and all he could do was stare. At his friend. His partner in so many things.

"I was going to rescue you," was all his numb brain could think of to say. "I had a plan. You know I always have a plan."

"Yeah. I know your plan." Her gaze slid beyond him. Up, past the leaning wall he'd used as cover, beyond the light. The gun dropped a notch. "Problem is, I wanted something more than just revenge and a new order."

"Jesus Christ!" She raised the weapon again; he froze mid-step. But he didn't shut up. He couldn't. His chest squeezed painfully as he flung his empty hand at her. "Why didn't you say something? We were friends!"

"We were friends because we had no choice," she said, jaw firming. "We were friends because they put us in the same goddamned room and told us how it'd have to be. Fight or die on the streets, remember?"

Yeah, he remembered. "Way I recall it," he replied evenly, "you were just as eager to fight as I was."

Amanda snorted. "You never could see past your own hate." Her finger tightened on the trigger.

A woman screamed.

Kayleigh.

The sound shattered the numb shock freezing his nerves, his muscles. Cut through the chains of disbelief.

No.

It didn't make sense; it didn't have to make sense. Amanda Green wasn't his friend, his partner, his sister-in-arms anymore.

~~Maybe they'd gotten to her. Thirty-eight days of~~ torture could break anyone.

Maybe she never had been the woman he thought. The soldier he'd trusted.

That made both of them, didn't it?

It didn't matter. Not at the moment. As anger clawed at his throat, he flung out his other hand, threw the rock curled into his fist with unerring aim. Amanda's eyes widened.

Her boots skidded in the mud, and though he heard her cry out—heard a bone-deep *thud* of flesh and stone—he'd already turned away. Leaped over the broken wall.

It took him less than thirty seconds to clear the distance. His skin itched as he waited for the flare of Amanda's witchcraft or the sharp report of a gun, but it didn't come. Every step away spiked his rage higher, pounding it through his chest.

Missionaries, Church soldiers, always ran in packs—pairs or more. That had been drilled into him since day one in May's camp.

Why hadn't he paid attention? *Shit!*

He scrambled up the steep incline and earned a boot to the face for his trouble.

White lights and every foul word in the book deto-nated through his head as pain crunched through his cheekbone. He slid down the hill, fingers scraping and clawing as he fought for purchase.

"Stop!" Kayleigh's cry. "Don't!"

Hang on. Shaking off the haze, he threw his weight back up, shoes sliding, kicking rocks and hand-sized hunks of rusted metal to the ground beneath him.

This time, there was no painful greeting.

Only Kayleigh, her sodden hair streaming like a whip as she bent double, her feet flailing, thrashing in the grip of the whipcord-lean man who held her back to his chest. Her face was bone white, the silver cuffs Shawn had wrapped around her wrists glinting as she brought both hands up over her head.

They collided with the man's nose. He cursed, muffled against her hair.

Shawn didn't know what the black-clad agent bit out, what command, but Kayleigh jerked sharply.

Shawn scrambled to his feet. "Let her go!"

The man spun, staggered as Kayleigh's weight pulled him to the side. The gun he held in one hand wavered with the momentum. Her eyes widened as she saw him.

"No, wait!"

The operative grinned, his bearded features masked beneath his hood—dressed the same as Amanda. Even carrying the same gun. "And there's mission goal number two," he said cheerfully.

Shawn's gaze dropped to Kayleigh.

Her mouth flattened. "I said . . ." She planted her feet, locked her knees, and twisted with all her weight. The man's gun arm swung with the effort to hold her. "Stop!"

The operative wrenched her to the side. Let her go so fast that Kayleigh spun, lingered on the edge of the outcropping.

No!

Shawn lunged for her. Earned an armful of tensile muscle as the Church soldier met him halfway. Over the man's shoulder, Kayleigh toppled.

Her scream as she tumbled out of sight rang in Shawn's ears. Ended abruptly enough that for a long moment, neither man moved.

Shawn gasped. He couldn't breathe. Couldn't take in enough air. He sucked in a lungful, recognized shock as it settled into his gut. Shook violently.

She wasn't supposed to die.

The arm in Shawn's grip flexed as the man frowned at the spot where she'd just been. "That's going to suck in the report."

Red sheared through Shawn's head.

Amanda, a traitor. Kayleigh, somehow something more. An innocent victim?

His own mistake.

Everything.

Everything demanded blood. Every hurting thing.

The man grunted as Shawn tackled him over the edge.

CHAPTER THIRTEEN

The impact should have rocked them both.

As the man struggled to shake off Shawn's grip, they hit the side of the outcropping, rebounded off the jagged remains of pipes sheared by the force of the toppled building.

Agony seared through his side as they rolled, over and over, a thousand different shades of pain popping like fireworks through his body. The man in body armor had to be faring better, but as they hit the ground, a soft, squelching *thud* of flesh and bone told Shawn it didn't matter.

Tangled in a horrifyingly twisted mass of arms and legs, it took him too fucking long to drag himself from the muddy pit sucking at his weight. The Church soldier was still, face-up in the muck, his eyes wide and staring.

The side of his head bled into the earth, washed

pink by the steady patter of rain. It leaked into the concave ruin of his skull.

Nausea welled in Shawn's guts. Splashed bile into his throat.

Death happened. Of course it happened.

And it never got easier to handle. No matter who counted on him. Or why.

Kayleigh. He turned, struggled to his hands and knees. Blood stained his sleeve, or maybe it was mud coloring the dark blue fabric black. He couldn't tell. Everything hurt, and his eyes wouldn't focus.

A concussion? Maybe. Wouldn't be his first.

"Kayleigh." It was a croak of sound. He cleared his throat, tried again. "Kayleigh!"

The rain hammered his back, driving fat droplets into his scalp and dripping off his nose. He shook his head hard, swayed on his hands and knees as the world tilted around him.

A soft, ragged groan from his right sharpened his focus.

There! A pale hand. He half crawled, half dragged himself across the rock-strewn ground. As he rounded the outcropping, he saw her. Splayed like a broken doll, one arm flung wide, the other crossed over her body.

Was she breathing?

Please, God, let her be breathing.

He dragged himself to her side, cursing as his body resisted. It hurt. Damn, it hurt bad enough that he wondered about the state of his ribs, his skull.

Hell, even his sanity.

But his muddy fingers, trembling, reached for her throat. Tucked beneath the tangled, sopping wet mass of her hair to search for a pulse.

His teeth bared, grim triumph, as a hard, steady

knock thrummed beneath his fingertips. "Good girl," he rasped, and forced himself to his knees. When the world didn't tilt over, he grasped at the crumbling wall, hauled himself all the way to his feet.

His head reeled.

No time. He didn't know where Amanda was, if he'd taken her out or if she waited for reinforcements. He didn't know what else could go wrong, didn't even want to consider what would happen if he passed out here in the ruins.

Carefully, slowly, he bent. Hoping she hadn't hurt anything serious in the fall, he fisted a hand into her jacket, hauled her upright. Her head lolled back on her neck, hair caught in her lips.

Shawn closed his eyes.

His legs shook. Arms trembled.

Why he paused, he wasn't sure. Except somehow, for some reason his cobwebbed brain couldn't figure out, it became very important that he drag his thumb across her mouth. Free the hair glued to her lips by rain and mud, smooth it back from her face.

"Please be okay," he murmured thickly.

Her lashes, spiky with rain, fanned over her pale cheeks.

Gritting his teeth, Shawn tucked his arm under her legs and groaned with the effort it took to stand.

Somehow, everything had gone to hell.

Consciousness hit like a truck.

Kayleigh groaned at the first cognizant pounding in her skull, winced when it blossomed into a bitter symphony of aches and pains. It started in her head, traveled down her neck, and plucked nerves in her shoulder that she hadn't even known existed.

Her back hurt, her hip felt brutalized, and oh, of course, her leg and wrist still played a jaunty melody together.

She raised a hand to rub at her forehead; didn't even consider how strange it was she could until warm fingers banded around her arm.

Fight!

Her eyes snapped open, adrenaline surging like an electrical whip. Her wild swing locked, forced back to her side as another hand flattened over her shoulder and held her down.

"Careful." Dark and rich, Shawn's voice pierced the rest of the fuzzy cotton clinging to her head. "It's all right, don't— *Kayleigh!*"

Her body went still, every limb shaking with effort. She blinked rapidly as his face, all hard lines and whiskered edges, shimmered into focus. He bent over her, the ends of his drying hair curling over his forehead. His grip gentled when she didn't try to hit him again, and over the streaks of mud coating his cheeks, his eyes searched hers intently.

He looked so worried. A mask of grime and concern. For her?

"I think I liked it better unconscious." Hoarse, but she managed it.

The drawn tension carving brackets into his mouth eased.

Kayleigh turned her head, blinking in the faintest glimmer of light, a needle-fine pinprick that nevertheless burned like a torch in the vast, devouring darkness tucked around them.

She sucked in a sharp breath as his fingers grasped

her forearm, let it out on a cranky "Ow, stop it," when a cautious squeeze sent shocks of pain up her arm.

"It's not broken." He didn't look back at her, focused intently on the limb he cradled gently between his callused, filthy hands. The faint penlight—jammed into a crevice and pointed at her—picked out dark smears of dirt, highlighted his bare chest, and painted his broad shoulders and wickedly contoured arms in shades of blue shadow and dusky skin.

Kayleigh frowned. "Where's your shirt— Ouch!" His gaze flicked to her face, eyelids tightening, but he didn't let her arm go. His fingertips skated over her abraded wrist. The skin, cracked and crusted, burned. "That's not broken, either." But oh, it hurt enough to make her flinch deeply.

"All right." Gingerly, he pulled her sleeve back down. Wait, not her sleeve. Kayleigh blinked dumbly at the navy blue fabric.

"Oh." *She* wore his shirt.

"Are you still cold?"

It hung on her, somewhat damp still but warmer than her suit jacket and smelling of rain, earth.

Him.

She resisted the urge to raise her arm to her nose, instead forcing an elbow under her. It grated on rocky ground, cushioned only faintly by her discarded blazer. Underneath the shirt, she could feel the clinging fabric of silk—now ruined beyond repair.

Shawn's hands slid under her shoulders, helped her upright. His arms framed her shoulders, his chest level with her face as he steadied her.

The contours under that thin light drew her gaze like nothing else.

The man had a warrior's body, she'd give him that.

As rough and edged as any of the lethal agents in her father's stable. A sprinkling of dark hair trailed to a point at abdominal muscles she suddenly ached to run her fingers down. See if they rippled under her touch, see if her nails would leave an imprint.

She shivered. *Virile masculinity* sounded much less sarcastic in her malfunctioning thoughts.

"The rain stopped," he said over her head, and she heard it in stereo: grim and deep, richly resonant through his chest. Another shiver forced her teeth together. "But everything's still damp. Sorry about that."

"I'm fine." She forced the words out, forced her back to straighten, when all she wanted to do was reach out, lay her head against that strong chest. Shock settled somewhere in her bones, nestled in the hole in her gut and crackled.

Shawn's grip eased at her shoulders.

This time, when he caught her arm in that implacable grip, she swallowed the ache in her throat. He made short work of the handcuffs, but at least he pulled the long sleeves down between the metal and her skin as they clicked closed.

She closed her eyes. "At least tell me what happened."

The fingers at her wrist tightened. She winced, but he was already letting go when she looked up, withdrawing across the narrow band of light. "You tell me."

Oh, God. She didn't have the energy for this. "I don't know who that man was," she said wearily, "but I'd guess one of my father's agents."

"You'd guess." He glared at the ground between them, shallow divots and scoring picked out in stark contrast by the light.

"Shawn, I'm his daughter, not his personal omniscient keeper."

"Don't you work at that lab project?"

She raised both hands to scrub one across her face. "He wasn't a Salem subject," she said through her fingers. "I know them all by face and name, and I didn't know him." Muffled as it was, it probably sounded like she lacked conviction, but she didn't care. Exhaustion ruled her body. Her mouth. "I should have just let him shoot you," she finished, bone-dry despite her rain-damp chill.

His eyes lifted, gaze still so damned hard, she didn't know if *soft* would ever apply to a man like him. "Why didn't you?"

"Come on!" She flung out her fingers, cuffs rattling. "Haven't we been over this?"

"He was right there, Kayleigh, you could have gone home."

"Don't you think I know that?"

"Then what? What were you *thinking*?"

She stilled. As the ruins sucked away his voice, plucked it from the ground between them and tossed it wildly, she tried to search his face, his eyes, and found . . . something painful.

Something angry.

At her?

She could have gone home, sure. But she'd seen Shawn come over that ledge, ready to fight for her. To save her from what he thought was a threat, and she'd meant it when she said she didn't want him dead.

The agent would have killed him. That's what missionaries *did*.

That couldn't be the issue. Did he want to be rid of her?

Well, of course he would. "Did I make the wrong choice?" she asked, her own voice softer. When he looked away, she shifted, pulled herself to her knees, and braced one hand on the ground, the other pulled taut against the chain. "Shawn?"

"I don't know." The words lashed. Shawn shoved himself to his feet, took two steps away until the dark swallowed all but the fierce glitter in his eyes, the penlight reflected back in obsidian and steel. "You swear you don't take people off the street, and I know it's a lie—"

"It's not."

His shoulders went rigid. "Don't." A lethal growl. "I saw her, Doctor. I've seen the evidence."

Kayleigh flinched at the return to an honorific she was beginning to despise on his lips. "You're not making any sense."

"I'm not making any sense? *Me*?" He laughed, a crack of sound that flung shards of too many conflicting emotions through her chest. She hunched, but there was no protection from the bitter fury he threw at her. "That was one of my friends back there! My people, *my* friend. Last I knew, the Mission had her, and here she is. Working for *you*!"

No. The magnitude of his accusation slapped her in the face, curled like fire in her belly, and brought tears of pain to her eyes.

She blinked them back. Her ulcer, the stress it came from, didn't matter. Not right now. "Impossible. We don't kidnap people and press them into service. Church agents are trained from childhood. It's—" *Safer that way.* Children adapted better.

Now he took a step back toward her, fists outlined at his sides. Clenched hard. "You still deny it?"

She pressed her own to her stomach. "Of course I do! Damn it, Shawn, I know where my people come from!"

"Innocents," he spat.

"*Missionaries*." When he only turned away with a rough snort of contempt, she leaped to her feet, ignored the throbbing warning in her body to reach out and seize his bare arm in both of her hands. "Listen to me!" The chain lashed at his skin; he didn't flinch.

Every muscle in his body went still, a taut, vibrating statue. Vividly hot to the touch.

Kayleigh stared at the silhouette of his profile. A nerve ticked over his temple, and the pulse beneath her palms thrummed hard. A rapid, angry staccato.

Bad move. She let go. Her fingertips tingled as if she'd pressed them into an electrical outlet. "Listen to me," she tried again, quieter this time. Cautiously. "The Salem genome—" When his shoulder jerked, she hastily amended the language. "The witchcraft DNA has been in house for a very, very long time, okay? The missionaries have a yearly physical, and we get genetic material from that. The two combined create the viable strain we use for our subjects." Mostly viable, anyway.

He stared at the ground.

"We haven't even made a new generation of actual subjects in, God, decades. Not while it's so unstable. We don't take people off the street," she told him fervently. "We never have."

His shoulders squared as he turned, lips flat and twisted into an angry sneer as he caught her upper arms. He dragged her close, until she couldn't possibly mistake a single furious syllable. "Pretty speech, Dr. Lauderdale, but you forget one very important thing."

Her smile was flat. Wan. "Just one?"

He wasn't amused. Not even a little. "I've *seen* the truth. All your official bullshit and party line won't make that go away. Your father—"

Kayleigh didn't know where she found the strength. The energy. All she knew was the words "your father" crossed his lips and she shoved with all her might, tore herself out of his grasp as she snarled, "*I am not my father.*"

He found his footing faster than she'd like, straightened, and yelled over her. "Then stop making excuses and own up to your bullshit!"

The tears she struggled to hold back burned, just a notch under the bile swimming in her stomach. Hammering at her ulcer.

Her sanity.

Nobody has to answer for anything now.

Parker Adams's accusation rang through her memory, unwanted and unwelcome and so sharp, it drowned out the rumble of Shawn's own, too similar allegations.

Not for crimes committed against innocent people on the streets . . .

They weren't right. They couldn't be.

She raised her hands to her face, dug her knuckles into her eyes. "Stop it."

"Open your eyes and see the truth, Kayleigh!"

You have no idea what your father's been up to, do you?

Her fingers jabbed into her forehead, drilled into the ache building over her eyebrows. "Stop."

Shawn's hand closed over her arm, just over her elbow. Warm, solid. "What you do is bad enough," he said tightly. "You're playing God up in your lab like lives don't matter." She jerked. "What he does—"

Open your eyes, sweetheart. Your father is butchering people.

"No!" She wrenched at his grip, slammed an elbow into his ribs before she realized the trajectory of her swing. He grunted with the impact, but he didn't move. Didn't stagger this time.

Kayleigh stumbled back, hands raised in mingled apology and frustration as tears spilled over her lashes.

She hated crying. *Hated it.* And he brought her to it every time.

Shawn didn't close the distance. "Stop taking potshots at me because you don't like the truth. The sooner you realize your part in this, the sooner you can—" The words cut out, his mouth twisting. The silence filling in for the worthless platitude crackled.

Through her tears, Kayleigh laughed bitterly. "The sooner I can what? Get on with my life?"

His expression, narrowed and suddenly so cautious, said it all.

There was no getting on from this.

The faint haze trapped in the penlight warned her that she'd reached her limit; a corona clung to Shawn's skin, so close it was as if he were dusted by gold.

Teeth clenched, she straightened under her own power. Tucked her bound hands against her chest. "I'm sorry," she managed to force out, a semblance of calm. The thinnest veneer of civility. "I didn't mean to hit you. I didn't mean to make the wrong choice. I'm sorry that your parents were killed, God, I'm so—"

"*Don't.*"

She couldn't stop, shaking her head over and over. "I'm sorry that agent turned against you—"

"Her name is Amanda." He scraped a dirty hand through his hair, leaving the curling ends sticking up in its wake. "She's a witch. *You* turned her against us."

A vein threatened to explode in her forehead. "Not," she said between her teeth, "me."

"Then your father!" The explosive accusation bit

hard, but not nearly as much as his snarled, "What the fuck is the difference?"

Full circle, and it drew blood.

All at once, the fight drained from her weary body. The damp chill on her cheeks told her that her tears fell unchecked now, but she couldn't bring herself to care. To wipe them away. As she turned, fists clenched over the chain binding her hands together, Kayleigh's shoulders rounded against the hole growing in her chest.

Her gut.

For a long moment, the silence twanged, tight as a coiled spring. Then, roughly, he muttered, "Shit."

Alarm flickered a moment too late. Rock crunched, a hand seized her shoulder, and before she could fight him off, Shawn turned her. Pulled her into his arms.

She stiffened. "Don't touch—"

He ignored it, tucked her hard against his chest and smoothed one broad hand over her back. "I'm sorry," he said, the sound both a murmur in his low voice and a rumble through his chest beneath her ear.

It was a day for sorry.

Kayleigh wanted to push away. Wanted to punch him in his handsome, rugged, stupid face and call him every name in the book, but her tears wouldn't stop. Even if it was his fault, having somebody hold her, somebody comfort her, was worth it. At least for now.

Her fingers curled against his chest. His warm, bare skin.

When she didn't shove him away, something in Shawn's rigid body eased. As if it melted away, she felt his muscles give, his shoulders protectively hunch around her as he gathered her into his arms and buried his face into her hair like he needed it, too.

Like she *mattered*.

A pretty lie.

It'd do. For now.

Kayleigh allowed herself to be comforted. To absorb the heat of his body and the whispered apologies he breathed into her hair and to think, just for a second, that it was enough.

She wasn't her father. But didn't she want to be?

One callused hand curled around her nape.

She shuddered. Raising her head, she scraped her borrowed sleeve over her eyes and met his. Close enough to see each individual eyelash in a thick, short fan of them, close enough to wonder if the gold dust she saw in his dark brown irises was really there, or just a figment of her eyesight's deterioration.

Heat simmered there. The heat of his anger, she recognized that much.

The rest she remembered from that moment in her car. The glint of barely restrained need. The heat of his body against hers, his throaty encouragement.

It echoed in her own skin, cradled against his. Another shiver shuddered up her spine. His fingers tightened at her back. "Are you cold?"

"Always," she whispered, shocked at her own raw honesty. "Shawn—"

His gaze darkened. "I can't keep apologizing to you."

She didn't want apologies. Not now. His mouth was inches away, lips soft and firm all at once, bracketed with all the things he carried with him: anger, aggression, *vengeance.*

Lights flickered at the corners of her vision.

He could end her. As easily as breathing, he could tear her apart. And even as she thought it, her vision flashed double.

He could heal her.

The alien thought terrified her. Hers and not hers. Again, with the pressure in her head. The weight in the air.

Her fingernails dug into the contoured lines of his chest. He sucked in a breath, nostrils flaring.

"Kayleigh, there's too much we don't—"

"Please." The word shocked her almost as much as the continued streak of honesty appalled her. *Please? How many times would she ask this man to kiss her?*

His arms tightened. Nestled against her, hips firm against hers, she knew how much his body had tuned in. The hard ridge under his stiff jeans zipper settled so achingly close.

So very much not what she needed right now.

Or was it?

Slow. Maybe she'd just start slow. She tipped her face up, thrilled when his thumb dug into the sensitive point behind her ear, cradling her head.

His lashes lowered, sparking a faint shimmer in her compromised sight. His mouth hovered scant millimeters from hers. So close, she could feel his breath. Drowned in the anticipation of his kiss.

She braced her hands against his shoulders. "Kiss me, Shawn."

"Kayleigh . . ." He closed his eyes.

His lips brushed hers, a feathered caress barely more than a breath.

Something aching and needy uncurled within her. Something hot and oddly welcoming.

He stilled. Opened them again, features drawn tight. "No."

Her gut kicked.

"No kissing. No unnecessary touching." Slowly, jaw thrust forward as if it hurt him to do it, Shawn let go, eased his body away from hers. The shock of cold air slipped into the space where his heat had been, curled in and froze her shaking core.

She clasped her hands to her chest, suddenly afraid that he'd see the ragged hole there. Shame burned.

"We've been here before."

She turned away. Disappointment warred with rampant relief. Pride and regret.

Always, regret.

"You're right, of course," she forced herself to say, ignoring the hollow pit in her gut. It hurt. The whole damned thing hurt. "I think I'm in shock."

"Shock." He repeated the word on a low rumble.

"Maybe a concussion," she continued with a frown. Her gaze skated over the narrow band of rock and debris picked out by the penlight. Where to go? What to do?

How could she hide?

"Okay, we'll go with that."

Her cheeks burned. Desperate to clear the last five minutes from her memory, she swung around, glared hotly at him when she realized he watched her the way she might watch a jumping spider. "And just so we're clear, you bas—"

A feminine voice called, "There you are!" In one split second, a hand reached from the outskirts of the dark, settled on her arm, and ended her forced fury on a startled shriek.

A shape loomed out of the ruins, and Shawn didn't think. He didn't breathe; he barely even considered his own ravaged body as he lunged past Kayleigh's wide-eyed alarm and seized fistfuls of synth-leather.

An impression of honey blond hair and a startled, "Oh shit!" turned into violent lethality as large, angry hands closed over his shoulders, ripped him away from the woman he'd seized.

A fist plowed into Shawn's face. He cursed savagely as the ruins flipped end over end. When the lights stopped flashing across his retinas—seconds too long—he rolled over, shoved himself to his feet, and threw himself at the broad, burly man closing in on him.

Another punch, fist like a truck, swung wide. Shawn caught the man's arm, teeth bared, and came in hard and low with an uppercut that felt as if he'd driven his fist into a brick wall.

A hard grunt, an exhale of surprise and pain from his opponent pushed Shawn harder. Faster. Another gut punch, and an elbow came down on Shawn's shoulder. He staggered.

"Wait, stop!"

A woman's voice, not Kayleigh's. Not Amanda's.

The man caught his swing, but Shawn feinted hard and drove his knuckles into a jaw made of iron.

"I said *stop*!" A clinging weight slammed into Shawn's back, sent him staggering as an arm banded around his neck. "Shawn," yelled the feminine voice in his ear, "we're friends—*ouch*." He twisted his fingers in her collar and hanks of her hair. "May sent us!"

He froze. With one arm bent behind his head, grip tight in the back of his feminine assailant's slick jacket, he stared directly across the line of a large, rough hand locked around his throat. The muscled forearm lifted another half inch, forcing him on his toes. "Let," growled a voice deeper even than his own, a rumble of violent warning, "her go."

A thin beam of light shattered the dark; the lethal

gaze of a man built like a brick shithouse stared right back. Shawn very carefully let go of the woman's collar on his back.

Kayleigh's voice cracked. "What . . . the *hell*?"

The weight on his back slid to the floor. The man in front of him relaxed a fraction. His fingers loosened, lowered, allowing Shawn the chance to breathe again without grinding his own esophagus against brawl-scarred fingers. Gray-green eyes flicked to his side, narrowed in a craggy face carved from granite.

Shawn wasn't a small man, but this guy made him feel it. He sidled one step away from the woman circling him, her fine, delicate features lit by a wary half smile. "Thank you for not killing each other. It's like watching two tanks go head-on." She adjusted her jacket, her smile deepening into elfin lines as the man beside her grunted.

The light jerked. Shawn spun, turning his back on the large man and the blond woman, caught the penlight as Kayleigh's trembling hand dropped.

"You okay?" he asked quietly, the back of his neck prickling with the awareness of two sets of eyes drilling into it.

Kayleigh sagged, but when he would have reached out to steady her, she took a step back. Her shoulders straightened just as quickly as her chin lifted. "Fine." Stubborn as hell. Until her cool fractured, gaze skimming over his mouth, his chest. "Are you?"

He fought back an exhausted smile. "Fine."

"If you two are done, uh . . ." The feminine throat clearing behind him brought a deep flush to Kayleigh's cheeks. Her face turned away, shackles clinking as she tucked her hair back behind one ear.

"Oh, for fuck's sake," rumbled the man. "Jessie."

"It's May," the woman said on cue. "And it's important."

Shawn turned. "What does she want?" And then, as the incongruity of the situation settled over him, his eyes narrowed. "How did you find us?"

The woman, Jessie, smiled faintly. "It's what I do. A lot, actually." She jammed her hands into her synth-leather coat, straightening her arms in a way that made her appear small and fragile. Especially next to her ham-fisted partner. "My name's Jessie, this is Silas. You're Shawn, and you—" Her gaze, tinted amber in the dim stream of light, flicked behind him. "You look terrible."

Kayleigh murmured something bemused. Silas's gaze narrowed a fraction as Shawn shifted; the not-too-subtle move placed him squarely in front of Kayleigh, blocked her from Jessie's speculative study.

The larger man, obviously the more impatient of the two, settled a hand on Jessie's shoulder. "Sunshine."

She winced. "Um . . ." She took in a deep breath, shoulders shifting under his hand. "We're here because your comm isn't working—"

"We're too far from a comm bank."

Her expression said, *No kidding* louder than words. "—and they need you back in the low streets. Like, now."

His jaw set. "Too bad."

"I'm not asking because—"

"I'm not going," he cut in.

"Fuck me sideways, already." The epithet thundered. Silas glared. "May's laid up in a low-street hospital, so anytime you're done playing the tragic outlaw—"

"Silas!" Jessie turned, arms outspread in outrage,

but Shawn didn't hear them. "*Tact.* You're as bad as Naomi sometimes."

May? Hurt?

Silas grunted. "We're wasting time."

Jessie made a similar sound, impatience and apology all rolled into one. "Shawn—"

He stopped paying attention. Couldn't. The blood drained from his head. A vision of May—her face lined with age, eyes sparkling, iron will and unstoppable energy—filled his mind. His memory.

She'd always been there. Always. *Just like his parents.*

For a stark, brutal moment, he forgot to breathe.

Not again.

He'd never passed out in his life. He sure as hell wasn't going to start now. Clawing his way back into narrow-eyed focus, Shawn didn't realize Kayleigh had grabbed his arm until he took a step forward.

Chain dragged across his skin, shockingly cold.

"Where?" he demanded over her, shrugging off her touch before any more of her heat seared into his skin. Branded him as the fool he was.

He should have been there. But no, he had to have bigger plans, didn't he?

"How did she get hurt?" If Lauderdale had sent his agents, somehow found her—

Black rage streaked across his vision.

"An earthquake," Silas told him, matter-of-fact.

It cracked through the blinding sea of scenarios his imagination formed. Shawn blinked. "What?"

"About two hours ago, a portion of the city rattled like a tin cup. The place came down around them." Jessie's face was a blur, but sympathy obviously colored her voice as she added, "Last thing she was demanding was you, so . . ."

His knuckles popped as he raised his face to the dark chasm. An earthquake?

"That's impossible," Kayleigh murmured behind him. "If it reached that far . . ."

"Oh, yeah." Jessie's voice flattened. "It's bad up there. Add panic and a lot of injured—"

He didn't need time to consider. "Take me to her," he demanded, and if they noticed the rough rasp in his order, they didn't ask him if he was all right.

He wasn't. He wouldn't be until he saw her.

Instead, Jessie gestured behind him. "What about her?" A beat. "Uh, and kinky jokes aside, why the handcuffs?"

Shawn didn't look behind him. Didn't stop as he passed them both. "She's Laurence Lauderdale's daughter," he said tightly, ignoring Jessie's gasp.

The chain clinked quietly, but Kayleigh said nothing. If she moved, if she even looked at him as he strode away, he didn't know.

He refused to look.

His shoulders itched, skin tight with anger and uncertainty and, shit, things he didn't even have the energy to explore. Not now. Maybe not ever.

"Keep her close," he found himself saying. "But don't trust her."

Only a fool trusted a Lauderdale. He knew that much.

He just had to remember it.

CHAPTER FOURTEEN

"**S**ir, another report from the edge of the mid-lows."

Director Lauderdale rubbed his forehead, gaze fixed on the spread of data fanned across his desk. "Where?"

The voice on the feed—one of many, and nameless in his focused memory—paused. Chatter filled the transmission background, the buzz of hardworking men and women fielding calls, cycling information.

"Just before Pike."

Carefully, Lauderdale marked off another red line. "Thank you," he murmured, but his attention no longer focused on the frequency. The map smiled at him, a crescent swath of red lines and shaded blocks.

Background noise filtered in from the open frequencies; words spoken in clipped, professional tones, faded to a blur as he stared hard at the visual representation of destruction.

Earthquakes. Mysterious and destructive; the earth itself giving rise to fury and frustration.

A shudder of dread seized the base of his spine.

He remembered. The fear, the chaos.

His wife in his arms as the first tremors struck.

"Director Lauderdale, the bishop's office is demanding an update." This new voice, female, sounded harried. Sarah? Susan? He leaned back in his chair, allowing his eyes to close for a brief, blessed second.

Matilda had always been so strong. So much stronger than their children. Than even he, some days. She'd held them all together.

Through the fires as devastated Seattle blocks fractured and collapsed so many decades ago, through the flood as the bay overwhelmed the shore in a fury of water and destruction.

His hands shook.

"Director?"

They'd made it through because of her. He had driven their stolen truck through the carnage left behind, he'd navigated a brutal path through devastation so thoroughly unforgiving that he still remembered details in a sea of faded memories.

A child's teddy bear, soaked through. A lifeless, bloated corpse left to rot in the crossroads of a once-busy thoroughfare.

So many of those corpses. Some places he'd driven through had laid them out like a nest, a blanket of tangled arms and legs and battered, broken faces.

They'd survived it. He and Mattie and what few of the initial subjects they'd been able to save.

"Director Lauderdale, what should I tell the bishop's office?"

Hospital patients, lab volunteers, some nurses, even

a doctor. And they kept stopping for more. Stragglers, survivors. Children, too.

That's what mattered. That people had stopped everything to help. That they kept on going, supported one another, helped one another.

He opened his eyes. *Sharon.* That was it. Sharon Jones. "Inform the bishop's office that I would like to arrange a meeting, Ms. Jones. One hour."

"Yes, sir, I'll schedule it right away." Relief colored the feed, even over the chatter. "What should I tell them in the meantime?"

Lauderdale studied the map in front of him, gnarled hands framing the bloody smile. "Tell them . . ." He was aware of the sudden dimming over the feeds, the hush that told him more ears than hers strained to hear.

His comm unit whispered a warning, a subtle thrum he felt against the desk under his hands. A glance at the screen, words enlarged for his failing sight, forced a scowl.

AG checked in. Op a failure. Advise.

Failure. Kayleigh was still out there.

The hope of a city on the brink.

Failure just wouldn't do.

His spine straightened, frail and aching shoulders setting with purpose. "Tell them that God will not abandon us now. That we must help our brothers and sisters and ensure that we remain calm, above all, to do it."

Her voice firmed. "Yes, sir."

Lauderdale stood, shuffled to the window and looked out. Not at the quad beneath the windowpane, filled to the brim with agents and employees scurrying like worker ants, but to the horizon. The sky was gray and cloudy—not black with volcanic ash as he remembered, no glowing red heart of a volcano pulsing like a jewel on the horizon.

But he remembered still. The tremors that came first and sudden, the quakes that sent cracks through the city streets.

The hysteria.

Kayleigh was a single entity, and if he was very lucky, Ms. Green had forced the kidnapper to change locations. He had to count on that. If God was feeling kind, she'd stay out of the earthquake's radius.

He could not sacrifice the future of New Seattle for one person, even if his chest hurt to consider it. He had to hope—trust—that she was every bit as strong as her mother.

Anything else could undo decades of planning.

Kayleigh.

"Ms. Jones, inform the media outlets to cease coverage of the demolished areas," he said quietly. The sensitive equipment had no trouble picking up the order. "I want full efforts on twenty-four-hour emergency analysis. Set up a press conference on the steps of the Holy Cathedral."

"Will I be informing Bishop Applegate's office about this?"

Lauderdale touched the glass. His eyebrows furrowed deeply. "No. Our spiritual leader will have a great deal of prayer on his mind. I'll inform him myself."

"Yes, sir."

"And Ms. Jones?"

A beat. "Yes?"

Lauderdale allowed himself the luxury of a smile. "Excellent work. Your department is invaluable."

Her tone warmed. "Thank you, sir. I'll pass it along."

She didn't have to. Those with ears on the channel would do it first, and it would spread like a wildfire. This time, when the frequency filled again with its white noise of directions and information, he detected a new thread; a subtle strengthening of resolve. Of purpose.

Good. Very good. They'd need that.

If everything stayed true to expectation, a few hours could see it turn so much worse.

Lauderdale had trained his people well. They'd be ready.

Make a better world.

This city would not fall for nothing.

CHAPTER FIFTEEN

Chaos.

The clinic—a small three-story structure built into the base of the higher tier's foundation—thrummed with the turmoil of harried doctors, grimly efficient nurses. Shawn felt the pressure of it hammering at him, drilling into his head, but he didn't have time for it.

Didn't care for anything but the room in front of him.

The whole district was in disarray, rubble left on the street where tenements and brownstones had crumbled. The quake had done a number over a wide swath, and he'd stared at the damage as they'd driven through it in a rusted, burnt orange pickup truck.

Now, it seemed a thousand miles away.

His hands fisted. Somewhere behind him, Jessie had taken Kayleigh to get her wounds bandaged and clothes changed; somewhere, he was aware of the scurrying din of overworked medical personnel.

But the narrow window in front of him, a transparent divide set into the door, seized his guts in an icy grip.

Through it, he could see that May's eyes were closed, her face slack. A wicked purple bruise rimmed over her eye, swelled to a bloody red before it vanished under white bandages.

Her skin gleamed sickly and pale, so different from the tough-as-nails woman he'd left behind only yesterday.

Two figures leaned over the bed, a man and a woman. He didn't need to see the kid's face to recognize Danny. He expected her grandson to be here. The woman, her magenta-streaked hair hiding her face in a choppy curtain, shrugged.

The murmured conversations ceased around him; Shawn heard only the rapid, panicked beat of his heart as he reached for the door handle.

The dull chatter of a radio peppered the air.

Two sets of eyes looked up in tandem. Hers, an exotic near-violet gaze, narrowed, but it was Danny's that flashed fire. "You son of a bitch!" he snarled, lunging for Shawn.

He braced, but a figure in the corner stepped out, hooked a wiry arm around Danny's chest. The action jerked the thin man hard to the side. A pair of glasses slid crookedly down his nose as he flinched, lines of pain bracketing his mouth. "Danny."

Jonas Stone. Even the single, soothing word fell in a perfect tenor Shawn would recognize anywhere.

"I want him out!"

Shawn's jaw cracked; his teeth gritted so hard, the

sound dulled the blade-sharp accusation in the kid's near-sob.

"Get him out, or so help me, I'll take him out myself!"

The woman perched on the edge of the bed straightened. "You idiots are in a hospital—" She pointed. "Either all of you *get the fuck out*," she snapped, such leashed menace in her authoritative, husky voice, "or you settle down like goddamned adults and shut the hell up."

Danny went still. The look Stone sent the woman was masked behind light brown hair longer even than Shawn's, but Shawn saw her roll her eyes at him.

The woman was beautiful. Exotically so, with some kind of Asian heritage, model-quality cheekbones, a mouth almost too lush for easy comfort, and an array of facial piercings that did nothing to soften the violence he read in her eyes, in the set of her body.

Even settled on a hospital bed, wearing a jacket made of blue buckles and straps clinging to every curve, Shawn recognized a trained killer when he saw one.

He'd gotten very good at spotting them on the streets.

Shawn shut the door quietly behind him. "I'm not here to fight."

"The fuck you—"

Stone's arm tightened around Danny's waist. "Danny, please."

Where May was thin to the point of whipcord lean, Danny was squarer. Not as rock solid as he could be with enough time, not yet, but the traces of youthful optimism that had always marked him had vanished under a mask of worry and pain. His eyes flung daggers at Shawn, while the man who held him back from his ill-advised threat captured the back of Danny's neck in a long-fingered hand and held on tight.

It was the kind of move he'd pulled on Kayleigh, and that realization made his guts wrench; uncomfortably sharp. Too damned close.

Shawn raised his hands. "What happened?"

"What happened?" Danny spat the words over Stone's shoulder. "What happened is that she wasn't even supposed to be there, you egotistical son of a bitch!"

"Danny." Stone's fingers tightened.

"It was his fault, she was looking for him!"

Shawn flinched.

"Hey." Stone reached up with both hands, caught Danny's face between his palms. Danny was taller, but the kid hunched, angry mask cracking as he rested his forehead against Stone's. "It's okay. Naomi's going to make sure your grandma makes it, okay?"

Naomi. Fuck's sake.

Danny shuddered, eyes closing. "I know. *I know.* I just—"

"We know." Stone pulled him to the side of the small room. When he glanced at Shawn through his frameless glasses, that shrewd mottled brown and green stare left him feeling exposed as hell.

His bare chest couldn't be helped until he found a shirt, but he'd haphazardly scrubbed the dirt off his exposed skin before coming in. He wasn't that much of a mess.

Still, he couldn't keep himself from looking away, even as his back straightened. The radio crackled overhead, another feminine voice delivering emergency instructions.

He turned to the woman, instead. "*The* Naomi West."

"That would be me." Her overly lush mouth quirked, a silver ring in the center winking beneath the dull fluorescent lights. "You aren't Satan and you haven't tried to take me on for the bounty, so I'm going to assume you're the Shawn they keep nagging about."

Charming. "Yeah." Take her on? Hell, no. Not even on a good day, and today was the farthest thing from it. Naomi West had once been one of the Church's top assassins. A hell of a missionary, by all accounts.

Now she was the resistance's second-closest guarded secret. Their very own witch healer. Shawn had never trusted her. He didn't trust anyone coming down from on high to suddenly mingle with the civil soldiers.

Then again, he'd never met her, either.

But as he approached the bed, a wary eye on Danny, he didn't stop to question why he wasn't grilling her. Why he was okay with having the healer here for May.

It was obvious. And he was a selfish bastard.

"Can you fix her?" he demanded.

"Shut up, of course she can," Danny muttered behind him. The kid had deflated, collapsed on the edge of a chair with his head in his hands.

"Hi, I'm Jonas," the man beside him said, flashing a smile that wasn't cheerful so much as oddly and determinedly reassuring.

Because Shawn looked like he needed it?

Fuck.

"In the flesh," was all Shawn managed. How was it that two of the four people in the highly classified resistance leader's room were ex-Church? When did that shift happen?

Naomi quirked a black eyebrow at him. "Is it true? Were you AWOL?"

The chair creaked behind him. Shawn didn't have to look to know Danny had raised his head.

He nodded. "Yeah."

"Come back for May?"

Shawn glanced at the radio. The serenely professional voice on it assured listeners that emergency services were functioning at prime efficiency, that everyone should remain calm.

His mouth twisted. "Mostly."

"Asshole," Danny muttered.

Shawn turned. "That was your freebie," he replied evenly, a phrase they'd both heard May utter many times.

The kid's dark eyes narrowed.

Jonas laid a scarred hand on his shoulder. "May was in Lucky Lou's headquarters." Unlike Danny, there was no blame in his voice. None in his gaze as it met Shawn's direct. His crystal-clear tenor was pitched to soothe. "The earthquake lasted about thirty seconds. For about half that, nobody knew what the hell was going on."

He knew that feeling.

"The whole building collapsed when Lou's underneath gave," Jonas continued. "She was just on her way out. Concussion, maybe some initial brain swelling."

Shawn's hackles settled slowly. He still wanted to drive his fist through something, but May would never forgive him if he chose Danny for the stress release.

He blew out a hard breath. "Will she be okay?"

Naomi shrugged. "I've already done most of the hard work. It'll take some time for her body to work out the kinks, but she'll be fine."

"Nai's damned good at what she does." Jonas's smile flickered. "Always."

"Flirt."

Shawn scraped both hands through his hair. "Do the other cells know yet?"

Danny raised his head. "Not yet. Most don't even know how to reach her."

"I've got people fielding requests," Jonas supplied. Silently, Danny's hand lifted. Interlaced tightly with his.

It was a gesture so intimate, so personal between the two men that embarrassment filled him. Shawn looked away, met Naomi's amused stare across the narrow room. That eyebrow was still hiked high.

He refused to flinch. "What's the breakdown, then?" Outside, voices were raised, a flurry of activity that warned him more injured had come in.

Naomi's smile, a deeply sardonic curve, faded.

"The breakdown," Jonas answered, his cadence easing into the now-familiar rhythm of his comm calls, "is that we have every cell accounted for save two. One is still working on stripping Lucky Lou's and one below."

"Below?"

"Sent after you," Danny muttered, sullen.

Shawn winced. He should have expected that. May would never let things rest the way he'd shaped them. "When do you expect them back?"

"Soon," Jonas replied. If he was aware that his thumb swept over Danny's knuckles, back and forth, he didn't acknowledge it. His other hand shoved his glasses back up on his nose. "But since you're here, let's get to the *real* issue."

The real issue? Aside from May's unannounced

nap, there was only one major problem Shawn knew of that would warrant this level of seriousness.

"If this is about Kayleigh," Shawn began, only to stop, mentally cursing as Jonas's eyes went round and wide behind his lenses.

"Wait, hold on—Kayleigh?"

"May didn't tell you?" When Jonas only stared, Shawn palmed his forehead with a rough hand. "Shit. Yeah, I have Lauderdale's daughter."

The bed creaked as Naomi looked up from whatever she studied in May's still features. "Wait, *Lauderdale*?"

"You're kidding." It was almost a laugh. Jonas shook his head. "The old man's throwing a shit fit right about now, I bet. No wonder May wanted you found. You know we need her, right?"

Shawn gritted his teeth, ignoring the pang of guilt. "What's the real issue, then?"

Jonas sobered immediately. "The issue is that I've been tracking encrypted chatter from the various hubs in the Church mainframe."

"You have access?"

Danny took a deep breath. "No," he said on the hard exhale. Strained, but at least he'd found middle ground between sulking and anger.

"The whole topside quad is on its own closed system," Jonas explained, gaze touching on Danny for a moment, then lifting back to Shawn. His brow furrowed. "I can crack the mid-low offices, but they don't have anything important there. Haven't for about a month, now."

"Less since breaking me out," Danny said, a mild snort.

Jonas returned his smile. "That didn't help."

Shawn watched their byplay, but his mind forged on. "Point being?"

"Point being," Jonas repeated, "anything coming out is encrypted like . . ." His free hand splayed, and for the first time, Shawn noticed his smallest two fingers bent crookedly. Broken, maybe, and never set right.

"Like hell," Naomi offered, "if May and Jonas had a security specialist for a love-child and named it the Devil."

"Nice," Danny drawled.

Shawn swiped one arm across his eyes, squeezing them shut as exhaustion plucked at his flagging nerves. "So we don't know what they're talking about or sending."

"No," Jonas agreed. His eyebrows rose over his glasses. "But I can tell you this. There have been three separate earthquakes, and none of them were reported in the local media."

"Which, by the way," Danny interjected, "is freaking weird. New Seattle's got a complex about things that make the earth shake, what with that whole witch-fueled Armageddon a few years back."

Naomi's smile returned. "Smartass."

"No offense," the kid added, leaning back in his chair and resting his head against the wall behind it.

"Eat me, kid," she snorted, as Jonas spoke over them both with a serious, "That's the part that worries me."

Shawn watched her lay a steady hand over May's forehead. The woman was made of edges and spikes; he could see her attitude on her face like a brand. Dangerous as hell.

Yet May trusted her. That meant something, right now. Hell, the old woman probably saw something of herself in the witch's defiance.

But if he cut her some slack, then wouldn't he have to give all of them a fair chance? Jonas. The dying ex-missionary Simon. The ex-Mission director the resistance had been protecting, Parker Adams.

Kayleigh.

Could he trust Laurence Lauderdale's daughter? No, of course not.

Did he want to?

Didn't he already?

"Shawn?"

He blinked hard, frowned as Jonas waved a scarred hand at him. "What?"

"Are you all right?"

"Tired," he said, as close to the truth as they needed. Tired, angry, frustrated.

Confused.

Where was Kayleigh now?

And why had his first response been to protect her? Here, in this room, and down below when Jessie had grabbed her arm. The way his chest had twisted when she'd asked him, all but begged him to kiss her still sent shocks of sluggish, simmering arousal through his body.

The way she'd screamed when that operative had pushed her over the ledge haunted his thoughts like a ghost he didn't fucking want.

"Okay." The man's tenor forced Shawn's attention back to the cramped room, the two sets of dark eyes watching him. Measuring him. "I was saying that a mega shit-ton of data scraped through my nets."

"So?"

"So," he repeated, a habit that was beginning to grate, "every packet corresponded with every quake by about an hour or so."

"Wait," Shawn interrupted. He raised both hands, as if to pause the train of ideas, of incredulity, that Jonas was throwing out between them. "Are you telling me the Church can *predict* the earthquakes?"

Naomi lifted her head. "That's impossible." When Jonas only raised his eyebrows at her, her mouth went lopsided. "Well, mostly."

"Mostly?"

She shrugged. "We know a witch who does the prediction thing, but I can't say he saw *this* coming. Exactly."

"Look, all I know," Jonas said, shifting his weight awkwardly, "is that the data waves didn't just come from the quad." Danny reached up, slid an arm around his waist, tugged him closer. Jonas leaned against his shoulder with obvious relief. The lines at his mouth eased, but the intensity behind his forthright stare didn't. "They were earmarked on Lauderdale's top clearance channels."

"So whatever is going on," Shawn said slowly, "Laurence Lauderdale knows."

And if he knew, did Kayleigh?

"I'm a witch." Jessie smiled at Kayleigh, a warm curve that matched the easy amicability in her light brown eyes. "Just so we're clear."

"Noted," Kayleigh replied warily. The handcuffs Jessie had replaced once her injuries were bandaged clinked in front of her as she tucked tendrils of her freshly braided hair back behind one ear. Two pain-killers without kick later, a change of borrowed clothes that made her feel like a slummer all over again, a snack to take the edge off, and she was feeling human again.

Mostly human. The cuffs still caught her by surprise when she tried to gesture, and the synth-leather pants and black tank top looked like something she'd have found on a low-street dance floor. She shifted, pulling down the edge of the shirt as it exposed more of her back than she was comfortable with.

"Sorry about the clothes," Jessie added, watching her with both sympathy and amusement. "You're about Naomi's size, and she has a weird sense of humor."

"That explains the bracelet," Kayleigh admitted, looking down at the black strap with silver spikes decorating her un-bandaged wrist. She'd almost left it in the bag Jessie had pressed into her hands, sure the bracelet wasn't meant for her. At the last moment, she'd picked it up.

It was a surreal symbol of how much she didn't fit in to this world. How much this world wasn't hers. It clinked against the cuffs in musical reminder.

If she got out of here with her skin intact, she'd keep it. A spiky souvenir.

"Pretty much," Jessie agreed, a quick smile crossing her wide mouth. It touched her eyes, lit them to warm honey, and faded again. "Naomi's a witch, too. Different circumstances."

"I remember her circumstances," Kayleigh said slowly, her attention narrowing on the witch beside her, "but they didn't include witchcraft."

"Things change."

"Not like that." Kayleigh was very sure. After all, she knew the genome better than almost anyone alive.

Jessie's smile, something much more mysterious, unnerved her. "Lots of things change," she said quietly. "Things that shouldn't exist, do. Things that aren't supposed to happen, happen. What is it they say? Life finds a way?"

"Not that fast." It made no sense. As far as Kayleigh knew, she still had Naomi West's original data on file. There had never been any sign of the Salem genome in her genetic workups.

Only witches carried the genome. Marked from birth.

"Is there a reason I should know that you're witches?" she added when Jessie only watched her expectantly.

"My mom came out of your Salem lab."

Kayleigh hesitated, her gaze trapped in Jessie's. Her smile hadn't faded, but Kayleigh wasn't stupid. Despite the fact that they both sat on the floor in what little space they could grab in the clinic hallway, she had little illusion about her safety.

Whatever kind of witch Jessie was, she'd seen powers that could conflagrate a body in seconds. Tear it apart.

Even bend it to another's will.

A pit opened in her stomach.

"You look worried," Jessie said, tilting her head. Her hair, a sandy shade darker than Kayleigh's, pulled back into a high ponytail, swung around her shoulders as she gestured. "Don't be."

"Hard not to." Kayleigh didn't know how to ask, but she tried anyway. "Was your mother . . . Did she—"

"Die horribly?" The witch looked away. "Yeah. But not because of that broken thing that makes your subjects—" She sneered the word, but not at Kayleigh. As if she couldn't avoid the edged emphasis. "—break down, I guess. She was murdered."

"Oh." Kayleigh held very still. This wasn't the kind of conversation she expected to find herself having, not with the pretty blond girl who'd saved her from the ruins.

Of course, what did she expect? Tea and cookies?

She blew out a hard breath. "Jessie, I'm sorry."

"You didn't murder her. You were just a kid when it happened," the woman added, glancing back at her with a quick smile. "You're what, twenty-eight?"

"Thirty."

"I'm twenty-nine. We were both teenagers then." Jessie drew her feet in, making room for a gurney as two tired-looking men in scrubs pushed it down the hall. "My mom's name was Lydia Leigh."

Oh. "Leigh."

The witch's smile tightened. "Yeah. Recognize it?" Kayleigh hesitated, long enough that Jessie tilted her head back and stared up at the flickering ceiling instead. "Let me guess," she said dryly. "You recognize it because of my brother."

"Caleb Leigh was kind of a big deal in the Mission. It was hard not to hear about it."

She chuckled, a husky sound. "Don't let him hear you say that. His ego's already impossible."

Present tense. Her eyes widened. "Reports said he was dead."

"Mm." A noncommittal sound. "How long have you been part of the Salem thing?"

The question slid in under a note of amusement;

Kayleigh stiffened as the answer sprang to her lips. She flattened them together before anything spilled out.

She was tired, but she wasn't stupid. And she wasn't among friends.

Jessie's smile faded. Her gaze dropped from the ceiling. "My mom escaped that lab in the old industrial district. She set it on fire."

Was she serious? She looked it; as if the things coming out of her mouth weren't as wild as they sounded.

But then, Kayleigh knew how wild the truth really got.

When she learned about the abandoned lab's location, she had wondered what caused her father to move it, leave the GeneCorp building behind, but the data had been sealed first, and then vanished. By the time she took over Mrs. Parrish's duties, it didn't seem important.

Her focus had been on the Eve sequence, not on the past.

"Your mom sounds very strong," she offered cautiously.

Jessie nodded. "She was. So am I. I guess you'd have to be, too," she added. She laced her hands in her cross-legged lap, smiled reassuringly at a young boy who passed, a teddy bear clutched in his arms. "I can't imagine having the guts to maintain something like that hellhole. All those people dying. All those kids."

Kayleigh winced. *Guts* was exactly her problem. "It's not . . . like that. Not really. New generations haven't been cultivated since—"

"Twenty-five years ago."

Almost exactly. "How do you know?"

Jessie smiled sadly and shook her head.

No excuses. It *was* like that, wasn't it? Subjects falling apart when they hit a certain age. Breaking down. New generations hadn't been created for years, but her dad was pushing. He wanted progress.

She'd been dealing with the sequence for mere months, but she'd already signed off on a list as long as her arm. Executions of degenerating subjects—*people*—whose witchcraft tore them apart.

Clean them up, her father had said. No evidence for the Mission to collect.

Missionaries hunted witches.

Sector Three had *made* them.

Progress demanded she do her part. Her father demanded . . .

She did, too. "I'm sorry," Kayleigh said, looking down. "I've only been working on it for a few months. That's no excuse, but . . ."

"I thought as much." A warm hand covered Kayleigh's, clenched against her own thigh. "I just wanted to tell you, so that you knew where I come from."

Slow. She was too slow. "Wait, twenty-five years . . ." Kayleigh very cautiously searched the witch's expression. "You?"

"Mm."

"A Salem subject?"

The witch shrugged, squeezing Kayleigh's hand as if *she* were the strange one, the out-of-place one. "Case subject one-three-zero-nine-eight-four." She rattled off the numbers like she expected them to mean something. Something specific, something important.

White noise filled Kayleigh's ears. Droned in her head.

They didn't mean anything. Not exactly. But she knew the format.

"Oh, my God," she whispered. "You . . . you *were* a subject."

"My mom—my *donor*," Jessie amended, grimacing, "rescued me. Rescued a lot of them, actually."

"But—" Kayleigh's mind raced. Impossible. It was impossible. At twenty-nine years old, Jessie should have already been suffering from degeneration. Even dead. Simon was the oldest of her surviving subjects, he'd made it to thirty.

If he wasn't dead yet, he would be soon.

She seized Jessie's hand in both of hers. "How do you feel?"

But the witch surprised her. Her eyes flashed humor, not pain. Not fear. "A few wild zingers through the witch sight now and again," she said, pitching her voice quietly to avoid attention from a small family bustling down the crowded hall. Kayleigh watched them navigate through the maze of stretched-out legs and piled belongings, children huddled together. "All in all, great since your mother fixed me."

Kayleigh's head came back around so fast, her vision doubled before it caught up. "That's impossible."

Her eyebrows pulled together. "You didn't know?"

"My mother is dead."

"Yes," Jessie agreed, but her hand tightened around Kayleigh's. "I knew her before—"

Kayleigh jerked her hand free. "That isn't funny!" Her insides twisted, pain lancing through her stomach.

Frowning, Jessie splayed her hands in the air, palm-out as if Kayleigh were a wild cat, hissing and snarling.

She felt like it.

"I'm serious. Matilda saved my life."

Oh, God. The hurt coiled in her chest was a thousand times worse.

Was this Shawn's doing? "Did he put you up to this?" she asked stiffly, lips numb and skin cold; anger and exhaustion swirled, a pit in her heart.

"Who?"

"Shawn!"

"No," Jessie said, surprise in her amber eyes. She glanced down the hall, past the people milling through it, settled on the fringe with their minor injuries. "Actually, I don't think Shawn knew her."

Kayleigh flinched. "Stop saying that."

"Honey—"

"You had to be, what, six when she died? Seven?" She shook her head hard, clambering to her feet as if she had anywhere to run. She didn't. Not here, surrounded by strangers. She turned, glared at the sea of patients. "I was eight years old. I don't remember you."

Behind her, the witch sighed. "We never met. Kayleigh, I'm so sorry, I had no idea—" She beckoned, gestured to the floor. "Your mom was alive and well when she saved my life. Mine and Silas's," she added, features softening. "Did you know she was a witch?"

"No, she wasn't." Kayleigh felt like a broken recording, looping over and over back on denials as her world spun more and more out of control. She shook her head until the ends of her hair whipped around her shoulders. "You're lying."

"She could see the paths laid out before someone," Jessie continued, hands laced at her knees. Her gaze was steady. Weighty. Merciless. "Choices they could make and how it might work out for them."

Oh, God. She was lying. She had to be. Kayleigh flung out her hands, fingers splayed, her chest aching, lungs feeling as if she couldn't get enough air. "Stop lying!" Faces turned, eyes flicked to her. Voices dimmed to a murmur.

She didn't care.

"Oh, honey, I'm so sorry—" Jessie stopped. Her eyes widened, pupils dilating so fast it was as if her eyes had gone briefly black in a thin band of pale brown. "Oh, shit." A whisper. "Shitfucker." Less so. "*Naomi!*" Her shout demanded the eyes of every stranger in the hall.

She clambered to her feet, graceless, harried. Grim. One hand slid on the wall, and Kayleigh reached out to steady the suddenly manic woman.

Froze.

A ripple of motion, a subtle wave of anticipation slid through the hall. Kayleigh's gaze skimmed from wall to wall as every hair on the back of her neck lifted.

The floor vibrated beneath her.

"Another earthquake!" screamed a young man beside them.

As if that were a cue, chaos erupted; the walls shuddered as a violent tremor shook the clinic, threw the patients inside into pandemonium. Screams filled the narrow space, and Kayleigh stumbled as a stampede of wild-eyed humanity crushed her against the wall.

"Kayleigh!"

An elbow dug into her ribs, a shoulder clipped hers, sent an arc of pain and choking claustrophobia through her senses. A fracture split down the plaster in front of her face.

The screams echoed, shrieks of terror and pain, and then, just as suddenly, it stopped.

The building went still. Panicked cries turned to

questions; the crowd faltered. Sobs trickled through the stunned silence.

"My baby!" The terrified cry sparked a new sea of them.

Suddenly, people shouted for nurses, for doctors. For help.

Hands grabbed her arm; Kayleigh spun, thrusting out her cuffed hands for balance, and caught Jessie's shoulder. "How bad are they hurt?" she demanded, already tucking the aftershocks into the back of her head.

That didn't matter right now.

The little boy sprawled on the tile floor and curled around his teddy bear mattered. The mother with her hand over her daughter's bleeding nose and lip.

The screamer in the crowd and the half-wild faces surrounding her; those mattered more than anything else.

Years of training kicked in. One thing at a time.

"The doctors can—"

"More injured coming in," a nurse called from somewhere by the reception desk. Even down the hall, her voice carried. "Betty! Get on the comms, call everyone in!" The intercom crackled. "We are on diversion. All personnel be advised, we are code purple."

"What is that?" demanded a woman who grabbed Kayleigh's shirt by her hip. She knelt, eyes glassy, looking through Kayleigh as much as at her. "What does that mean?"

She bit her lip. "Every bed is full."

"Fuck me," Jessie whispered. Her grip tightened on Kayleigh's arm. "It's going to get worse. The amount of injured coming in—" Her voice broke.

Kayleigh blew out a hard breath. Her gaze swept the chaos, the order a band of tightly wound nurses and personnel tried to make of the front desk eight feet away.

"Uncuff me," she said, even before she'd even consciously made the call.

She could help. She was a geneticist, sure, but she'd done all her requisite clinicals. Still did them every year.

"What?" Jessie closed her eyes, as if she were having trouble concentrating.

"Jessie? Jessie!"

Shock? When she opened them again, they weren't entirely clear, still dilated, but intensely focused. "I'm okay."

Kayleigh thrust her hands out, jaw set. "Uncuff me. I can help."

A crack of thunder split the barely controlled madness. The whole clinic shuddered, but it didn't feel the same as the aftershocks. The hall rocked suddenly, threw people to the floor, slamming them like dominoes against each other. Jessie seized Kayleigh's wrists.

A blast of cold air ripped down the hall like a vacuum, sucking dust and plaster debris with it.

The intercom crackled once, shorted on a series of sparks as the lights popped and fizzled to darkness.

"Then help," Jessie shouted in her ear. " 'Cause the whole east side just came down!" Her voice cracked. Strain, a sort of detached focus.

The cuffs came off. Kayleigh didn't even notice as they clattered to the floor behind her.

Too much. There was too much happening around her, too many secrets unfolding beneath her. The lab, her mother, her father, her *life*.

She didn't know what was what; didn't know who lied, whom to trust. Shawn was a mystery, Jessie a witch, her father—

No. Not here. Not now, when the world around her collapsed on itself. She couldn't do anything about them, about her past, about the future.

This? This she could do something about. One injury at a time.

CHAPTER SIXTEEN

Everything hurt, knocking skull to pounding aches shooting through his spine, but Shawn didn't slow down until a grim-faced nurse pushed an open bottle of water into his hand and pulled him to the fringe.

"Before you collapse," the man ordered, but was already turning away.

The argument died on Shawn's lips.

Lifting the bottle to his mouth, he drank slowly, gaze skimming across the wreckage of the clinic and neighboring facilities.

A whole wing had slid into rubble, rocked loose by the earthquake that had rattled four city blocks in either direction. The city was in chaos; radio stations were breaking silence, emergency channels counseled calm while newscasters covered the wrecked areas and fought to stay on the air. Two had already gone dark, and Jonas continued to maintain every feed, every frequency he could juggle from the nearest resistance safe house thirteen blocks southwest.

The New Seattle Riot Force had mustered, ostensibly to help, but Shawn noticed how the few media reporters who'd arrived had quickly disappeared again.

Shawn had found a shirt, but now it was as bad as his first, covered in dirt and plaster dust and smears of blood. Not his.

He'd spent two hours helping move the wounded. Helping dig through the rubble.

Carrying the dead.

And he'd spent just as long watching Kayleigh.

What kind of fucked-up world was it when he worked to rescue injured people and couldn't stop thinking about the woman who was supposed to be his enemy? This whole city's enemy. Daughter of a monster; leader of a witch factory.

Possibly in possession of information relevant to all of New Seattle.

And he liked her. He just had to come to terms with that, because every time he turned around, she was there.

He took another drink, his gaze sliding to the triage tents set up hastily in the street. He found her easily, her pale hair a beacon in the flickering streetlights. At this time in the evening, there wasn't a chance in hell this street would see any other light.

They'd set up generators for more lights, and now they afforded Shawn the opportunity to watch Kayleigh work among the other medical staff.

She moved like she belonged. Like she knew the routine.

But she looked like something out of Shawn's world. Her borrowed synth-leather pants hugged her body in sleek lines, painted every slender curve in black matte. The heavy spiked bracelet around her wrist forced a lash of amusement, tempered by the white bandage circling the other forearm. She had to be hurting, but she didn't complain.

She'd never complained, had she? She fought. Argued.

Strong girl. Much stronger than he gave her credit for. Still so ignorant about so many things.

Her tank top cupped her small breasts, offered a teasing peek at beige lace when she bent to check on a patient. The rough guise didn't match the delicate bra he was positive she didn't mean to flash—this street-ready outfit wasn't anything like her so-prim topsider armor—and the knowledge of it settled somewhere in the base of his spine. Burned, pulsed, a steady pressure.

Everything had gone to hell.

May was safe in another location, recovering thanks to Naomi's efforts, but still too weak to risk being seen in public. The hospital was in disarray, the street filled with huddled, frightened people, with volunteers, with injured.

Rubble and debris had been swept aside in the two hours Shawn had worked to clear the immediate clinic grounds.

Earthquakes, witch factories, traitors turned friends and friends turned traitor.

Yet here he was. Clutching his water bottle like it could somehow give him the answer to everything. To his life, his choices.

The world.

Her.

Kayleigh touched a young girl's hand, smiled down at her with none of the grim solemnity she'd displayed as she worked. Tireless, steadfast.

Shawn knew better. Knew the effort it took to put on a mask of reassurance for those who demanded answers.

His heart twisted as the girl flung her arms around Kayleigh's neck.

Kayleigh herself wrapped both arms around her little body and clung for a moment. Just a breather.

He knew that need.

Felt it fist in his heart.

He'd rocked her world in every way but the one he wanted to, and it kicked him in the ass to understand that. To realize it in himself.

He wanted her, but more than that, he wanted to sit down and work this shit out. He wanted her to understand where he came from and why.

He wanted to understand her.

Damn it. He just *wanted*.

He couldn't. He should have pulled her out of that first aid camp, slapped those handcuffs back on her, and dragged her somewhere quiet to grill her about her father. About these earthquakes. About Jonas Stone's intel.

He fucking *couldn't*.

As if she could sense his interest, his stare, she looked up, found him almost instantly. Their gazes collided, and it was like a punch to his chest. A grip around his throat.

Her eyes gleamed with barely held-together restraint, even across the street, haunted and hopeless and dark. Her cheeks were pale, features drawn.

He raised his water bottle in silent salute.

Her mouth tilted up at one corner, and with a deep breath, she pulled away from the child.

He couldn't ask her now. Not when she was so obviously at her breaking point.

His comm vibrated against his side. He unclipped it from his waistband and cracked it open without checking the number. "What?" Weary, even to his own ears.

"How bad?" came Jonas's greeting, and for once, the man's voice was just as strained over the fuzzy line.

Shawn didn't even have the energy to gloat. *Welcome to the resistance.* "Bad," he said instead. "The clinic lost one of its two wings when the foundation gave out, and we've been moving people into the street. No more aftershocks, but it's a hair away from mass hysteria over here."

"Damn."

No kidding. Shawn watched Kayleigh direct the young girl to a small knot of children, watched her place both hands at her lower back and stretch. "How's May?"

"She'll be fine with time," the man replied, quickly and without pussyfooting around the subject. Shawn respected that. "Naomi's magic did its thing and she's awake, but it'll be a while before she'll be at a hundred percent. That's not why I'm calling, though."

"What's going on?" Shawn turned away, hunching a shoulder to dull the white noise of the city street behind him.

"It's topside news. So far, they've got the most stable feeds, but it's all blocked past the sec-lines."

Shawn frowned. "Did they get hit?"

"Not exactly, and that's the problem."

"Spit it out, Stone."

"Jonas, okay?" But he continued without prompting. "The Bishop's dead."

Shawn's frown deepened to a scowl, eyebrows furrowing hard. "How?"

"The official topside reports are saying debris from

the quakes, tragic accident, and so on, but they're not even trying on this one." His easy tenor hardened with the implied insult. "We're not stupid. The quakes didn't rattle the city that far up, and far as any of my sources say, Bishop Applegate was still topside."

"Jesus Christ." The repercussions reached out, scored through the thinning remnants of Shawn's calm. He turned, eyes immediately searching for Kayleigh. "This means—" *Fuck.* She wasn't there.

"Yeah." Jonas's voice thinned. "Laurence Lauderdale is officially head of Holy Order of St. Dominic."

Shawn's fingers clenched around the unit. "Keep me informed," he managed, a bare thread of civility as the growl leaked through his teeth. "I have someone to question."

"Shawn!"

He paused, waiting.

"Go easy. There's no evidence she knew."

"There's no evidence she didn't," Shawn replied, and shut down the line.

Of course she knew. There was no way she didn't know that her own father had planned the most thorough coup in New Seattle's bloody history.

His shoulders slumped.

Was there?

The only bit of privacy she could find came in the form of a clinic room. Evacuated due to cracks from floor to ceiling, plaster dust coating the single narrow bed in white powder, it showed no further indication of falling apart.

Even better, no one would think to look for her here.

Maybe it wasn't the smartest move she'd ever made, but she needed space. Kayleigh sagged on the edge of the bed, staring down at the comm she'd stolen from a patient on the street. He wouldn't miss it, not while he remained unconscious.

She'd return it before she left.

Unlike hers, his family might want to get in touch.

Her throat ached from holding back tears for so long; her chest hurt so badly, it drowned out even the steady burn in her stomach.

So many injured. So many people caught in the tragedy that had already defined generations of people. She'd tended broken limbs and bleeding lacerations; abrasions and burns and head wounds.

She'd worked tirelessly, sometimes aware that Shawn watched her from wherever he worked. Sometimes mindless and grim as she bandaged, taped, sutured, and hydrated.

The ones she couldn't help weighed on her. Nameless, broken.

Now, she sat alone and empty, staring at the indicator on the comm screen. The one that assured her no one had tried to call her line.

No one had left her a message.

No one had noticed that she was alive but the man who'd taken her from that life.

The doubt eating at her swallowed another portion of her mind. Her heart.

Was he right? Was Shawn right about everything? Parker, too?

Was she the blind one?

Her hand slid to the side pocket of her pants, a narrow slit barely enough to hold money—which was probably the point. These weren't the kind of pants one wore for anything but drinking, dancing, maybe a one-night stand.

Not her life at all.

The small cylinder in her pocket pressed against her thigh.

The door thudded as a weight pushed against it. Kayleigh's head snapped up, comm falling from nerveless fingers as the door handle cranked and the panel slammed against the wall.

Shawn filled the frame, his features worn and taut with a thousand different things—each as familiar to her as the faces of her own demons. Anger, frustration, exhaustion, accusation.

"The Bishop is dead."

Kayleigh blinked, momentarily caught off guard. "What?"

"Tell me you didn't know," he demanded hoarsely.

She slid from the examination table as he strode inside, the door slamming shut behind him. Plaster rained down in a fine gray cloud. "*What?*" Sharper. Stunned.

He didn't stop, didn't slow. His muscles rippled beneath his pale green shirt, stretched the fabric taut as he caught her upper arms in both hands, fingers tight in her flesh. "Tell me you didn't know," he repeated, gaze boring into hers.

Her heart lodged in her throat as he lifted her to her toes, a casual display of such easy strength.

She wanted that strength.

"I don't know what you mean," she whispered.

His lips slanted into a hard line, gaze flicking to the ceiling for one brief second of reprieve. It didn't last. "Good enough," he said, and roughly pulled her against his chest. She staggered, braced herself against the broad wall of his chest, and electrical sparks shivered from fingertips all the way to the sudden pressure between her legs.

She caught his shirt in both hands and didn't stop there. Why should she?

She dragged up the hem of that shirt, scraped her fingers across the hard contours of his abdomen, his chest. His nostrils flared as his head tipped back, an angry, rough sound caught in his throat.

Stupid move? Maybe.

Smart hadn't gotten her anywhere. Logic hadn't earned her any points.

This time, this once, she was going to be deliberately stupid. While she could.

He shrugged out of the shirt, let it fall to the floor, and reached for her again. This time, when his hands closed on her bare midriff, she didn't gasp as he lifted her. Didn't struggle when he placed her on the edge of the exam table and stepped between her legs.

"What happened," she panted as his palms splayed across her ribs, "to no unnecessary touching?"

A smile, fierce as the rest of him, touched his mouth. "This is necessary." Kayleigh arched as one rough hand palmed her breast over her lace bra. "So fucking necessary."

"Yes," she groaned, senses shorting out until there was no clinic or tragedy or kidnapping. Until there was only him, only her, separated by a fine barrier of synth-leather and rapidly thinning oxygen.

This is where she wanted to be. So similar to that exchange in her car—so different in every way.

He hooked her tank top, tore it over her head with less finesse than urgency. It thrilled her to her toes. The desperate need on his face as he stared at her, as his gaze skimmed her mouth, her throat, the small shape of her breast beneath her bra, sent an answering flame to her belly. This time, it didn't hurt.

This time, she didn't care that he was virtually a stranger. She knew what she needed to know. Expected nothing of him but what she demanded now.

Shawn hooked the straps of her bra, pulled it down. The sound he made echoed an answering ache in her body, and she bent back, resting her hands behind her to thrust out her breasts for him to taste. To lick.

He obeyed her wordless command. His tongue flicked one nipple, and she jolted. His lips closed over the hardened flesh and she bit back a wild sound.

"No." He seized her waist, jerked her to the edge of the table, fitted her so snugly against his erection that she couldn't stop herself from crying out, head falling back. "I want to hear you. I want your voice."

Embarrassment filled her, heat climbed her cheeks, but he didn't give her time to consider the demand. His mouth closed over one breast, nearly taking the whole of it into his mouth and suckling deeply. The sharp pressure, the pinpricks of near-pain, rocked her down to her soul, and she cried, "Oh, God!" as his teeth scraped over her flesh.

He transferred to the other breast, licked and sucked even as he rocked hard between her legs.

Sparks flew across her skin, across her vision.

Her hips rolled and he gasped against her damp skin. "More."

With so much pleasure. Kayleigh locked her legs around his waist, caught the nape of his neck with one hand. The shape of his erection, thick and hard and perfect behind his zipper, only teased her. Tormented her.

Tormented them both.

"I want you inside me," she whispered, pleading and demand and aching need all in one. She didn't care if that husky sound came from her, didn't care that the door was unlocked behind them. "Shawn, please, *please* don't make me—"

He kissed her. Finally, *oh, God*, finally, his mouth, damp from the attentions he'd laved on her, closed over hers. Took her lips in a kiss that demanded everything, held nothing back. Her lips opened for him, her eyes closed as his tongue swept into her mouth to give her only a portion of what she craved.

His body in hers.

His need fueling her own.

Frustration warred with stark raving need; arousal turned her body into a liquid mass of nerve endings and wicked hunger. One hand speared into his hair, clenched hard as he drove his tongue between her lips, groaned deep in his chest as her tongue flicked out to meet his, slid against his own.

His hands fumbled at her zipper. She almost laughed, but couldn't tear her mouth away to do it.

He wasn't nearly so in control as he let on.

The knowledge set off fireworks in her body. To think she drove him to this. Made his fingers shake as he tore open the button on her waistband and eased down the zipper. She wiggled when he pulled at the fake leather fabric, slid out of her flats with ease as he lifted his mouth away long enough to tear the pants off her legs. Her underwear went with, matching beige lace.

He gave up when one foot cleared the fabric; Kayleigh didn't care. Bared to his gaze, she stilled, sucking in a shaking breath.

He stared at her like she was a treasure. Like she was some kind of fragile princess too delicate to touch. Too important to risk breaking.

Kayleigh didn't want that. Not from him.

She spread her legs.

His gaze locked on the blond patch of hair she revealed to him.

"Touch," she ordered huskily. "Touch everything."

He sank to his knees in front of the table, his features rapt. "Kissing first," he whispered, his intent clear.

Kayleigh fought the urge to snap her legs together as he braced both large hands at her inner thighs. This . . . this wasn't what she wanted. She wanted hard and fast and unthinking. He'd already proven that he could make her come by herself; she wanted *him*.

This was . . . "No," she whispered, "I can't. It's too—" Her words ended on a shuddering cry as his tongue slid across her already-wet flesh. Her voice cracked, back arching, as his lips closed over the sensitive bead of her clit.

Intimate. It was too damned intimate, and he didn't care, dragging his tongue over her, plunging it inside, tasting her as thoroughly as if she were his favorite dessert. Over and over, he licked and sucked and bit so gently that her fingers clenched in his hair, urged him on until he bit harder and her orgasm spiraled sudden and turbulent. Her hips lifted off the table, her throat closed on a wild sound.

He gave her no recovery time.

A hiss of a zipper, the slick whisper of synth-leather rustled, and suddenly his erection nudged at her swollen, sensitized flesh. He bent over her, braced a hand beside her head.

The other caught her chin, held her head when she would have looked away. "Kayleigh."

"Yes," she gasped. She rolled her hips, shuddering as her flesh rubbed over his skin, tight and hot. So good. Her orgasm, eased on a teaser, coiled hungrily in her skin again. Eager. Ready.

"Kayleigh," he gasped again, cords in his throat standing out as his fingers tightened into a white-knuckled fist beside her. "Christ, tell me you're safe."

Safe? Safe from— Oh. She nodded fast. "Every year." Part of her health plan. It was good, sometimes, to work for a hospital. "Shawn. *Now*."

Her nails raked across his shoulders as she locked her ankles at the small of his back. His breath hissed out.

His hips moved; the hard flesh nudging her own stroked across her clitoris. Kayleigh stopped thinking. Stopped breathing.

The head of him pressed against her body. Slid in her wetness, teased so unbearably that she cursed; a harsh word that brought a surprised laugh from Shawn.

A laugh that ended on his own repeated curse as she pushed herself up on her elbows, locked her lips around one flat nipple, and bit hard.

He thrust inside her, a jerk of his body she didn't think was entirely on purpose, but she didn't care. He was inside her. Touching her in every way that mattered. He groaned long and loud, bent over her on the exam table, his elbows keeping his weight steady, and thrust again.

Kayleigh lost her mind. She knew, somehow she knew it'd be good, but as he filled her, as he stroked inside her, sweat gathering on his skin, on hers, all she wanted was more.

More him. More of his rough, whispered demands, more of the thick, full feeling inside her body as he slid inside her, over and over, slick flesh in flesh. The pressure inside her body built, so fast. Too fast. She wanted it to last, wanted to linger.

Wanted to enjoy this precious, brief moment in time.

Shawn shifted. His fingers dug into her hips, tilted her in a way that forced his erection to rub against the most sensitive spot inside her. Allowed his body to grind against her clitoris with every thrust. The cool fabric of his pants, pulled down at his hips, slapped against her flesh, a delicious contrast to all his heat.

His eyes glittered, skin pulled taut over his cheeks, muscles in his shoulders and arms tight with the effort he took to control himself.

To please *her*.

She sobbed out his name, cupped her own breasts, fingers tight around her nipples. A flush grew across Shawn's golden skin, his eyes flared. "Fuck," he rasped roughly. His movements jerked, rhythm wild as she plucked at her own nipples, moaning. Encouraging. "So . . . fucking beautiful . . . Kayleigh!"

Her name on his lips, on a ragged groan as he threw his head back and fucked her like she'd never dreamed, ended every hope she had of outlasting him. Her climax ripped through her, tore a sobbing note of pleasure and pain from her chest, her lips; the intensity arched her back, her neck.

His hips pumped hard against hers, eyes nearly black as he watched her squirm, watched her shake. Teeth baring, his masculine growl underscored hers as his body gave, as his erection jerked and leaped inside her. He half collapsed with the force of it, hands splayed on either side of her on the table, sweat gleaming on his face, his shoulder. His chest.

He was beautiful. Raw male, strength and aggression and possession.

As Kayleigh's heart thudded wildly in her chest, as her body wrung every last drop of pleasure it could from this moment, reality slowly settled in.

It never took long.

She closed her eyes.

This was everything she'd hoped. Everything she'd never found in the so-polite men topside.

Shawn was everything she couldn't have. Shouldn't want.

His breath, hot on her shoulder, hitched.

He raised his head, a question forming in his eyes, obvious as he took a breath.

Kayleigh smiled to keep from screaming at the injustice of it all. "Pants," is what she said instead, her voice raw. "Door's still unlocked."

Amusement softened the somewhat shell-shocked shape of his rugged features. "Point."

When he withdrew from her, she sucked in a breath, vision flickering like a faulty lamp. God. She still wanted him. Craved more of him.

He caught her face in one hand as she sat up gingerly, bent to press his mouth to hers in a kiss that wasn't anything like the ones they'd shared before.

This one, soft, gentle, lingered. His lips caressed hers, caught softly and made her breath lurch. Her heart picked up speed all over again.

Kayleigh turned her face away. "Pants," she insisted, injecting the word with more humor than she had it in her to feel.

His chuckle tore at her heart as he bent, picked up

his own shirt and allowed her to clean up, struggle back into the borrowed synth-leather hanging from one leg.

Palm the cylinder inside the pocket.

When she was dressed again, when she'd managed to keep her back turned to the point where she was sure her face didn't betray her every thought, she turned to find him shrugging back into his shirt. His hair stood nearly on end, curly ends tousled from her own fingers.

His muscles flexed as he pulled the hem down, gaze meeting hers across the narrow room. Tangling over so many words.

He still tried. "Kayleigh, I—"

She didn't dare let him finish. "It's okay," she said quickly, an ache in her throat. She crossed the distance, wrapped her arms around his waist.

To her dismay—to her shame—she took that moment. A fleeting breath, where everything was going to be okay. Where things were exactly as they should be. She took it and held it and filed it away.

Later. She could cry over it later.

But she had to *know*. And nothing down here would explain it. Not as her father could.

As she'd force him to.

Shawn's arms closed around her, hands tight at her back. "It's not okay," he said against her hair. "Everything's just—"

"Messed up," she whispered. Her thumb caught the cap of the small syringe. It fell to the floor.

Plink.

She felt the stillness in him. Felt his body tense as he straightened, as he looked down at her.

As the needle slid home into the skin at his back.

The question in his eyes banked. His fingers dug into her flesh hard enough to leave bruises, teeth bared, but the plunger depressed. "Why?" A thousand questions in one ragged syllable.

How their roles had reversed.

Kayleigh swallowed tears. "I'm sorry," she whispered. "I'm so sorry." Within the space of that useless apology, she watched his muscles go slack. Caught him as he staggered, guided him to the clinic floor.

His eyes were already closing as she knelt over him. His whiskers rasped against her palm, echo of the burn she could still feel between her thighs.

He'd sleep. And she'd make sure that someone found him.

It was the least she could do.

She stood, her limbs like lead. Her thoughts, just as heavy. Numb, slow, she unsnapped the bracelet she'd thought a great souvenir. Dropped it by his shoulder.

It didn't belong topside. Just as she didn't belong down here. She had questions to ask, people whose lives depended on her.

She needed answers.

Shawn Lowe would never let her go to ask them.

As she reached for the door, her fingers trembling, the first of her tears—shame, bitter and hollow—slid over her cheeks.

CHAPTER SEVENTEEN

The helicopter lifted over New Seattle, the *whup-whup-whup* of its rotary blades earsplittingly loud even through the headphones Kayleigh wore. Beside her, the pleasantly conscientious New Seattle Riot Force officer assigned to her for protection remained focused on the digital readout cupped in one hand.

Whatever he was saying into his mic, it wasn't on the same frequency as Kayleigh's headset.

Finding an NSRF officer hadn't been that difficult. Her picture had been sent to every law enforcement agency from topside to the mid-lows; a fact that mollified some of Kayleigh's helpless anger. *Some.*

None of them knew what was happening topside. No one could answer her careful questions.

The fifteen minutes spent waiting for a lift back topside, tension thick as a blanket on her skin, and shoulders itching as they organized the effort, had drained what anger was left.

Now, she pressed her hands against the window of the aircraft, staring down at a wide swath of destruction carved like a crescent into New Seattle's silhouette.

The quake fractured up the side of the layer cake, an offshoot from the Old Sea-Trench whittled underneath a portion of the city foundation. As the helicopter glided over it, rising higher into a sky slowly darkening from pale gray to oil, she watched lights bob and flicker along the newly formed crevasse. Lanterns, flashlights, generators sparking as they fueled electricity to the ravaged blocks.

Somewhere down there, Shawn was . . . was what?

Angry at her? Feeling betrayed?

Relieved?

She didn't know him well enough to even hazard a guess. All she knew was that he'd never understand.

The headset muffling the worst of the noise crackled to life in her ears. "Just a few more minutes, miss," said the officer. His voice was kind, his demeanor had been nothing but courteous since he introduced himself.

Officer Matthew Wilkinson. Probably a husband or father. He had that look; that kind of wary sympathy a well-trained man reserved for the opposite sex during times of stress.

He treated her like a victim, she thought, nodding politely. Treated her like something fragile.

She wasn't. Her head hurt, she could have happily eaten a four-course meal by herself, and she was willing to threaten homicide for a cup of strong coffee, but she wasn't made of glass.

Most of her, anyway. Her heart felt a little brittle.

Stupid, really. Too late, Kayleigh remembered why she didn't date casually.

She'd never really perfected the art of separating body and mind. If she had, she'd have long since conquered her ulcer and insomnia.

She leaned back into the uncomfortable seat as the helicopter banked smoothly, pilot guiding it over the Holy Order quadplex wall as a spate of technical babble filtered over the headsets. The pilot offered a thumbs-up, and beside her, the officer leaned across the small gap to capture her attention.

She followed the line of his finger. "We're going to land behind the Holy Cathedral," he said, a surreal time lapse between the shape of his mustache-framed mouth and the words filtering through the frequency. "There's a landing pad just there."

The courtyard, framed by the four rectangular buildings comprising the quad, teemed with people as the helicopter skated overhead; employees in business dress, some in the all-black of the Church's operatives, scurrying like ants from one side to the other. Most moved from the blackened frame of the Mission building, a section swathed by dark blue tarp, to the Magdalene Asylum, while some split to and from the civics building.

The cathedral rose tall and imposing over it all, a beautifully ornate frame from the courtyard side. The real display faced out, where the topsiders would come in for Sunday Mass up gorgeously carved white steps and move inside beneath the highest cross decorating the steeple.

As the helicopter crested the sloping roof, she found the circular landing pad, wide enough for two vehicles and already hosting one.

Her guts clenched, a sudden jolt of fear. Of nerves.

Officer Wilkinson touched her arm. "Is there anyone we should call for you, Dr. Lauderdale?"

His eyes, a very clear green, were compassionate.

She summoned a smile as the bird dropped gently. "No, thank you. I know where to go."

"Are you sure?" The landing skids hovered, just a few feet separating the landing pad and the helicopter. Kayleigh grabbed the edge of the seat as the machine tilted under the pilot's skillful handling, touched down.

"Absolutely," she assured him, unbuckling her harness. "Thank you, sir, I'm grateful for the ride home." And for the jacket, which bore the NSRF tag across the back.

The officer nodded, unlatching the door. "Keep your head down and clear the landing pad before you straighten," he ordered. "You just got home, let's keep your head attached."

This time, her smile felt a little more real. "I'll do that. Thanks again."

"No problem, miss. Be safe."

Given everything that had happened in the past few days? The things that needed to happen now? Kayleigh just couldn't promise.

At least her vision wasn't going double on her anymore.

She slid out of the passenger bay, offering a quick wave to the pilot, who nodded solemnly back, his gaze hidden by the helmet he wore. Keeping her head down as directed, she hurried to the edge of the landing pad, buffeted by the wind from the rotary blades as the helicopter lifted back into the air.

Home. Once, anyway.

Kayleigh wasted no time. She crossed the quad, ignoring the sideways stares she received from people not otherwise occupied on an errand. In her synth-leather pants and NSRF jacket, probably looking every bit as worn down as she felt, Kayleigh wasn't surprised when a murmur rose in her wake. Some spun to watch her go.

She ignored them.

Her father would be in his office. God only knew, he never left it anymore. She entered the Magdalene from the front, waved to the desk clerk, whose eyes rounded. "Doctor!"

"I'm going up, buzz me in," she ordered, as if it were the most natural thing in the world.

"Yes, ma'am." She hit the panel, unlocking the far door that led to the internal corridors of the hospital.

Normally, Kayleigh would have used the side door, or come up the elevator direct from the parking garage. All of her keys, her pass cards, everything had been left in her car, wherever Shawn had abandoned it.

She wouldn't be here long enough to get them changed.

The ride up the elevator was interminably long. The silvered panels gave her too much time to study herself. To avoid her own shadowed eyes in the mirror.

She looked like a common street girl, like she'd spent all night long grinding on a dance floor, around a pole, hell, even underneath a man; she looked as if she'd come home too late, too worn, too used.

She raked both hands through her hair, still struggling to push it into some semblance of order as the doors opened.

The director's office, a three-piece suite with a reception area, a conference room, and her father's own well-appointed space, opened right off the elevator.

A harried, dark-haired head rose from the desk beyond the initial foyer.

Eyes widened behind thick-framed glasses. "Dr. Lauderdale!"

"Evening, Patrick." She strove for calm, she really did. But as she walked out of the elevator and into the familiar comfort of her father's office, as Patrick Ross rounded the desk, shock clear on his usually so-polite expression, her façade crumbled. "Is . . ." Her voice shuddered. "Is my dad in?"

"I— Dr. Lauderdale, we heard you'd been kidnapped." He reached out as if he'd take her arm, paused, and adjusted his plain black tie instead. "Your dad—Director Lauderdale is on a press conference right now. I don't know if you heard, but there was an earthquake. Bishop Applegate had a terrible accident, it's been a nightmare." As he spoke, her father's assistant seemed to pull his usual polished veneer back into place, brick by efficient brick.

Kayleigh's only crumpled. "I heard," she whispered. Her shoulders rounded, but she couldn't stop. Couldn't keep herself from shaking as hours and hours of stress, fear, anxiety—so much guilt—boiled over. "I . . . I lost my comm down there, I don't have clothes . . . I need to talk to him, Patrick."

To his obvious horror, tears filled her eyes. She knuckled them away impatiently, but they wouldn't stop. Not even when Patrick plucked tissues from a box, shoved them into her hands.

"Okay." It was barely a breath of sound from the well-dressed man. Grimacing, he checked the watch on his wrist, looked up to the blank screen mounted on the wall as if it would give him some kind of clue. When she sniffled into a tissue, he winced. "Stay here,

Doctor. There's water in the bar and some of the director's usual snacks. I'll . . ." He practically wrung his hands as he backpedaled to the elevator. "I'll get him. It might be a little while. Just . . . stay." Patrick retreated into the elevator, nodding at her as the doors closed.

What a mess. She couldn't stop crying, couldn't keep her usual façade of calm and efficiency up any longer. She tried; damn it, she scraped what dignity she had left around her, and it only fractured further.

Her stomach burned, badly enough to remind her of everything she'd done. Everything she had left to do.

Kayleigh lasted all of three seconds in the silence of the office.

It would take them some time to extricate her father from a press conference of this magnitude. If the bishop really was dead—

Tell me you didn't know.

She grabbed at her head as Shawn's voice filled it.

Of course she hadn't known. How could she? She wasn't omniscient, she'd told him that before. Kayleigh had been so busy helping the victims of the quake, how could she know?

Desperate to clear her mind, to focus on something besides the intensity of dark brown eyes tearing through her, going blank with forced sedation, she reached for the remote. The widescreen lit soundlessly.

Her father liked to keep it on the news. Kayleigh often did, too, when she wasn't preoccupied with her own project goals.

"—somewhat unbelievable reports of unlikely rescuers," said a solemn, black-haired man in the frame. His eyes, unnaturally blue in his pleasant features, stared out with grave yet carefully modulated charm.

"Sources from below the sec-lines are telling us that victims of the previous quake and subsequent tremors have been rescued by witches."

Kayleigh's smile, wan and strained, edged into a muffled snort as she rubbed her face with both hands.

The Salem agents must be out in force.

"One, a girl described as 'no more than sixteen, with short hair and freckles,' allegedly used nothing but her voice to lift a ton of rubble out of the way of stalled emergency vehicles."

Impossible. Sixteen? There was no one in the Salem Project listings that young.

Kayleigh's hands clasped together, pressed tight enough to mute their trembling to a dull vibration.

The man smiled briefly. "Reports are uncertain as to where this girl is now, but civilians and medical personnel in the area are calling her the Good Witch in gratitude."

She didn't laugh. She could barely breathe.

Witches helping people? Witches outside Sector Three?

More like Jessie and Naomi?

Unbidden, her thoughts circled back around. To Shawn. To the blank rage distorting his features as the sedative put him down.

Did he know about this so-called Good Witch? Was she one of theirs?

Did her father know?

Abruptly, the news feed cut, blipped once, and shifted to a new location. Kayleigh shook her head, squinting as the picture in front of her blurred.

"All stations should now be aware of current events. The Church is here," her father said, his voice strong and clear despite the hunched shoulders and gnarled fingers curled into either side of the podium. Kayleigh stared up into the monitor, her mouth parting on a soundless note of surprise as her vision sparkled. As the light of the screen fuzzed, building a pale halo around it. "We know this is a difficult time, but all citizens of New Seattle must remain calm."

Her guts turned, churning as camera bulbs flashed, lights popping like sparklers and sending a fresh splatter over her suddenly deteriorating vision.

She rubbed her eyes, stepped back, and bumped into Patrick's curved desk.

"We have deployed agents to every law enforcement office in the city," Director Lauderdale continued, his faded blue-gray eyes staring not at the crowd, but at her. Through her. Directly into the camera. His lined, weathered features—always so familiar—now looked alien. Strange.

When he tilted his head as he moved, his eyes left icy trails. An afterburn of pale blue. "Magdalene Asylum staff have been relocated with priority to the most harshly affected areas, then spread out among the other hospitals, clinics and triage centers for unavoidable diversion."

Diversion. He expected catastrophic injuries.

Kayleigh squinted, and when that failed to clear the haze, scrunched her eyes closed.

Hundreds of thousands dead.

She swayed. The desk hit the small of her back, and she gripped the edge without being fully aware that she'd done so. Not until her elbow swept the stacked in-box to the ground.

Papers fluttered. Pens scattered across the floor.

It could be less, whispered that confident, knowing part of her brain she didn't know what to make of. *It could be so much less.*

The pain struck hard and sudden, mirror of the first migraine that had ever put her in the hospital. The office turned sideways as her father's voice echoed through her head.

"Stand firm," he said. "This disaster will not end . . ."

Her vision went black.

" . . . together, in the name of our late . . . We will—" *We will. . .*

Her fingernails snagged in the plush carpet.

Make a better world.

CHAPTER EIGHTEEN

Hard hands closed around Shawn's shoulders. His back collided with the twisted portion of the chain-link fence still standing guard around the ruined husk of the GeneCorp facility, knocking the wind out of him.

Shawn didn't fight back.

The man pinning him to the swaying metal looked like hell slapped into a human shape. His features were sallow, cheeks gaunt and sharp bone structure stark and nearly white beneath his thin skin. His eyes, snapping hazel and glassy enough to explain the heat saturating through the man's palms to Shawn's shoulders, bored into his, lips peeled back from bared teeth.

Simon Wells, the ex-missionary, was falling apart.

"You *had* her?"

The snarled demand fisted Shawn's hands against the fence behind him. "I had her," he confirmed tightly. More than had her.

He'd held her. Tasted her.
Fucked her.
For what? *Nothing.* It'd meant nothing to her. Or
to him.
Yeah, right.
His shoulder blades scraped against rusted metal as
Simon shoved him hard, let him go to stalk a few feet
away. The chain link fence clanged wildly.

Simon was tall, taller than Shawn, but whatever
compact muscle had once defined him as a dangerous
agent of the Church had weakened, gone ropy with the
disease claiming him day by day.

The jeans he wore didn't quite fit, his shirt baggy.
But there was no mistaking the lethality of every
trained movement as he turned, flicking away the
rainwater as it drizzled over them both. "What happened?"

Behind him, three figures made their way across
the shattered lot, one limping between arm crutches.
Jonas. His voice, pitch-perfect, drifted across the lot,
punctuated by the muted *thunk* of his crutches colliding with pitted asphalt. Naomi, her magenta-streaked
hair and piercings catching what little light filtered
from above, nodded and quickened her pace.

Shawn's jaw locked. "She got the jump on me." The
words curled in his gut like acid.

Simon's incredulous snort was a sucker punch to
the solar plexus. "Please," he scoffed, "she couldn't
jump a legless dog."

"Shut the hell up."

He hadn't meant to say the words. Definitely hadn't
intended to give the ex-missionary any more ammuni-
tion to throw in his venomous attack, but Simon's eyes
widened, then narrowed just as fast.

"You stupid son of a bitch." The man's fists clenched, a muscle jumping in his cheek as he squared up, nose to nose, and pure scorn dripping from every word. "You let Lauderdale have the cure for a piece of ass?"

Shawn jerked. "Fuck your cure," he snarled.

The man grabbed his collar. "*You* fucked my cure," he threw back, vicious. Shaking with it. "You fucked the only woman who's got the goddamned cure, and then you let her run back topside like some kind of slumming whor—"

He moved, fast. Explosive. Suddenly, Shawn's fist drove into Simon's face, sent the man reeling, fingers ripping from Shawn's collar. Threads snapped, fabric tearing free.

Simon reeled, spat out a mouthful of blood. Murder in his sunken eyes, he spun back, took one step.

Shawn met it.

Arms wrapped in bright red vinyl snaked under his, jerked his elbows together, and brought him up short. "Knock it off!" a woman said behind him.

"Guys." Jonas's voice. Strained.

Simon drew up, fists clenched at his sides, nostrils flaring with every breath as Shawn wrenched at Naomi's grip. Blood trickled from Simon's nose.

A foot slammed into the back of his knee, dropping him to the gravel so efficiently, it took him a second to realize the jagged edge of gravel digging into his kneecap hurt like a bitch. "You're both fuckheads," Naomi declared.

"Guys, please," Jonas said as he and the sandy-haired man who walked with him finally cleared the lot. "There's bigger things at stake, here." But apology laced the words. "No offense, Simon."

Simon shook his head, back of his hand lifted to blot at the thin line of red trailing over his lip and chin.

The scarred man beside him only folded his arms over his zipped-up black jacket and stared at Shawn. The light picked out raw creases of corrugated skin on the left side of his throat, trailing ridged fingers up along his jaw to twist one side of his mouth into a permanent smirk.

There was nothing funny about the serious, overpoweringly blue eyes leveled on Shawn.

He met that gaze, held it even kneeling. His jaw firmed. "What?"

"I'm Caleb Leigh."

"Good for you."

Naomi's fingers closed on the back of his neck. "Hey, asshole," she said in his ear, her husky voice growing more amused by the second. "You're surrounded by people who all like each other a screwton more than you, so be nice."

Jonas winced. "Nai . . ."

"Okay, and if you do, *I'll* be nice," she added.

"Thank you." Shifting, shoulders hunched over the braces that allowed him to walk, Jonas jerked a head back to the facility. "We found the remains of a digital reader under some wreckage. It'll take more time than we have to get the data off it, if anything is left, but maybe we can find Simon's information with enough effort and a whole bucket of luck."

Shawn rose to his feet as Naomi's grip eased, shaking off the lingering sting in his fist. Simon glared at him, but he rubbed at his head as if it hurt and said nothing.

Caleb looked up at the twinkling neon. A narrow band of shadow cut through the usual blanket, a void where the destruction had wiped out a swath of buildings, electricity. Lives. "Cure or not, this isn't over. If what I *saw* was right, it's only just beginning."

"What you saw?" Shawn frowned. "What do you mean?"

"A vision." This new voice came on soundless feet, and Shawn shifted to see a tall, elegantly featured redhead in denim and too-big flannel step out of the shadows beyond the lot. Her copper hair was pulled into a tight braid, severely drawn back from her face, and her blue eyes, cool as winter, met his without hesitance or reservation.

His eyebrows rose. "Parker fucking Adams."

Simon shifted. Just enough that nobody could mistake his point. "Curb it," he ordered, quiet but far from gentle.

The new woman—her face plastered on every feed and every bulletin from the lower city slums on up—circled the group. The hand she placed on Simon's arm did nothing to ease the man's tension, but he covered her fingers with his own. "You know as well as I do what May says," she said, her gaze on Shawn. "I know you don't trust me or Simon, but I'm telling you that we've got no more love for the Holy Order than you do."

"Maybe less," Simon muttered.

Shawn doubted that. Still, she was right. He didn't apologize, but he inclined his head to the ex-Mission director to show he was willing to listen.

This was where he'd try his newfound theory. The one that said maybe, just maybe, May knew something he didn't about these people. Traitors to their own cause. Maybe the saviors of his?

What options did he have? "What vision?"

"A few weeks back," Caleb said, matter-of-factly as if he weren't rocking back on his heels on a broken, pitted lot of an abandoned witch-making lab, "I *saw* a vision, something about the future."

"Here or something in the distance?"

Parker tilted her head. "You put your faith in witchcraft, Mr. Lowe?"

His eyes narrowed. "Is this the missionary asking?"

Her fingers tightened on Simon's arm as the man tensed. "No. This vision affects all of us."

"It basically said that Laurence Lauderdale was going to be responsible for hundreds of thousands of people dead," Simon said tightly. "A mountain of corpses."

Shawn shrugged. "What, like the witch labs?"

"Worse," Caleb replied, and though it was a quiet syllable, it cut through Shawn's lingering annoyance. His pride.

The ache in his chest.

Somehow, the way the blond kid spoke, it carried weight.

Parker's red eyebrows furrowed. "If Jonas's data is correct and he somehow knows how to predict the earthquakes, he's not letting the people in the danger zone know. We have to find out what he's doing and why."

"We have to do more than that," Simon said, curving one arm around Parker's waist. "Incoming, Jonas."

"I . . . can't argue what you guys aren't saying." Jonas's gaze flicked beyond the group. Headlights turned a corner, panned over the gritty lot. His glasses' lenses flared brightly and went transparent again. "Who brought in the cavalry?"

The van, dirty white and bearing the scars of time

and hard wear, settled close enough to paint them all in gold.

"Argue what?" Shawn demanded as the door opened. "What's not being said?" Danny hopped out, turned, and helped a familiar sandy blond woman out behind him.

"Of course," Jonas added, as Naomi snorted.

Shawn wasn't sure what the joke was. He didn't care.

Jessie hit the ground, didn't even pause before jogging over to the group. "Everything's quiet for now," was her greeting, followed by Danny's added, "No more aftershocks, but there's a citywide curfew officially in effect to get people off the street. Far as I can tell, there's at least one Church-sanctioned witch with every police and riot force unit, now, and they're *mean*."

"What are we talking about?" Jessie added, circling them to nudge a shoulder against Caleb's.

The similarities, though he was taller and she obviously older, struck Shawn immediately. Siblings.

Simon, squinting, muttered, "That's the last of us here."

Parker frowned up at him. Worry drew a deep weft in her brow. "Are you all right?"

"Usual song and dance," he murmured. She laid a hand on his chest, which he covered with one of his own.

"Party in the GeneCorp lot?" Naomi's amusement was made of something sharp. Cutting.

"Seemed as good a place as any," Jonas admitted, reaching up, arm brace hanging from his forearm, to rub at his forehead as if it hurt. A lot of that going around. "We found Kayleigh Lauderdale's reader, but it's not that helpful. She wasn't dumb enough to carry the syringe with her, so we're discussing options. After three weeks, that stuff's been analyzed to death. If the cure exists, it's in the topside mainframe."

"So, we're not looking at options," Simon translated, lifting his gaze from Parker's deeply concerned expression. "One. Singular. We get up there, we figure out what the fuck is going on, and then we kill the son of a bitch."

"I don't think killing Lauderdale will—"

Oh, yeah, it would. "I volunteer," Shawn said immediately, cutting off Jonas's calm voice of reason.

"So do I," Simon added. "I want that son of a bitch to go down screaming." The venom in his voice earned a surprised raise of Shawn's eyebrows. "And if we're damned lucky, Kayleigh will be up there with that goddamned syringe."

Caleb half turned, his square features pulled into a tight frown. Shawn noticed his gaze settled on Parker, whose mouth flattened to a thin, white line.

He glanced at Simon. "Parker—"

Simon let her go. "She knows the score."

"Damn it, Simon," she whispered. So much pain, so much wanting wrapped in raw apprehension.

Shawn looked away before he turned Simon down flat.

Their relationship, their arguments, were none of his affair. He needed manpower, and by all accounts, Simon Wells hated Laurence Lauderdale as much as he did.

If they found the cure up there, well, so much the better.

Naomi sighed, shaking back her wet hair as she casually planted an elbow against Shawn's shoulder. He didn't stagger under the sudden weight, but the look he shot her went ignored as she grinned fiercely. "You're all a bunch of morons and I'm going, too."

"No," Jonas cut in, flashing her a steely look that wiped her smile. "We need you with the wounded, Nai. No one else can do what you do."

The elbow on his shoulder jerked away. "Shit-fucker." This time, the hand that shoved through her wet hair smacked of impatience. "You need someone who's up on Mission protocol."

"I can—"

Danny slipped a hand over Jonas's mouth, forcing the thinner man's eyes to go wide behind his spectacles. "Don't even say it. Don't even think it."

Jonas gripped his wrist, sliding his hand down. "They need someone," he pointed out, but Danny only shook his head and declared, "We need you more than they do."

For a long moment, nobody spoke. Shawn studied them from beneath furrowed eyebrows, one hand clenching and unclenching at his side.

A lover's thing?

No. For once—maybe more than just for once, maybe in a display of maturity Shawn hadn't ever given Danny credit for, the kid said flatly, "May's in no shape to keep the information flowing. You're master of the wave, Jonas, you're the only one who can do what she does, even without her gifts."

Color suffused Jonas's cheeks. "Oh."

Parker, silent and still since Simon's offer, raised her head. Strands of her hair clung to her cheeks in a wet gleam of copper, but her eyes were cool, icy calm as they settled not on Jonas, but on Shawn. "I'll go."

Next to Caleb, Jessie's head came up hard. Her eyes narrowed.

Was he the only objective one here?

That was laughable, given he couldn't close his eyes for two seconds without imagining what it had felt like to have Kayleigh writhing beneath him. Crying out his name. Begging for more.

Betraying him when he was at his weakest.

The blind leading the clinically insane.

His smile was tight. "Fine," he snapped, glaring at Simon as the man opened his mouth. "We need someone who knows the Mission inside and out. Can you name anyone else?"

The man hesitated. His features darkened. "No."

"Then it's done."

Naomi threw up her hands. "Why did I give up my gun again?"

Caleb smiled, but it wasn't an easy expression. The scar tilted it to a lopsided edge. "Because you're smarter than you look."

"Fuck you, Leigh." She looked up at the sky, and as if this was everyone's cue, Shawn watched as they all followed suit.

That black void cut across the view only emphasized the point.

"I'm going to need your girlfriend," she added to Caleb after a moment's pensive silence.

"Fiancée."

"Whatever."

Caleb's smile betrayed more than a trace of gruff affection. "She can be there in an hour."

Shawn didn't know what else had somehow been conveyed in that simple exchange, but it didn't matter.

Let Naomi do what she did with the sick and injured. Let Caleb do what he needed to do with the visions or whatever he did. Jonas would direct Simon,

Parker, and Shawn topside for the kind of operation he'd waited sixteen years for.

Parker tucked her hair back over her shoulder. "We should get ready."

Jessie's mouth tightened. "Parker—"

"Bigger things at stake," she said over the witch's protest.

Shawn didn't even bother to translate. "Meet at the garage in two hours." That should give them all enough time to prepare. To talk.

To say their good-byes.

Shawn couldn't begrudge them that much. Even it was more than he ever got. Too damned close. He'd let her in too close, trusted her too far, and he'd paid for it.

Never trust a Lauderdale.

As they shouldn't trust him. The taste of his own medicine burned a hole in his gut.

He wouldn't make that mistake again.

So why, he thought as he turned away from the group, did he volunteer for what amounted to a suicide mission?

"Hey, Shawn?"

He paused.

Jonas's familiarly awkward footsteps approached. "I have something for you, if you want it."

CHAPTER NINETEEN

The nurse in wrinkled purple scrubs watched Kayleigh sign her name with a flourish, her stern features set into disapproving lines. "Once more, Dr. Lauderdale, I have to stress that we really should keep you for observation—"

"No," Kayleigh cut in, not for the first time. "I'm fine, thank you."

Around them, the hum of the hospital seemed muted. More than half the staff had been transferred to high-risk areas below the sec-lines, leaving a skeleton crew to maintain the quieter topside streets.

Kayleigh wasn't going to stay in that bed any longer than she had to. Wasn't going to stare at the plain white ceiling, listening to machines monitor her heartbeat and her vitals, and think about all the things she didn't have answers for.

Jessie and her mother. Parker and her accusations.

Matilda Lauderdale.

The Eve sequence.

Shawn.

Her father hadn't come to see her. Nobody had come to check on her but one doctor in a hurry and her father's assistant, who'd briefly and conscientiously dropped off a bag of clothes, a new comm, and a large vase of flowers he claimed came from her father. He hadn't stayed past a cursory check-in.

Kayleigh didn't need the attention. Didn't need the extra burden.

She handed the readout to the nurse, who was already imprinting her thumb to the lock. "I'd like a copy of my file, please," she added.

"Notes show we have it sent directly to Director—"

"Send it to me," Kayleigh interrupted evenly. "Right now, please."

The nurse shrugged. "Nothing has changed from your last stay, according to the charts, but . . ." A few seconds as her fingers skated over the reader. "Flagged for delivery, Doctor."

"Thank you." Kayleigh zipped up the dove gray cashmere sweater that wasn't hers, hiding the pale blue T-shirt beneath. The dark-wash designer jeans fit surprisingly well, but at the price tag, she'd have been more surprised if they didn't. Patrick must have sent out for new clothing. The items were informal enough to get her from the hospital to home without much impact on her surroundings, but she wasn't going home.

Her father had dodged her calls. Fine. She'd get half her answers herself, and confront him with the rest.

The intercom overhead chimed. "Code blue, south wing."

"Excuse me," the nurse added, already turning away.

"Wait," Kayleigh called to her retreating back. "Can you buzz me into the elevator?"

Obviously harried, the nurse reached across the desk, thumbed the switch inset into a panel of them, and gestured. "Quickly, Doctor."

Kayleigh smiled her thanks, slung her new tote over her shoulder and quickly made her way through the far door. The same door she'd stepped in to visit her father.

She wasn't going to try again.

The comm in her hand chimed, a pretty bell-like tone, as she reached the silent elevator. Kayleigh checked the screen. Two messages.

As she stepped into the reflective elevator, giving herself a cursory glance to make sure she'd managed to at least put herself together with Patrick's delivered supplies, she scanned the text.

So glad you're feeling better. Go right home and get some rest.

Her father. The fact that he was still up didn't surprise her. A lump formed in her throat as she stared at the innocuous words.

He knew she'd left. Probably got word the instant she'd signed the checkout documents. He had time to send a note, but not to call her.

He was busy. Of course he was busy. A pall hung over the city, thick as smoke. Even she felt it from the dubious haven of her hospital room.

The bishop was dead. The Mission in disarray.

There was no one else to grab the reins and keep the city from falling apart.

The gravity of the situation didn't make her need for answers any less important.

Kayleigh rubbed the back of her neck as her thumb pressed the comm screen.

This time, the message that filled it scrolled for a few seconds before it stopped.

The elevator car slowed. When the doors opened, she stepped out, but she wasn't focused on the corridor in front of her. That hadn't changed; a hasty scan showed her white walls, fluorescent lights, all the same things she'd come to expect for so many years.

She strode rapidly down the simple hall, eyes on her comm screen.

The chart filling it was detailed and precise.

She read it twice. Heart rate, oxygen levels, vitals all strong. She was deficient in several vitamins—she made a mental note, clinically detached, to increase her supplements. Beyond the surface data, past the diagnostic notes, the deeper genetic details scrolled in a flurry of data that might have read like gibberish to anyone else.

She wasn't anyone else.

Kayleigh read it a third time.

Her footsteps drew to a stumbling halt.

A fourth.

Her hands began to shake.

She could see the paths laid out before someone, Jessie Leigh had explained.

By the time Kayleigh pressed her thumb to the security lock outside her laboratory door, a vein throbbed, pounded, in her forehead. It took her two tries to get the retina scan properly.

The door hissed open, released compressed air as the tumblers disengaged. She pushed inside, ducking under the hanging flap of plastic, ignored the dark offices lining the lab proper, ignored the shrouded machines and silent worktables.

"Computer," she said, her voice breaking. Clearing her throat, she tried again. "Computer, wake up."

"Imprint verified."

She had no time for that. Grip white-knuckled around the comm, Kayleigh circled the main table as lights flickered to life in a path behind her. Ahead of her.

She didn't see it. Didn't notice as the computers at her workstation blinked on.

"Call up all data on unknown matter analyzed eight days ago," she whispered. When no mechanical voice assured her of its progress, she repeated it, louder.

"Displayed," said the pleasant voice. "Computer fourteen, monitor number one."

Her stomach turned, over and over, torn between fear and fury and pain.

The chart was wrong. Of course it was wrong.

It couldn't be wrong.

Kayleigh tossed her comm to the table as she passed it, strode into her office, and dug through her desk until she found one of her kits.

"Power up blood analysis," she ordered, her voice louder than it needed to be. Sharper than the quiet hum of machines warming, equipment thrumming gently.

"All units powered and ready."

"Pull file Lauderdale, Kayleigh—classification seven-seven-three-six—from my comm."

"File acquired," the computer assured her.

There were papers on her table. Trays of samples she hadn't even thought about in days, notes from her techs. It seemed a lifetime ago that she'd hunched over this table as Shawn watched her from the stool behind her.

With one jerky motion, she swept it all to the floor, threw the lid off her kit.

"Display beside analysis from unlabeled sample," Kayleigh demanded, even as she shoved her sleeve up. The tourniquet pinched as she wrapped it around her own arm; the needle pinched more.

She filled two vials with her own blood, guts churning.

What other excuse was there?

She slapped a gauze pad over the small wound left behind, taped it sloppily into place. "Prepare analysis."

No use speculating until she had facts. Her own facts. Surely something had gone awry. Something strange, a mixed file or . . . or . . .

Or Laurence Lauderdale had lied.

Her fingers shook as she slotted one vial into the DNA sequencer.

"Analyzing," the computer reported, and she wanted to throw something at that pleasant, even voice.

Kayleigh held her breath. When her lungs started to clamor for air, she exhaled hard, jamming her fingers into her hair and digging her nails into her skull as she waited for the results.

Ten minutes. Lab Seventeen had been outfitted with the fastest and most cutting-edge technology available anywhere. Ten minutes was a far cry from the week of laborious analysis the old genome sequencers used to require before the fall of the old city.

Ten minutes seemed a lifetime.

"Locate active news frequency," she demanded. "Volume to six."

Without confirmation, a woman's voice filled the speakers wired into the lab. "—as the death toll pauses at forty-three confirmed cases, with over fifty more in critical care or missing. There have been no further aftershocks and many are hoping that this is the end."

Kayleigh didn't sit. Tension all but vibrating from toes to scalp, she gripped the edge of the table and stared instead at the mysterious liquid she'd taken from Parker.

Great since your mother fixed me.

Her mother. *Her* mother. How did Matilda Lauderdale know Jessie Leigh? How did she know Parker Adams?

They'd always told her that Matilda died when Kayleigh was eight years old, a disease they'd worried Kayleigh had inherited. All the tests when she was a child, the yearly checks; they'd all come back clean.

Kayleigh had never looked at her own charts. Why should she? Since she was eight years old, her father had always taken care of it.

She'd never bothered to study her own sequencing the way she studied everyone else's.

Everything came down to genetics. Her mother, brilliant and gifted, had known that. That had to be why she'd made Simon.

But for what purpose? Why had she bothered having Kayleigh if she already had Simon?

Why was it that her entire history, her own family, now seemed a lie?

Because it was. Jessie had tried to tell her.

"Further reports from the most damaged areas of the quake zone are heartening," the newswoman continued, her voice somehow managing to be both cheerful and serious. "Among the most surprising, wanted felon Phinneas Clarke—once the owner of the now-defunct topside resort Timeless—organized the search and rescue for a man's family after the man was allegedly refused help by New Seattle Riot Force officers."

The Salem witches were broken, their sequencing incomplete. Defective. Matilda Lauderdale had been working on it when she died.

Or . . . or not died.

Kayleigh glared at the screen closest to her, eyes tracking across a string of letters. Adenine, thymine, cytosine, guanine. The four bases were all there in the mystery fluid, but it wasn't right. There were patterns in the sequence, extra genes she'd never expected to find. Had never seen before.

Links between the bases that meant nothing. Garbage. Her techs had been right.

But why had Parker been carrying the mystery fluid?

"After neighbors helped rescue the man's youngest two children from the ruins of his home, witnesses say Clarke—actively wanted for questioning and suspected heretical associations—quickly vanished."

Where had the stuff come from?

How had Matilda fixed Jessie?

"*Augh!*" Kayleigh stamped her foot hard, sending a spike of pain through her arch.

Twenty-five years ago, Kayleigh had been five years old. GeneCorp had shut down, moved, and all new generations halted.

Why?

Lydia Leigh had set it on fire, according to the subject's living daughter.

"All across the metropolis," the news anchor droned, "topsiders and low-street locals hold a collective breath."

Kayleigh scowled at the screen.

Why didn't her mother restart the program? Why didn't her dad?

Matilda Lauderdale's illness had become apparent. That's what Kayleigh had been told. And without Matilda to fix the broken sequencing, any subjects they created would die.

She couldn't remember. Why couldn't she remember her own mother clearly?

A shrill beep knifed through the news chatter. "Analysis complete. Data compiled. Monitor—"

"Yes, yes," she muttered, ignoring the labeled screen as figures filled a third panel on the bank of six.

Kayleigh's eyes darted over it. Trembling, she keyed down. Again. The bases were there. The data, there.

The proof . . . *there*.

Her knees gave out from under her.

As she collapsed onto a stool, Kayleigh Lauderdale stared at the incontrovertible evidence of her parents' duplicity.

The Salem genome.

Kayleigh had the witch allele. Her mother had been a witch.

Was that what was wrong with her eyes? With her head? Was that what was triggering when she looked at someone and just *knew* the things she did?

Why hadn't anyone told her?

Think. There was always opportunity to take advantage of, always a solution to every problem. She just had to think like her mother.

Only she didn't know how her mother thought.

"With Bishop Applegate dead and no clear line of succession—"

"Radio, off!"

The woman's voice ended mid-word.

No, she didn't know how Matilda thought, but she knew how her father operated. How his mind worked, and that meant Matilda did, too. She'd made Simon, and if her father had known, he never let on.

Why? Why hide from her own family?

What could her mother have done that was so bad?

"Focus," she murmured, frowning at the flickering screens. She couldn't think emotionally. That wasn't how a scientist operated. She had to think rationally, logically.

If Kayleigh wanted to hide something from the world, what would she use?

Plain sight.

People saw only what they wanted to see. Her gaze narrowed on the screens, flicked from her own chart to the junk analysis.

Obeying gut instinct, Kayleigh snagged a pencil, paged through her own genetic sequencing, and wrote out the bases. The collection of letters that earmarked each genetic line. Wrote until her paper was filled with letter after letter, until she flipped it over and started again.

For thirty minutes, she labored in silence, brain working the puzzle. Churning it through the analytical filters that had allowed her to tear through her work in school and, later, in this very lab.

Ding! The comm chimed cheerfully at her elbow.

Kayleigh snatched the unit up, plucked the earpiece from the case, and affixed it to her ear, eyes on her scribbled notations. "Dr. Lauderdale."

Silence met her habitual greeting. Silence, and the faint whisper of an active frequency.

Her pencil moved between two notations.

Then her focus fractured as a deep, masculine

voice said quietly, "I wondered if you'd gone back home."

The pencil lead snapped. Kayleigh's head came up, but there was nobody to see; nothing but empty lab and the sudden crush of too much memory, too many unspoken words in her chest. "Shawn." A whisper.

"You sound surprised."

More than she'd ever wanted to be. Surprised, a little relieved.

Scared.

"What are you doing calling me?" she asked, laying the pencil down very carefully. "It's not safe."

"For you, you mean?" The scorn infecting the frequency line dragged sharp nails across her nerves.

She blew out a hard breath, propping her elbows on the table surface to dig the heels of her hands into her eye sockets. "For you, you idiot."

"Try another one."

His voice. Damn it, she'd done so well blocking out his voice. First, the hospital had allowed her to sleep without dreams. Then, this . . . this new discovery. Focusing on the puzzle beneath her elbows, the mystery of her medical charts—

Who was she kidding?

"Shawn, I—" Her throat closed around the words she didn't know how to say.

How could she admit to the man who'd kidnapped her that her father was flawed? That he'd hidden the greatest secret of her life from her?

That she was a witch.

She couldn't.

"You shouldn't be contacting me," she said instead, husky. Ragged. "It's over."

"Yeah." A grunt of confirmation. "You made that

very clear when you knocked me out." Anger lashed across the feed. "How long did it take you to make that decision, Kayleigh?"

She squeezed her eyes shut. "Please, don't—"

"Was it spur of the moment?" he pressed on, over her, ignoring her protest. His voice was implacably tense, all but vibrating through the tiny mic clipped to the shell of her ear. "Or did you come up with the plan when I was fucking you on that table?"

Kayleigh's back straightened. "You did it first."

"So, that's how we're playing it. An eye for an eye?"

"No!" She practically growled the denial. "You wouldn't understand."

"Oh, yeah? Because way I *understand* it, honey, I was balls-deep in your body and all you wanted was—"

Her hands flattened against the table surface so fast, the sound cracked through the lab. Returned a flat echo. "Stop it!"

Silence filled the feed. Tense. Heavy.

Kayleigh held her breath, stared sightlessly at the scribbled notes between her fingers as the comm line crackled.

"Kayleigh—"

She flinched. "I don't—"

"Ask me how I am," Shawn said, but there was nothing sharp in the weary demand.

She licked her dry lips. "How . . . how are you?"

"Tired," he answered immediately. Quietly. "Confused. Torn."

A wild kernel of something warm and dangerous unfurled in her chest. "Torn?"

"You're a Lauderdale."

Was she? Kayleigh raised her gaze to the glowing

monitors in front of her, the ache in her throat intensifying as the words built, jumbled together.

"You're everything I swore I'd hate," he said roughly. "I don't sleep with people I hate, Kayleigh. Ever."

She closed her eyes.

"I . . ." A beat. A breath. "I don't blame you. My pride's stinging, but I don't blame you for doing to me what I did to you."

"I don't need your absolution," she whispered.

"I know." He hesitated, and this time, she swore his deep voice shook as he said, "I'm going to need yours."

What did that even mean?

"I just wanted you to know that," he finished, finality obvious on the frequency.

It didn't matter. In his eyes, she was a Lauderdale. How much of one only came down to blood and genes and logistics, but as far as Shawn was concerned—as far as he'd always care—she was raised by his enemy.

"Thank you for telling me." The ache carved a hole in her chest and threatened to leave her heart bloody and raw on the floor, but she couldn't let on. "If it's all the same to you—"

"Kayleigh."

Her hand jerked as she reached for the comm. "If it's all the same," she repeated louder, over his deep, rich voice. The way he said her name.

Like he might actually care.

"I have to go," she whispered. "I . . . There's work to do before I—" *Ruin whatever life I have left.* "I have to go."

"Remember this later. Promise me you'll remember what I said."

Pain lanced through her heart.

She squeezed her eyes shut again, forced them open to glare at the papers strewn across the table. "Don't contact me again, Shawn. This . . . It never happened."

Her finger hovered over the button that would disconnect the line. Froze.

For a long moment, he said nothing.

End it. Her hand shook, her stomach twisted.

Shawn took a slow breath. "That," he said, just as measured, "is where you're wrong."

The connection severed. Kayleigh looked down to find her nail embedded in the rim of the button, the unit silent and dark again.

Very slowly, she let go of the comm unit. It didn't vibrate again. Didn't chime or light up or any of the things she hadn't yet reprogrammed it not to do.

He didn't call back.

Numb, Kayleigh picked up her pencil, clicked the lead back into place, and returned to the puzzle in front of her.

This, at least, was quantifiable. Something she could fix. Figure out.

Work with.

With the pieces finally in place, she found the pattern. After forty-five minutes, she sat back. Tears filled her eyes—elation, fury, grief so profound, it filled that hole in her chest, drained it into her stomach where it burned like hell.

Her mother had been so brilliant.

So damned clever.

The liquid inside Parker's mysterious vial wasn't garbage. Not under the right circumstances.

She reached for her comm, keyed in her father's number, and let it ring. When it went to his mailbox, she did it again. And again.

Her shoulders drooped, eyes squeezing shut as her forehead settled against her scribbled notes.

The line clicked once. "Kayleigh, can this—"

"What else don't I know?" Her greeting, drained of everything that had ever been warm, scraped even her own nerves raw. "What else aren't you telling me?"

"Slow down, Kayleigh." Her father's voice, in comparison, hadn't changed. Thinned as it was by age and she could only imagine what kind of stress, it nevertheless carried a professional clip that told her he wasn't alone. "I'm very busy right now. The state of emergency—"

She flattened her free hand on the table, forced herself to sit upright. "The Eve sequence," she interrupted. "I have a lead."

The suddenness with which he changed tactics ripped another hole in her stomach. She hunched, hand shifting to her abdomen, as he ordered crisply, "Send it to me right away."

"I can't."

"Why not?" Irritation? Or impatience?

She stared at her notes, glanced at the three filled screens in front of her. "It's . . ." She tapped a few keys. The comm in her hand vibrated softly. "It's just data right now. I think it's viable, but I need a working test."

Background noise peppered the line as her father fell silent. Then, "We should discuss this in person."

"I think," Kayleigh said as she slowly slid from the stool, "that would be a really good idea."

"I'll have Patrick set up an appointment."

She almost said no. Almost demanded his attention now, this minute; but stomping her foot had never gotten her what she wanted. "All right," she agreed, digging the heel of her hand into her forehead. "We're going to have a lot to talk about, Dad."

In the grand scheme of things, she'd already waited thirty years for answers to questions she never knew she had. He would confess everything.

This time, she had all the cards.

She could wait a few more hours.

CHAPTER TWENTY

"**T**his is goddamned the dumbest thing we've ever done."

Shawn looked up into the dark, only vaguely picking out the soles of Simon's boots hanging above him. Black on black, the man was all but invisible as he scaled a cable.

On the ground, Silas Smith wrestled a taut cable into place, the muscles in his shoulders and arms bulging as the line jerked in his gloved hands. He watched Simon's progress up the cable carefully, square jaw thrust forward in intense concentration.

It was his deep baritone that grunted the words.

A muted glint of red on Shawn's left signaled Parker's shaking head. "That's saying a lot."

"Sorry, kids." Jonas's voice filtered to all of them, his easy tenor a welcome distraction from the grim cold settling over New Seattle. "If the sec-lines weren't locked down, this would be a lot easier."

"You're telling me," added a feminine voice that caused Silas's head to tilt faintly.

"Jessie, why are you on the line?"

"Someone had to keep an eye on the S-Team," she said brightly. Parker's chuckle turned into a poorly disguised cough. "Jonas has his hands full with the computer stuff, so I'm your bird's-eye view. Sort of. We're the J-Team!"

His eyes flicked to Shawn, exasperation underscoring the effort it took to keep Simon's cable from swinging.

Shawn shrugged, touching the mic on his ear to turn it and leave it transmitting. "Simon?"

"Fuck, already," the man gasped, clear on the comm line they all shared, but echoed faintly in stereo from above. The line wrenched to one side. "Not the . . . easiest thing . . ."

The amusement faded from Parker's expression, leaving her quiet and hunched against the autumn chill.

On the very edge of the city, on the tier just below the sec-lines, security was supposed to be nearly impossible to get through. At least, for normal people. The city had never counted on Jonas Stone, or the insanity of a couple of morons with a mission.

Nobody could expect some enterprising fools to scale the next tier up, and they didn't have the means to watch it happen with Jonas's electronic genius at work. The man had hacked into the system, blacked out a swath of the street they'd be climbing into, and redirected the security cameras.

All so they could go topside and murder a man. And, if they were lucky, find the data Kayleigh didn't know she had.

Shawn looked up, past the dark blot that was Simon's struggle. He hadn't been this high in the tiers for a long time. Without the sea of neon and lights speckling the canvas, he felt out of place. Lost.

Then again, maybe it wasn't his location.

Why had he called her?

That was a dumb question, and he knew it. Shawn liked her. Wanted her to reconsider everything, give up her life for him.

Just like that.

Could someone really *like* somebody so fast? No committee to talk it over with the rest of his thoughts? His goals?

A hand touched his arm. His head jerked up, furrowed eyebrows deepening to find Parker watching him with shadowed concern. "Are you okay?"

Silas grunted as the rope twanged hard.

Shawn's attention slid to him, ready to offer an additional grip if needed, but the cable steadied. "Fine," he said abruptly.

Her eyes, bleached of color in the near-dark, narrowed a fraction. A smile, all but invisible. "You seem torn."

Torn. Exactly the word he'd used with Kayleigh.

But he didn't have to be, did he? She'd made her choice. Work, the Salem Project.

Her father.

She'd turned him down. "No, I'm fine."

"You're worried about Kayleigh." Her pronouncement set his teeth on edge.

"I'm nearly at the top," Simon declared on the line.

Hyper-conscious of Silas's straining presence only a few feet away, of the ears on the frequency, Shawn jammed his gloved hands into his jeans pockets, shivering some as the cooler air up here ghosted across his nape. "I don't have to worry about Dr. Lauderdale."

Parker, her arms folded across her flak vest to conserve her own heat, tipped her face up to the night. To Simon, now invisible as he crested the top. "She's . . . complicated."

"She's an adult," Shawn countered evenly.

"Sort of."

Yeah, and wasn't that the sticking point? He withdrew his hands, tugging his gloves up on his wrist. "Look, whatever you're getting at, I don't really care." Another lie. He was pretty good at those.

He'd have to be. This was the way it needed to be.

"Parker," Silas rumbled. "Next."

"You're all so damned tough, aren't you?" The whole observation came on a sigh. Shaking her head, she passed Shawn, tightening her own gloves. "Take it from me, Mr. Lowe. Life is short." As Silas recoiled the cable around his wrist, pulling it taut, she grabbed the line in one hand, glanced over her shoulder.

Something bleak and haunted filled her eyes. Shaped her shadowed features, carving black lines in the dark.

"Too short to play games," she added.

Shawn looked away.

"Got it?" Silas asked, offering a hand as a step-up. Parker placed her booted foot in them, caught the cable as he boosted her up with one powerful lift of one arm.

"Come up nice and slow, sweetheart." Simon's encouragement.

Parker's huff, almost a laugh, as she shimmied up

the rope. "I aced . . . climbing . . . in training, Agent Wells. Save your . . . pity."

Despite his worries, his lies—the sinking sensation deep in his gut that he'd fucked up everything without even knowing quite how—a smile tugged at the corners of his mouth.

Silas only shook his head, a gesture he watched the big man do often.

Resignation? Or, as Shawn was beginning to suspect, a strange sense of balance with the world and his place in it.

It took Parker less time than it had taken Simon to scale the distance. Another sign of Simon's failing health.

Shit.

"You're up," Silas told him, a deep note in the dark. "Ready?"

No. Maybe not as ready as he thought.

"It's none of my business," Silas continued slowly when Shawn didn't move. "But I've seen things that some would call evil. Seen some good people make damned poor choices." The man shifted his weight, awkward. Suddenly uncertain. "Don't know Kayleigh. Don't much like the situation. But she seems like someone stuck."

"Stuck?"

"Yeah." He shrugged, the outline of his hand slashing through the air. "Make the best of what you've got, right? Seems like she's done just that."

Two men standing in the dark, this close to a heart-to-heart. About Kayleigh fucking Lauderdale. Jesus Christ.

Setting his jaw, Shawn sidled around Silas's broad shoulders, flexed his fingers around the cable. "If she's so stuck," he found himself saying, "then why the hell didn't she get out while she could?"

Silas's answering sound, a wordless reverberation, turned into a matter-of-fact "Maybe she didn't know it was an option."

Maybe Shawn hadn't made it clear enough.

"Or," Silas added, "maybe by the time it came around, she was already trapped."

Hell.

Too late now. Way too late. A team of resistance fighters infiltrating topside to murder her father?

Yeah. That boat had sailed.

He rolled his shoulders. "Let's get this done."

Silas said nothing.

Of all four sides of the Holy Order's quad, the cathedral was the quietest. At its max capacity, Kayleigh suspected it could hold the entire topside population in all its wings, foyers, and pews, and as a landmark, it stood as the highest, brightest beacon of New Seattle.

Aside from Sunday Mass, it rarely held more than a few clergy at any given time. Although press conferences were often held on the Holy Cathedral's steps for the backdrop, the press were forbidden to operate within its walls. At the bishop's orders, the interior was to provide a sanctuary of peace and safety.

Or so it was reputed.

To Kayleigh, the vaulted ceilings and ornate interiors echoed hollowly with her footsteps, magnified every whisper. Angels, cherubs, and Jesus Christ looked down from a vaunted place on high, beautiful glass windows set into the ceiling, but it wasn't the

Son of God's likeness that held the most prominent positions.

St. Dominic watched all from every corner, every pedestal and window and icon. Where cherubs clustered, there he waited. Where angels heralded, he stood and listened. He watched everything, heard everything. Gold and marble and polished wood—prohibitively expensive since the fall.

The cathedral had always been opulent. Normally, it didn't bother her. She barely noticed when she came for Mass.

Tonight, as she made her way through the nave and passed under the watchful eyes of St. Dominic's marble likeness, she felt exposed. Raw.

A heretic on hallowed ground.

She clutched her digital reader to her chest. "Dad?"

"In here!" The cathedral took her voice, his, threw them around until they whispered eerily in a loop. Repressing a shudder, Kayleigh hurried across the nave, rounded the marble statue.

The cathedral proper unfolded in front of her. No light shone through the large window arrayed into the wall, but it didn't need it. Even without the unearthly glow the stained glass picked up, it was a stern piece. Violent crimsons and regal blues, an expensive, detailed accounting of St. Dominic at the height of his life.

The inquisitor.

When full, the cathedral was impressive. Empty, and it became intimidating. The lights were kept low, lamps affixed to the corners and arrayed at key points to offer visibility without glare.

A soft, muted corona hovered around each.

Her father stood in front of the massive altar where the bishop had often stood, his hands clasped behind him as he studied the choir balcony overhead. He looked so frail on the carpeted steps, a tiny, stooped figure only a breath away from collapse.

Kayleigh's heart lurched. The edges of the lights brightened as the nimbus increased.

She waited for the pain to hit, the headache that would accompany her ocular warnings. So far, only her vision flared. She had time.

He didn't turn as she approached, though her footfalls—stifled by the lush crimson carpet—announced her arrival. "Why are we meeting here?" she asked.

"Ah, Kayleigh." Her father's mottled head gleamed beneath the cobweb-fine fringe of white hair clinging to his scalp. "Right on time, as always."

Faint praise. She climbed the stairs, but hesitated before clearing the altar landing. "Dad, what happened to Bishop Applegate?"

His thin shoulders stiffened. "Why?" When he turned, his expression was sad, thin mouth set in a resigned slant. "Will you repeat the things the media has spun?"

"What things?" She frowned. "What are they saying? I've only been hearing news about the earthquake."

"News," he muttered. "Like that will help them."

"Dad?"

His pale eyes focused on her again. Exhaustion telegraphed through every brittle line of his body as he sagged. "Don't mind me, sweetheart. It's been a trying few days." He didn't reach for her—but then, Laurence Lauderdale had never been one for casual affection. Instead, he stepped off the landing. Wobbled enough that she offered a hand, which he took in obvious gratitude. "Bishop Applegate had an accident. Investigators are still trying to put it together."

Carefully, step by step, she steadied her father as he made his way to the cathedral floor. "That's terrible."

And . . . and very hard to swallow.

A sudden accident? *Sudden?* Just in time for everything else?

"Unfortunately, we're all too busy with the earthquakes," he continued once he straightened his suit jacket. The smile he gave her, perfunctory but not unkind, sobered as his gaze landed on the reader in the crook of her arm. "Is that the Eve data?"

She looked down at it. Her arm tightened across the frame. "Yes."

"Good, we'll need it."

Yes. She knew that much. "Dad, I need to ask you something."

His bushy white eyebrows rose. "Speak plainly, Kayleigh, we need to leave quickly."

"Then you need to be straight with me." Plain was the only way she could frame it. It came out on a rush. "Did my mother really die when I was eight?"

Those eyebrows fell. Knotted. For a moment, Kayleigh wondered if she saw impatience under his wrinkled, so familiar features, but when he sighed, shoulders rounding, all she read was dismay. "I knew you'd ask me this one day."

He will lie.

She raised her fingers to her temple, wincing as that haze reached out. Enfolded her father. Her own skin. Conflicting thoughts sparked.

He has no choice but to tell the truth.

Two paths. Choices laid out before someone.

Was this what her mother had seen?

"Your mother . . ." His nostrils, large in his aquiline nose, flared. "Your mother left us, Kayleigh." When her mouth fell open, he added quickly, "It wasn't anything you did, never think that. She had so much talent, she was so brilliant. You're like her in so many ways, but she couldn't . . ."

Kayleigh looked down at her reader. The data she'd stored there, the backups she'd made, made it feel as if it weighed a thousand pounds. "Mom found the Eve sequence, didn't she?"

"I don't know." Honesty, there. She'd stake her life on it. "I do know that she engineered the fracture."

"But why?"

He sighed deeply. "I ask myself that every day, sweetheart. Our vision was so closely aligned for decades. And then I caught her . . . dabbling." Pain filled his eyes. Bent his old, fragile body until he seemed breakable as glass. "I should have known when she took active interest. She'd always loved me, I know it, but we were older already. And then she . . ."

She watched him struggle with the words, for the first time in her memory watched her father fail to find them.

Her throat dry, tongue thick with fear, she whispered, "Was mom a witch?"

He went still. "Why do you ask?"

"Because I saw my charts, Dad."

"Ah." Another pained sound, almost a sigh. "I'd hoped to spare you that knowledge, too."

Kayleigh took a step backward, anger welling. Fighting for purchase beside hope. Terrible, painful hope. "So you didn't mean to lie to me?"

"Not a lie," he corrected, stern reprimand creeping into his features. His shoulders straightened as much as they could, finger thrust at her. "You had the allele, like your mother, but you displayed no talents beyond your intelligence."

"All witches have the allele," she pointed out, struggling for calm. Rational. "Abilities are inevitable."

"All witches have the allele," her father said, a smile pulling at his mouth, creasing his eyes, "yet not all those who have the allele are witches."

"That . . ." Kayleigh looked down at her reader. "Dad, that flies in the face of everything we ever taught people."

"It needed to be taught."

"At what cost?" She looked up, stricken. "How many innocent people were sent to the fires for having the gene?"

"They aren't important!" He turned, faced her directly. "Please understand, sweetheart," he pleaded, "I wanted to spare you the humiliation of a witch's stigma. I didn't dare let the Church get its hand on you. Your mother . . . Hiding her abilities was easy. She saw people, saw what they were capable of. God only knew how it'd manifest in you."

"But it didn't."

His thin, wrinkled lips vanished beneath a grim frown. "Until now. I know, sweetheart. I suspected it with your first collapse."

"You knew?" Kayleigh flinched. "And you didn't tell me! You let me wonder what was wrong?" Her father said nothing. She took a deep breath. Facts. She needed the answers. "What changed? Why now?"

"Your mother died several months ago," he admitted, simply. As if it were only a detail. "Simon made sure of that."

"Simon?" Kayleigh sucked in a hard breath, choked

on it as too many words surged to her throat. "Simon killed her? But he—"

Her father's eyes, mirror to hers, turned flinty.

She paused, stared. Then, slowly, so slowly as her lips shaped every word with unraveling care, she whispered, "Simon . . . worked for you. Dad?" She couldn't avoid the question. Couldn't not ask. "Did you . . . ? Did you find her without telling me? Did you kill her? Did you send her own blood to kill her?"

A lie will destroy everything.

"Dad? Did you kill Mom?"

It welled up in her. Something heavy, thick like cobwebs clinging to her skin, weighing her thoughts. As she watched, the shape of her father split into two, superimposed on top of one another.

One crumpled, apology wrenched from his lips, sobs in his thin chest.

The other let out a hard breath, a long-fingered, frail hand curving over his eyes. "I had wondered if your mother's death might have caused a subsequent reaction."

She shook her head, uncomprehending even as that first image reached out a frail, trembling hand. "I don't . . . What's going on, Dad?"

He lowered his hand, eyes flinty, now. Cold. "Science finds a way." *Life finds a way*, Jessie had said. So simply. "With Matilda's death, her powers somehow transferred to you. I intend to study how. Patrick."

"Sir." The voice came from behind her.

"Escort my daughter to safety." The sobbing man faded, leaving only one version of her father behind. He turned his back.

Fingers wrapped around her upper arm, jarring her out of her reverie. "Dad!"

Another arm, clad in designer business wear, reached past her face. Kayleigh's eyes widened as a rectangular box, colored wire twisted into place from every corner and merged beneath a simple plastic cap, skated past her vision. "The device is ready to go at any time."

A figure in Mission black armor beckoned from the far door.

"What is that?" When he took the device from Patrick, ignored her, Kayleigh took a step forward. The hand at her arm tightened. "Dad, is that a bomb?"

"Don't be ridiculous. It's merely a switch."

A switch. She cringed. "Dad, what are you doing?"

He smiled without looking at her. "What we've always done, sweetheart. We're making a better world."

Patrick pulled her back down the aisle.

"Dad!"

CHAPTER TWENTY-ONE

Getting up to the Holy Order quadplex turned out to be easier when Jonas could control the outside security. Inside was a whole other matter. Everything the quad pulled from was on a closed circuit, which meant Jonas needed juice.

Shawn followed Parker, admiration for her growing as she made her way through the blackened portion of the Mission building. Most of the debris had been cleared, and aside from the occasional mutter as she worked out the altered floor plan, she led confidently and without excuses.

When they found a panel covered in thick plastic, it was the work of moments to pull it off, power up the machine, and follow Jonas's explicit instructions.

It took ten minutes, but as Parker signed off the cracked account, Jonas's breathed "*Yes*" reeked of success. "Give me five minutes to tap into the cameras."

"Think this will work?"

Shawn shrugged at Simon. "If he's half as good as May believes, he'll make it work."

Parker kept her gaze on her watch, coolly marking the time.

At three minutes, the line crackled. "You want the cathedral," Jonas said, urgency thick in the feed. "Go!"

"There's a connected corridor," Parker said without missing a beat, and Simon added, "I know where it is."

They sprinted through halls that showed little wear, each pulling a gun in case they ran into trouble.

When they ran into trouble.

The weight of Shawn's borrowed Beretta was much lighter than his usual weapon of choice, but it fired bullets and he couldn't complain. Without taking a five-man excavation team back into the ruins, he'd have to make do.

They ducked into open, cubicle-staggered offices where the signs of fire damage and violence colored the walls. Bullet holes riddled plaster stained brown. Parker's features frosted over.

"The quad is full of people," Jonas said, keys rattling and clicking behind his report. "Most are employees, they don't seem to be focused on anything else but their errands."

"Good," Shawn said. Fewer people around, the better.

"No one's idling, anyway," Simon added.

"You all right, Simon?"

"Fuck off," the man muttered, and Jonas shut up.

Within a few minutes, Parker pushed open a double-wide door, eased into a narrow hall, and vanished around the corner.

Shawn followed, blinking as the Holy Cathedral of St. Dominic unfolded in front of him.

The place was massive. Larger than anyplace he'd ever seen.

"One to the left," Simon muttered, "two across the way. Four waiting in the quad." The words slurred, as if he had trouble remembering to enunciate. "About twenty beyond."

"Simon," Parker murmured.

"*Go.*"

The mission was more important.

They fanned into the cathedral proper.

Color splashed from every direction, crimson and blue and mellow gold, but Shawn didn't have the luxury to care about art. All he saw was Kayleigh, fighting as a thin man in designer clothing dragged her through a far door.

Every muscle tensed; violence turned every nerve into a throbbing well of fury.

"Easy," Silas rumbled quietly.

"Fuck easy," Shawn snarled, and stalked out into the open. He leveled his weapon on the old man at the base of the altar steps, finger tight to the trigger. "Call them off her!"

Kayleigh gasped, her eyes widening as she saw Shawn first, then the group behind him. She thrashed in earnest, grabbed the door frame to scream, "A bomb!" It echoed, lashed back in the vast emptiness of the cathedral. "There's a bomb— *Let me go.*" She vanished through the door, a man's curse following.

Laurence Lauderdale turned slowly, awkwardly as if the motion pained him. White hair drifting around his thin scalp, he tilted his head at the group, bemused.

Rage tightened to a narrow tunnel of hatred so intense, it raked venomous claws through Shawn's stomach. His chest.

This was what he'd waited for. Sixteen years, *right here.*

Silas pushed past him. "On it," was all he said.

"We'll take them," Parker said, flanking Shawn. Her mouth was a thin, white line, her eyes chips of ice. "Handle Lauderdale."

"With fucking pleasure." Simon strode across the crimson carpet bisecting the aisle, his gaze on the old man, gun lowered at his side. "What are you up to, old man?"

"Simon." The old man's voice quavered.

"Get the location of that bomb," Jonas ordered. "Is there anyone around?"

"Just him," Shawn replied.

"Be careful, he's a wily bastard."

"Simon's got him engaged," Shawn said quietly, but his attention only half focused on the plan. On the order.

The man he'd come to murder, the monster, had changed. Stooped and gnarled, he was almost unrecognizable compared to the suited man who'd knocked on Shawn's door that day. He'd been a distinguished man sixteen years ago, standing straight and polished and so untouchable. Confident as he'd spoken with Shawn's father.

Pitiless as he'd watched his people gun Shawn's family down.

"Hey." Simon's acknowledgment cut like glass. *"Dad."*

Shawn's gaze jerked to Simon. *Dad?* That made him . . .

Kayleigh's brother?

And here Shawn thought his was a screwed-up family dynamic.

Why didn't she tell him Simon was her brother? Why didn't she trust him enough to confide?

Stupid questions. He never gave her the option. Never pretended he had any plans for the future.

Lauderdale smiled, wry and grim all at the same time. Hands tucked behind him, he let his chin droop. "So, that's the way of it, then. I wondered if you were mine as much as hers."

"Don't tell me you didn't know," Simon growled.

"I'm sorry to say I didn't. Not that it changes anything." Eyes the same color as Kayleigh's, vivid even across the dimly lit cathedral, turned to Shawn. "I see you've made friends."

Behind them, Silas ran across a pew, surprisingly light-footed for such a large body. Parker was already gone.

Kayleigh would be rescued. She wasn't his problem. She wasn't his plan.

Had never been part of it for longer than it took to get his hands around her father's throat.

His fist clenched as the door closed behind Silas.

His guts churned, dread building into bile. He couldn't abandon this, everything, now. Not for a woman. Not even for her. She'd have to understand

She never will.

So be it.

He strode around the central pedestal, gun lowering to his side as he glared at the wrecked old man watching them both with weary eyes. "You have nowhere to run," he warned. "So you may as well tell us everything."

Simon's laugh was rough, gummy. "Start off with the location of that bomb."

"Hm?" The man tilted his spotted head. "Which one?"

"Guys!" Jonas's voice cracked through the mic in his ear. "That place is *wired*. I'm tracing the source, but it's— Did he say 'which one'?"

Another line clicked into place. "I'll *look*," Jessie announced, emphasis on the word.

"Jessie, *don't you*—" Gunfire cut Silas off mid-order, and Shawn jerked his head as the sound left his ear pulsing. "Be careful, damn it!"

Simon glanced back at Shawn, a sidelong frown over his shoulder. Something red and viscous gleamed at his upper lip, smeared over his forearm as he dragged his sleeve across it. Blood, thin and watery, and tinged with too much yellow to be healthy. "There's a shit ton of people fleeing the gunfire," he warned. His eyes seemed cloudy, shoulders jerking as if he fought to stay upright. "We need to move fast."

Could they move fast enough?

"Why the hell are you wiring this place up?" he demanded of the old man. "What's your angle?"

"Because there is no room for it in the future," Lauderdale replied as if he answered a simpler, more obvious question.

"That doesn't answer anything."

"Doesn't it?" He smiled faintly. "It's a symbol, this place. A beacon of hope and stability. That's why it has to go."

That made no sense. "You're going to blow up your own—"

Lauderdale shifted, one hand coming up in a sudden arc.

Every alarm in his brain clanged at once. Shawn's head jerked to the side, eyes widening. "Simon, get—"

The warning died as a gunshot tore through the cathedral air, slammed wall to wall, built on a sea of echoes. They drilled through his eardrums, left them ringing.

Simon, caught half turning, staggered.

"What happened?" Jonas's demand, peppered by a terse, strained echo from Parker.

The smell of gunpowder wafted across the cathedral. Sweat bloomed across Shawn's forehead, his shoulders, dampened his palms as he watched Simon topple to the ground. The pungent metallic odor of blood followed.

Lauderdale stepped back onto the altar steps, holding up a narrow black box in one hand as the other dropped his weapon. It thunked as it hit the carpeted stairs, a hollow sound mirroring the dull *thud* of Shawn's heartbeat.

Rage seized his throat. "You never had problems pulling the trigger, did you?"

"Shawn?" Parker's voice, cracking faintly under the strain he imagined she must be feeling. "Simon!"

The old man stood silently for a moment, his gaze fixed on Simon's still body. Then, thoughtfully, "You could have shot me, boy. What's stopping you?"

The taunt, matter-of-fact as it was, plinked something dark and ugly in his brain.

The line crackled faintly, as if interference hovered just on the edge of the channel. "What happened?" Jonas demanded.

Fingers shaking, he reached up, depressed the tiny button on the mic. The line went dead. "That was your son!" he snarled.

There was no answering emotion in the old man's wizened regard. "Will you shoot me for it, Shawn

Lowe?" At his name on the bastard's lips, Shawn jerked, guts twisting. Nausea filled his belly, bile in his throat. "Oh, yes," he added, almost a sigh as he held that switch between them. "I remember you now."

The observation burned like acid.

"Why shoot him?" Shawn demanded. "What was the point?"

"Failures come around." Lauderdale glanced at the still, sallow figure at Shawn's feet, and his eyebrows twitched. "He would have died anyway, you know. There's no stopping degeneration. Not yet, anyway. I did him a service."

"Is that your excuse?" Shawn gritted out between his teeth, "Is that why you killed my parents? A *service*?"

Lauderdale waved the switch in front of him in denial. "I pulled no triggers. Your parents overreacted. I am not responsible for that!"

"Overreacted," Shawn spat. "*You* killed them! And it ends here. Now."

Lauderdale's face tipped to the ceiling, but if he studied the art painted there or saw something else in his old brain, Shawn couldn't tell. Didn't care.

This man had murdered his family, and he would pay. *And so would Kayleigh.*

His finger jerked against the trigger. Stilled. His teeth gritted so hard, the joints in his jaw popped loudly.

It's not about her. It never was. Not for one second did he think—

"What about Kayleigh?"

His heart hit the back of his throat and lodged there. "She has nothing to do with this!"

Lauderdale watched him, a shrewd half smile on his

thin lips. "Ah. You can always tell when a man goes soft." He raised his free hand, rubbed it over his balding head. Awkward. Impatient. "Knowing what you know of my daughter," he continued, rational to the bone, "will you shoot me, son?"

"Don't call me that."

Again, that gaze settled on Simon. Blood darkened the carpet, turned red fibers nearly black under Shawn's boots.

When the man shrugged, stooped shoulders rolling with it, he said, "Shoot me, then. I will be beyond caring." He flipped the cap off the box he held, thumb nestling on the trigger. "What you young people don't and have never understood is that it isn't about me. It's never been about *me*. This city will fall, and when the dust is settled, they'll come together again. The way they used to. The way they *should*."

"You're crazy!"

The man shrugged again. The motion jerked, as if being upright pained him. "I have been called worse by better men."

Shawn wanted to kneel and check Simon's throat for a pulse. He wanted to pull the trigger, damn the switch and the bomb and Kayleigh . . .

He couldn't damn Kayleigh.

Shawn eased one step closer to Simon. His skin was pale, clammy, everything too still. No breath that he could see at a glance. No sound.

Shit. *Shit*.

"Where are the bombs?" he demanded grimly.

"Out of your reach," Lauderdale assured him. "Even if I told you, you'd never make it in time."

"This cathedral isn't that big."

The old man's laughter was dry as brittle bone. "It

doesn't stop there, my boy. It has never stopped at the Church. You're too young to understand what I saw back then. How the people came together, how they helped one another."

Shawn squeezed his eyes shut. "At least tell me why you went after my father. Why the warrant?"

"I don't really recall," Lauderdale said promptly, and Shawn snarled a word that earned a brief frown. "All of you street people are the same, aren't you?"

He ignored that. "You're lying."

"My dear boy," Lauderdale said as he cradled the switch between gnarled hands, thumb firmly in place. "Why would I bother lying? To be honest, there were a lot of reasons I could think of off the top of my head— employment opportunities, medical necessity, even simple interrogation. But I think the likeliest is . . ." He hummed a wavering note. "This was fifteen years ago?"

"Sixteen."

"Ah." As if it all made sense, he nodded. "The chances are good that his was one of the records selected from the medical files."

Shawn's gun lowered a fraction. "Selected? Selected for what?"

"Back then, I had all medical records sent through filters," Lauderdale explained, pleasant for all he stood on a church altar with a bomb switch in his hands. "Your father's genetic sequence was ideal for the Salem purposes."

He knew it. He'd known it then—suspected something to do with that fucking witch factory—and now, confirmed, he stepped forward. "Is there anything in this city you haven't corrupted?"

"Me?" He raised the switch, brandished it. "I've corrupted nothing! I've watched this city crumble bit by bit, cowed under Church rule and drowning in its own poison."

Gun firm again, Shawn bared his teeth. "Bullshit," he snarled. "Your family is no more than a collection of butchers." *Unfair*, his heart argued.

The demon in him didn't care. It hungered for blood, demanded justice. Vengeance.

"My family? You mean Kayleigh." Her name earned another punch in Shawn's chest, a reminder of everything he stood to lose.

Had lost already.

Lauderdale shook his head, smile slipping. "No. Kayleigh is brilliant, but she lacks the . . . stomach. The will, you understand. I couldn't tell her my plans."

Kayleigh? Lacking will? Shawn scoffed, rage banking enough to recognize that bullshit for what it was.

"We did things differently back then," Lauderdale admitted. "Still would, if I had the right help. Mattie understood, at first. Saw the light at the end of the tunnel." He winced. "Before the tunnel grew too long and the ground too . . . *cluttered*. No, Kayleigh doesn't know where the lab came from. How we operated. Maybe I shouldn't have coddled her."

"Coddled?" Shawn flung his free hand at the cathedral around them. "You call this *coddling*? You planted a bomb!"

"No." Surprise laced the reply. And regret. "This is . . . necessary." The man gestured with the box, and the sweat on Shawn's shoulders turned to ice. "This . . . this cathedral is an afterthought. A stain. We won't need mementos of the Church when this is over, don't you see? It's not about you or me or religion anymore! It never was. It's for *them*. For the people! The same people you claim to fight for."

Shawn closed his eyes. Took a slow, deep breath, and raised the gun.

This is the way it has to be.

"This is the end of the road," he announced, his voice rebounding back at him from every direction. "Tell us where all the bombs are, and—"

"And what? You shall have me tried?" Lauderdale studied him for a long moment. Ignored the weapon, the threat. "There is no force that can try me now. Everything I have done, I've done for the betterment of this city."

Such bullshit.

"I regret nothing." When his eyes flicked aside, focused on something behind Shawn—ghosts or God only knew—he nodded. "Good genes," he finally said, as if to himself. "I always knew it. My Mattie had a flair for the dramatic, but nobody could see it like she could." He turned his back, head tilting up as he studied the face of the red-robed figure set into stained glass.

"Hit that switch," Shawn warned, "and you're a dead man."

One hand, the hand with the black box, edged out from his side. "My dear boy, I have been dying for years." His thumb moved.

Shawn's heart stalled.

As the world tunneled to a single moment, he pulled the trigger. Two gunshots cracked in the silence.

CHAPTER TWENTY-TWO

A third operative hit the ground, wheezing through his cracked faceplate. Parker lowered her gun, her face pale in the quad lights as she raked a stern eye over the huddled mass of bystanders hovering at the fringe.

Kayleigh stared at the carnage. Three agents down, one—a petite figure going hand to hand with the much larger Silas—showing signs of wear.

She took a step forward.

Parker's arm came up, blocking her. "Stay out of sight," she ordered, in the same cool tones Kayleigh had always earned from the Mission director.

She raised one hand, wrapped her fingers around Parker's wrist. They shook. "I didn't know," she said intently, staring at the scattered, cowering crowd. Some were on comms. Calling for help, maybe. "Parker." A beat. "Director Ad—"

The woman's shoulders didn't relax under the synth-leather jacket she wore—the same style she'd seen on Silas, on Shawn. But her eyes, always so cold, softened. Gently, she disengaged her wrist. "It's Parker," she said, and if it wasn't the warmest thing, it didn't freeze, either. "And I believe you. Mostly."

Silas shifted as a boot cracked against his knee. He grimaced, caught the agent by the throat, and lifted her.

Kayleigh winced as he slammed her against the cathedral wall, once. Twice. Plastic fractured.

The crowd gasped.

Parker glowered at them. "Go home," she ordered, every word an arctic command.

Some turned. Others stared.

One, a woman in crisp business attire, frowned. "Weren't those Church agents—"

Kayleigh caught Parker's shoulder as the ex-missionary's grip shifted on her gun. The pale quality of her cheeks turned sallow.

The director had never liked blood. That she was willing to spill it now told Kayleigh everything she needed to know about the importance of their mission.

"Everyone, leave the area," Kayleigh ordered, less chilly, but she knew how to wield her reputation. Parker may have been the famed ice bitch of the Mission, but *she* was a Lauderdale.

Some nearly sprinted. Others took their time, but some people just wanted a show. She had no time for it.

"Some of them called for the riot force," Kayleigh warned, turning back to the red-haired woman. Soldier, really. The difference was astounding after only three weeks.

Parker nodded once. "Silas, wrap it up!"

He grunted. When the agent's hand came up, a trick Kayleigh had seen her do already in this fight, he wrapped his fingers around it. Kept her from using the magic that had stopped Kayleigh in her tracks with sheer kinetic strength. Silas squeezed until the witch cried out, sharp even through the spiderwebbed face-plate covering her features.

"Give up," he growled.

Suddenly, Parker stiffened. She raised her fingers to her ear, tendrils of red sliding over them as she turned swiftly. "What do you mean? Where's Simon?"

At the same time, Silas spun, giving his back to the crumpled agent. "Get away from the wall!" he roared.

Parker was already grabbing Kayleigh's arm, wrenched her off the paved walkway and into the scrub bushes planted beside it.

Her heart surged into her throat. "What . . . Where's—"

She had no chance to finish.

A clap of thunder echoed from somewhere nearby. Within a nanosecond, a shudder vibrated the quad ground. Kayleigh hit the dirt, Parker half sprawled on top of her.

The next instant hit like a shock wave.

It tore through the air, ripped apart everything in its path. Parker's body rocked, lifted half off Kayleigh's shoulder, and she cringed as a sheet of red whipped over her face. The world spun, heat licked over her exposed skin, seared everything it could reach. The ground shook and rocked, screams punctuated a ter-rible rumble, cracking stone and shattered glass.

Kayleigh covered her head, squeezing her eyes closed, and prayed.

It couldn't end like this. Nothing was resolved.

All the things she'd meant to say, all the truths she needed to know, hadn't seen daylight yet. She needed them to see daylight.

An arm curled around her shoulders, flattened over her as the rumbling faded, as abruptly as it came.

The screaming didn't stop.

Kayleigh opened an eye. Opened both, and flinched as dust turned seeing anything into a gritty ordeal. Half over her, Parker hacked out a lung full of plaster and obliterated stone, blood gleaming at her temple. "Where's Simon?" she croaked, probably into the comm they were all wired into.

"What happened?" Kayleigh struggled to sit as Parker, splayed awkwardly and cradling one arm to her chest, stared blankly. What little color had burned into her face, soot and dirt and the flush of heat drained.

Over the woman's shoulder, desolation settled.

"Oh—" *Oh, God. No.* The words congealed in Kayleigh's chest. The prayer, unspoken.

That heavy weight in her head slammed into place around her, pushed thick fingers through her reality.

The cathedral lay in ruins.

The walls, no longer recognizable, had buckled, folded in under the weight of the roof above it. Half of Jesus Christ's face gazed solemnly out over the destruction, glass gleamed under the few lights that had survived the blast.

Chunks of stone teetered, splintered remnants of pews and crosses and marble statues fanned in a wide arc, carried on the blast.

Kayleigh's hands shook as she scrambled to her knees.

"Simon." Parker's whisper scored ragged furrows

across Kayleigh's heart. Sank into the bruised and battered flesh. "Simon, check in!"

Her vision crossed. Parker doubled, but before Kayleigh could see either—bleeding grief into her own skin and shaking so badly that she couldn't even see straight enough to focus on either figure—she reached out. Caught Parker by the shoulders and pulled her into a hard embrace.

She's pregnant.

The thought slammed into her skull with the certainty she was coming to understand meant truth. Real truth, the possibility of it and the paths leading to it.

She'll lose the baby.

The woman in her arms trembled, eyes closed, but her hand fisted in the back of Kayleigh's splinter-studded sweater.

"We have to—" Her voice broke.

She had to do something.

Kayleigh took a deep breath. "We have to pull the injured away," she said crisply. "Set up a triage just by the—the wreckage."

Parker let her go. Stepped away. "Silas!"

A rumble, hard to hear through the sound of people sobbing, crying, must have translated in Parker's comm because the woman nodded.

Very calmly, she plucked a small device from her ear, picked up Kayleigh's filthy hand, and pressed it into her palm. Saying nothing, she turned away.

The woman made it six feet before she dropped to her knees in the bushes and retched.

Kayleigh fastened the mic to her ear. "H-hello?"

"Kayleigh?" Silas's deep baritone. "Where's Parker? Is she hurt?"

"Throwing up," she whispered. As she wanted to. "We need medical people as soon as possible."

She surveyed the damage, the carnage of the cathedral. Blocks tilted sideways, slabs of stone hanging precariously. Injured sprawled where they'd been thrown, some huddled, others standing, shock glazed in their eyes.

Every sparking light slammed a halo into place. Her vision went spotty.

"Get to the south side of the cathedral," came an order, an unfamiliar voice with the crystal clarity of true tonal quality. "Silas, move your ass, big man, I need a pickup!"

Her heart seized.

"On it," Silas said, and she saw his large silhouette across the dusty span of what had once been the cathedral steps.

She moved as if in a trance. "I . . . There's people . . . They're hurt."

"We've called a team," the man said, firm but not unkind. "Kayleigh, my name is Jonas. Is Parker hurt?"

"Shock," Kayleigh said, as if from a distance. "She's in shock. She needs help before . . ."

"Doctor!"

Silas's call roared across the quad, echoed in the comm. Her head jerked up. She flinched, already ducking just in case something else might come out of the rubble and attack her.

Too much. She'd already lost everything, what else— *Parker's baby would grow strong.*

"I need your hands!"

How? What path could possibly exist to allow the

woman to survive the shock Kayleigh herself couldn't remember how to breathe in?

"Okay, Kayleigh?" Jonas's voice. Calm. Forced, but even. "I've seen you at work, I need you to pull it together and go help him."

Her fingers curled into fists.

"People are trapped, Kayleigh. They need you."

Taking a deep breath, she scrambled over a mound of rock and stone, barely flinched when the sharp edge sliced her palm. "I'm here. What—"

Silas's shoulders twisted. A large slab of painted plaster teetered and fell over, and he cursed when the stone beneath it failed to move. The once beautiful fresco turned to shards of color and scorched black at his feet.

Sticking his fingers into a crack, he planted his boots, squared up, and pulled with all his might.

Tendons stuck out in his neck. His shoulders bulged, arms cording with effort. His growl turned into a strained groan, and the slab shifted.

Kayleigh hurried forward just as the whole piece snapped with the effort, broke at a seam, and teetered outward. Silas staggered out of the way and coughed as dust exploded into a gray-brown haze.

She flinched, choking on the particles and waving her hands in front of her face.

A stooped silhouette limped from the ruin.

Kayleigh's world ceased to exist. Her vision snapped back into place, halos gone.

As the dust billowed around them, as the shattered lights hissed and buzzed and flickered on and off, the silhouette turned into two.

"Dad . . . ?"

He stepped out of the cloud. Blood matted one side of his face, his hair was practically gray with plaster, his jacket shredded, soot and grime coating everything that was left.

Her heart, shriveled for days, wrenched. "Shawn!"

"Thank God," Jonas breathed.

Supporting Simon's arm over his shoulder, he half dragged the staggering man with him. Forced him to move, to keep upright despite the blood painting his worn T-shirt black.

Her fisted hands clenched at her stomach as they cleared the hole.

The dust swirled.

No one else came out.

Kayleigh swallowed hard as brittle brown eyes met hers from a mask of blood and dirt.

The comm in her ear clicked to life. "Get out." Jessie's voice, barely recognizable as it slanted high and shrill. "Get out, *get out from under cover.* The bomb's in the Old Sea-Trench—Oh, God, right now, everyone!"

Silas didn't even stop to ask. As Kayleigh shook her head, confused, he roared, "Go!" and grabbed Simon's free arm. With inhuman strength, he pulled the half-conscious man across his shoulders, shoved Shawn out of the wreckage.

Kayleigh caught him as he staggered, wobbled when his full weight collapsed on her shoulders.

His breath expelled over her face, surprise and pain.

"Parker!" Silas yelled. "Move it!"

A muted sound cut through the lingering litany of groans, cries. Questions. Like thunder, but much weaker than the terrible blast that pulled down the cathedral.

It echoed for a moment, muffled and deep.

Shawn clung to her, agony and terrible strain in his eyes, his set jaw, but he moved when she pulled him. "What was that?" he demanded, hoarse. "What's in the Trench?"

"Parker," Silas barked, "Simon's out! Jessie—"

The ground shuddered. Parker, a young woman clinging to her shoulder, dragged another victim away from the ruins. "What's happening?" she demanded.

"All agents!" The comm in Kayleigh's ear hissed, spat gibberish for a lengthy moment before it coalesced into a jarring "—surge detected."

Shawn's arm tightened around Kayleigh's shoulder, and suddenly, the balance shifted as she staggered. His fingers fisted into her sweater, kept her upright.

Broken stone and gem-bright fragments of glass juddered in place.

"Brace for impact!"

It was the longest thirty seconds of his life.

The ground didn't shake; it swayed. Like a sailboat caught in a storm, it heaved back and forth, wrenched itself right out from under him.

Kayleigh collapsed, and he snarled out a curse, more, as he forced his body to move, catch her, fall to the ground and cover her head, her body with his own. Rock bounced, buildings shuddered.

The dust flew, made it hard to see, but he heard the full thunder as it rolled on and on; heard screaming as the earthquake shook and trembled and forced the quad to dance.

Molding disintegrated. Piercing shrieks of pain punctuated Kayleigh's gasps beneath him.

Glass shattered in a wild sheet of shrapnel, windows exploded outward as building frames buckled and bent.

He buried his face in her hair, jacket pulled up to protect their heads in the only way he knew how as fragments of glass and mortar peppered his shoulders, his back. She shuddered violently beneath him, at least partly the fault of the quake rolling the city like a boat on vicious waves.

Her fists dug into the ground. Shawn covered one with his own, squeezed hard as she buried her face against the crook of one elbow, nose to the ground.

I'm here.

He almost nearly wasn't; almost died there in the cathedral, Simon in his arms instead of the woman he wanted. "Hold on!" he roared.

Everything fell still.

His voice died in the tomblike silence settling around them. Rang like a hollow bell through Shawn's aching head.

Nothing shook. Nothing trembled.

Slowly, very cautiously, he pulled the jacket from over his head. Bits of molding and shards of glass skittered off the synth-leather facing, speckling the grass.

People—shocked, traumatized—milled like stranded sheep. Some bent to help others up, others curled up on the ground and refused to move. Tears, prayers, shocked dismay, he heard it all as if from a distance.

Then the earpiece crackled to life. "Sunshine?" Silas's dark voice. "Jonas, do you copy?"

Kayleigh struggled to her feet. Shawn caught her arm, helped her up. Dirt smeared over her cheek, plaster rained from her hair as she shook her head hard.

A dull echo rang faintly in his ears; he didn't doubt they all suffered from it.

The quad, already ruined by Lauderdale's bomb, spread out before them as it always had. Trees, lawn, surrounding buildings acting like the walls of the courtyard. Only now, it tipped. Very subtly, as if it were his vision and not the physicality of the landscape, but he couldn't deny it. The whole courtyard slanted, skewed.

Glass glinted beneath struggling lights, diamonds buried in the manicured lawn. Some trees had toppled while others remained upright, and a portion of the Mission building had crumbled inward like paper.

Whole segments of the buildings now gaped out over nothing, a view of the horizon peeping through where steel and glass should have been.

Kayleigh dragged a finger down her cheek, peeled her hair from the mud it clung to. "This isn't right," she whispered.

Silas bent, clasped Parker's forearm and lifted her from the muck, but his attention turned inward. "Jessie!" he said again. "Answer me, sunshine."

The line fuzzed in Shawn's ear. He winced.

"*Fuck.*"

Kayleigh turned away from the spectacular array of destruction. Her gaze met his. Held. "My dad?" she asked softly.

Whatever equilibrium the earthquake hadn't stolen left him. He took a step back, swaying with the effort. Clutching his arm, ignoring the throbbing ache lancing from hip to shoulder, he looked away.

He could lie. But why?

"I had to take the shot," he said tightly. For all the good that did any of them.

"Simon's breathing," Parker called.

"We have injured!" cried another man.

"Help is on the way," she shot back, crouching by Simon's still body.

Kayleigh's chin drooped. She half turned, fists clenching and unclenching, and he winced as her hair slid over her cheek. Hid her expression, a tangled curtain.

"Kayleigh—"

Bzzt! The sound stuttered in his ear. Shawn touched two fingers to the mic. "Jonas? Jonas, can you read me?"

"Jessie, damn it," Silas growled, and barked, "Someone wrap a sleeve around that leg!"

Kayleigh strode away, unsteady enough that she flung out her arms for balance, but with her shoulders straight. Set.

Determined.

"Kayleigh," Shawn called, then swore and cupped a hand over his ear as the frequency shattered into indecipherable gibberish. He half turned, one eye on her slender, rail-stiff back.

She bent at the corner of the quad, sifted through rubble and stone.

"—*zzt*—read me? Th—" The mic hissed and spat.

"Jonas, this is Shawn, can you hear me?"

"Tell him we have wounded incoming," Parker called, features set so hard that lines bracketed her mouth, even under a mask of dirt.

"Jonas!"

"—ounded by the tru—. . . help from th—. . . *hsst*," spat the mic. Jonas's voice, recognizable in spurts. Was he getting anything back?

"We need a way off this quad," Silas called.

Shawn glanced up, frowned as Kayleigh knelt and

fished the remains of a rectangular pad from the ground. Glass slid off it in a thin, shattered sheet. Her jaw worked, eyes blank.

That part worried him. Anger, he expected. Grief. Accusation, something.

Blank emptiness was a reaction that curled in his gut and kicked. Hard.

"Hey!" A feminine voice, shaky, but familiar.

Silas whirled, raised a forearm as if expecting a blow, but the woman in black body armor didn't land the punch or kick she could have.

She raised her hands.

"Amanda, don't!" Shawn yelled.

Crack! Glass unpeeled from the flimsy frame hanging crookedly from the Magdalene. It hit the ground behind Shawn, splintered, metal frame clanging as it bounced.

He ducked, one hand lifting to protect his head even as he prepared to launch himself at the petite witch he'd once called friend.

Her palms turned backward. "I can get you away from here," she called, loud enough to be heard over the others.

Silas didn't turn away from her, didn't dare give her an opportunity. "Bullshit."

"I can. I *will*."

"Your call, Shawn." Parker sent him a glance filled with urgency. "He's going to bleed out if we don't get him to West soon."

Amanda watched him, too. "You have no reason to trust me, but I'm telling you I can help."

The choice was his.

Trust her. After everything she'd done, the shit she'd pulled down in the ruins, could he? Could *they*?

Given everything at stake, what choice was there really?

"Then lead the way." Shawn turned as sirens lifted over the ambient cacophony of post-disaster. People helped each other, carried the unconscious out of rubble, guided others to sit. Some gave over coats, others helped bandage wounds.

He couldn't imagine what was happening below.

Kayleigh left the corner, stumbled over cathedral rock and uneven ground, but she didn't stop. Didn't slow. Ignoring everyone, she followed Silas as he bent, pulled Simon over his broad shoulders and retraced Amanda's steps through the far edge of the cathedral's twisted foundation.

Swallowing his heart, he forced his agonized body into a jog. "Kayleigh."

She jerked, caught herself, and wrapped her arms over her stomach. "No," she whispered, lost in the ambience, but loud and clear over the mic.

He hesitated. Dug the heel of his hand into his eyes.

That was the choice he'd made, wasn't it?

Letting the gap widen between them, Shawn touched his mic. "Jonas!" It didn't shake. Good for him. "We have wounded incoming. If you can hear this, wounded are incoming."

"—end he . . ." *Bzzt!* "—ight awa—"

Confirmation, if it was even that, died.

"Shit," he whispered again, and hurried after the group.

The landing pad beside the cathedral had all but melted, ripples frozen in the asphalt as if a giant finger had shoved them in place. The helicopter that once claimed it now roosted all too close to the edge of the drop-off segregating the Holy Order quad from the rest of topside's highest tier. Debris clung to the scuffed paint, but the blades were clear.

Amanda wrenched open the scuffed cargo door. "This should work."

Wordlessly, Silas clambered inside, ducking as he carried Simon like the man weighed nothing. Within moments, a large hand extended, pulled Parker after him.

Kayleigh stared into the interior.

Shawn held his breath. Halted on the edge of the landing pad, in case she saw him and decided not to go with.

Please, he prayed silently. His fists clenched. *Please, Kayleigh.*

He could live without her love. He'd managed thirty-three years, he could keep on going. He could live without her kiss, without her touch.

But he wanted to live with her somewhere nearby. Somehow. A friend? An acquaintance.

Someone he could see every day.

Selfish. He knew it. She'd hate him forever, but if she'd only hate him up close and personal, he'd cope with it.

She looked down at the comm in her hand.

Raising her chin again, she seized the edge of the helicopter and pulled herself inside.

Thank you, God.

Amanda turned, her light brown eyes sharp as glass. "You coming?"

Yeah. With a brick in his chest and every joint screaming, he limped across the rippled landing pad. "Hey, Amanda."

She hesitated.

"If you ever turn on us again," he said, reaching up to hook a hand into the passenger seat harness, "I will kill you."

Her mouth hiked up faintly at one corner, a touch of humor that didn't reach her light brown eyes. "Deal," she said softly. "I'm—"

"Don't." Shawn buckled himself into place. "Just fly us down."

CHAPTER TWENTY-THREE

New Seattle had become a fractured city. Not just politically, but in every literal way.

For the second time in as many days, Kayleigh sat inside a helicopter circling the city that was all she knew of the world. Outside the protective walls, just visible in a sea of black, the earth was desolate and cracked, fissures opened along the path of the Old-Sea Trench. She could trace it by memory—every school-child knew in what direction the fault line reached out—but now she could see it, clear as day.

Portions of the city looked as if claws had been taken to the streets. The layer cake tilted, ruptures slanting from lower tiers to upper looking more like wounds bleeding shadow than the fissures they were.

Lights flashed, neon still popped and brightened as if nothing was wrong, yet as the helicopter sank below, Kayleigh touched the cool glass beside her and knew she was looking at the end of an era.

The earthquake must have triggered somewhere in the fault line. The ensuing tremors jerked the city back and forth, and the tiers had shifted like a house of cards on the razor edge of collapse. The engineers had done well; fifty years of effort didn't end in the obliteration of the city as before.

But it was an end.

"Come on, Simon, stay with me." Parker hadn't stopped murmuring. Her voice remained calm, low. Soothing. The very fact she hadn't started screaming brought tears to Kayleigh's eyes.

She was strong. Her baby would have a fighting chance. It was all Kayleigh could hope for.

Her tears didn't fall. Gritty and dry, it was as if her body refused to lose anything more.

She looked away from the window.

Dark eyes met hers. A spark inside Shawn's gaze quickly banked to stony resolve, and they slowly closed.

Exhaustion carved deep grooves into his blood-caked features. His head lolled as the helicopter circled, hands tucked into his jacket. It hid the scrapes, the blood and dirt ground into his knuckles.

Her father's blood?

"Jonas, do you copy?" Silas kept trying the comm. His voice, like Parker's, remained low, as if afraid to tip over the balance of eerie calm in the cargo bay.

The woman flying the chopper said nothing.

Shawn had called her Amanda. Even while searching for her comm, she'd heard the pain in his voice.

His friend. His lover? Maybe once?

Kayleigh's throat ached as she closed her eyes. Good for him. Them.

Maybe he'd find some peace.

She must have dozed. The next thing she knew, a warm hand curved over her shoulder and Shawn murmured, "Kayleigh. We're here, Kayleigh."

Groggy, eyes crusted over, she scrubbed at her face as a flurry of activity outside the open cargo door greeted her.

Generators thrummed loudly, a racket drowned only by the helicopter's blades slowing.

"Phin!" Silas called.

A handsome, dark-haired man jogged into view, wasted no time in helping Silas carry a clammy, bone-white Simon from the helicopter. "How bad?" he demanded.

"We need Naomi," Silas roared back, both men hunching under the blades. "Where's Jessie?"

"The shake knocked out communications," the man yelled back. "She's fine, with Jonas."

Palpable relief softened Silas's grim features.

Shawn slid out of the cargo door in their wake, turned and offered a hand, but Kayleigh had already moved. Insides quaking, she hit the broken pavement on feet that felt like bricks, squinted in the eye-shattering light flooding the makeshift landing pad.

Tents made of tarp and plastic rippled in the helicopter's squall, people ducked as they hurried back and forth across the field of equipment, parked vehicles and more. Somewhere, a generator failed, and a quarter of the lights flickered.

Shawn's hand dropped as she passed him silently.

"Out of the way," a woman yelled. Kayleigh stepped back as a jaw-droppingly gorgeous woman with three eyebrow piercings and a lip ring pushed by her. "How bad is it?" she asked, echo of the man named Phin, who smiled in welcome and just as quickly fell solemn.

"Naomi! Thank God. Gunshot wound, maybe some damage from debris," Parker said rapidly. "He's been bleeding steadily."

The woman called Naomi—the one who'd loaned out her clothes, and Kayleigh could see the street-chic flair mimicked in her tight shredded jeans and vinyl-patched crimson jacket—pointed back the way she'd come. "Meet him at the first triage station. Go!"

"Wait." Phin caught the back of her head, pulled her close for a hard, fast kiss. "I'll be at the second station. Don't overstrain yourself."

Naomi grinned, lots of teeth. "Won't. I've got a battery."

The man glanced beyond her, his gaze skimming off Kayleigh to fall on another woman, who nodded as she passed. This one, short and curvy, held out a small can. "And I brought you one of Jonas's boosters," she announced, less encouraging than skeptical. "At his insistence."

Phin raised his hands, moving back. "Take care of her, Jules."

She stared at the chaos, enfolded in an icy blanket of shock.

A hand caught her arm.

She looked up, everything unfolding in slow motion, and found Shawn looking down at her. His face, so hard beneath his mask of blood and dirt, framed eyes that glittered in the flooding light. "Kayleigh. Please listen—"

Her gaze slid away. Whatever energy she had left pooled to the soles of her feet. Leaked out. "What is there to say?" she asked dully. "You took the shot. It's done."

"Don't. Please, don't."

Her laugh tore through her empty chest. "Despite everything, he was my dad. I need . . ." She turned; his hand slid away. "I need time." Lifting her fingers to her ear, she plucked the mic from it. Held it out.

Face carved in mud and stone, he took the black device.

"Parker!" A man, too boyishly handsome to be over thirty, jumped from the edge of the lot. He waved his hands. "Parker, we need your help, now!"

"But Simon—"

"I know, I know, but Jonas needs—"

Too much. It was all too much. Kayleigh stepped away from the chaos, from the shouting debate that ensued behind her. Hollow and cold, she clutched her rescued comm to her chest and went in search of something. Somewhere.

Anywhere.

"Move."

Jessie heard his approach seconds before Silas shoved open the storefront door. The tiny bell strung at the doorknob jingled.

Braced against the back of Jonas's chair, she looked up from the string of gibberish the man hammered out of his keyboard. "I'm fine," she said automatically. "We lost communications due to the impact, nobody here specifically is hurt. Is Parker okay? Tell me she's okay."

Silas didn't stop. Didn't say anything.

She knew him—knew him like she knew her own heart—and nothing short of reassuring himself would do. Until then, it was like talking to a wall.

"Parker's fine, I sent her for a quick checkup." Jonas leaned out from his chair, one thin elbow braced on the table. Bags under his eyes told the same story everyone else was already singing the refrain to: exhaustion, nonstop effort.

Unlike most everyone else, though, Jonas was the glue keeping the resistance cells organized for the citywide rescue efforts. With the resistance leader still under care, even with Naomi's stretched-thin help, Jonas was all they had.

Silas stepped around two harried volunteers who stopped dead, took one look at the fierce intensity all but burning up the air around him, and hastily got the hell out of his way.

Jessie straightened ruefully.

"You guys." Jonas sighed. "You know I love you both dearly, but if this is going to be one of those moments, get the hell out of my command center."

Not that it was much of one. The place was a wreck, many of the clothes it had once displayed now distributed among the needy, the rest shoved aside to make room for the tech.

Jessie laid a hand on his shoulder. "Got this," she murmured.

Silas reached her just as Jonas chuckled softly. The man turned back to his computer, ignoring Jessie's muffled sound of resigned amusement as callused fingers encircled her wrist, and without a single word, turned and dragged her back out of the store.

"Send Parker in if you see her," Jonas called. "And hurry up, Jess, I need your eyes."

The door swung shut.

Her amusement died as Silas rounded on her.

Under the grime, gray-touched green eyes blazed at her, fury entangled with stark fear. "That," he growled, entangling his fingers into her hair and tipping her face up, "will never fucking happen again."

She didn't cringe when he bodily moved her from the doorway, tucking her up against the front facing. Glass thunked hollowly behind her, but it didn't hurt. She trusted him. With more than just her well-being.

"I'm sorry." She met his furious stare and, as she was trying so hard to remember how to do, didn't lie. She didn't have to lie anymore, not with him. "I went into a vision to try and *see* the connections Lauderdale had. After a few false starts, I followed one all the way to the Trench."

He was silent, fingers tight at her scalp.

"He'd set up a serious bomb right in the crevice. Judging by the looks of things, it wasn't his first." She slipped one hand up his shirt, warmth filling her. His heavy muscles leaped under her touch, his heart hammered against her palm.

The fire in his eyes altered.

She didn't have to lie to change his focus. Hiding a smile, Jessie said very seriously, "I was fine. I was careful and didn't cross the boundary between *seeing* and affecting. Jonas says that Lauderdale must have been trying to find that perfect spot to trigger an all-new city-busting earthquake. Silas, that thing was freaking huge."

"God damn it, sunshine, you could have—!"

"No," she cut in quickly. "Don't go there. Matilda's cure left me more stable, remember? I was never in danger from the bomb. When it blew up in the Trench, it hit that earthquake nerve because there was the first shake, then I *saw* the rest. That's when I tried to warn you, but I had literally seconds as the shockwave spread."

"Fuck me," he rasped, leaning down to rest his forehead against hers. His eyes closed as he inhaled deeply through his nose. "Communications dropped, I didn't know . . ." He couldn't finish the statement.

Jessie didn't want him to. "Hey." As she pushed up on tiptoes, her lips found his with unerring accuracy; his fingers tightened in her hair. Between one breath and the next, he stepped forward, pinned her between his hard body and the unyielding storefront glass. A rough hand tilted her head, and the reassuring kiss she'd intended altered into a mind-blowing, heart-pounding mesh of lips and tongue and breath.

Thunk! The glass shuddered as a fist pounded once from the inside.

Jessie startled, eyes flying open, but Silas only palmed the glass over her head and rumbled, "Fuck off, Stone, she's busy."

Jonas's laughter, beautifully serene, trickled out. "Sorry, Smith, I need her back."

"You don't get her."

She grinned up at him, lips tingling. Skating her nails gently over his ridged abs, she withdrew her hand and promised, "Later. You need a bath, and I need to help."

Blunt fingertips slid over her cheek. The manic fear was gone from his eyes, but the lines carved into his dust-smeared face didn't ease. "Don't wear yourself out. Juliet's with Naomi."

"I'm good."

"I know you are, sunshine. That's why I worry." He straightened his arms, a modified push-up that flexed powerful muscles. It sent zingers of appreciation from toes to forehead. "I'll bring food in an hour."

"I'll find a dark corner where we can . . ." Jessie licked her lips. "Eat."

His chuckle, as much thunder as laughter, followed her back into the store.

"All right, Jonas," she said, feeling much more at ease. "Where else can I *look* for you?"

CHAPTER TWENTY-FOUR

"I couldn't believe it when they told me who you were." Juliet Carpenter sat on the edge of a cooler dredged up for Kayleigh's use in the small tarp tent, the wilting edge of a patchwork blanket sliding off the plastic top beneath her.

Kayleigh smiled at her, but with hesitation. For the past twenty-four hours, she'd managed exactly five hours of exhausted sleep, untold hours helping the endless train of injured as they came—some under their own power, others carried by volunteers. She'd worked herself to the bone, threw herself into every task she could. Avoided addressing anything but the triage line of fractures, lacerations, worse.

It was easier than coping.

Now, she faced a tent full of expectant faces and wasn't sure what she was supposed to say. "I'm sorry?"

"No, don't be."

Easy for Juliet to say.

She was much shorter than Kayleigh had pictured when she'd first gone over Mrs. Parrish's old files. Operation Wayward Rose, one of Sector Three's most classified missions, had focused on finding Juliet Carpenter, for reasons Mrs. Parrish had never made clear.

It was the same mission that had killed her.

Now here Juliet sat, right in front of Kayleigh. Her figure was notably curvy beneath her street-worn jeans and definitely too-big sweater, and her skin had that quality of pale reserved for the majority of people who didn't see the sun much. She'd spent, according to the data Kayleigh had acquired, twenty-five years in the low streets, which explained it.

Her short, choppy black hair gleamed in the fluorescent white light. She tucked it behind one ear, drawing attention to lighter brown roots contrasted at the crown of her head. She was pretty. Not like Parker's classic beauty or Naomi's downright intimidating sex appeal, but in a warm sort of way.

Kayleigh could see why Caleb Leigh had a hard time letting her out of his sight.

Or maybe, she thought as he glowered at her, arms folded across his chest, he had a hard time letting Juliet into Kayleigh's sight.

He loomed behind her, scars outlined in sharp relief by the generator-fueled lantern clipped to the bar over Kayleigh's impromptu work desk.

Still alive, and definitely kicking.

Lounging behind him, propped on the only chair his designated nursemaid had been able to find, Simon watched them with tired but razor-keen eyes. She felt like a bug under a microscope. Of them all, only Juliet and the dark-haired young man introduced as Danny—

under strict orders to keep an eye on Simon and make sure he rested, much to both men's chagrin—seemed to hold no animosity toward her.

Simon, however, seemed to hate the world. She couldn't blame him. He was starting to look rough only a few weeks ago, but now he looked like hell. Cheeks sunken, drawing more attention to the contrast of his sharp cheekbones, and bruised circles under his jaundiced eyes gave him a skeletal appearance she found disturbing on too many levels.

Not the least of which was the knowledge that his degeneration labored in the last stages. She wanted to ask him questions, mark his progress, help in some way, but he watched her with such open hostility that she wasn't sure how to try.

Manufacturing the Eve sequence would be a start. She had hours, maybe. The wounds he'd sustained had taken a terrible toll. If Naomi kept using her purported healing powers on him—and Kayleigh's fingers itched to get samples of *her* DNA to study—then maybe she had days.

Kayleigh wound a plastic strip around Juliet's arm, slanting Caleb a wary look as he shifted impatiently.

"Don't mind him," Juliet said, amusement thick in the dismissal. "He's half convinced you're out to poison me or kidnap me or cook me up and feed me to the wounded."

Caleb, any boyish good looks he might have possessed long since hardened into stark, edged planes, glowered. "She's a Lauderdale."

The reminder hurt. It was supposed to.

Forcing herself not to wince, Kayleigh twisted the tie in place and said soothingly, "You're going to feel a pinch."

Juliet closed her eyes, her free hand reaching up to her shoulder.

A scarred hand claimed it, held it tightly. "You sure you want to do this, Jules?"

"Yes." A harsh whisper, and Kayleigh didn't waste time. Quickly, before the girl could change her mind, she inserted the needle into the thick vein at the crook of Juliet's arm.

Juliet flinched, a whimper caught in her throat. Her knuckles went white in Caleb's.

"It's okay," Kayleigh murmured. "Almost done." She released the tourniquet, drew three vials of blood as rapidly as she dared. "Jessie warned me you'd feel this way about needles, so I'm being fast as I can."

"Comes from spending your life poked and prodded by them," Simon said, and if his voice wasn't quite cutting, it hadn't warmed by any stretch.

"It's fine," Juliet said between her teeth. "For God's sake, Simon, be nice."

"No." Kayleigh didn't look at the injured man as she withdrew the tube and pressed a swatch of gauze to the woman's skin. "He doesn't have to be."

Someone, one of the men, snorted.

She couldn't be sure who as she added softly, "Put your fingers here, hold it in place."

Juliet did as suggested, her pretty light green eyes serious as they flicked to Simon. "I don't hold her accountable."

"I do," he said.

"She didn't make us."

Kayleigh winced, collecting the three capped vials and turning back to her microscope. "It's okay," she started, only to shrink, ducking her head, as Simon growled, "We're just as much Mattie's as she is."

Danny breathed out a sigh. "Calm down, Simon, or Parker's going to be pissed."

"Parker's not here," he retorted, and turned his hazel regard back to Kayleigh. She felt it boring into the side of her head. "What's the point of bleeding us, Kayleigh? You're only reinforcing the comparisons between you and—"

"Oh, for the love of—" Juliet shifted on the cooler, heightened color flooding into her cheeks as she snapped, "Leave her alone, Simon!"

Caleb's hand rested on the back of her neck, a silent reminder of his presence.

Simon frowned at her. "Hey, I'm on your side."

Kayleigh carefully placed a slide of blood under the lens, her shoulders hunched as the debate surrounded her.

"Well, I'm on *her* side. Jesus, it's like she hasn't had enough to deal with. Just like us." Juliet tipped her head up, met Caleb's lifted blond eyebrow. "Tell him that he's an idiot, would you? Maybe he'll hear man-speak."

The scarred side of his mouth lifted as incredibly blue eyes turned to the injured Simon, who met his gaze with a scowl. "You're an idiot."

"Fuck you, Leigh."

With a *hmph* of disdain, Juliet shifted, the plastic cooler creaking. "Kayleigh— Can I call you that?"

"Please," she returned, not looking up. "First name's fine. I think maybe I shouldn't broadcast the family connection."

"Yeah."

The microscope wouldn't be a huge help, not yet, but she wanted a control of each sample, a first glimpse at the strain she was dealing with. Of the four samples she had, three had come from the GeneCorp lab. From them, Simon's genetic strain had come directly from her—from *their*—mother, but Juliet's and Jessie's were a different strain, each mapped on the Salem pattern. And then there was Kayleigh's.

The untampered witch allele as a control.

"Kayleigh," Juliet continued, oblivious to her focus, "you know that we're all from GeneCorp, right?"

"Mm-hm."

"Well, I should tell you that—"

"Jules, wait," Caleb inserted, but she spoke over him loudly, "My name isn't actually Juliet."

It took her a moment, but the silence following this announcement filtered through her concentration.

Kayleigh raised her eyes, gaze blurring some as it focused from the eyepiece to the earnest green eyes staring at her. "I beg your pardon?" Why would it matter?

Simon watched in silence, scowl black and braced, and Danny hovered behind him, a hand rubbing the back of his head in abashed uncertainty.

Caleb's stare promised murder if she got this one wrong.

What was going on? Kayleigh's eyebrows knitted. "I'm sorry, I don't know what's happening here."

Juliet smiled weakly. "I mean, it is my name. My sister named me. When I was born, though, my name was Eve."

For a long moment, nobody moved. Even Kayleigh blinked at her, the words circling her head sluggishly.

When they finally sank into her brain, she very carefully put the vial she held down on the tray with the other two.

Caleb tensed, a wall of leashed menace behind

Juliet, but the girl tilted her head. "I had a case number and everything, but I was also Eve."

Eve. Twenty-five years old.

GeneCorp.

Her mother.

"Eve," Kayleigh repeated.

Juliet nodded.

"Eve, as in the Eve sequence?"

"If I say 'in the flesh,' will that get me glared at?"

Kayleigh didn't have the heart to smile. "She did it. She actually managed to unlock the puzzle. But . . ." Her gaze turned inward, flashed through all the data she'd managed to send to her comm, before the device had fried in the cathedral.

The puzzle was in her brain. That unknown liquid that was so much garbage until it paired with the Salem gene, that was it. Somehow, it factored in to everything.

"How did Parker get that vial of stuff?" she asked quietly.

Caleb grumbled for a moment, then said more clearly, "We thought it might give her an edge over you."

"Me." Kayleigh laced her fingers tightly together before anyone could see how badly they shook. "Because she was trying to find out what was happening in Sector Three, right?" Two nods. One stare.

Danny jammed his hands into his pocket and looked downright embarrassed. "Grams locked on to that fact, too. Parker sort of . . . became a pawn."

"Like you," Juliet added, not unkindly.

Kayleigh nodded back, but for what reason, she didn't know. Eve. Her mother had done it, after all. "But where did the syringe come from? Was . . . was my mother manufacturing it from wherever she was hiding?"

Caleb's eyes narrowed. "Jessie found it. After Matilda—"

When he stopped suddenly, Simon continued with a candid, "Matilda killed herself, Kayleigh."

"Oh, God." She didn't mean to say it. Didn't know how to bottle it up inside as her stomach kicked viciously. As if something black and raw and ruined tried to force itself up through her chest. "Suicide? But Dad— He said you did it, Simon." This was worse, somehow. So much worse. "Why? Why did she—"

Abandon everything for a second time?

"He was half right. I'd been sent to finish the job," Simon said bluntly. "She'd become a liability." But as Kayleigh stared at him, fingers clasped to her chest, the hard edges of his anger softened. Deflated. "Christ, I'm sorry. That was harsh. Kayleigh, I swear, if I had been even ten minutes sooner, I could have stopped her."

Caleb shook his head. "No way. She was damned good at what Naomi calls her 'mysterious stranger' routine. Trust me, nobody could have stopped her. She did what she did because she knew it was best."

"Best?"

Simon's mouth twisted. "Your— She killed herself so I wouldn't have to. I needed pieces in play, and she . . . I don't know, she knew that or something."

"Matilda was a good woman," Caleb said flatly. "A scary woman, but everything she did was to make this"—his unscarred hand lifted, waved to encompass her, Juliet, the tent, beyond—"happen. I can promise you that."

Kayleigh wanted to scream, but all she did was turn what she hoped was a calm face to Juliet and whisper, "Thank you for telling me. That'll change how I go about reproducing the sequence."

Simon gripped the arms of the chair. "Can you?"

She nodded, once. "I'm positive. And with Ev—" She caught herself. "With Juliet as a base and a trip to pick up some equipment, I can do it in a matter of hours, after all."

"Kayleigh, I'm sorry. I heard—" Juliet caught herself, amended whatever she was going to say with, "I know everything that happened must have hit you really hard. I just wanted to tell you the truth right away."

It was Kayleigh's turn to nod. And then, because she couldn't help herself, she blurted, "Are you my sister, too?"

In her peripheral, Simon bolted upright. Whatever color he had drained from his face, as if it never occurred to him. "Oh, for fuck's sake."

"Simon, damn it, sit down before Parker kills me!"

He sat, rolling his eyes at Danny. "She's weird about blood, relax."

Kayleigh watched Juliet, who looked taken aback. "I . . . Er, no? Maybe? I don't know."

Well. The pragmatic part of her mind kicked into gear, forcing her to sit up straight, reach for the microscope slide with brisk efficiency. "I can find out," she said simply. "It just seems that since my mother . . ." Her throat ached. "Since Matilda took a direct hand in Simon's genetics, and I think maybe mine somehow, if she . . . if . . ." If Kayleigh had so much more family than she'd ever dreamed, maybe she wasn't so alone after all.

Maybe it wasn't enough.

She couldn't finish her thought. Didn't know how to frame it. The reality of it, the weight of the whole, crashed down on her. Kayleigh's head dropped, chin to chest, and she took a sobbing breath.

"Oh, Jesus," Caleb said, on the verge of masculine panic.

"*Shit*," Simon swore.

Plastic creaked, and suddenly, Juliet's arms wrapped around Kayleigh's shoulders.

"Jules—" Caleb hovered, hands upraised. "God damn it, Simon, did you have to be so harsh?"

Kayleigh choked back another sob, blinking fast to keep tears from falling. "I'm fine," she managed, only to shudder out a broken laugh as Juliet countered, "No, you're not, and it's okay."

"Aw, look at her," Danny said quietly. "She's not at all like the scary monster I'd pictured."

"Shut up, Granger." Simon's voice hovered somewhere between indecision and apology.

Kayleigh held very, very still until the horrible hole in her chest filmed over with the barest filaments of calm. She didn't cry, she was done with sobbing over the things she couldn't change, but she sniffed back the threat of tears and whispered, "I'm all right."

Juliet's embrace loosened.

Another hand, larger, squeezed her shoulder. Then, Caleb's voice. "If you have everything you need, we should go."

"Okay, honey?"

Honey. Just like Shawn called her.

Shawn. Damn it. She'd gone hours, nearly a full day without allowing herself to think about him. The fragile stitches holding her insides together strained as she took a deep breath, forced him—his smile, his rich laugh, the way he'd caught her arm with such naked pain in his eyes—down deep where she couldn't touch it again.

One life-altering debacle at a time.

"I have what I need," she said, pushing her hair back from her face and smoothing her hands down her borrowed sweater. The maroon garment hung on her, too big in the same way Juliet's was, but Naomi had given her another pair of pants. If Kayleigh felt stupid working in a medical tent wearing synth-leather pants, she didn't have the luxury to worry about it.

Juliet rose, pulling her sleeve down over her arm. After murmured good-byes, Caleb escorted her out.

Danny lingered by the entrance, dark brown eyes—so much like Shawn's, her traitorous memory whispered—questioning.

Kayleigh resolutely stared at her table, the separate vials of blood, as Simon stepped past the cooler. "You shouldn't be up—" she began, only to end it on a "What?" when he sank to his knees at her side.

Hazel eyes dark with pain, Simon braced one hand against her leg, the other clenched on the back of her chair. "Listen to me," he said, so intently that it was almost a growl.

Wide-eyed, she glanced at Danny, who met her look with a shrug.

She tried logic again. "Simon, Parker needs you to not overexert yourself."

He ignored her, letting go of her leg to cup her cheek; a gesture that would have sent her nerves into a melody of anticipation had it been Shawn.

But it wasn't. It was Simon.

Her brother.

She wished she'd known.

"I owe you an apology so many times over," he told her, every serious note striking like a hammer. "Kayleigh, I played a lot of games up there—"

"Don't," she whispered, reaching up to cup his hand against her cheek. She drew it away, but held it tightly between her palms as he frowned at her. "Simon, I wasn't any sort of angel. I didn't know what my—" She caught herself. "What our mother had done. I didn't know anything about it, but I don't know now that I would have done anything differently. Not then."

Simon, to her profound surprise, smiled. Haggard as it was, the skin around his nose and mouth reddened by degeneration, it still lit something wicked and sharp in his eyes.

That was the Simon she'd known.

"Lauderdale had this thing, didn't he?" Simon's tone was wry. Knowing. "You never wanted to disappoint him."

"You did."

"I went out of my way," Simon said, "even before I knew that Mattie had used his genes for me, too."

Kayleigh blinked. "Did she?" Not just a half brother, then? She didn't have the strength to let this one blindside her. "Okay."

He shrugged. "But the choices I made were mine alone, and I didn't make them for any of the right reasons." His mouth curved, turned crooked. "Not until Parker. Kayleigh, don't blame yourself."

"There's no one else to blame for how I lived my life," she told him, honesty so sharp, she knew that he saw her bleed. His smile faded. "We're responsible for our own choices, I can live with that."

"Can you?"

She shrugged and let go of his hand.

He rose, cursing under his breath.

Danny scraped both hands through his black hair, squinting up at nothing. "You know what? I think I'm going to go check on . . . uh, something else."

Kayleigh let him go without comment. Instead, she sprang to her feet as Simon winced, one eye squinting. She seized his arm. "Sit down," she ordered, but her tone softened, gentled because she didn't know how else to handle him. His illness, his impending fatherhood.

His death? God, where was her newfound power when she needed it?

She needed to fix something, damn it. She couldn't touch her own messed-up world, but maybe she could do something good for him. For Parker.

"This is the deal," she told him, guiding him back into his chair and ignoring his muttered curses. "You rest until I have this fixed. I'm going to have you patched up soon."

"Kayleigh." He thrust out his jaw. "Yell at me, if it'll make you feel better. Do something. You've been walking around for hours half dead, and Shawn's worse."

"I don't want to talk about Shawn," she said evenly. Folding her arms over her stomach, she sighed. "And I'm not going to yell at a dying man."

"You need to let it—"

"Simon," she cut in, injecting her voice with steel, "you are *dying*. It's my fault—" She flung up a hand. "Shush. It's at least my responsibility. And Parker is pregnant, so you do what I say or—"

Too late, she realized his mouth hung open. That he'd snapped upright in his chair, his fingers clenched around her wrist.

She winced. "Um."

"You're sure?" When she nodded warily, something she'd never seen before slipped into his eyes. Bright. Serious in a way that had nothing to do with a threat to handle. Under the strain and exhaustion, under the dull glaze of degeneration, something resolute flickered to life. "How?"

She guessed he knew the mechanics. "I just . . . I think when Mom—our mom died, her abilities started to come to me. Medically, Simon, I can't be sure. But I . . . just know."

For a long moment, he stared at nothing. Kayleigh disengaged from his grip, waited for him to collect his thoughts.

She knew the feeling.

When he did, she saw them file into place with an almost audible click. "We need to talk."

"No, we don't," she demurred. Because if he started talking, he'd bring up Shawn again. She'd fielded it once already, she didn't have the energy to do it again. Shawn was done. Over.

They'd all made their decisions.

"Fuck." It was half a laugh, half a despairing sound. "You should see your face. You're hurting so badly."

"Simon, I don't want to talk about anything but your prognosis."

"Kayleigh." Simon touched her hands. "Listen to me. Shawn didn't kill Lauderdale."

"Please, he took the shot—"

His mouth twisted. "Shawn took the shot, but he's shit with a gun. He missed. I didn't."

CHAPTER TWENTY-FIVE

Naomi sat outside the fourth triage station, a tin can of half-warmed soup cradled in both hands. Exhaustion drummed through her body like a mantra; she was tapped of everything she'd ever had and then some.

So many wounded.

Her head fell back against the crate she leaned her back against, one of a handful scoured out from stockpiles all over the city. Inside were supplies to be distributed among the wounded.

People had really surprised the fuck out of her.

"Excuse me." The easy, masculine voice peeled through yawning layers of fatigue, curved her mouth up into a weary smile. "This seat taken?"

Without opening her eyes, she tipped her head. "It is now."

Phin settled to the ground beside her, his shoulder

warm and solid where it braced hers. "How are you holding up, witchy woman?"

By a thread. "Oh, you know," she murmured, rattling her half-empty tin can without removing her forearm from the brace of one knee.

"That great, huh?" Fingers touched her cheek, tracing tendrils of magenta-streaked hair from the glued-on mask of sweat stuck to her face. She opened her eyes, unable to help the little kick her heart gave as Phin's warm chocolate eyes smiled into hers. "When was the last time you slept?" he asked gently.

She licked the warm metal ring pierced through the center of her lip. An action that drew his gaze, even as his mouth hiked at one corner. "Are we talking the kind of sleep where you get a whole dream all the way through?"

His chuckle was as much a physical stroke as it was a mental balm for her soul. "I'm going to assume that's a no."

"That's definitely a no," she confirmed, too tired to argue as he plucked the can from her fingers. He set it down, pulled her hand from her knee, and dug his thumbs into her palm.

Every muscle from hand to shoulder gave out at once.

Her eyes drifted closed again, appreciative moan earning an answering sound from him. It was easy to forget sometimes that Phin wasn't just the topsider he'd been born as, that he'd earned his stripes and more down in these streets. Naomi spent a lot of time trying to protect him; he spent a lot of time calling her on her shit.

But when he got his hands on her, all bets were off. Pleasure rippled through her as his fingers dug into her fatigued muscles, easing corded tendons with the skill of a masseuse. He'd practically been one, once.

"How many more wounded need your help?" Phin asked.

"Not sure." She groaned as his fingers left hers, only to ease into a sigh as he found her other hand. "I've got the current emergencies under control and Juliet's gone for the night. If anyone else is carried in . . ." She'd have to get her ass in gear.

With what, she didn't know.

"Okay." Phin moved, denim rustling as he shifted against the crate. Before she could argue—and she knew that *he* knew she'd argue—he slid an arm under her bent knees, another behind her back. Her eyes snapped open, but by the time her sluggish brain caught up, he'd repositioned her in his lap.

Now, with her legs over his hip and her cheek pillowed by his chest, he ordered, "Sleep. I'll stay here and keep a lookout."

Her elbow dug into his ribs as she propped herself upright. "Phin, you're as tired as I am."

His teeth gleamed very white in the glow cast by the scattered lanterns. "I'll win."

"Only because I let you," she retorted.

His arm folded around her shoulders, tugged her back down to his chest. "Whatever helps you sleep, my love."

Maybe a few minutes. Naomi was used to long hours, she'd spent her life in the Mission. The extra draw this witch-healing crap pulled out of her, though, that was something else.

Muffling a yawn, she wriggled into place. Smiled as she heard him hiss out a careful, not-quite-silent breath.

"Why, Mr. Clarke," she murmured, fingers easing up around the side of his neck. The warm skin there tensed. "I do believe you're not all that tired."

He laughed softly. "Body is willing," he admitted against her hair, "spirit is thinking a nap sounds like heaven. Sleep, Naomi. I promise to be here."

Her heart shimmered. There wasn't any other word for it. As lights flickered behind her eyelids, she took a deep breath, let it out on a murmured, "I love you."

Phin rested his chin against the top of her head. His heart beat steadily beneath her ear. "I know."

Her mouth quirked. "Ass."

He said nothing, only hummed a sound that was as much acknowledgment as humor. As the generators thrummed loudly, voices rising and falling in arrhythmic patterns of the makeshift camp, Naomi nestled into Phin's embrace and let herself sleep.

How long was Shawn going to torture himself?

A good question. Danny's intervention—a clipped, "You are a complete tool, you know that?"—hadn't done anything but tell Shawn everything he already knew.

So here he was, standing outside the small tarp-covered tent Kayleigh had turned into her own lab, fingers clenched around metal and nylon. Rain pounded the street, seeping into all the places it hadn't used to. The newly formed canyons carved into the overhead tiers made for a hell of a lot of scrabbling as people hurried to get supplies out of the wet.

Shawn had done everything to keep tabs on her but visit himself. Danny's additional, "Just go talk to her. Please?" hadn't so much made up his mind as goaded it.

Now he didn't know what to say.

"Hi, I'm a complete tool," while accurate, didn't seem the right tone.

There was nothing to knock on, so he settled for a tap against the tarp. Rain jumped from the surface, splattered over him. He barely noticed. He'd been soaked through for an hour now.

"Come in."

Kayleigh's voice slipped out from under the flap, wrapped around Shawn's throat. Slid into his heart.

I need time.

How much time? How long before he could reach out again, see her smile? Watch intelligence spark to life in her eyes as she puzzled over a project.

Anything, God, but this silence.

Seizing his courage in both hands, Shawn took a deep breath and ducked under the tarp flap.

The light inside blazed, blinding all on its own. The small area was stacked with crates, many placed just to get out of the rain, while an improvised worktable held an old microscope, three plastic trays, and a small refrigerator dug out from God knew where. Cords intersected the crates, powering the appliances.

In the farthest corner, Kayleigh looked up from a small notebook, pen falling still. A radio peppered the silence, the voice—not one of the polished big media anchors; he'd bet one of Jonas's feeds—quiet and serious.

For a long moment, all Shawn could do was stare. Drink her in. Stand in the entrance to this cluttered, makeshift space and think of all the things he wanted to say.

And all the horrible ways he could fuck it up.

Rain dripped from his hair, slid down his jaw. He wiped it away with an impatient hand.

Her face carefully went blank. "Shawn."

This was a bad idea. Guts roiling, he took a step back. "I can come back—"

"No." She put the notebook down, rising from her perch on one of the crates. "Stay. We . . . I think we should talk."

Talk. Fear gripped Shawn's heart. What was left of it, anyway. He hadn't felt all that whole for days. He looked down, studied the crates, the single chair propped against the table. Anywhere but at her.

Just looking at her made him *want*. All the things he never let himself dream of, all those soft and warm things he'd sworn to abandon in his search for vengeance.

Obviously uncertain, she rounded the first barrier. The sleeves of her red sweater nearly covered her fingers, and the baggy quality hid the body he knew waited underneath.

His gaze snagged on matte black. "Are you wearing synth-leather again?"

Kayleigh looked down at her own legs, at the bare feet peeping from beneath the too-long hem. "Naomi." As an explanation went, it was enough.

Abruptly, Shawn felt a chuckle well up. It made it half out of his mouth before he strangled it, clearing his throat. "You look nice."

But she knew. Somehow, she knew what he thought, what he felt, because red climbed her cheeks and she ran an uncertain hand through her hair, rumpling it even more.

An innocent gesture. One that shot straight to his gut in a completely different way.

He'd wrapped that hair around his fist. Held her as he'd kissed her. As he'd claimed her.

Shawn's fingers curled into fists, amusement dying. Metal spikes jammed into his palm. "Kayleigh, I came for a reason."

"I know." Her own fingers clasped together. "I'm glad you did."

That stopped him. Glad?

Achingly aware of the narrow distance between them—of how easy it would be to step over the crates, the stacked supplies; of how much easier it would be to turn around and walk away—Shawn held his breath.

She didn't look at him. "The world's a mess. Everything's different."

That was as true as anything he'd ever heard in his life. Everything would be different forever. In so many ways.

He nodded once, but didn't dare say anything.

"In less than a week, I've lost everything I ever cared about." Her fingers twisted, now wringing together. Ink stained her index and middle fingers in faded blue. "My home, my work, my . . . my parents. Both of them."

Oh, Jesus. "Kayleigh, I'm—"

"*Don't.*" An often-enough refrain between them, tight with pain and barely repressed anger.

Shawn's jaw locked.

She didn't look at him. He wanted her to look at him.

"I'm not a complete fool, despite what people think," she continued after a moment. Her voice, husky with emotion, all but vibrated with the effort locking in her fingers together so tight, they gleamed white and yellow. "I know what my dad did. I can deduce the rest. I know exactly how much I helped him and how much damage I—" Her mouth flattened. "*We* caused."

Oh, for God's sake. He couldn't take this.

Chest tight, a vise of anger and impatience and the fragile threads of a love so unsure that he didn't dare name it, Shawn jumped over the first pile of crates. His shoulder tweaked a warning; he ignored it,

Kayleigh's head came up, eyes wide as he vaulted the second.

She took a step back, he didn't let her take another. Closing the distance in a matter of seconds, he wrapped both hands around her upper arms—metal pinged as it clattered off plastic siding—and dragged her to her toes, nose to nose. "Stop it."

Shock warred with anger. "Let me go."

"No." Never again. He shook her once for emphasis. "If we're taking responsibility, then we're both going to take the fucking responsibility," he growled. "I knew who you were when I kissed you in that car."

She flinched.

"I knew who you were when I cozied up to you topside, and I sure as shit knew what I planned to do even as you straddled my lap and I watched you come apart around my fingers."

Her cheeks reddened, eyes turning smoky blue as she sucked in a sharp breath.

Shawn refused to let it sit there. "I'm sorry. I'm so sorry, Kayleigh, for everything. Up until a few days ago, you weren't anything but a name."

He let her go as she pulled, steadied her when she stumbled. But he didn't let her turn away, backing her against the farthest pile of stacked containers when she tried.

She raised her chin.

He wanted nothing more than to seize her face between his hands and kiss every last thought out of her head; out of his.

That wouldn't fix anything.

Instead, he grabbed the edge of the crate behind her head. Trapped her between his forearms.

"We're going to have this out," he said roughly. "We *need* to have this out, and if you hate me afterwards . . ."

"I have never hated you!"

"Well, I hated you," he shot back. Rain slammed into the tarp overhead, pattered loudly as his declaration filled the narrow divide between them.

Kayleigh, suddenly still, searched his eyes.

"A coalition of witches have banded together to help rescue efforts," said the quiet radio voice. "With the Church in turmoil—"

"I hated you," Shawn repeated, dragging the words out as his pulse slammed in his ears, "before I met you. For years, I hated everything that had anything to do with the name Lauderdale. It wasn't—" He stopped abruptly.

"Personal?" The way she framed the question told him how much bullshit that really was.

His head dropped, eyes closing. "It was beyond personal," he admitted. "It became . . . a poison. Something I kept eating because . . . because it was all I had—*Christ.*" His hands fisted by her head, arms tensing. "You got under my skin, Kayleigh. I don't even know how it happened. One minute, I was planning how to get you out of that lab, and the next, I caught myself laughing."

She swallowed, a flex of her throat in his peripheral vision. Her hands, pressed against the crate behind her, spasmed.

Shawn took a deep breath, smelled that acrid tang of New Seattle's rain, the whisper of antiseptic and whatever chemicals she used.

And her. Somehow, it always came down to her.

Her fragrance filled his nose, that clean scent he'd thought was soap, the warm reminder of her body as she'd wrapped around his in the car. In that hospital room.

So close now.

His cock stirred; he gritted his teeth. This was not about sex. It wasn't about red-blooded attraction. He needed her to understand that.

He didn't know how to say it.

"Shit," he muttered.

Her chest jumped beneath her sweater. The sound accompanying the sudden, jerking motion strangled.

Shawn's head rose slowly.

Amusement, caught somewhere between all her doubt and solemnity, turned her eyes to polished glass. Gray and blue laughter; a flicker of it at her lips. Slowly, so slowly that he could have turned away if he wanted, her hand rose.

Cupped his roughened jaw.

Shawn swallowed a groan. "God, Kayleigh." He turned his face into her hand, squeezing his eyes shut. "Tell me you don't hate me, still."

Her steadying breath shook. "We're going to have to start over." Though the tension didn't completely leave her body, her balance shifted. She stopped trying to meld with the plastic crates. "We're going to have to redo every conversation, every gesture. Our whole history is built on lies and mistrust, Shawn."

"I'm prepared," he swore, opening his eyes. He searched her features, her own stare, *willing* her to see his sincerity. Feel it in every word. "I'll start over right now. My name is Shawn Lowe. I—"

Her hand slid to his nape, pulled him forward so quickly that his words tangled on his own lips. On hers.

If this was a prank, Shawn was an easy mark.

His fingers slid into her hair, cupped the back of her head as he took over the kiss; slanted his mouth across hers and groaned out loud when her lips opened.

Her tongue touched his bottom lip. Slid inside his mouth to dart against his, and he nearly fell out of his skin.

Suddenly, it wasn't about words. There weren't enough words to show her, to tell her, to make her understand. Her hand slid under his wet shirt. Where it touched, he felt branded; where her fingers skimmed, he burned.

This. This was what mattered.

He raised his head, panting for breath. Her breathing mimicked his, eyes hazy, rainwater trailing down her cheek from his hair.

Shawn let her go, trailed his fingers through the strands of her hair that streamed like silk between them. He stepped back.

Her hand fell to her side.

Shaking in his skin, Shawn pulled his wet shirt over his head. It hit the tent floor with a damp *splat*.

Kayleigh's lips parted. Her eyes pinned to his chest, lit to a diamond flame that did as much to stoke his own need as broadcast hers.

His fingers stalled at the button to his jeans. "Are you sure?"

When she shook her head, it was a knife to his gut. Very carefully, he forced his hands back down to his sides.

"Maybe," Kayleigh murmured, fingers toying with the hem of her sweater, "we don't have to redo *every* conversation."

He tilted his head, not daring to breathe.

As her lips curved, she tugged the sweater up over her belly. Her ribs. A flash of blue beneath turned into a T-shirt she stripped off with a single tug. As the light blazed with stark clarity, Shawn stared at the most perfect, beautiful woman he'd ever seen and forgot how to think. Even how to breathe.

Kayleigh Lauderdale in nothing but skin-tight black synth-leather was every man's wet dream.

But he wasn't dreaming now, was he?

The zipper hissed down. Matte black parted to reveal lavender satin, too damned delicate to belong down here.

He sucked in a hard, throttled breath.

Rain dripped from his hair, traced his shoulder, his pectorals. Kayleigh watched a drop slide down to his abs, licked her lips.

"Say it," Shawn rasped.

Her cheeks darkened. "How—?"

"Your eyes just went electric." He spread his arms wide. "I've seen that look twice. I never thought I'd—" *Crave it.* "Say it, Kayleigh."

"I . . ." Her fingers curled into her waistband. "I want to lick you."

Jesus fucking Christ. Every nerve in his skin went nova-hot. Her jaw shifted; he clenched his teeth, clenched every muscle into lockdown. His erection strained at his zipper, so hard, it hurt.

I want to lick you.

Any damned day of the week. "Do it."

Her lashes flared. "Really?"

He was going to die. "Really," he repeated through his teeth.

The hem of her pants scraped against the floor as she approached. One hand curved over his chest, fingertips just stroking his nipple. He let out a hard breath from his nose.

When she leaned forward, weight braced on that hand, her breath painted a hot brand against his shoulder. Her tongue darted out. Once, twice.

Her teeth closed over the ridge of one muscle, and he nearly jolted right out of his mind. His fists clenched so tight, joints cracked. "Jesus."

Her mouth licked, kissed, nibbled across his chest. He couldn't stand there and watch her blond head tucked so close to his skin, couldn't watch her feast at his flesh and not grab her, so he tipped his head back and stared fixedly at the tent roof.

It rippled beneath the rain.

He didn't give a good fucking damn about the rain.

Kayleigh licked a path down his abdomen, and his cock jumped greedily. She found the vee of muscle between his hipbones and made a wild, hungry sound, and he started counting backward.

When her fingers dipped into his waistband, he forgot the numbers.

The fabric gave too easily. As his dick pulsed in the colder air of the tent, as Kayleigh's breath ghosted across the sensitive skin, Shawn gave up entirely.

"I am not man enough for this," he growled, jamming his hands under her arms and forcibly lifting her.

She yelped, surprised. "But I want—"

"Later," he promised roughly, and planted her ass on the nearest crate. Guiding her legs around his waist, he caught her by the nape, dragged her closer until there was no room for anything between them but skin and sweat and all-consuming need.

He kissed her like he was starving. Slanted his mouth over hers and drank in her moan as he ground himself into the leather-clad vee of her legs. Her back arched, forcing her breasts against his chest. Lips catching, tongues sliding wetly, he feasted at her mouth and rubbed his aching cock against the material covering what he really wanted.

The sensation sent fireworks through his body. A spring coiled tightly at the base of his spine.

Too damned soon.

He cupped her face in both hands. "Kayleigh."

She shuddered.

"Kayleigh," he whispered, sliding his hands from her cheeks, skating across her shoulders. Her arms. Her chest jumped as she sucked in a breath; his erection did the same as he cupped her breasts in his palms, ran a thumb over both nipples. She threw her head back, eyebrows knitted tightly in fierce concentration.

He chuckled. He couldn't help himself. "Relax," he whispered. "Remember?"

Her eyes opened, wild blue. "No." She dug her fingers into her waistband, peeled the synth-leather down her hips. Every rock of her body brought him that much closer to her, made him that much hungrier.

Shawn hissed as she curled her fingers around his cock. "This is where," she told him brokenly, "you get the job done."

This time, his laughter fractured on a groan.

He seized her hips, pulled her to the edge of the crate. Her body opened for him, aroused and swollen and so wet, he could smell their mingled fragrance: rain and musk, sweat and need.

As the head of his cock stroked against her, nudged her clit, she arched against him, legs tightening around his waist. Everything faded. The tent, the crates, the bright light. Everything but Kayleigh, flushed and sweaty and needy.

Ready.

He hesitated.

Her ankles locked at the small of his back. "I have never been so sure of anything," she whispered huskily. "Make love to me, Shawn. Right here. Just like this."

He dragged his fingers up her back. Reveled in the way it made her shiver, loved the way it forced her body to slide against his. He bent, seized her mouth in a slow, drugging, openmouthed kiss that flew in the face of every demand riding him, riding her.

"I love you," he whispered against her lips, and thrust home.

Neither of them lasted long. To Shawn's undoing, it was Kayleigh who fractured first.

CHAPTER TWENTY-SIX

Somehow, Kayleigh ended up straddling his lap as the sweat cooled. Shawn ran his hands up and down her back, a light caress causing her to shiver.

He shifted, his hand flattening at the small of her back. "Are you—" His voice rasped. He cleared his throat. "Are you cold?"

"Mm." Kayleigh didn't lift her cheek from his shoulder, not yet ready to face the harsh light of her tent. The radio droned on, the rain peppered the tent tarp, and somewhere, they still had to have a conversation. A real one, with complete sentences.

I love you.

Lust. The moment. A thousand other things that he could have meant.

But as he'd entered her body, eyes fierce and glittering with barely controlled need, it had felt so real. So . . . true.

She'd been so close to saying it herself, but Kayleigh *knew* herself. She liked them big and rough and bad. She'd never been able to separate sex and emotion.

Was that what this was?

"Jessie!" Silas's voice boomed through the thin tarp tent.

Kayleigh froze. Arm locked around her back, Shawn stopped breathing.

Footsteps marched past the tent wall, a mere foot away from the two naked people entwined amid the supplies. Jessie's curse was as recognizable as Silas's baritone. "For the last time," she growled, frustration apparent in every clipped word, "*I* am not the pregnant one! Stop nagging, Silas."

Kayleigh winced.

"It's pouring rain," Silas retorted, his voice now so close, she could reach out and probably poke him through the tarp. "You haven't slept, and you're out here looking for something else to stick your fingers in."

Shawn's hand settled over Kayleigh's waist. She jerked, raised her head to squint at his wildly wicked eyebrow.

Heat seared her cheeks.

"There's too much—" Silas must have done something because Jessie's protest ended on an, "Oomph!" Then, sharply, "Silas Smith, you put me down this second."

"I'm not waiting for you to come to your senses," he grumbled, his voice fading slowly. "You don't have any."

"At least let me check on Parker!"

Slowly, Shawn's fingers eased along the inside curve of Kayleigh's hip. Skimmed across her still sensitized flesh.

His eyes darkened to near black, dilated as she took a sharp breath.

"Parker is with Simon," they heard. "Leave them alone. You want someone to check on, I could use—"

Whatever it was he could use shut Jessie up. Silence filled in behind them.

Kayleigh shuddered as his fingers plucked at her clit. Her fingers locked in his hair, heart juddering as he rubbed and teased and pinched.

The flesh still inside her twitched. Hardened.

"Oh," she managed, her head falling back.

"There you go," he whispered. "That's what I like to see. Relax, honey."

"C-can't." Her hips jerked; his nostrils flared, a muscle jumping in his jaw. Clever fingers playing her body, he braced his free hand behind him, lifted his hips under hers.

As quickly as that, her second orgasm unfurled inside her skin like a banner, a wave of sensation somehow more sluggish than the first. It filled her from belly to chest to head, colored her world and forced a lingering cry from her lips.

"Yes," he said, rough need and awe. "So beautiful."

It was so easy to love him.

As she came down, shuddering, Kayleigh scrubbed both hands across her face. "You're . . . really good at that."

Wisely, he said nothing to that. Instead, he cupped her cheek as she had him, thumb stroking over her bottom lip. "Everything is starting over," he said, so serious. So determined. "The city doesn't have the Church anymore, the witches are getting noticed for their good deeds, too."

Her throat ached as she stared at him. Tears hovered, but she'd made that promise already, hadn't she? She wouldn't cry.

Not for what she'd lost.

"You're going to cure Simon," he continued, sitting upright and spreading both hands over her naked back. His erection, full and tight inside her, triggered another wave of sensation.

How did he do this to her so easily?

"Parker's pregnant—"

"How did that get out?" she asked, shaking her head. "I didn't tell anyone but Simon."

Shawn looked at the tent tarp. "Same reason I think everyone will know that I'm not going to kill anyone who says hi to me anymore."

She winced, but it came on the heels of a sudden snort of laughter.

He sucked in a breath. "Jesus, don't do that." Gently, he pushed back her hair from her face. "I guess what I'm trying to say is that, with everything else starting over, we can, too."

Her hips twitched. He tried so hard, she watched the fight in his taut features, but Kayleigh smiled.

She had his number.

Capturing his face between her palms, she very slowly raised her body. The shudder rippled across his muscles. They corded with effort. "If this is love, Shawn Lowe," she said softly, "then you're going to have to teach me how it goes."

His hands opened over her hips, fingers tight. "I can do that," he managed.

"My prior experience with it is—"

"Yeah." Smoothly, he pulled her back down onto

his erection, filled her so tightly. She gasped. "I promise, honey. I'll do more than get the job done."

"I'm going to hold you—oh, God."

"Yes." The smug note in his voice broke beneath a husky groan. "You damn well better."

Jonas Stone leaned against the converted shop door. The autumn chill in the air was the damp, clingy kind; the sort that curled into a man's coat and bit deeply.

The street was quiet, tents still and stragglers looking for warmth in the buildings that hadn't crumbled, the other tents set up across the way. If he listened past the generators, he could hear a faint murmur of ongoing conversation. Voices, families, friends.

Strangers helping strangers.

He'd never seen anything like it.

With the help of people whose names he'd never known but resolved to learn, despite the constant rain and influx of wounded and refugees, the whole street was looking better after a few dedicated days of effort.

Aftershocks had blasted through a few times, but none was as bad as the first. After a while, people learned to wait them out, and clean the mess when it worked itself out.

Three tents away, just visible across the open square, Simon Wells ducked out of the smallest medical tent. His smile, the first Jonas had seen in a very long time, eased something tense and worried in his chest.

Whatever he said, Jonas could guess. Parker leaped into his arms, legs wrapping around his waist as he swung her around and around.

Kayleigh Lauderdale had come through.

Another stranger. Another person helped. And with the cure in hand, the resistance could reach out to the remaining Salem agents who suddenly found themselves without purpose.

A cold breeze ripped through the door.

"Come inside and shut the door," came an aggravated order, a gravelly voice that still made him smile to hear. Obediently, Jonas limped away from the open air, eased the shop door shut.

May sat at the computer Jonas had occupied until today, her eyes bright and alert. No sign of the godawful bruise she'd sported until just recently remained; no trace of her injury from the falling debris marked her.

That was another one he owed Naomi.

Lounging beside her, hip propped against the table, Danny watched him with a dreamy kind of half smile.

Jonas smiled back, even as heat slid into his face. His ears.

May beckoned him. "You were right. Three of the cells reported back. Two found more of those bombs laid around the Trench."

"That's ballsy," Danny said. He could have offered a hand to Jonas, could have offered a lot more than that; but slowly, he and Jonas were figuring out the boundaries.

There weren't many in the bedroom—Jonas was positive his ears were red as fire now—but Danny had learned that Jonas was capable, even with his twisted legs. Crutches or not, he could get around, and he walked at his own staggered pace.

But it helped that Danny was damned good with his hands. In a lot of ways.

If May noticed Jonas's hot cheeks, she ignored it.

"My guess is that he intended to detonate each one until he found the sweet spot."

"Which would have triggered another massive earthquake, exactly like the city buster fifty years ago," Jonas concluded. "Damn. He really wanted to bring the whole thing down."

The old woman rested a bony elbow on the table, running her hand through her short hair. "I can't believe it."

"Why not?" Danny asked, shifting over so Jonas could lean against the table beside him. His hip settled against Jonas's, a warm line of solid masculinity. Support. "The man was crazy. You should have heard him going on about the Church and what a blight it was."

May shook her head. Sorrow, frustration, carved deep lines into her features. "How could anyone who lived through that hell want to do it again?"

Jonas touched her shoulder.

Without looking away from the screen, she reached up and took his hand.

It was such a familial gesture, the kind of thing he always imagined between loved ones, that Jonas's heart stalled.

He must have looked like he'd swallowed glass. Danny reached out and interlaced his fingers with Jonas's other hand, his snort of laughter muffled.

But warm amusement faded.

"I was fourteen years old when the quakes hit," May said, her normally tough-as-nails tone gone quieter. Soft. Jonas glanced at Danny, whose mouth settled into a crooked, unhappy slant. "I remember dreaming about it beforehand. So did my mom. Every witch I'd met who'd been alive since then, they all sensed it coming."

He frowned. "That . . . I didn't know."

"No." She squeezed his hand. "When the witch hunts started, we didn't dare explain. We didn't even know what it meant. How would that go over?"

"Not well," Jonas murmured. "I'm sorry."

"It wasn't your fault." She let go of his hand, but only so she could stand. "But it was mine that I didn't tell my dad."

What was he supposed to say? Jonas was a trouble-shooter—or had been, once upon a time. What could he say to this? To make it better?

Even tolerable?

May didn't seem to expect anything. "He thought me and my mom were in a city up north, visiting family. Divorced, you know." Her smile was brittle. "I sometimes wonder if he survived Old Seattle's fall."

"You can't kick yourself about that," Danny said, frowning. "Grams, you've spent your whole life saving people."

Her gray hair glinted in the monitor's glow as she stared down at the keyboard.

Jonas touched her arm. "Tell me about him?"

"He was a cop, back before the Riot Force neutered them. Good man, spent a lot of time undercover and on the street. My mom didn't . . ." May chuckled, a raspy sound. "She wasn't ever meant to be a cop's wife. He was amazing, though. She always loved him, even if it wasn't enough. He called me Lene, and he didn't take shit from anyone."

"Sounds like his strength lives on in you."

May looked up, eyes crinkling. "I think he would have liked you, Jonas. The both of you." She reached out, pulled Danny into a hug, and linked her arm through Jonas's. "Just for the record, you know you boys make me proud."

"Just for the record, Grams," Danny said, kissing her cheek, "you're the only grandmother for me."

She laughed then, shaking her head. "I'm leaving."

"Where are you headed?" Jonas asked, surprised when she rested a hand on his shoulder to kiss his cheek. The gruff resistance leader had a soft side.

That she showed it to him was humbling.

"I'm going to set up another base near the sec-lines," she said, striding for the door. Shorter though she was, older, a little bit more frail than when she'd started, Jonas couldn't help but admire the tensile set of her shoulders, the confidence strumming through her whipcord body. In old jeans and a baggy flannel, buried in the coat she threw around her shoulders, she was exactly the right kind of grandmother for him, too.

Her brown eyes gleamed over her collar. "You've got this one well in hand, Jonas. I'll be taking Amanda with me."

"Are you sure that's wise?"

A shrug. "She's done the worst she can do, and she's come back from it. More than most can say. She'll need time and some help, but she'll be strong again."

"Wait, why aren't you staying?" Danny asked, straightened from his slouch.

"Because it's not over, Danny." May adjusted her collar, buttoned up the coat against the chill. "The head is gone, but the body of the Church remains. They'll send in more from the other cities. We'll need to keep fighting for a while, which means people like Amanda Green can get some cathartic release."

"But . . ." Danny's expression hovered between endearing and dismay. "Can't you stay with us?"

Her gaze pinned on Jonas, silent words that he didn't need to hear to understand.

Jonas, his smile rueful, nodded. "I'll watch over everything," he promised.

Like her, he didn't have to give voice to just what. The operation, the cells of people, the tech.

Danny.

"I know you will." She reached for the door.

"Hey, Grams?" When she hesitated, Danny called, "I love you."

Her head tilted, a faded gray in the dark brown coat. She looked over her shoulder, her smile odd. Her eyes, bright with something Jonas couldn't decide was tears or not, flicked between them. "I love you, too, Danny. You take care of that man of yours."

Jonas ducked his head.

Danny's palm slid against his as he raised Jonas's hand to his mouth, pressed a kiss to the back of it. The love apparent in his smile nearly undid Jonas right there.

So this is what it was like to have family.

The door swung shut behind her.

Jonas cleared his throat. "Danny—"

He turned Jonas's hand over, pressed another kiss to his palm.

The heat of embarrassment flipped over, started an all-new heat radiating outward from his hand.

"Okay," he said, giving in all at once. To Danny, to this new world; to himself. "I love you. And I love your grandmother, too." Danny's smile curved against his palm. "And I still don't know what this means, but—"

"Hey, angel?" Danny's tongue flicked out between Jonas's fingers. "That's good enough."

It really was, wasn't it?

So much had changed, so many things would have to be relearned, but as Jonas sighed into Danny's kiss, as the square outside welcomed strangers to shelter—as a new order rose from the ashes of the dead—it seemed good enough.

For now.

EPILOGUE

"You did a good thing," Shawn said as the tent flap closed behind the pale but exuberant Simon. His shouts echoed, Parker's mingled tears and laughter a wrenching reminder of how close it had been.

From Shawn's perch on one pile of still-unsorted crates—the best seat in the house, he figured—he'd been able to watch Kayleigh as she walked Simon through the medical explanation her patient barely tolerated.

Simon's nerves had been palpable. So had his distress.

The man, Shawn reflected, had a hell of a lot to live for.

Kayleigh rubbed her forearms, her forehead crinkled as she stared sightlessly through the blue tarp. Simon and Parker's voices faded into the constant buzz of the electrical generators.

Shawn bit back a smile. Knowing his dedicated doctor, she was running scenarios through her head. Medical reports, whatever it was that doctors did with patients. She'd been distant for a couple of days, starting almost from the moment Shawn had put his shirt back on the first time; maybe he ought to take it off again.

Then again, with his luck, one of the witches would wander right back in just in time to catch him half naked and all but begging for it.

Oh, yeah. He'd beg, if he had to. He wasn't above dirty fighting. With Simon now cured, Shawn intended to claim his lover's time for himself. "Hey," he offered. "Don't look so worried."

"Mm?" When she glanced at him, fog-blue eyes only half aware, he laughed outright. Color crept into her cheeks, framed by strands of golden hair lit up like a corona where it escaped her messy ponytail. "Sorry," she added, turning away from the tent access. "I just . . ."

"Worry a lot?" He didn't need her to tell him that. "I know you did everything right."

"Maybe." Her mouth turned down, gaze flicking past Shawn to the workbench she'd glued herself to. "I hope so. I want . . ." She paused, worried brow wrinkling deeply. "I just want everyone to know I'm trying."

He unfolded from the crate. "Hey," he said again, but this time in gentle reprimand. "They know, honey. You've been working yourself into exhaustion for two days. You saved his life, and that's just the start."

"But, what if—"

"That's it." He didn't let her finish, didn't dare let her put words to the number of fears filling her head. "Come here." He held his arms out.

His heart skipped a half beat when she hesitated. Then, shoulders slumping, she leaned into his embrace.

Only to stagger mid-step. Her hand shot out, collided with his solar plexus as her knee cracked into his. "Ouch!"

"Christ," he groaned at the same time, tightening one arm across the small of her back.

Her weight sagged against his forearm, ponytail slapping his face as she bent to rub at her bare foot. "Ouch, *ouch*," she muttered, with all the emphasis of a curse. "Damn it!"

He almost laughed. Swallowed it just in time. "Score one for grace and pride. You okay?"

"I stepped on something."

Shawn's arm loosened as she bent, and this time, the breath he sucked in had nothing to do with surprise and everything to do with the sight of her blond head swinging all too close to the semi-permanent hard-on he'd been sporting since the moment they'd met.

He cleared his throat. "Er, while you're down there . . ."

Kayleigh didn't bother to muffle her laughing snort. But as she came back up, hobbling slightly on the ball of one foot, the glint of metal and matte black nylon in her hand turned simmering heat to a rising tide of embarrassment. "What is this?" she asked.

Knowing his luck, the flickering electric lantern only highlighted his red ears in perfect contrast. "Um." He rubbed the back of his neck with a suddenly damp hand. How had they avoided finding it for two damned days? "It's a spiked bracelet."

"I know what it is," she replied patiently, eyes snapping with silent laughter. "Thanks. Why is it here?"

And of course, during all the makeup sex and serious discussions, the hours spent helping the refugees and the displaced, he'd forgotten the flimsy excuse that he'd hidden behind to get here. The plan he'd made.

Until she had to go and impale her foot on it.

He frowned down at her slender, bare feet. "Are you okay? Did it break the skin?"

"No." Kayleigh dangled the black band from one finger. "Did you bring this back?"

He looked up, fingers digging into his own neck. Damn it. Now, it seemed stupid. "Yup." He dropped his gaze from the blue tarp ceiling when it refused to help him out. "That was me."

"To leave on the floor?" Her eyebrow hiked.

"No." Ah, fuck it. Shawn reached out, snagged her around the waist again, and hauled her closer to him; chest to chest, thigh to thigh. She gasped, hand flattening against his chest, and he trapped it there with his free hand. "I don't have a ring."

She blinked at him. "Sorry?"

For a doctor, Kayleigh Lauderdale could be a little dense. He took a deep breath. "It was the only thing I had to work with," he explained, mentally wincing at the taut strain filling his own voice. Around them, blocked by the thin tarp, the city crackled and hummed. Voices chattered, even a tinny radio played music from somewhere, but he blocked it all out.

Who cared if they could hear him make a fool of himself? She was worth it.

He focused only on her. Her face, her wide eyes. The shape of her mouth, slightly parted, as if she were forever on the verge of interrupting.

The woman he loved.

"I know it's not your usual style," he continued, pushing on despite the fire heating up the back of his neck now. "But it was so damned hot when you wore it before, and I thought, Jesus, what the hell did I have to lose?" Except everything. "I thought I'd give it all I had, ring or not. It was a stupid excuse, but damn it, woman, you're all I want."

Kayleigh's fingers tucked into the buttoned seam of his shirt. "Shawn?"

"I was hoping that you'd think it was cute enough to at least let me get a foot in the door—"

Her eyes lit with laughter. "Shawn!"

"—and I couldn't bear the thought of letting you—" Shawn stilled. "What?"

Her body leaned into his, the hand holding the spiked bracelet sliding over his shoulder to curl around his overheated nape. As her beautiful face dissolved into smiles, she asked huskily, "Anyone ever tell you that you need to relax?"

"More than a few times." His hand mapped the small of her back, shaped the warm skin beneath her sweater. He couldn't help himself; didn't even consider stopping.

He had her. All he had to do now was keep her.

"Kayleigh Lauderdale." He cupped her cheek, thumb grazing over her bottom lip. "Will you take this spiky, badass bracelet and—" His throat closed. "And marry me?"

The bracelet hit the floor with a tiny, muted ping. Her fingers tightened on the back of his neck, her other palm somehow tucked between his askew buttons and flattened, warm and soft, over his heart. It thudded against his ribs. "I'll marry you," she whispered, her lips so close, his mouth tingled as her breath warmed his skin. "You're going to have to sweet-talk me into the spikes."

"Good enough," he rasped, and kissed her. His heart surged into a frantic beat; his blood warmed, his body stirred.

This was it. This was forever.

Somehow, the buttons of his shirt came undone. One popped free, clattering to the ground. Kayleigh's sigh, muffled against his mouth, coaxed an answering, uninhibited chuckle from somewhere deep in his chest. Someplace he'd thought he'd lost years ago.

He'd thought Laurence Lauderdale had taken that part from him.

Now, a Lauderdale was showing him that he'd never lost it. Not really. Her fingers splayed over his chest, dug lightly into the muscle. Her eyes shimmered as her lashes rose, color high in her cheeks. "Did they tell you about my newfound abilities?"

He nodded. "Some."

"Okay." She dragged her tongue over her lips, and his cock tightened all over again. Never, ever enough. "Just so you know," she whispered, "you made the right choice."

"I know." Threading his fingers into her loose ponytail, framing her head, he tilted her head up, smiled down into her cloud-blue eyes. "I don't need witchcraft to tell me that."

A tear caught on her lashes. "I love you, Shawn."

"Yup." He caught the damp bead with his thumb, smoothed it away. "See what you get when you relax, Doctor?"

Her laughter filled the tent, his heart; that aching place in his soul that had festered for too long. Clutching her to him, Shawn breathed in her warm, clean scent. Held it until his lungs ached.

Next year, he'd take her to the ashes of his old home.

Of his parents' home. By then, he would be ready to finally say good-bye.

With Kayleigh by his side, he could start his life—their life—fresh. There was no better time to do it.

No better woman to do it with.

"So, you'll marry me?" he asked, desperate to be sure. "Really?"

Her mouth hiked up into a sexy, mind-altering curve of wicked promise. "Really. And if you're lucky, I'll even wear the spikes." Her teeth nipped at his bottom lip. "And nothing else."

"That'll make it awkward for our friends." Seizing her by the hand, he dragged her deeper into the tent. "Best ceremony ever."

God, he loved it when she laughed.

Want to know how it all began?
Check out

BEFORE THE WITCHES

An e-orginal novella from

KARINA
COOPER

and
Avon Impulse

CHAPTER ONE

"**W**hat's her name?"

The voice came as if through a fog, each syllable laced with a leer so thick she could practically taste its acid on her tongue. Ekaterina Zhuvova blinked away the thick cotton of exhaustion filling her head, gaze focusing with some effort on the two men standing at the back of the small living room.

"Elena," Ivan said, nodding with almost paternal pride at the red-haired woman leaning back against the couch, her full breasts pushed up by her position. She raked a lascivious gaze over the stranger's tall body. "She is most experienced with making a man forget a few hours, eh?"

This man wasn't like the others Katya had seen come and go from this house before. He wasn't as tall as some she'd entertained, but he was clearly strong enough to hold his own and still a foot taller than her petite five feet and two inches. His shoulders were broad, chest tight with muscle beneath a navy blue cotton T-shirt and a button-down open flannel shirt. Long legs encased in worn denim planted with near military precision, though his shaggy, slightly spiky black hair told her whatever his demeanor, he wasn't active duty. Ex-military? Private contractor?

A taste for foreign girls developed overseas and couldn't kick the habit? She knew *that* type, all right.

"Her?" The man's gaze settled on her, and Katya looked away. *Please, don't pick me.*

"Katya," Ivan said, and the warmth left his voice as he turned his head. She lowered her eyes before he could see her anger as his mouth worked, but he didn't spit. She knew he wanted to.

"No good?" the man asked, his tone lazily assessing.

"*Ved'ma,*" Ivan explained with a shrug. She barely kept from wincing, schooling her features into calm.

"Is that her name?"

"No." Ivan eyed her. "She is strange one, even in my country."

"Strange." One eyebrow rose.

Ivan grinned. "She is knowing exactly what a man likes. This is both good thing and bad. I save her for the men who are less sure of self. She is very good with first-time, eh?"

She was beyond blushing, but the flush staining her cheeks now was anger. She ducked her head before she said something guaranteed to put her in lockup.

Ivan was half right. She'd always been good at reading people. She didn't know how or why, but she always knew when a person was lying. It wasn't the same as what Ivan was suggesting, but she'd gotten damned good at that, too.

Her talent wasn't the gift he made it out to be. It had made for a rocky childhood in St. Petersburg's destitute streets. Cast out by the neighborhood children, they'd hunted her into the desperate sanctuary of her mother's single-room flat, forced her into frightened isolation. Their jeers still haunted her dreams.

Ved'ma, ved'ma! Ubyeii yee!

She'd found no solace from the adults who felt threatened by a little girl with an uncanny grasp of deceit. It was no wonder she'd bartered everything she had, including her own body, to get to America.

In America, they didn't care about witches. That belief had proved true.

They were too busy paying for her physical prowess to care about any other talents, and the time they spent lying to her meant she got damned good at reading between the lines. She knew a lot. She knew what was truth and what was lie. She knew how to ask the right questions, and how to translate the half truths and lies. Men spent a lot of time lying to themselves. Especially when screwing a strange girl in a dingy house.

Her gaze flicked back to meet the client's, and this time, she didn't look away.

His mouth tightened. "What about the one in the chair?"

Dismissed. Thank God. Katya angled her shoulder against the wall. If she sat, if she so much as perched on the end of the couch by Elena, she knew she'd fall asleep. She was beyond fatigued. Brutal nightmares had filled her dreams all night long, and she'd dragged herself out of bed this morning feeling as if she'd been awake for years.

Every time she closed her eyes last night, she'd dreamed of death. Fires, floods, scenes of wildly absurd apocalyptic chaos. It was as if her brain had taken all her plans and launched off into a thousand worst-case scenarios, each culminating in the ludicrously detailed destruction of the world. She woke up at least a dozen times, sweaty and shaking.

Now, it was all Katya could do to keep her eyelids open as a Russian pimp and a stranger discussed human beings like they were at some kind of flea market.

Tomorrow was the day. The day she and all the other immigrant girls trapped in this hellhole would be free. The day that all her plans would come to fruition. Almost everything had fallen into place, with the sole exception of the police aid she'd tried to ask for only this morning. They'd denied her. Refused to believe her.

She hated this country, sometimes. It would be different once she was free. Once they were *all* free. The girls knew what to do. They were ready.

Terrified, but ready. One more day.

And every hour closer made moments like *this* feel impossible to handle.

Another man. Another sweaty session on a stained mattress. Another lie batted through her lashes and strained through a smile she'd long since learned to cultivate. She didn't think she could do it.

"I want her."

She was sure she looked like hell warmed over, so even with Ivan's impatient gestures, it took her too long to realize that the mysterious man with the dark hair and five o'clock shadow had chosen her.

Katya straightened again, keenly aware of the client's assessing gaze as she approached the men. She didn't dare say anything. This was the bargaining moment, the time when only Ivan could speak. Business, he called it.

Human trafficking was definitely a business.

Ivan was a large man, more girth than height, but he was as hard and worn as brick and not given to patience. His thick jowls and caterpillar eyebrows gave him the appearance of a bulldog; a reputation equally as earned. He was their warden. Their money handler and their guard.

Only he didn't guard *them*. He guarded the men who paid to screw them.

And occasionally skimmed from the honey himself. He lowered his head and glared at her in silent warning.

Behave, or she'd live to regret it.

"You tell her what you like," he said, snagging Katya's arm. "She will do it. *Anything*." She bit her lip, swallowing a startled sound as the large Russian swung her around, then shoved her hard into the other man's chest.

Large, strong hands closed over her shoulders.

"She is hellcat." Ivan leered, one fleshy eye closing in a wink.

"Good."

The only two other girls not already occupied watched with impassive faces as Ivan shook a finger under Katya's nose. "You be good girl for this one, eh?" he told her, his accent thick enough to serve borscht on.

Unlike hers, his accent was all natural.

Katya nodded, forcing her lips up into a wide, wicked smile. At the same time, she arched her back, forcing the curve of her backside into the stranger's groin.

His fingers tightened on her shoulders. "What's the cost?" the man asked.

Ivan arced a fleshy hand through the air. "This one, she is thousand more than negotiated," he said, and Katya's eyes widened.

A thousand American dollars *more?* Impossible. Ivan's boss didn't barter his girls for that much, at least not these girls in this ramshackle Renton brothel. Did the always absent Mikoyan know about this arrangement?

Who was this man that Ivan would demand more money? A politician? A new money launderer? Someone with a business angle that Ivan's boss wanted to squeeze for everything it was worth?

Dark brown eyes met hers briefly, then skated away. "Fine," he said tightly. "Jesus Christ."

"Of course, she is more expensive, but you want her. Next time," Ivan added as he gestured to the room, "maybe you try another."

"Right." The man nodded to the small backpack on the floor. "Mikoyan's cut is in there. Count it while I'm busy," he said flatly, and didn't bother with any more pleasantries. Shifting his grip on her arm, he hauled her bodily out of the cramped living room. There was barely enough room in there for a couch and a television, much less five more people.

Katya stumbled as he pulled her purposefully toward the stairs. Behind them, the sudden blare of the television flickered to life.

"You are *hurting* me!" she protested as he jerked her up the stairs and into a cramped room.

The door clicked quietly into place, leaving Katya locked inside with nothing but a dirty mattress and the man who'd just purchased her for the hour.

He didn't pay any attention to her accented protest, his fingers hard on her biceps as he spun her in place.

Her pale hair slid into her eyes as he seized both arms and tucked her tightly against the door.

His dark brown eyes met hers, his face so close she could smell remnants of his aftershave. Something like fresh sawdust and pine. His angular features were suntanned, darkened by a five o'clock shadow that looked more like it was getting on toward ten.

He looked intent. Focused. And he damn well needed to let her go. Adrenaline forced her blood to surge, wiping away all traces of exhaustion.

She twisted; he pinned her shoulders back against the door. "How good is your English?" he demanded.

Katya stared up at him. That was his reason for holding her? He wanted to *talk*?

Her gaze trailed to the neck of his T-shirt, to the telltale bulge under his left shoulder. A matte black edge peeking from the open flannel made her eyes widen. A gun?

A cop? She sucked in a breath.

Those long fingers dug into her flesh.

She snapped her gaze back to his, her heart pounding in her ears. "Is good," she managed, deliberately thickening the Russian accent that still colored her otherwise excellent English. Pulling her persona around her like a shroud, she let her body soften against his.

Watched his pupils dilate as the lush curve of her breasts pushed into his chest.

Cop or not, he was a man. And all men had an easy button.

One more day, she told herself. One more man.

"I am understanding English very well," she purred. The tension at her arms lessened. Deliberately, she drew her tongue across her full lower lip.

His gaze pinned there, a whole lot warmer than it had been a moment ago.

"Well enough for hearing what you are wanting," she added huskily. A muscle leaped in his jaw as she leaned forward, pressing her lips against his chin. "Well enough for obeying. You like me?" Her mouth brushed against his whiskered jaw. "You want me, you are asking just for me, *da?*" Her lips drifted lower, explored the cords tense at his neck.

At his collar, just above his T-shirt. His skin was warm.

Her stomach clenched. To her surprise, not all of it was fear. Or disgust.

He jerked as her tongue slid out to taste the hollow of his throat. Suddenly, his hands constricted again, pushed her back against the door. The panel shook.

His eyes were hard. "Who are you?"

"Katya." That wasn't a lie, and he'd heard it already.

"Your *real* name," he said tersely.

For a moment, she froze. Paralyzed by indecision. She could ask him if he was on the take; she'd know the truth the instant it left his lips. But if his answer was no, she'd be in a world of trouble. He'd haul her to Ivan and she'd be left trying to explain why she was asking questions of the clients.

Especially questions about police.

No, she couldn't ask. He'd bartered for an hour of her body. Good cops didn't do that.

She frowned. Pouted, really. "Why?" she demanded petulantly. "Katya is not pretty?"

"Now."

Fine. "Ekaterina Mikhailovna Zhuvova," she said, so smoothly that she watched him blink at the on-slaught of blurred syllables.

"Where are you from, Ekaterina Mikhailovna Zhu-vova?" His echoed accent was damned near close to perfect.

"Moscow," she lied. St. Petersburg, actually, but it was all the same to Americans.

"Why were you at the police station this morning?"

Katya's eyes widened. So he *was* a cop. And given how buddy-buddy she'd seen him get with Ivan, not the kind of cop she desperately needed.

Her mind racing, she watched the intensity, the suspicion in the dirty cop's features and recognized them for what they were. He was grilling her. Why? Did he have reason to suspect her?

The ability to *hear* a lie wasn't going to help her deliver her own pack of them. Her heart slamming in her chest, she managed, "Station? You are police?" She tried to shrink back, but he hadn't let her go. She didn't have to fake the fear in her voice as she begged, "*Please*, do not arrest me. Do not hurt me!" She allowed herself to shake in his grip, watched with some satisfaction as his expression banked to sudden surprise.

Then fury. He was . . . offended?

"I'm not going to hurt you," he growled. It resonated like honesty.

It didn't matter. "You are police," she cried, as if it explained everything.

"Yeah, but I'm not— Son of a bitch." He let her go.

She slid out from between his body and the door, but the only place to go was deeper into the tiny room. Any farther, and she'd be on the stained mattress.

The signal he expected, but not the one she wanted to send.

She'd had enough of this filthy room to last a lifetime. The water-stained walls, single mattress, and bare, scuffed floor would be indelibly imprinted on her brain forever.

She just had to last one more day. Which meant playing by this cop's rules. She clasped her hands under chin. "You are here to arrest Katya?"

The cop grunted. Then, seamlessly switching gears—and again surprising the hell out of her—he said in passable Russian, "I am not going to hurt you, Katya. I just want to know why you were at the station." So the bastard knew her language.

And he was still telling the truth.

Katya's shoulders rounded. She dipped her chin, letting her hair slide over her face in a light golden curtain. "They picked me up," she lied, this time in the same language he almost didn't butcher. "They were asking me questions. I told them I was visiting my sister."

The cops had claimed they needed more evidence than just the word of an illegal immigrant like her. Now she knew why. A cop on the take.

Why wasn't she more surprised?

He watched her as if trying to read the truth in her eyes, and she met his gaze squarely. *Believe me*, she prayed. Seven girls counted on his gullibility.

Katya started as he crossed the small room. She backpedaled, her stomach twisting around an icy knot of anticipation. Her heel hit the edge of the mattress, and she jerked.

He caught her arms, but there was nothing restraining about it this time. He steadied her gently. His brow furrowing in tacit concern, he said, "My name is Nigel Ferris." *Truth*, whispered the tiny signal in the back of her brain. "Did you tell them that you were a—"

He hesitated, and she barely kept from laughing outright. Was it possible? Did he have trouble shaping his mouth around the word "whore"?

A dirty cop with morals. Now she'd seen *everything*.

Forcing her features into a mask of terrified sincerity, she shook her head until her hair swung. "*Nyet!* I say nothing."

His face shuttered, and she slowly took in a deep breath. Did he believe her? If not, she could end up very dead, very quick. There'd been girls who vanished before.

Lies spoken about their whereabouts.

Distraction. She could do distraction.

She stepped into him. Closed the distance between them, slid her hands up his chest. A part of her mind fragmented at finding him hot to the touch, even through his T-shirt. His muscles leaped under her palms; his heart slammed against her hand.

He wasn't as unaffected by her as he wanted to be.

And rightfully so; her role demanded she dress the part. Her too-thin T-shirt was white, her bra sweetheart pink and clearly obvious beneath it. It left two inches of her waist bare, hugged tight by low-rise jeans.

She looked edible. Fresh.

She looked like every other Russian girl off the boat who had ever been forced into prostitution.

And she knew how to act the part.

Rising up on her tiptoes, she hooked her fingers into the collar of his shirt and said in her accented English, "You will not hurt Katya?"

His jaw shifted. His body all but vibrated against hers. Most men would have had her on her back by now.

Was he shy?

She flicked her tongue against the column of his throat. He sucked in a breath. "Katya will not hurt you," she murmured. She nuzzled the skin behind his ear, and his head moved. A fraction of an inch. Reluctant as hell, but there.

"Katya will make you feel nice," she whispered, just before she sank her teeth into the sensitive skin of his earlobe.

The sound he made was guttural, leashed taut.

So he had the same button as all the other men after all. The same weakness that would buy her the time to figure out what to do with a dirty cop.

She smiled against his skin.

A smile that faded as he once more caught her shoulders, wrenching her away. His eyes blazed in stormy black and brown; a wild intensity that ratcheted tension through her as he stared into her own.

Her heart leaped into her throat. "I—"

"They'll know if I don't," he muttered hoarsely, but more as if he spoke to himself than to her. Without warning, he pulled her hard against him. Caught her face between his palms and tipped her face up with impatient fingers.

Katya gasped.

He covered the sound with his lips, pulled the air from her lungs on a low, angry noise that did nothing to dull the sudden heat flushing her chest. Her stomach, and lower.

His lips were warm, firm against hers. Demanding. He didn't coax, he didn't wait; Katya had long since learned never to expect it. He tilted her face up, thumbs at the corners of her mouth, and swept his tongue inside to taste her.

Her breath shuddered. The sensation seemed to light a fire in him; he dragged his tongue across hers. Teased it, coaxed it to follow back into his own mouth. The world simmered around her, danced wildly as if caught in a heat wave.

His eyelashes were black, she realized. The skin across his high cheekbones was taut, flushed with control and arousal, and his body against hers was rock-solid and— *Oh, God.*

For one moment, Katya forgot about her situation. She forgot about the other girls she was so desperately trying to protect; forgot about their jailer somewhere in the small house.

She forgot about the plans to escape this hellhole and the police who had turned her away.

There was only Nigel Ferris; dirty cop with a mouth to die for.

She closed her eyes. His hands left her face and she fisted her fingers in his shirt, hauling him closer. Begging him wordlessly to continue feasting from her lips. Tasting her soul. He groaned again. His arms came around her, dragged her off the floor. Wild, wanton, she wrapped her legs around his hips and tangled her fingers into his short, wavy hair.

He sank his teeth into her lower lip and she arched. The thick length of his erection ground against the front of her jeans and her skin caught fire. Gasping for breath, she could only moan helplessly as he held her as easily as if she were made of feathers, ground himself against her, devoured her identity and her willpower with a bruising kiss that would be sure to leave her lips swollen when he was done.

Arousal filled her so hard, so shockingly hot and fast, that she reeled.

It had been too long.

Why? Why a cop? A bad cop, even?

And then his hand crept under her shirt and she forgot that, too. Her world was suddenly composed of the feel of his callused palm against her naked waist. Her ribs. And then hard and warm over the soft pink cup of her bra. She thrust herself into his hand, her fingers tight at the back of his neck.

"Not a good idea," he groaned against her mouth, each syllable a throaty curse. "Wait, stop, I— The hell!" He staggered, jarring Katya out of her reverie as somewhere beyond that door, girls screamed.

Her eyes snapped open.

"Shit!" Nigel dropped to his knees, still cradling Katya against his chest. "Get down!" He dropped her, and arousal flipped over to utter confusion, total fear. A raid! Were they being shot at? Was that—

"The floor," she gasped, struggling to push herself to her hands and knees. "It's moving!"

He didn't say anything, flattening a hand on her back. Katya grunted gracelessly as he pushed her to her stomach, and yelped as he covered her body with his. She felt dwarfed. Smothered.

Sick to her stomach.

He pushed her head down, folded his arms over her. The house shook and trembled around them. Plaster cracked, dingy white dust sifting to the floor as it rolled. Her stomach pitched and yawned; one ear plugged abruptly, and vertigo slammed into every nerve still trying to find mental footing.

Through the vee between his protective arm and the floor, she watched the mattress shimmy and vibrate its way to the other wall. Plaster fell in clumps, and she felt him tense over her. Heard him grit out something hard and painful.

He was protecting her. The dirty cop, the man who'd bargained with a Russian pimp for an hour of sex, was protecting her.

Katya's hands fisted as the room shuddered.

Who the hell was this man?

And why did she suddenly feel that she'd seen this earthquake coming?

Next month, don't miss these exciting new love stories only from Avon Books

Any Duchess Will Do by Tessa Dare
Griffin York, Duke of Halford, has no desire to wed, but when his mother forces him to pick a bride, he decides to teach her a lesson . . . by choosing the serving girl. For Pauline Simms, tolerating "duchess training" is worth the small fortune the duke has offered her, even if it is just play-acting. But as Pauline inadvertently educates Griffin of the love within him, both must face the biggest challenge of all: Can a roguish duke convince her to trust him with her heart?

Surrender to the Earl by Gayle Callen
Audrey Blake just wanted a favor, not a fiancé. But when Robert Henslow, Earl of Knightsbridge, appeared on her doorstep willing to help her take ownership of her rightful property, she couldn't turn him down. Not even with a fake engagement on the line. Yet it's Robert who yearns to prove to her how much they have to gain by making it real—and convincing her to submit to the most blissful passion.

The Secret Life of Lady Julia by Lecia Cornwall
One kiss led to another for Lady Julia Leighton, but when the roguish stranger disappeared from her betrothal ball, her life was forever changed. Now seeing Julia again years later, Thomas Merritt is utterly bewitched, even if they can never be together. Now in a Vienna rife with political intrigue, Thomas harbors a perilous secret—and the only person who can aid him is the woman who has captured his heart.

*G*ive in to your Impulses!

These unforgettable stories only take a second to buy and give you hours of reading pleasure!

Go to *www.AvonImpulse.com* and see what we have to offer.

Available wherever e-books are sold.

AVON**IMPULSE**

IMP 0811